THE BIRTH OF THE DRAGON

"Alfred's in labor," Tom said, "The young Negwenya is ready to breathe fire with the coming dawn."

Riena shuddered and stretched out her hand to rest on the Zulu warrior's pregnant belly.

"The Negwenya's child is in there," Tom said. "Can't you see him?"

She could see a shape, moving gently, first from side to side and then up and down, like a water snake caught in the weeds.

"I'm not going to sit here and watch him die," she said. "If I can forgive him for what he did to me, surely you can do the same."

Tom didn't move. There was no way he was going to help that bastard, he thought. He took Riena by the hand and half-carried her out of the house.

Tom turned to face the house. He didn't have time for a second step. With a roar that muffled the cry of a newborn generation, the shanty burst into flames. Flames licked the sky and he stared awestruck as they formed themselves into the shape Nkolosi had drawn in the dirt—the pointed ears, the curling tail, the wings ready to unfurl.

Suddenly the Negwenya began to move. Sensuously. Lazily. Dancing t〔...〕 of Nkolosi's laughter.

"Run, Tom," Riena yel〔...〕

"Run."

RITE
OF
THE
DRAGON

Janet Gluckman

LEISURE BOOKS ❦ NEW YORK CITY

*For Mike, Debbie and Stefi,
because they kept believing
and for all my other friends
who wouldn't let me give up.*

A LEISURE BOOK
Published by
Nordon Publications, Inc.
Two Park Avenue
New York, N.Y. 10016
Copyright © 1981 by Janet Gluckman
Printed in the United States

AUTHOR'S NOTE

South Africa is a Lorelei. Her visible charms mask a dark and violent nature. While she makes lovers of all South Africans, she allows only the minority to worship her in the sunlight; the majority, in servitude, must stay in the shadows.

One day that majority will revolt and claim its place in the sun. A force stronger than the apathy of well-being created by adequate food, shelter and clothing will unite South Africa's non-White majority in the cause of dignity. It will have to be a power as natural as eating, breathing and making love, for if it is to create a single sense of African purpose it must do more than neutralize the Lorelei's power; it must supersede tribal hatreds, the urban African's denial of his heritage, the Coloured man's state of limbo and the lethargy of those who care—but not enough.

In *Rite of the Dragon,* such a force is embodied in the person of Nkolosi—witchdoctor, commander of ritual and practitioner of an art that has been handed down to him through generations of belief in its power. That belief has made him healer, matchmaker, arbitrator, judge, jury and executioner, not just at times of great moments but daily, habitually.

In Africa that is the norm.

What then if a man like Nkolosi, realizing the extent of his power, takes it upon himself to become a catalyst in a political movement?

Therein lies the premise of this book. Although *Rite of the Dragon* is a work of fiction, the events and characters add up to what I saw and experienced growing up in South Africa. I was born there; I lived there for more than twenty years. Even now I think of it as the most physically beautiful country in the world. The book may well be the accumulated result of an overactive imagination. I don't know. What I do know is that the following explanation of South Africa's classification system is real enough. I have included the definitions for the sake of clarity. The parenthetical comments are mine; the system is not. Please absolve me of any responsibility for its existence.

Janet Gluckman

European: All White people. (Afrikaans is promoted as the national language in an attempt to create a South African language. Not all Whites are racists. Many resent Afrikaans and promote the slow integration of all races. Others want instant equality but fear the results after so many generations of apartheid.)

Bantu: Official nomenclature for all Blacks. The word means "people." The Bantu were once called Natives and now wish to be called Africans. (The derogatory term for Blacks remains "kaffir.")

Coloured: People of mixed origin, more often called Cape Coloured or Cape Malay because most of them live in the Cape Province (colloquially known as "Capies").

Asiatic: Chiefly people of Indian origin, but also Chinese and Malays; they stay culturally intact but have no citizenship. The Japanese are classified as "honorary Whites" (for the purpose of continued trade with Japan).

BOOK
ONE

1

Tom Sibanda lay sweating in the tall Zeekoevlei grass. His eyes were closed but he was not asleep. He was concentrating. Blocking out the day so that he could feel the dandelion fluff being carried to him by the summer wind. He had to be able to feel it against his skin or his game didn't work; it was hard enough to convince himself that they were snowflakes when he'd never seen any. With his eyes open, it was impossible. Riena was lucky, he thought. She swore she had seen snow once. It couldn't have been December, of course. No matter how many times they played "Jingle Bells," December would still be the middle of the summer. Maybe if those dumb announcers played it in June, he thought, it would snow in Cape Town too. Still, the game helped, when it was very hot. Like today.

"Come on, Tom. Building this house was your idea and now you're not helping."

"Coming," Tom said. But he didn't move. It was his thirteenth birthday. He had the right to lie around and do nothing. Not that he expected Riena to understand. What did eleven-year-old girls know, anyway? It was Alfred who should have understood. Kept her off his back. His half-brother was even dumber than the radio announcers, Tom decided. And cocky, too. Strutting around like a bantam just because some Whitey had told him he was a Zulu and could live with their father while Tom had to stay with his mother. How could someone else tell you what you were!

He opened his eyes and lifted his arm. Inspecting it. Turning it around the way his mother examined a piece of meat at the corner store. It's at least as dark as Alfred s, he thought. He was like his father, too; not

11

olive at all. Not like Riena, but then she wasn't a relative. She looked Coloured for sure, even if her grandmother had come from Basutoland, like Riena said.

Closing his eyes again, Tom remembered the first time the White man came to the house to tell him they couldn't all live together anymore. How could they have been a family one day and not the next? So what if he and his mother were classified Coloured and his father and half-brother were classified Bantu. Black. He didn't understand why it mattered. In the beginning, he'd kept asking his mother to explain. And she'd tried. It hadn't made any sense to him; it still didn't.

"Tom, I can't carry this all by myself. It's too heavy."

"I'm coming, Riena," Tom said again. A summer day's for doing nothing, he thought resentfully, forgetting that the hideout had been his idea. It was for planning all of the things he was going to do when he was grown up; the books he was going to write. He pictured himself six foot tall, instead of only five foot three. Maybe he would grow up to be a witchdoctor, he thought. Like Nkolosi. Then if people ordered him around, he could punish them the way Nkolosi did. He would be the one giving orders. And he'd have a secret helper—one that obeyed his every command, the way the Negwenya obeyed Nkolosi. Only maybe it wouldn't be a dragon; he'd think of something else. He looked at his thigh and tried to imagine a tattoo there, where Nkolosi carried the sign of the Negwenya. A two-headed snake would look impressive, he thought.

Tom stood up and grinned. The first thing he'd do was order his helper to turn Alfred into a Whitey. Serve him right. "See if you'd run around boasting about being a purebred then, Alfred Mtshali," he said. He picked a small bug off his leg and squished it between his fingers. "Thomas Mtshali. Thomas Sibanda." He repeated the two names a few times. Though he didn't like to admit it, he was getting used to his new name, the one they'd given him after his father and Alfred had moved into the *location*.

Staring out over the *vlei*, Tom imagined himself being

quoted, the way people always repeated Nkolosi's words. "Sibanda says. . . ." He liked the sound of it. He'd do good things, too, he thought, the way Nkolosi did sometimes. Cure people. Help them get food. Make them send their children to school. . . .

"Tom!"

This time there was no ignoring Riena. Something was wrong, something much more important than the fact that he wasn't pulling his weight with their project.

"Where are you?"

"Over here. Under the bush."

Under which bush, Tom thought, hearing the hysteria in her voice. Yanking at his shorts, he ran in the direction he hoped was right. He found her by almost tripping over the leg that she was clutching with both hands. She was crying.

"What happened? What's wrong?" He knelt down beside her.

"It was a *boomslang*, Tom. You said they didn't bite but they do. They do."

"Get your hands away so I can see." Tom's voice was patient, the way his mother's was when she was afraid something really bad might have happened. She's probably just scared, he thought hopefully. He'd never heard of a tree snake biting anyone before.

"I can't let go. I can't. It hurts too much."

"Come on, Riena," Tom said, wondering where Alfred had disappeared to. He always managed to disappear when things went wrong.

Slowly, Riena released her hold on her leg. She was right. There it was, swelling and red and puffy.

"We're going over to the *vlei*," Tom said. "When we get there, I'm going to use my knife and. . . ."

Riena clutched her leg again and started to wail.

"You wanna die, or you going to do what I tell you?" He sounded much surer of himself than he felt. "Where the hell is Alfred?"

"He said . . . he said he was going to get Nkolosi. I told him to call you but he said I would die if Nkolosi didn't come. He said treesnakes only bite Coloured people who've been bad and had a spell put on them. He said. . . ."

She began to cry again but allowed Tom to help her up. Damn Alfred, Tom thought. Always acting like a big shot. Shooting off his mouth and saying things like that so he didn't have to stick around when the going got rough. Oh! well. It didn't really matter. He was used to taking care of Riena. He'd been doing it ever since his mother had found her wandering around the streets and taken her in.

"Come on, Riena," he said, helping her hobble toward the water. "Hey, if you could live through Sharpeville, guns going off and blood and all that stuff, you can live through a little old snake bite."

When they reached the edge of the bracken water, Tom helped Riena sit down. Taking out the old pocket knife his father had given him, he opened it and flashed it through the dirty water. It was only a pretense at hygiene but it was the best he could do. Before either of them had time for second thoughts, he slid the blade into Riena's flesh and put his lips to the geyser that rose instantly from the wound. It wasn't until he could no longer stand Riena's screams that he stopped sucking and spitting. Sucking and spitting.

"Shouldn't we tie something around it? I'm going to bleed to death," Riena said, between sobs.

Tom rinsed his mouth several times to try to get rid of the metallic taste of her blood in his mouth. Then he reluctantly examined his surgery. The blood that was running down her leg was showing no sign of stopping. He looked down at the shirt he was wearing. His birthday gift. The new one his mother had made for him and given him that morning. Alfred's wearing an old one, he thought, willing his half-brother's return but knowing it wasn't going to happen. Cursing, he took off his shirt, removed one of the sleeves with his bloodstained knife, and bound Riena's leg.

"Think it's okay now," he said, flopping down next to her. She had stopped crying but every once in a while she took two or three quick breaths involuntarily,

14

the way everyone did after they'd been crying that hard. She's pretty gutsy, Tom thought, finding it difficult to admit that about a girl—even one who had been orphaned at Sharpeville. He felt a little bad about having reminded her of that and wondered again how she'd ended up a thousand miles away from home. All the way from Johannesburg to Cape Town. That was three years ago and she still refused to talk about it. If he ever had an adventure like that he'd want to talk about it to everyone who'd listen. His mother had told him that Riena used to live in the *location*. At Sharpeville. Until a policeman shot her mother in the back during the riot. His mother said that she didn't have anyone left to take care of her, except the relative who'd brought her to Observatory and dumped her there. Too much trouble for some people to have a kid hanging around, his mother said, so Riena had come to live with them and he was even more confused. She could almost pass for White yet she'd been living in a Bantu location. He'd heard his mother tell a friend that someone must have paid to have her reclassified but when he'd asked about it, his mother had told him not to talk about it anymore.

Suddenly, lying there in the sun, Tom felt a peculiar sensation. It had nothing to do with fear that he hadn't done the right thing, nor was it pride that he had. Whatever it was, it made him forget that he wasn't supposed to like girls and he reached for Riena's hand.

"Don't worry, Riena," he said. "I'll take care of you. I'll always take care of you."

2

"That sonofabitching Zulu's dropping out of school. Stop him, Nkolosi," Tom Sibanda said. He stared at the back of Alfred Mtshali's charcoal neck until it blended into the trees at the edge of De Waal Drive.

"Aren't you overreacting?" Nkolosi said, tilting his head to catch the last rays of the afternoon sun before the Atlantic devoured it.

Tom tried to analyze the complexities of his hatred for his half-brother. It had been ten years since the day Alfred had run out on Riena, the day the treesnake had bitten her. She had almost lost her leg because of the time lapse between the bite and Tom's first aid. Not that he'd been wild about Alfred before that day, Tom admitted to himself, but somehow that had been the seed of what he felt now.

He released a pine cone from his grip and watched it do an adagio against the slope that led to the university entrance.

"Alfred's the first Black man they've let into this engineering school," he said, examining the indentations the cone's scales had left on his palm. "He was opening doors for all of us."

"Quit whining, Sibanda. Maybe Mtshali's tired of playing guinea pig. Or maybe he's bored with going hungry to pay for his books. Isn't it his prerogative to give up his potential to fill his belly?"

"Selling out is one thing. Joining the South African police force is another. With help like his. . . ."

". . . Have you ever considered helping yourself? At least he's learned to make bombs. All you ever do is cover pages with useless words that end up in the rubbish. You complain and assume everyone else will do the dirty work."

"So he's learned to make bombs! That's just what the Nationalists expected. You can be sure they'll use it as their rationale for refusing to allow another Black man into this place. And the Liberals will pat themselves on the back and tell each other how hard they tried."

"What exactly is it you want me to do?"

Humiliate him, Tom thought. Send the Negwenya to turn him into an object of contempt so that he can feel some of the emotions he's so casually inflicted on others all of his life.

Before he could say anything, the witchdoctor smiled. "It's my Negwenya's services you want, isn't it?" he said. "Neither of us come cheap, you know."

"I can pay your price. And your Mata Hari's."

"Can you? Our price might not be money."

"What, then?"

"You'll know when it's demanded of you."

"If you'll order the Negwenya to punish Mtshali I'll pay your price, no matter what it is."

"I can order her into his dreams to seek the source of his worst fears," Nkolosi said.

". . . Will you order her to take him as her lover?"

"I can't dictate the form his discipline will take, Sibanda. My Negwenya makes that decision herself. Once she's taken possession of Mtshali, he will determine his own punishment."

Nkolosi knelt and drew in the sand and Tom watched the Negwenya take shape, her dragon ears pointed, her tail curled, her wings in repose.

"You know she can be a passionate and consuming mistress. You must hate Mtshali very much," Nkolosi said.

Tom Sibanda tried to recollect a time when he hadn't hated his half-brother. It was so long ago, it was ancient history. Before the hue of his own palms and the color of the quick of his nails condemned him to a mulatto no-man's land between White ritual hatred and the Black struggle; before they told him he was a *kaffir* and he found out it meant "man without a soul." Not like Alfred Mtshali, whose parents were both Zulus and whose palms had no trouble passing the closest scrutiny.

"What's Riena doing these days?" Nkolosi said, trimming the dirt from the tips of the Negwenya's wings.

"I haven't seen her for a while."

"Don't lie to me, Sibanda, not even about something that trivial," the witchdoctor said. He dug his long nail into the sand to complete the Negwenya's eye.

"Since you know I'm lying, you must know that she spends her time down at the docks, sleeping with sailors." Tom found it almost as difficult to think the words as he did to say them. Picturing her in her corrugated iron shanty at the docks. Servicing johns in a broken-down shack rented to her by a righteous Afrikaner minister whose Sunday sermons rarely failed to touch on the evils of prostitution.

"White sailors?"

"How the hell would I know?"

"I thought she was a history teacher." Nkolosi was enjoying Tom's discomfort.

"She was. Until some bounty hunter reported her for including slavery and civil rights in her American History courses," Tom said.

Nkolosi stood up and cleaned his hands on the sides of his trousers.

"Will you send the Negwenya?" Tom asked. He was staring at the dragon as if he expected it to move.

"Does Mtshali believe?"

Tom nodded.

"Do you?"

Tom nodded again, surprised that Nkolosi needed to ask the question. No one who had grown up the way Tom had would dare entertain doubts about the witchdoctor's power. Or the Negwenya's. Nkolosi had demonstrated his knowledge of the ancient arts, had succeeded too often, for anyone to question them. He commanded no less fear and respect than his father before him. And his father's father.

"Then it is done," Nkolosi said. "I'll gather the *Likkewane,* the lizards, for Mtshali's pillow. They will let him know the Negwenya is courting him. I promise you he won't sleep much."

For the moment, Tom thought, that was enough. But if Alfred impacted his life one more time, he'd be less compassionate.

"The payment?" he asked, as Nkolosi began to move away.

Nkolosi only laughed and kept on walking.

Tom waited a week before he went to see Alfred. In his cop's uniform, his half-brother looked like any other sellout.

"You seem tired. Have you been sleeping well?" Tom asked. Alfred's puzzled look told him his half-brother had not made the connection between Tom and the lizard carcasses that had forced him out of his bed and onto the floor. "I heard you were lonely," Tom went on. "I thought I'd provide you with some companionship."

Light dawned on Alfred's face.

"Did you think the lizards were an accident? Didn't it occur to you that you'd earned yourself a courtesan?"

"You can't mean that, Tom."

"Oh, I mean it all right."

Alfred was beginning to look frightened. "Make her stay away," he said.

Tom laughed. "You know I don't have control over her," he said. "Take care. I hear she's a most demanding mistress."

"I'll go to Nkolosi."

"You'll have to find him first. And for that he has to want to be found."

"You know where he is. I'll follow you till you lead me to him."

"You stupid *kaffir*. A few weeks with the force and you think you're Sam Spade." Tom grinned at his choice of detectives. Then he turned to leave. There was nothing more Alfred could say to interest him.

Alfred, not about to submit that easily, followed.

At first Tom enjoyed the sport of leading his half-brother from shebeens to churches, through alleyways, on trains and buses, but after a few days he tired of the game. Deciding Alfred would eventually tire of it, too, he picked up the threads of his normal life. Though he'd tried to lie about it to Nkolosi, part of his routine was a weekly visit with Riena. He saw no reason to cancel because Alfred was dogging his trail; no matter what Riena had become, he looked forward to seeing her.

They met, as usual, under the town hall clock. Hugging each other affectionately, they dodged Cape Town's morning traffic and went across the street to the parade grounds.

The parking lot had given way to a flea market. "Let me buy you something," Tom said, holding up a piece of cheap costume jewelry. She shook her head and walked on. Stepping over the discarded gift boxes and ribbons that littered the sidewalk, she mingled with the Whites and Coloureds, Malays and Indians, Zulus and Xosas, homogenized by their bargain hunting and rubbing shoulders as if they were all equals. That was probably what drew Riena there every week, Tom thought, watching her tug at the hem of her short cotton skirt and swing her hips with practiced carelessness. She was beginning to look like a tart.

"I'm not going with you to see Ma today," she said when he caught up with her.

"Why?"

"I'm tired of lying to her and telling her stories about the kids in my class. Besides, I have a date."

"Anyone I know?"

"No."

Before Tom could question her further, Riena veered off to the left, between two fruit stands and away from the flea market.

"Where are you taking me?"

"There is something I want to buy. But not here," Riena said.

"What?"

"Violets," she said.

It was a long time since Tom had been to the flower market. It was flanked at one end by the general post office and at the other by Adderley Street's constant traffic. Masses of flowers in wooden tubs seemed to grow out of the concrete. Roses. Gladioli. Carnations. All of them so perfect that they didn't seem real to Tom until Riena had bought her violets and he saw her shiver as their moisture penetrated the paper wrapping and dripped down her arm.

Riena leaned slightly backwards against the wind as they exited the alley. Tom, thinking she was about to fall, darted forward to catch her. The sudden movement allowed him a glimpse of Alfred and he considered saying something to Riena. She had interacted so little with him, however, that it seemed pointless to involve her in their quarrel.

"Are you meeting him down there?" Tom asked, realizing he was being led down the Heerengracht toward the docks.

"Yes, I'm meeting him 'down there,'" Riena said, imitating Tom's contemptuous tone. She said no more until they reached the shanty. It wasn't until she had raised her hand to knock at the door and said: "Come in and meet Jake," that Tom became aware of her degree of apprehension.

"Is he a customer?"

"Jakes's my lover, Tom." Riena said, softly. "I'm going to have his child." She put her hands over her ears as if to block out the sound of his anger.

"You goddamned whore!" Tom shouted with no regard for anything but his own feeling of betrayal. The door was open and his words, bouncing off the shanty's walls, echoed back at him. The were punctuated by a tugboat, bellowing as it guided a clumsy ward into the shelter of Duncan Dock.

"I love him," Riena said. "He's an American. He's going to send me a passport."

Tom Sibanda turned from the look in her eyes and stood in the doorway, watching a cable car sway up Table Mountain. The edges of a late southeaster whipped his face, and he felt fear for Riena settle like a permanant deposit between his skin and the air. Crossing the classification lines "for the purposes of miscegenation" was illegal. She was risking jail. And for what? Love him, my ass, Tom thought, stepping forward and kicking the door shut behind him. She wants to get out of here, like the rest of us. She always did. Even when they were children she'd sworn to leave South Africa.

The whirring of an electric motor somewhere out of sight triggered an assault wave of memory. It reminded him of the incessant hum of his mother's sewing machine and of Riena, ten-year-old hands clutched over

21

her ears to deaden the sound. It was a gesture that had become habitual; she did it still when faced with something beyond her control. Like a few minutes ago, standing at the door. She'd done it then.

Tom tried not to think about Riena in bed with that White man, his body pressing down on hers. Instead he remembered Riena the child, lying under the yellow and orange weave of her Bantu blanket, staring at the vibrating kerosene lamp that stood next to his mother's Singer and chanting: "I won't be like her. I won't stay here forever." Over and over again. Not knowing that she was shouting beneath the protection of her hands.

That house of ours was enough to corrupt anybody, Tom thought; Ma's compulsive cleanliness sending her to the bottle of Dettol like an alcoholic. The pine smell mixing with machine oil. The machine her God, taking precedence over his needs and Riena's.

Furiously, Tom pushed the memories aside. He was not ready yet to have his anger diluted. Nor did he wish to speak to Riena, now or any time in the future. He had managed to come to terms with her prostitution but this was a different kind of betrayal. Grinding his teeth, he stalked up the Heerengracht.

It did not occur to him to look around for Alfred. Had he done so, he might have seen his half-brother step out of the shadow of a storage shed, buttoning his uniform jacket as he moved toward the door of Riena's shanty.

3

Tom wasted no time getting to a liquor store. He took his purchases home and spent the rest of the day getting progressively drunker. When he woke up the next morning, he opened a new bottle and started all over again. His supply lasted for the better part of two months.

Sobering up at last, Tom found himself with no job. Worse than that, he had nothing left of the novel he'd been working on for a year. He retained a vague memory of having sacrificed it to some goddess of the water, imploring her to regurgitate it as a bound best seller. Which body of water eluded him completely. The hurt caused by Riena's love affair had dulled to a steady ache. Not so his hatred for Alfred; that had, if anything, intensified.

That night Tom went to see his half-brother.

"Did you find Nkolosi?"

"I found Riena instead," Mtshali said.

The look on Alfred's face filled Tom with a nameless terror. "What did you do to her?"

"I arrested her. Fucking White man got away."

"You did what?"

"My patriotic duty."

"Why?"

"Why?" Mtshali laughed. "That's easy. You punished me with the Negwenya. I saw a way to hurt you."

"By punishing Riena? Doesn't your conscience keep you awake at night?"

Mtshali shrugged. "The Negwenya keeps me awake."

"Riena's been your friend since we were children."

"To me she's just a woman. I'm a Zulu, remember." Mtshali grinned. "I didn't grow up with her the way you did." He paused. "How do you think it will feel to have a White relative? You did know she was pregnant, didn't you?"

Tom's first instinct was to drive his fist through his half-brother's grin. The trouble was, he had never been much of a fighter. Besides, a cut lip would heal.

Once again, Tom went to see Nkolosi.

"I was expecting you," the witchdoctor said, without looking up from his cross-legged position on the ground. This time, the Negwenya was already clearly drawn in the soft earth.

"I want him to die," Tom said, without preliminaries.

"That decision was made some time ago."

"How? When? Order the Negwenya. . . ."

". . . I told you, I can't make demands. She's decided he's to die; the means, too, must be her choice."

Forgetting the respect he owed Nkolosi, Tom cursed roundly. He expected to be reprimanded but Nkolosi's eyes simply hardened.

"Riena's belly was filled with child when Mtshali arrested her," the witchdoctor said.

"You knew that?"

"There is nothing I don't know."

"And the Negwenya?"

Nkolosi nodded.

"Then she must also know how he deserves to die."

"I know what you want, Sibanda. Now I must ask the Negwenya what it is she wants. Come back tonight and I'll tell you if her desires match yours."

"I'll wait here."

"You will do as I tell you," Nkolosi said quietly.

Tom retreated. When he returned, Nkolosi was ready. "The Negwenya says Mtshali dreams of hunger and sweats when he thinks of Riena in labor," he said. "She has determined to make sure Mtshali's belly is never empty again. She will take him as her lover tonight."

"Will she plant her seed in him?"

"In seven months his belly will have swollen like a pregnant cow's. By then the young Negwenya's scales will have hardened inside him and Alfred Mtshali will be ready to breathe fire."

"Will the fire kill him?"

"Would it not kill you?"

"And my payment?"

Nkolosi laughed. "I promise you that will come. Now go and inform Mtshali."

Tom found his half-brother at the local shebeen.

Savoring the responses to each carefully chosen word, Tom told him of the Negwenya's decision. "Her son will grow a little more each day, until you will no longer be able to button your jacket. In seven months the scales will have hardened, and he will be ready to breathe fire," he said, repeating Nkolosi's prediction.

24

Mtshali, his hand unconsciously rubbing his stomach, swayed and leaned against the wall.

"You'll be able to feel the scales, Mtshali. The tail will uncurl, and you'll watch it push out your flesh like. . . ."

The Zulu's knees buckled. With a look of contempt, Tom spat on the floor and left.

For three months Tom tried repeatedly to see Riena. He was no less angry at her betrayal but the memories that came to him at night had softened him enough that he wanted to see her. The authorities' refusal to allow him visiting privileges was consistent and did not include an explanation. He made no effort, however, to see Alfred, even when he heard that his half-brother had left the force and moved into their old hideout. He told himself it was intelligent to avoid an unpleasant confrontation but in truth, he was scared. And it wasn't only Alfred's anger he feared; he wanted to avoid contact with the Negwenya who was surely watching over her son as he became visible under Alfred's stretching belly.

After half a year had gone by, six months of wondering when Nkolosi would exact payment and what that payment would be, Tom sought out the witchdoctor.

"You have not been to visit Mtshali. Why?" Nkolosi began, as if they had not been apart for six months.

"I was afraid of the Negwenya," Tom said, admitting his fear because he was sure Nkolosi knew of it anyway. "How is Alfred?"

"How would you be? Your half-brother is big and growing bigger. And he is in great pain."

"What does he do out there at the *vlei?*"

"Talks to the frogs. Makes bombs. He has made one for you."

Tom stepped back as if he had been struck. He stumbled over an exposed root and barely saved himself from an undignified fall. Nkolosi threw back his head and laughed.

"The bomb is for you to *use,*" he said. "I instructed him to make it."

"Has it anything to do with my payment?"

"It is *my* fee." Nkolosi was no longer laughing. His eyes were expressionless but the corners of his mouth showed renewed amusement. "Go to Mtshali and get the bomb. Seven months from the eve of the day the Negwenya entered Mtshali's body, you are to blow up the women's section of Roeland Street Gaol."

"But Riena is there," Tom said.

It was not Nkolosi the witchdoctor who responded; it was Nkolosi the radical. The political activist. Tom had never seen him play that role before, though he'd heard it rumored that the witchdoctor was also the leader of Africans for Independence. As a dedicated believer in the pen being mightier than the sword, he had stayed away from the AFI.

"I warned you payment would not be easy," Nkolosi said. "Dead women make good publicity."

"And if I refuse?"

Apparently assuming his command to be stronger as magician rather than as soldier, Nkolosi resumed the mantle of witchdoctor. Crouching, he directed his right hand in the design that was becoming all too familiar to Tom. When he reached the tail, he drew it lovingly, his long nail creating intricate patterns with a circular, flowing motion.

"Stop!" Tom said. His eye caught the silhouette of a *Likkewaan* sunning itself behind a rock. He felt a chill, despite the summer heat.

"I knew I could rely on you," Nkolosi said. He put the finishing touches on the Negwenya's tail, then slowly and gently erased the image.

Tom delayed going to see Alfred until his fear of Nkolosi outweighed his revulsion at the idea of what he had to do. Three weeks after his visit to the witchdoctor, he finally drove around the mountain to Zeekoevlei. To the shack where the three of them—he, Alfred and Riena—had talked of growing up and going to college and getting married. Pretending they could be anything they wanted to be. Like real people. White people.

"Get the hell out of here, Sibanda," Alfred screamed when he saw Tom. He was in bed. A sheet, strung across the window, protected him from the sunlight and kept his face in shadow. Tom couldn't see his half-brother's face, but the voice was that of a very old man.

"Since you don't appear to be leaving," Mtshali said, when he had calmed down, "would you care to see beneath this blanket?"

Tom shook his head, knowing full well Mtshali would take no notice. "Nkolosi sent me for the bomb."

"You'll look at your handiwork before I show you mine," Mtshali said, throwing off the covers.

His belly was enormous. Even in the dim light, Tom could see that the flesh was taut, its black surface patterned by waves and ridges. He watched, fascinated, as a large protrusion moved back and forth, a centimeter at a time, pulling the flesh along with it in a pendulum motion that synchronized with Tom's heartbeat.

"Is that. . . ."

". . . The tail. It is never still." Mtshali sat up with extreme difficulty. "The bomb's in the corner."

He might as well have been talking to himself. Tom was gone. In the garden. Retching as if he were trying to expel some evil being from his own body.

A week later, with only a few hours to go before the job had to be done, Tom went back to collect the bomb. Then, unable to rid himself of the image of Riena's body splattered against the walls of her cell, he dialed the number of Roeland Street Gaol and asked to speak to Warden Piet Barnard.

"Empty the cells," Tom warned. "The jail's going to be bombed."

"You and who else? You're the tenth caller this week."

"This call's for real," Tom said.

"Where would you suggest we put all the prisoners, man? Out on the streets?"

"I don't care where you put them. Just get them out of there."

"What can you hope to achieve by killing your own

people? You must know they won't let me empty the cells.''

"There it is again, that anonymous 'they,'" Tom thought. The world's scapegoat. And his, too. "I've warned you, Warden. That makes it your choice as much as mine. If you do nothing, you'll be as responsible as I—we—are for their deaths. And they will die, you know."

"There have been too many false alarms. No one will listen to me." Barnard's voice held a note of pleading. "Don't those lives mean anything to you?"

"They're expendable," Tom said coldly. "Just as you and I are."

The harsher he sounded, Tom thought, the more likely Barnard would be to believe him. He was already convinced that the man cared and he wanted to say something more, something that would strike whatever chord it was that would make the warden take the risk of offending "them." He waited for a moment before replacing the receiver. Hoping. Praying to a God he'd thought he'd long since abandoned.

That God had, apparently, abandoned him. He heard a click at the other end of the line. Forgive me, Riena, he thought. For what I am about to do—forgive me.

4

Dynamite is non-discriminatory.

Mtshali's bomb caught even the rats by surprise and mingled their remains with black flesh and brown limbs and grey blankets.

It also blew a jagged, body-sized hole in the south wall of a corner cell.

Tom knew he had no business staying so close to the prison but he crouched in the shadows, watching the area around the service gates turn into a bizarre disco-theque. Sirens wailed. Sentries danced a grotesque Watusi between their posts and gyrating strobes bounced in a crazy kaleidoscope off the thousands of glass fragments embedded in the top of the surface of the prison wall. When the khaki-clad guard at the gate slicked back his hair and raised himself lightly on his toes, Tom half expected him to use his rifle as a cane and break into a soft-shoe.

"A boiler accident," a voice said close to him.

Tom recognized the warden's voice and froze. The man was standing at the outer edge of a concrete yard that separated the service gates from the burning building.

"Any survivors?" a second voice asked.

"I don't think so."

"Could this happen again?"

"Probably," the warden said. Tom could hear the same hesitation he had heard before in the man's voice. Then something drew his attention away from the con-versation, and he watched a figure emerge from the hole he had blown in the wall.

"Come with me," the warden said loudly to his hid-den companion. "I'll see if I can get you a list of the dead."

The deliberate way in which he moved out of the path of the survivor told Tom he had surely seen the fig-ure too. He watched it come closer. It was wrapped in a prison blanket and looked more like a moving rock than a human being.

Forgetting the pain she had caused him, Tom willed the figure to be Riena. His mouth filled with the metallic memory of the blood he had sucked from her spindly young leg and he smiled, remembering how she hated being called "*stokkies*" by all of the boys because of her skinny legs. By the time she was fourteen and her legs stopped resembling sticks, the nickname had stopped bothering her.

The figure was more than halfway across the con-crete before Tom dared to look closely at its face.

When he recognized its contours, it was all he could do to restrain himself from calling out to Riena. He dug his nails into his palm and concentrated on the pain, forcing himself to remain silent.

"Where the hell d'you think you're going, lady?"

Tom couldn't see the questioner but he assumed it to be one of the guards.

"Home," Riena said.

"You work in there?"

By craning his neck, Tom could see the guard's face. He watched Riena relax her hold on the blanket and imagined the man's eyes sliding from the curve of her breast to her bare toes and ankles. Clever, Riena. Very clever, Tom thought, waiting to hear the guard's reaction to her nudity. If there was anything that could get her out of there, it was the promise of her body.

"Where are your clothes, woman?" The man's tone was relatively gentle.

"In there," Riena said. "Lucky I got out with my bloody life."

"If you're hurt I can get the ambulance boys to take a look at you," the man said. "If not. . . ." He took a step forward.

"I'm fine. All I need is a hot bath," Riena said.

She let the man fondle her for a moment. Satisfied, he opened the gates for two ambulances and waved her through. She stumbled into the dimly lit parking lot, and Tom caught a side view of her pregnancy. He had hoped she might have lost the baby in prison, but the white thing was still growing inside her; the sight brought on a surge of the old contempt. Then, seeing her collapse against the nearest car, instinct took over.

"Riena!"

She moved her head slightly.

"Riena. It's Tom."

As if her adrenalin had stopped flowing after her charade with the guard, Riena allowed herself to be led to Tom's car. She didn't react at all until she felt the movement of the wheels, and even then all she did was cross her hands over her breasts to warm her hands in her armpits and cover her nakedness.

The gesture touched Tom. He leanded sideways and pulled the blanket over her. "It won't do to get arrested now for obscenity," he said lightly.

"Where are we going?" Riena asked, speaking for the first time.

"Zeekoevlei. To visit Mtshali."

"Alfred? What for?"

The two of you can help each other give birth, Tom thought. "Go to sleep. It's a long drive," he said, offering no explanation.

Like a child used to obeying orders, Riena settled herself against the seat and closed her eyes. She held her hands around her extended belly, as if protecting the infant inside. Seeing her do that, Tom felt his anger at her returning. He concentrated on keeping the wheels of the car as far away as possible from the edge of the cliff.

Executing De Waal Drive's convolutions made the sand road to the hideout seem like an easy ride, despite the familiar potholes which jerked Riena awake.

"Is Alfred allowed to live here now?" she asked. "Have things improved that much?"

"Allowed?" Tom laughed. "No. He's not allowed to live here. But the animals and the weeds don't give a damn. This is still White territory but no one cares."

He stopped the car and told Riena to wait while he got out and opened the trunk to remove a small kerosene lamp. "Alfred won't let anything resembling fire in the place, but I can't stand that perpetual darkness," he said, helping her out.

"The mosquitoes haven't changed. Don't they know they're supposed to sleep at night?" Riena asked, brushing her face as they approached the shack. The screeching of the gulls, whose sleep they had also disturbed, followed them inside.

"The place stinks," Tom said. He fumbled in his pocket for matches. "He's turned it into a giant womb."

He lit the lamp. As it flared, Riena doubled over. "I'm in labor, Tom," she said.

Tom ignored her until she straightened up. He was

about to speak, to tell her about Alfred, but his half-brother's voice preempted him.

"Negwenya!"

The word was barely intelligible, the fear unmistakable.

"Alfred's in labor, too," Tom said, as Riena doubled over again.

When the pain had subsided she straightened up, though with difficulty. Tom could see by the look on her face that she understood what was happening.

"The young Negwenya is ready to breathe fire with the coming dawn," he said.

Picking up the kerosene lamp, he led the way into Alfred's room. Riena followed. The room was littered with stacks of unwashed dishes and with the paraphernalia of making bombs. Underwear—dirty judging by the odor—covered the chair next to Alfred's bed.

Riena sat down on the bed and stretched out her hand to touch Mtshali, her face torn between disgust and pity.

"Why haven't you taken him to a hospital, Tom?" she asked quietly. Her right hand was resting on the Zulu's pregnant belly, her left anticipating the next pain from her own womb.

The figure on the bed shook and turned to face the wall. "Go away; it's no use. Leave me alone. If I'm alone, she'll come for the child and it will all be over."

"Can't we get him to a hospital? Show him x-rays? Convince him there's nothing there?"

"The Negwenya's child is in there. Can't you see him?" Tom said. He leaned over and tugged at the light blanket that covered the Black man's swollen belly.

"In God's name force him to get medical attention," Riena shouted, recoiling from the sight of Alfred Mtshali's undulating skin. She could see a shape, moving gently, first from side to side and then up and down, like a watersnake caught in the weeds.

Her own child demanded attention and she bent over. When the pain passed, she lifted her head and wiped her face on one of Alfred's undershirts. "I'm not going to sit here and watch him die," she said. "If I can forgive him for what he did to me, you can surely do the same."

Tom didn't move. There was no way he was going to help that bastard, he thought.

"I'm not having my baby in this place," Riena said, standing up.

"The fire," Alfred croaked. "Get it out of here. The Negwenya doesn't like it."

Tom glanced out of the window at the lightening sky. He didn't care about Riena's White bastard. As far as he was concerned, it could burn with his half-brother. He did care about himself; he wasn't ready to let the Negwenya take him. Nor, he admitted to himself, did he want to be responsible for hurting Riena. He had risked that once, and once was more than enough.

Holding the lamp in one hand, Tom half-carried Riena out of the house. When they were some distance away, he released his hold on her and she sank to the ground.

"I won't be the first woman to give birth here," she said, drawing her knees to her chin. "Help him, Tom. Get him out of there before the Negwenya takes him."

Allowing himself a split-second of doubt, Tom turned to face the house.

"Now, Tom. Please."

She checked to see if the head of her child had appeared. Tom, who had turned to look at her, averted his eyes. Rising slowly from his haunches, he stepped forward, moving into the sun's first rays.

He didn't have time for a second step. With a roar that muffled the cry of a newborn generation, the shanty burst into flames.

Tom, near enough to feel the heat, watched their hideout burn as if a giant match had ignited the world's largest junkpile. Flames licked the sky and he stared awestruck as they formed themselves into the shape Nkolosi had drawn in the dirt—the pinpointed ears, the curling tail, the wings ready to unfurl.

Suddenly the Negwenya began to move. Sensuously. Lazily. Dancing to the tune of Nkolosi's laughter.

"Run, Tom," Riena yelled, placing her son on her stomach so that she could cover him with her prison blanket. "Run. We'll be all right till someone comes."

Though he wanted desperately to take Riena at her word and run, he knelt in the grass and stroked her hair. "I'll carry you to the car and take you with me," he said.

"They prepared me for natural childbirth in prison," Riena said, "not for the Grand Prix."

Tom looked up at the sky, where the Negwenya hovered over them. Nkolosi, he thought. He had to get to Nkolosi. In a futile last gesture, he tucked the blanket around Riena. Then he was in the car, flooring the accelerator, bumping his way off the dusty road and onto De Waal Drive.

With fear running a marathon in his head, Tom took De Waal Drive's curves at reckless speed. For three miles he refused to look in his rear view mirror. When he did, the Negwenya was so close that he could read the affection in her eyes. She was floating, keeping the distance between them constant, her wings only half-extended.

Forgetting about everything except the need to outrun his pursuer, Tom sped through town, over High Level Road, and onto Marine Drive. He wound past miles of ocean at sea level, past deserted beaches waiting for Cape Town's sleeping sun worshipers to assume their positions on the sand, then up again, over a mountain pass, the sea dropping further and further below, and back down, thousands of feet, until he was at sea level once more. And driving. Still driving, toward a harbor now, fishing boats coming closer, rocking violently in the curve and splash of water rebounding from a long wooden pier. Enticing the car closer. Closer. Daring him to plunge between the whipping masts and the rough quay that held the waves at bay.

Tom's foot jammed the brake.

The perfume of seaweed mingled with salt. Fishermen, drawing their nets up against the wind, looked curiously at him and two teenagers, astride their bicycles,

34

turned away disappointed that he hadn't driven into the water. Sorry to let you down kids, Tom thought, clutching the steering wheel and breathing hard. Then, jumping out of the car, he ran onto a stretch of beach that was protected from the intrusion of the open sea by a semi-circular barrier of rocks.

As a shadow overhead cut out the sun, he saw Nkolosi, cross-legged, drawing with slow, semi-circular movements. "I paid the asking price, Nkolosi," Tom said, panting. He dropped onto his knees.

"You paid my price," the witchdoctor said. He laughed erasing the image in the sand. "The Negwenya will be lonely without your half-brother. It seems she finds you attractive. She has already bought your services, so perhaps this time she will be a less demanding mistress. I trust you will be an attentive gigolo, Sibanda."

Tom felt the shadow of the Negwenya protecting his neck from the sun. He watched Nkolosi unfurl himself and stand up to his full height. He wore no shirt and his muscles rippled under a shiny layer of sweat.

"We'll be seeing you, Sibanda," he said evenly. "Now go."

Go, Tom thought. Go where? No matter where he went, Nkolosi and his Negwenya would find him.

"Go, Sibanda!"

When Tom stood up he was taller than Nkolosi, yet he felt infinitesimally small. He looked down at the sand crab that had moved slowly over his shoe and clung there now, seeking refuge from the burning sand in the shadow of his trouser cuff.

"Negwenya?" he said, afraid to look up, sure he would be greeted by the avaricious eyes of a courtesan.

"She's long gone you fool," Nkolosi said. He turned on his heel and padded across the sand away from Tom, his hardened soles barely leaving an indentation to prove he had been there at all.

Suddenly Tom was aware of the sun, beating mercilessly into the back of his neck where the Negwenya's shadow had protected him. With a slow, tentative motion, he looked up. The sky was clear. A few wisps of clouds, a seagull, a kite spinning its tail on a downward spiral. There was nothing else.

5

With the sand crab still clinging to his foot, Tom walked down to the water's edge and stood there for a while, trying to piece together his thoughts. No matter what it was he examined, he returned to the Negwenya. It was as if she had become his vortex. When he started to think about Alfred, he saw images of the young Negwenya, floating away on a mattress of smoke. When he tried to analyze Nkolosi's words, the memory of the cold shadow on his neck made him shudder, and he pushed that aside too. He tried to make some order out of the next day, the next week, the next month, but any contemplation of his future without the insidious presence of Nkolosi and his . . . what? He had started to think servant. Subject. Slave. But Nkolosi's constant references to her choices belied anything that simple. What little sense of logic Tom had left told him that Nkolosi and the Negwenya were really both manifestations of the same force.

Feeling utterly alone, Tom trudged to his car. He drove aimlessly until he came upon a young African woman, an infant tied to her back in a sunburst blanket. She smiled and waved at him, her beaming face framed in a spiral of orange turban. He caught a flash of a tiny black head, peeking out of its pouch. It looked so comfortable in its woven womb. He thought of Riena, drawing her child into the coarse folds of a prison blanket, waiting to be found and hoping that whoever found her would be friend and not foe. Someone who would help mother and child get out of sight before the fire trucks arrived. He felt a twinge of guilt at having left them there, lying on the ground, and consoled himself by remembering how eminently sensible Riena was. By now she would surely be tucked away in some safe refuge. . . .

Refuge, Tom thought. That was what he needed. Not that runing away was going to provide safety for the long term, but he could use a soft bosom, a sympathetic ear, someone rational to remind him that he was living in the twentieth century, not in the dark ages.

He played with the images of various women: Carla, who could drink him under the table; Vera, who was incomparable in bed; Lisa. Cross-eyed Lisa who actually listened when he spoke and responded in a relatively intelligent fashion. He enjoyed each one of them; each one had often given him what he needed. But now, today, what he needed was Riena. Even tired and despondent, she would understand his needs, he thought, realizing that he no longer felt any anger toward her. She would perhaps not lend him her bosom—he grinned, his sense of humor beginning to restore itself—but her shoulder would probably do just as well.

Feeling a great deal better, Tom took stock of his surroundings. He was on High Level Road, heading away from Sea Point toward town. In fact, he thought wryly, if he kept heading in the same direction, he'd end up at Roeland Street Gaol.

Without stopping to wonder how she'd get there, Tom decided that the most obvious place to look for Riena would be down at the docks. He'd always liked watching the ships anyway, and if memory served him right, the circus had set up its tents down there. They would make for a pleasant distraction while he waited around to see if Riena showed up.

The usual line of cars waited to pass inspection at the entrance to Duncan Docks. As Tom inched his way forward, he caught the sound of a circus elephant, trumpeting its answer to the Mouille Point foghorn which, ignoring the brilliant sunshine, issued its warning across the ocean.

When the customs official finally waved him through, Tom parked near a loading dock and headed toward the Big Top. He could hear the snap of canvas against canvas as the tent's entrance flaps responded to the rising wind, and he gladly lost himself in the changing tempo of circus hands and dock workers, businessmen and prostitutes, quickly becoming a part of the choreography of the foreshore.

"There's no freak show, Ma. Why isn't there a freak show? I wanna see a freak show," a child wailed, somewhere out of sight.

The whole fucking world's a freak show, kid, Tom thought, remembering how badly he'd wanted to go to a circus when he was a child. He'd finally earned the two and sixpence for the ticket by selling flowers. Stolen flowers. He had hidden the money and kept it for almost a year, waiting for the circus to come back to town. By the time it did, Riena had come to stay with them. He'd gone anyway, alone, but his pleasure had been spoilt by guilt that he hadn't found a way to buy her a ticket too.

"Something wrong, boy?"

A sudden pain in his stomach had stopped Tom in midstride. He leaned up against a crane, stifling his urge to look up into the sky in search of the Negwenya.

"No, sir. I'm fine, sir," he said, straightening up.

The White man grinned. "I suppose you *kaffirs* get gas pains the same way we do," he said.

His voice was kind enough. One man sympathizing with another. He seemed unaware of the implied insult. Tom wanted to put his fist through the man's teeth but the satisfaction was hardly worth a jail sentence. He nodded politely and said: "Just a little hungry, sir."

The man put his briefcase between his feet, reached into his pocket, and held out a coin. Not wanting to draw any more attention to himself than he already had, Tom grinned politely, did a small obligatory shuffle, and took the coin from the man's outstretched hand. When the man moved away Tom flung the money aside in distaste, his pleasure in the docks gone. As he headed toward Riena's shanty, he tried to remember when he'd last eaten. He couldn't. Looking up at the sky, he grinned sheepishly at his not so latent paranoia.

Tom knocked lightly at Riena's door. There was no response. He tried once, and then again. Convinced that no one was there, but equally sure that Riena would be back later, he decided to find something to eat and return to wait for her. Half an hour later, his stomach pains gone, Tom was back. Looking for an inconspicuous place to wait, he settled on the spot where Alfred had hidden before Riena's arrest. It was sheltered from the sun and faced away from the mainstream of traffic. Besides, it pleased his sense of irony that Alfred's treachery had saved him some legwork.

Several hours later the circus band, blaring forth a Sousa march, woke Tom from a surprisingly dreamless sleep. The sun had moved low over the ocean and he was drenched in sweat. He stood up and squinted at the doorway he had intended to keep under surveillance. It was still shut and there was no sign of life, no sound coming from it.

He was debating the efficacy of hanging around with darkness imminent and had just about decided that Riena wasn't going to show up after all when the music stopped.

"Sure you'll be all right now, Riena?" a voice said. It was soft. Vaguely familiar. "I still think you need to see a doctor for sure. You only gave birth this morning and that was a long drive."

"I'm fine. Really.

The second voice was Riena's. Tom pulled back against the side of the shed, waiting for her companion to leave.

"What about food? Do you have anything to eat in there?"

"I'll be okay, honestly Miss. . . ."

". . . for heaven's sake, Riena. How many times do I have to tell you to call me Deanna?"

"Some habits are hard to break. M . . . Deanna."

"Will you phone me if you need anything?"

"I will. Honestly. And thank you."

"What for?"

"For taking my baby to Ma. For the clothes. For bringing me here."

Riena sounded close to tears. Her door clicked open and shut, and the other woman's heels faded away. The circus band began another of its marches and Tom left his hiding place. He crossed quickly to the shanty which looked as uninhabited as it had before.

He tried the door. It was locked. As he had done earlier, Tom knocked lightly, once and then again.

"Tom!" Riena didn't try to hide her relief. "Come in and close the door. For a moment I thought you were one of my old tricks. . . ." She left the sentence hanging and walked over to the bed. "I'm going to lie down."

She looked pale and haggard. In pain.

"Who was that woman talking to you?"

"Deanna Rosen. She's one of Ma's customers. Don't you remember her?"

"I never took much notice of Ma's ladies."

Riena opened her zipper and stepped out of a floral skirt that was noticeably too long.

"Is that her skirt?"

"Yes." Riena lay down and turned laboriously on her side to face Tom. "Why don't you make me some coffee?"

"Later. First tell me what happened."

"Miss . . . Deanna . . . came to Zeekoevlei looking for Alfred."

"For Alfred?"

Riena nodded.

"Would you mind telling me what a nice, White, Jewish lady was doing looking for him?"

"It's not all that complicated. She was one of his teachers at the university. His mentor, she said. Said he was one of the best students she'd ever had. She couldn't understand why he'd drop out so close to his degree."

"So she went looking for him at Zeekoevlei? Why not

40

the *location?*"

"Don't be so damn suspicious. She went there first."

"Why did she wait so long to look for him? He dropped out almost a year ago."

"Nine months." Riena felt her stomach. "I have no idea why she waited but I'm bloody glad she did. If she hadn't come along when she did, I'd probably be back in jail by now."

Tom moved across the room and sat down on the bed, placing himself in the curve of Riena's body. He leaned over to smooth out her frown with his fingertips. "Was it very bad?" he asked.

"The birth? No. It wasn't bad."

"Not the birth. The explosion." He took her hand.

"What d'you think it was like, Tom? Seeing the mutilated bodies of people who'd become my friends; being envious of their commuted sentences."

"At least you weren't physically hurt."

"Wasn't I? My arm's numb, Tom. I'm not sure exactly what happened. I remember feeling something warm trickling down my arm. It was dark, so I tasted it. When I realized it was blood, I decided I wanted to live after all. That's when I walked out."

"Let me look at your arm," Tom said. He felt only the slightest guilt for having caused the injury. His stronger emotion was pique—he'd wanted to talk to Riena about his own troubles, not give medical aid.

"You really ought to go to the emergency room," he said, examining the wound. It had begun to suppurate and needed to be lanced and dressed. A shot of penicillin was probably also in order.

"I'm not seeing a doctor," Riena said firmly. Tom started to argue, then stopped. He could hardly blame her for not wanting to go to a hospital.

"Do you think they know I got away?" Riena asked.

"Unless the ambulance crews took a proper head count, they'll probably just list you with the dead."

"I'm not so sure I'm alive." She sounded pitifully tired. "If I am, it's just barely."

"Don't give up now," Tom said, abandoning all

41

thought of getting her to a doctor. "Survive, lady. Even if you have to do it one day, one hour, one minute at a time." That's all the struggle she can handle right now, Tom decided. She was penniless. A convicted criminal with no papers. If she was trying to assess her chances for a new life, she was probably coming up with realities that were none too pleasant. As for resuming her old life, by the looks of her she wasn't going to be able to do that for a while.

"I have a first aid kit and antibiotics at my house," Tom said.

"I don't. . . ."

". . . It's that or gangrene. I'll help you dress."

Riena moved as if she were hanging onto consciousness by the barest thread.

"Did I hear you thanking that woman for taking your baby to Ma?" Tom asked, not because he really cared about the fate of her White bastard but rather to deflect Riena's thoughts from her physical pain.

"Son, Tom. His name's Jacob. I couldn't very well bring him here, could I?"

"No. I suppose not."

"He'd have gone to Ma if I'd had him in prison. I was used to the idea of not taking care of him myself."

"Is he. . . .?"

"Yes. He looks White. And I won't say I'm sorry because I'm not. I have no reason to be."

Tom recognized the firm set of Riena's mouth. The discussion appeared to have started her adrenalin working again.

"You can't still hate me because of Jake—or can you?"

"I never really hated you, Riena," Tom said, helping her put on her shoes. "What I hated was the thought of the two of you together—in bed. . . ."

". . . Making love? Do you think color has anything to do with the way people feel inside? Do you think his sperm is any different than yours? Let me tell you something about yourself, Thomas. You're at least as prejudiced as any White man I know."

Though he knew Riena's words were partly born of hysteria, they were hitting home and Tom had no answer to give her. His hatred for Whites had become as automatic as breathing. It was almost impossible for him to face it and evaluate it because he could not remember a time when it had not existed. His judgment of the White man had never veered from its bitter path. Now, meeting the look in Riena's eyes, he realized that if she was to be his haven, he would have to reexamine his indiscriminate contempt. Or at the very least, subdue it.

6

Tom supported Riena to the car. She stood against it while he unlocked the door, molding herself into the metal contours as if she hoped her aching body would appropriate some of its solidity. By the time she had crawled inside, shielding her injured arm as best she could from contact with the seat, Tom had started the engine. She rubbed her eyes, as if her vision had clouded, and Tom could recognize pain and fatigue in the slope of her shoulders.

"Sleep," he ordered, edging into the semi-darkness that was swallowing the cranes and storage sheds around them. The circus, not yet fully alive for the evening performance, gained an ethereal quality from the mist that habitually rolled in at dusk, and the foghorn's ghostly howl followed them out of the docks.

"I can sleep later," Riena said. "First I want to know why you came looking for me here. I suspect it wasn't entirely altruistic. And what happened to the . . . Negwenya?"

"She followed me," Tom began. He looked over at Riena, struggling to find a comfortable position, and decided that was not the time to air his fears. "Later," he said, echoing her. "I'd rather talk about you. How much time did you have left to serve?"

"I don't know. They gave me an indeterminate sentence."

"What happened to your lover? I presume they tapped him on the wrist and told him to go home." Tom couldn't help the sarcasm that crept into his voice. "Have you heard from him?"

"No. I'm sure he's been writing but you know they'd never let the letters through."

They again, Tom thought. The same they who didn't listen to warnings. "How did you meet him, Riena? Was he one of your johns?"

"Tom!" She sounded more weary than angry. "He gave a lecture. I went to hear him and . . . it doesn't matter. What have you been doing with yourself, Tom? Living off the fat of the land while you write, or have you been self-supporting?"

"I went on a drunk after that day at the docks. Didn't come out of it for two months. I haven't written anything since then," Tom said, deciding not to tell her about his manuscript. "I drove for Van Der Merwe for a while after that."

"The Nat politician?"

"Yes. It didn't last long, though."

"Why?"

"I'm not sure. Since then I've pretty much been living from hand to mouth. The occasional poker game—whatever I can pick up. I haven't been starving."

"And your book? It's not going to write itself."

"I'm not sure there's any point in going on with it. If it ever sees print, they'll lock me up; if it doesn't, it's an exercise in futility."

"Can't you write an a-political novel?"

"I've tried. No matter what I begin to write, it ends up having political overtones—undertones. It doesn't really matter. Nothing changes and my writing about it isn't going to make a damn bit of difference."

"Are you saying nothing's changed in the last eight or

nine months? That's not what I heard."

Riena looked in no shape for one of South Africa's interminable political discussions. Nonetheless, she obviously wanted to talk about the state of the nation. She'd told Tom once that it helped her to talk about the horrors of the system, as if verbalizing them excused their existence. For him, talking simply heightened his sensitivity. That was why he had begun to write about it—until even that became too painful.

"I hear there's a public beach in Port Elizabeth that's allowing mixed bathing," Riena said. "And that some Catholic schools now have integrated classrooms."

"Which is fine if you happen to be Catholic. When the Dutch Reform Church does that. . . ."

". . . Dreamer. Anything else?"

"A few 'Whites-only' signs have disappeared. We can go to five star hotels and restaurants and dance at the Carlton—provided we use the non-European toilets."

"What about sports? Jobs?"

"We now have mixed teams—but still no mixed audiences. Jobs? *Capies* may now work as hairdressers, wait on Europeans at Stuttafords and Garlicks, be secretaries. . . ."

". . . at equal pay?"

Tom laughed. "You can't be serious."

Riena's eyes were closing. "Go on talking," she said. "I can hear you."

"There's one other thing," Tom went on. "You may not be a European but you can make vacation plans just like the white folks. Travel by air. Sit anywhere on the plane and be waited on by a European stewardess."

"What on earth possessed them?" Riena mumbled.

"Some international regulation governing commercial aviation. Wait! Let me not forget the icing on the cake! Foreign Blacks, Kenyans and such, may now eat in any South African restaurant. Some of them even socialize with Europeans. Lucky bastards, aren't they?"

Tom's bitterness was lost on Riena. She was asleep. To his amazement, she looked as if she were smiling. Perhaps, he thought, she was picturing herself with her

45

lover, lying on the sands of a Port Elizabeth beach.

With Riena asleep, Tom had to face his mounting terror. Each mile took them closer to his house, and though he wasn't fooling himself into believing that he would be safe from the Negwenya elsewhere, going home seemed like issuing her an invitation to the dance. He tried telling himself it was absurd to believe in her at all, but each time he had himself nearly convinced, he was bombarded by images of Alfred in various stages of his grotesque pregnancy. He was so immersed in his thoughts that he almost missed his narrow driveway. He had to stop the car and back up, and in doing so he barely avoided hitting an elderly man who had stooped to retrieve something from the gutter.

The old man straightened up, his leathery face a study in bewilderment. His skin looked distorted and yellowed in the car's headlights and his Salvation Army shirt hung two sizes too big around his spare frame. He held out his arms to warn Tom of his presence, a suburban scarecrow imitating its fellows who dotted the Transkei. Why aren't you there, old man, Tom wondered. In the new homeland where the authorities have sent the elderly. People like his grandfather, whose roots were in neither world, told to: "Go home and act like an African."

It hadn't surprised Tom that his grandfather obeyed without question. There was no other way left for the old man to behave. Not even all of the young ones rebelled, Tom thought. And those who did stayed on in windowless corrugated iron shacks, on land they could never own. They exploited each other, and accepted being exploited by the Europeans, because the urban veneer of civilization was irresistible. Somehow the tall glass buildings and department stores helped them cling to their foolish dreams of a larger future. The trouble was those damnable African drums. They kept penetrating that veneer . . . no matter how desperately we pretend to turn a deaf ear to the primitive beat of our ancestors, he thought angrily, eventually the rhythm penetrates. And even if it had any chance of dying, the

46

Nkolosis would keep it alive.

"Where are we?"

Riena sounded confused. She started to sit up and clutched her arm.

"Pain?"

"Yes. And I just remembered why I'm not in my prison cot." She lay back and adjusted her position as if she were seeking the warmth created by her own body.

"Come on," Tom said, helping her out of the car. "I want to take a look at that arm." She's young, he thought. She'll make a fast recovery.

Suddenly he was aware of the soft murmur of voices floating through his kitchen window.

The police, Tom thought automatically, knowing full well that they didn't need a warrant to enter and search his home. But when nobody came up at them from the bushes he discarded that theory. Then he heard the clatter of a coffee cup against the porcelain sink and he grinned. At least it wasn't the Negwenya; she would hardly be drinking coffee and chatting at his kitchen table.

The front door was unlocked and he pushed it open.

"What the hell took you so long, Sibanda?"

The question floated down the dark corridor on a faint beam of light from a kerosene lamp, wafting its way on waves of coffee and stale beer. The words stagnated around the edge of a scream as Riena, now fully awake, sensed some kind of insidious evil.

"Wait here," Tom whispered, holding a hand none too gently over her mouth. "And shut up."

He released his hand and watched her lean against the wall, relax, and jump as the crunch of a beer can punctuated the anonymous male hum that came from the kitchen. She slumped onto the floor and rested her head pathetically against the wall.

"What the hell took you so long, Sibanda?" Nkolosi repeated.

Tom had left the front door ajar and he could hear the crickets making love outside. Somewhere a dog barked. In the softness of the summer night, he noticed

47

for the first time the guttural quality of Nkolosi's voice.

Glancing once more at Riena who hadn't moved, Tom walked into the kitchen and closed the door behind him. He was sure Nkolosi could hear the pounding of his heart.

There were three men in the room, Nkolosi and two others, both Africans. One was young, no more than twenty-one or twenty-two. He had an ugly, raw scar on his left cheek and he looked none too happy, an expression which Tom would learn was permanent. The second man was older, judging by the white hair that contrasted sharply with his chocolate skin, yet his hands were smooth and his face was unlined.

"What are you doing here, Nkolosi?" Tom asked, trying to sound calm. "And who are they? This is still my house I think. . . ."

". . . Sit Sibanda!"

"I prefer to stand."

"Sit! It is time to talk."

"What about?" Tom asked, sitting down.

"Africans for Independence. You're about to volunteer for service to the cause."

"Oh Christ, Nkolosi!" Tom exploded, "I'm no political activist and I'm not about to become one." He said it without thinking.

"Setting an explosion is not exactly a pacifist move, nor is killing—even if the dead are prisoners of the state," Nkolosi said, "though I do understand that you did it under duress." He smiled, pleased with the impact of the words.

Here it comes, Tom thought.

"You paid me in blood, Sibanda," Nkolosi said, unsmiling now. "The Negwenya, as you know, prefers to be paid in love and affection."

Tom shuddered.

"You should be grateful to me. I interceded with her on your behalf. She had grown very fond of you and wasn't easy to convince. She's not yet given up all hope of gaining your affection, so I'm sure if I told her you'd prefer. . . ."

Tom held out his hand, palm outward, as if to ward off an attack. He was being given a choice of shedding more blood in the name of equality or succumbing to the affections of the Negwenya. Given time, he could convince himself that pacifism was a road leading nowhere; there was not enough time in the universe to alter his fear of the Negwenya.

"Will she leave me alone?" he asked.

"I can make no guarantees. She has a very strong will. But if you do as I say, she may become bored and find a new lover."

"What is it you want of me?"

Tom's mouth was dry and the words stuck on his tongue.

"Sit down." Nkolosi's voice was benign. "If George here can spare a beer. . . ."

A barely perceptible thud stopped him in midsentence. George, preparing to crunch yet another in his never-ending series of empty beer cans, heard nothing. The other man, the older one, sensed rather than heard the soft sound. Without saying anything, he stood and walked past Tom to open the kitchen door. He narrowed his eyes to accustom them to the darkness and made out Riena's shapeless form, huddling somewhere between the wall and the floor.

"What the fuck is that?" he asked quietly, directing his question at Tom who walked into the passageway, lifted Riena by her good arm, and led her into the kitchen.

"That," Nkolosi said, "is Tom's other female problem. Riena Parker, I believe."

Riena backed away, terrified by the same nameless fear which had attacked her before in the corridor.

"Good looking bird," the younger man said. He opened another can of beer and stood up.

"Don't you touch her," Tom said sharply, surprised at the extent of his own reaction.

"We'll deal with the matter of the woman later," Nkolosi said. "Get her into the bedroom and then get back in here, Sibanda. No one's going to touch her—for

49

now, anyway."

George looked at Tom as if he wanted to slit his throat.

"She could prove useful to us," the older man said softly.

"I intend her to be," Nkolosi said. "Put her in your room for tonight, Tom. We're going to be talking for a while anyway. Simon, make some coffee and sandwiches. She'll be no use to us if she starves to death."

The older man nodded and got up. Tom thought he saw a measure of compassion in the man's eyes and wondered just what kind of threat Nkolosi was holding over his head. It was possible that the man was a willing member of the AFI. George surely was. He looked as if he derived great pleasure out of violence but there was something gentle about the older man.

"My room's the one furthest from the kitchen," Tom said, guiding Riena one more time down the dark corridor. He opened a door to show her the bathroom and took a dressing gown off a red plastic hook on the back of the bathroom door. "Here, wear this," he said, handing it to her. "It won't fit, but it's the best I can do. As you probably gathered, I wasn't exactly expecting company." Riena made no move to take the robe, so he draped it around her shoulders. "Get into bed and I'll bring you some food as soon as I can," he told her. "Unless you want me to check your arm first. Is the pain very bad?"

Riena shook her head.

"You'll be okay," Tom reassured her. "We'll talk tomorrow. I promise."

Riena tried to smile and thank him, but the words failed to emerge.

"Go to bed," Tom repeated, leading her to his bedroom door.

"Wash," she said weakly.

"Tomorrow," Tom said again. He opened his door, turned on the small bedside lamp that functioned from the main switch, and pushed her gently inside the room. He was worried about her wound, but that would have to wait. At least for the moment she was safe, something that could easily change if he kept Nkolosi waiting too long.

He shut the door firmly and turned his thoughts away from Riena's welfare to concentrate on his own. One step at a time, he thought, one baby step at a time. He tried to remember everything he'd heard about the AFI. It wasn't much. The membership guarded their identities closely, and for good reason. He did know that Africans for Independence did not tolerate emotional involvements of any kind; as far as they were concerned, neither family nor friendship was a necessary part of the life of a revolutionary. According to the little he had heard, any involvement was considered to be a major obstruction in the fulfillment of one's duties. Insurgence and compassion were, according to their tenets, incompatible.

And there was one other thing Tom knew, the only thing of which he was certain: the most highly valued commodity in the AFI was boldness. With that in mind, he approached the kitchen door and pushed it open as casually as if he were about to sit down to a friendly game of poker. If he was going to play the game, he thought grimly, it made sense to learn to play it well.

7

"Sit down, Tom," Nkolosi said, without preamble. His face was impassive, his eyes as expressionless as onyx. "What do you know about the AFI?"

Tom shrugged. "I've heard that it's a communist organization, that its members want equality now, and that it has no scruples about the means it uses to gain its ends."

"You're relatively well informed." Nkolosi sounded

51

surprised.

"It is a communist group then?"

"We prefer to think of ourselves as free agents. Russia is simply one other means to the ends you spoke of," Nkolosi said.

Tom walked over to the stove and poured himself a cup of thick black coffee from an aluminum pot, flinching as the plastic handle burnt his fingers.

"Anyone who believes there is such a thing as a perfect ideology is a fool, Sibanda," Nkolosi said.

"So all you really want is to drive the European into the sea. . . ."

". . . No. That's what George here wants," the witchdoctor interrupted. "He wants their cars and their money. . . .

". . . A true capitalist," Tom said bitterly.

George, his temper ever ready to surface, started to get up. Simon put a quieting hand on the younger man's shoulder.

"And you, Simon? What is it you want?"

"Simon's our resident Swahili. He came here illegally during the trouble in Kenya. We gave him a new name, new papers, and an education in exchange for his commitment to us," Nkolosi said, answering for the older man. "He wanted to be an engineer, so we sent him to Russia on a submarine, right Simon?"

"Now you're keeping your part of the bargain, is that it?" Tom said. He didn't ask about Nkolosi's motivation. It was evident that the man had an Hitlerian lust for power and needed no sentimental commitment to a cause.

"You're wrong, Sibanda," Nkolosi said quietly. "I have all the power I need." There wasn't the slightest sign of emotion on the African's face. "I want to see my people. . . ."

". . . Your people? Which are they? Your tribe? All of the Blacks? The Coloureds? All South Africans?"

"I want equality."

"At any price?"

"At any price."

You can hardly fail, Tom thought. You and your seductress have people like me by the shorts. The AFI will take care of the rest—the unbelievers. Those who don't fear magic, do fear bombs.

"One more thing," Nkolosi said. "AFI members cannot have personal attachments. It interferes with their efficiency. In your case, Sibanda, remember that you're still spoken for."

Coming from Nkolosi, his name sounded like a curse, Tom thought. "Riena could be useful to the organization," he said, repeating what someone had said earlier, though he had no idea how he could back up his statement if challenged.

"We could check her out. We do need another woman for our Jo'burg operation." It was Simon who spoke this time.

"Her name is Riena Parker, like our new brother here told us," Nkolosi said. "She was raised by his mother and, yes, she could possibly be useful to us. If we can persuade her to join us. Do you think we could do that, George?"

At the mention of his name, George returned to a fully upright position. He was immediately ready to do whatever was required of him. Except for his single interruption, he had spent the duration of Nkolosi and Tom's conversation in a beery half-sleep. Tom had the distinct feeling George would need little encouragement to 'persuade' anyone to do anything. He was a mercenary, pure and simple.

"When I have completed whatever it is you want me to do, will that free me from . . . from. . . ."

"How will you 'persuade' Riena to cooperate? Does the Negwenya perhaps have a lonely brother?" Tom sounded bitter.

"Riena has a son," Nkolosi said evenly. "He was born in the Negwenya's shadow; perhaps she will want to claim him as a playmate for her own child."

"You bastard." Tom forgot both his own vulnerability and his contempt for Riena's White-skinned child.

"I think you're forgetting yourself, Sibanda."

Nkolosi's tone was sharp. A reprimand. "You and the woman will do as I say."

"If she lives. She was hurt in the explosion. I think her wound is infected and she's had no time to recover from having given birth."

"She will live. I will see to it. As for the birth, I'll take care of that, too. I promise you, she'll be fine."

"Not if you don't let me take her some food and dress her arm. Give her a shot. . . . ."

". . . Shot! That's the European's answer to everything, isn't it? When we've finished talking, I'll show you how to take care of a wound."

Tom had no reason to question Nkolosi's talents as a healer. He had no doubt that the man was at least as competent as any trained physician.

"You did well with the explosion," Nkolosi went on. "The papers called it an accident, but as we of the AFI predicted, nobody believes that. Cape Town's buzzing with rumors and Piet Barnard's resigned."

"Barnard's resigned. Why?"

Nkolosi's only response was a shrug. Tom started to ask another question but decided against it. His only contact with Barnard had been over the telephone when he'd called to warn him to empty the cells, and he was certain he'd be in trouble if Nkolosi knew he'd done that. He'd felt a strange kind of anguish in the warden during their conversation. *"I've warned you, Warden. That makes it your choice too, not just mine. You'll be as responsible for their deaths as we are if you do nothing and they die. And they will, you know. They're expendable, Warden, just as you and I are."* It seemed too far fetched to believe, but perhaps Piet Barnard had taken him seriously and, having done nothing about emptying the cells, felt responsible for the dead inmates.

"You and the woman will obey orders!" Nkolosi was saying.

Tom had no idea what he'd missed while he thought about the warden. "Orders?"

"I'll fill you in on the details in a moment. Let me

backtrack first. Three of our AFI representatives have been granted an off-the-record hearing with Van Der Merwe and his committee. When they reject our proposal. . . ."

". . . when?"

Nkolosi shrugged impatiently. "Stop dreaming, Sibanda. They'll never agree to our terms. Not even with Van Der Merwe directing things. The man doesn't have enough power . . . yet."

Tom thought for a moment about Daniel Van Der Merwe, Nationalist Member of Parliament dedicated to the cause of separate development. He had driven the M.P.'s car for nearly a year and they'd hardly exchanged three words of unnecessary conversation. Nkolosi must be talking about a different man.

Nkolosi's mouth bent in an imitation of a smile at Tom's incredulous expression. "Van's been having a tough time with his conscience lately. He's not sleeping well. . . ."

". . . How do you know?"

"Nothing mysterious. His maid's a loyal AFI member. She has eyes and ears—and Mr. Van Der Merwe talks in his sleep. It appears the *Meneer* has a tough problem to resolve. He's fast rising to a position where he could become Prime Minister, if he toes the party line. The trouble is, he's not sure anymore that he believes the Nationalist claptrap. He's ready to look around for a more personal source of power."

And you know all about that, don't you, Nkolosi, Tom thought. "Is he a communist?"

Nkolosi threw back his head and laughed. "You're so naive, Sibanda," he said. "The love of power does not concern itself with ideologies. Van Der Merwe will use whatever power he finds. Or whatever I find for him."

"Does the Negwenya take White lovers too?"

Nkolosi's eyes hardened and Tom saw that he had taken too many liberties.

"Your orders," Nkolosi said. "By the time we get word that talks have broken down it will be Sunday morning. We'll be ready by then. . . ."

". . . Ready?"

Nkolosi nodded but didn't explain. "You and the woman leave for Johannesburg at dawn today."

"How? Why?"

"By car. And I told you I would explain everything. Patience. As I said, in a few hours you and she will be on your way to Johannesburg."

"A thousand miles is a lot of driving, Nkolosi, especially since Riena's arm will still be in bad shape. Couldn't we wait until sundown? It'll be scorching in the veld in the middle of the day."

"You'll look less suspicious during the day," Nkolosi said. "And you're to drive straight through."

Tom started to protest but the look on Nkolosi's face told him it would do no good. "Where do I take Riena once we get to Jo'burg?" he asked.

"To Arthur Cohn's house. In Houghton."

"Who the hell is Arthur. . . ."

". . . Cohn. He's a newspaperman, the head of OPI."

Tom looked puzzled.

"Overseas Press International. Mighty well informed man, Mr. Cohn, and keeps powerful company."

"What's Riena supposed to do there?"

"She's replacing the Cohns' maid."

"What happened to their present one?"

"She was uncooperative. She'll be taken care of. By the time you get there the Cohns will need a new maid, take my word for it.

Again Tom had no cause to doubt Nkolosi's efficiency. He wondered how it was possible for one man to have eyes in so many places. As for the man's removal procedures, he suspected they were best left unexamined.

"What exactly are Riena's orders?" he asked. "And mine?"

Nkolosi, his eyes boring into Tom's, gave him his instructions. By the time he'd heard everything, Tom had begun to wonder if the Negwenya's arms weren't the lesser of the two evils.

"It's a beautiful plan, is it not, Sibanda?" Nkolosi said

rhetorically when he'd finished.

"Beautiful! It's hideous," Tom said, trying to integrate what Nkolosi had told him into something his rational mind could accept. Step one: he, Tom, was to be instrumental in causing a bloody riot. Step two: Riena was to be part of a large scale plan to hold fifty prominent South Africans, and some of their families, for political ransom. And then there was step three. A lunatic plan that had every chance of success: using Johnson's Dairies to poison South Africa's major milk supply. Millions of people dying. . . .

Nkolosi turned his head slightly toward the kitchen window and nodded, as if in greeting. Tom followed the witchdoctor's glance. A shadow moved across the glass, momentarily blocking out the moon.

"It's a beautiful plan, is it not, Sibanda?" Nkolosi repeated softly.

Slowly, Tom felt himself nod.

"Riena's new name will be Elizabeth Riess," Nkolosi went on calmly. "She'll be given new identification papers. You'll be given a Pass; same name, but for the time being you're Bantu."

"Why?" Tom asked.

"You're supposed to be one of Johnson's drivers. All of his drivers are Bantu. Simon will have everything ready for her by morning. For the rest, she's to act as a servant and carry out the orders I've just given you. From now on she's a member of the AFI and subject to our rules. Tell her if she makes any attempt to get in touch with her family. . . ."

Nkolosi stood up and left the kitchen. Tom started to follow.

"Get her some food," Nkolosi ordered. "I'm going outside to collect what I need for her wound. I'll be ready in fifteen minutes and I'll want your help."

Nkolosi left, with George following him out.

Simon stood up and stretched. "I'd better get to those papers," he said. "I'm bushed. Was the woman badly hurt in the explosion?"

"It doesn't look pretty."

"Sorry, man. Nkolosi will take care of it though. *Kwakheri*. Goodnight."

" *Kwakheri*," Tom said, repeating the unfamiliar Swahili word.

Then he busied himself in the small kitchen, cleaning up and trying not to think of anything except the mundane tasks he had set for himself. He waited for a fresh pot of coffee to perk and put several slices of sweet milk cheese and tomato on two pieces of bread that were drying around the edges. As soon as the coffee was ready, he poured a cup, making it light and sweet. Then he put the sandwich and coffee on a small tray and carried it to his bedroom door.

"Riena, it's Tom," he called out, before opening the door. "Best I could do," he said. "It's not Fracarlo's, but it's edible. You must be starving." Fracarlo's, he thought, pushing the door open with his shoulder. The Europeans give their servants the same for a week's work as they pay for one order of Fracarlo's lasagna and crepe suzettes. Maybe the AFI has the right idea. He looked down at the coffee slopped into a chipped saucer and at the miserable sandwich and felt a familiar tightening of his bowels.

"Riena," he said, more sharply than he had intended.

There was no reply and he moved closer, wondering if perhaps she was dead and instantly ashamed of the thought that that might save him a great deal of trouble.

But Riena had not responded to Tom's conversation because she was curled up on one side of his double bed, fast asleep. Tom put the tray on the floor next to the bed and turned her over as gently as possible to check her arm. The three inch gouge that cut deeply into her flesh looked ugly. It was red and puffed around the edges. The center, though crusting over, was oozing thick yellow pus.

Tom went over to his closet and pulled out a Red Cross first aid kit, one he'd acquired for no particular reason except that it diminished his feeling of dependency; if the *Tsotsis* attacked him on a Friday night, at least he'd be able to dress his own wounds.

"Get me a dish of warm water, Sibanda," Nkolosi ordered.

Tom whirled around and found himself only inches away from the witchdoctor who had stolen soundlessly into the room. He stood quietly, a shallow basin balanced across his hands. He seemed to be having difficulty holding it still and Tom, sickeningly sure it held something that was alive, looked away.

8

"Go on man!" Nkolosi ordered. "Move. We don't have all night."

Tom moved quickly, skirting around Nkolosi who was blocking the most direct path to the door. A sour smell permeated the room and Tom could hear a faint rustling which seemed to come from the basin that Nkolosi was carrying over to the bed.

Not at all sure what he would see when he returned, Tom left the room. It took him no more than a minute to find a small container and fill it with lukewarm water.

"God!"

Riena's scream sent Tom hurtling down the corridor, water splashing.

"What the hell are you doing to her?" he yelled, charging into the room.

"Did you bring the water?" Nkolosi sounded as calm and sure of himself as a Harvard professor doing nothing more extraordinary than conducting an experiment he'd conducted a thousand times before.

Riena's quiet was of a different order. Anesthetized by terror, she stared blankly at the snake that was being waved slowly back and forth over her wound. Only her eyes, riveted to its gyrating tail and moving with it, proved that she was alive.

"Soak those in the water," Nkolosi ordered, gesturing with his head at the small odorous mound of grasses and herbs that still lay in the basin that had held the snake. He took a firm hold on the writhing creature and, with a practiced twist, removed its head and tossed that into the far corner of the room.

Taking hold of what was left of the snake in one hand, Nkolosi picked up a stiletto. Poising it in the air with a steady hand, he said: "Squeeze them out and hold them near the woman's arm. When I've opened the wound, remove the pus with that towel over there and stand ready to put the poultice inside."

Tom's stomach was reacting violently. He could feel it convulse as Nkolosi lanced the wound, and again when, as gently as he could, he removed the pus from Riena's arm. Riena didn't move even then. Something clicked in Tom's head and he remembered the hypnotist at the circus, the gyrating watch, the blank stare of his subject. Preoccupied, he didn't notice Nkolosi shift his hold slightly on both knife and snake, and it wasn't until the creature's blood began dripping into the wound that he realized what the motion was that he'd seen on the periphery of his vision.

In a couple of deft movements, Nkolosi had removed the snake's smooth skin.

"Out of my way," Nkolosi said. He bent over the wound which was bleeding surprisingly little and, like any physician binding his patient with surgical tape, bound Riena's arm with the tough skin of the gutted snake. Then he stood back to survey his handiwork.

"Riena," he said, his voice satisfied. "I want to ask you some questions."

"In the name of God, leave her alone, Nkolosi," Tom said. His hands were stiffening from a coating, the ingredients of which he could only guess at, and his stomach ached from its continuous convulsing. He wanted nothing more than to leave the room and go outside to breathe the clean night air. But something held him there, a kind of fascination that spoke of the power of his ancestors.

60

"She's not in pain," Nkolosi said. "Riena. Who was the father of your child?"

"Jake." The word was slurred but unmistakable.

"Jake who?"

"Jacob Prescott III."

Nkolosi straightened up and smiled, a genuine smile for the first time.

"Is that all you wanted to know?" Tom asked.

"It's all I needed to know," Nkolosi said softly. "Jacob Prescott III! Tonight the Negwenya will join in my celebration." He laughed at Tom's puzzled look. "Jacob Prescott is the nephew of Philip Prescott—United States Senator. Announced candidate for the Presidency of the United States of America. The circle will move until it closes. . . ."

The witchdoctor's voice trailed off but he seemed wide awake. Fresh. Tom wondered if he ever slept.

"Enough," Nkolosi said. "You will learn it all eventually. There is still the matter of the woman's recent childbirth to be taken care of, if she's to have the strength to complete this assignment. I warn you, you may not have the stomach for this, Sibanda."

"What are you going to do, Nkolosi?"

Tom sounded terrified and Nkolosi snorted derisively. "I'm going to remove what may be left of the afterbirth and dry her milk, so that her breasts do not leak and cause her pain."

"Why should you care about her pain?"

"I don't. But I do care that it not distract her and cause her to make a mistake. For the same reason I intend to convince her that her son was born a month, and not a day ago. Even our women sometimes suffer from—what is it the European calls it? Postnatal depression?"

Damn him, Tom thought. He has the power of the ancients and the knowledge of today. Add to that the cunning and resourcefulness of a jackal, and you have an adversary who cannot lose.

"Bring me the empty basin," Nkolosi said, going back to the bed. He removed the covers from Riena and

61

shifted her body slightly so that he had room to sit down beside her. She lay naked and still, seemingly in a deep and peaceful sleep.

"Riena," Nkolosi said. "Open your eyes."

She did as she was told but her eyes held the same vacant stare as before.

"Pull up your legs, Riena," Nkolosi said quietly.

When Riena obeyed, her movements stiff and jerky, he leaned forward and parted her legs slightly.

"The basin," he said.

Tom handed it to him and stood mesmerized as the witchdoctor coached Riena, forcing her to contract her muscles in imitation of labor until she expelled what was left of the afterbirth into the basin that had held the snake. She writhed on the bed and sweat poured down her body at the physical exertion, yet the expression in her eyes didn't change.

When she lay still, Nkolosi stretched her legs and replaced the covers. Then, placing his extended hands over her breasts, he said: "There is no longer any milk in your breasts, Riena. You do know that, don't you? If you understand what I am saying, nod your head and say yes."

Slowly Riena opened her mouth. It looked as if she were struggling to say a foreign word which would not slide comfortably around her tongue.

"Say it, Riena," Nkolosi ordered.

"Yes." The word was recognizable, but the voice was not.

"When did you give birth to your son, Riena?" Nkolosi asked.

"Yesterday," Riena said, in the same strangulated tone.

"No, Riena. Your son was one month old yesterday. If you understand me, say the words. Say: 'my son was one month old yesterday.'"

Riena opened her mouth and tried, but this time the words would not emerge. Nkolosi bent closer and took her face in his hands.

"Look at me," he ordered. "Now say: 'my son was

one month old yesterday.'''

Tom stepped closer to the bed. He felt a need to help Nkolosi, to urge Riena to say the words being forced from her.

"My son was one month old yesterday . . . my son was one month. . . ."

". . . Enough. You may sleep now," Nkolosi said, closing her eyes with his fingertips. "In the morning you will remember nothing except that your son was one month old yesterday." He rose from the bed and, still holding the basin with its bloody contents, led Tom from the room. "Clean yourself up and then check the woman to make sure she's resting well," he said, as if nothing untoward had taken place. "Be sure to get some sleep yourself, Sibanda. You have a long and tiring day ahead of you tomorrow."

A hundred questions raced through Tom's head. Most of all he wanted to ask why there had been no incantations, no calling upon the ancient gods.

"There was no need for any of that," Nkolosi said. "One must not abuse the power."

"How did you know. . . ." Tom began, but he found himself talking to the darkness. The witchdoctor had disappeared, sliding like a lizard into the night. Tom thought he heard the faint flutter of wings and then there was silence. He arched his back to stretch his tense muscles. Shower, Riena, sleep, he thought. Especially, sleep.

Fifteen minutes later, Tom was back in Riena's room. She was moaning slightly, as though a nightmare were disturbing her sleep, but she didn't wake up when he angled the Venetian blinds against the encroaching dawn.

Shutting his bedroom door quietly, Tom went into the kitchen and poured himself a cup of coffee to take out onto the porch. There was no way he could sleep yet, not until he made an attempt at sorting out some of the things he'd heard. Barnard, Van Der Merwe, Cohn, he thought, leaning against the brick wall that framed the porch. They were all moderate men who believed that reason was still a viable weapon. The trouble was that while fifty years ago it had made sense to talk about the slow uplifting of the Coloured races, it probably didn't any more. Tom looked at his watch; it was two in the morning. In less than four hours he would be on his way to the Karroo; that left a maximum of three hours for sleep. He shook his head as if to clear it and lit a cigarette, thinking about the fact that Riena knew nothing about the plans that had been made for her future. He was going to have to tell her that she'd exchanged one prison for another and the prospect did not please him. As for himself, he wasn't at all sure what kind of bargain he'd made. It seemed to him that he was being forced to take inordinate risks with no guarantee that doing so would rid him of the Negwenya—or Nkolosi, for that matter. As for the question of his conscience, that was better left unexamined. He felt like a neophyte gambler, playing against a marked deck. With no shot at inspecting the cards, it was a sucker's game. Unfortunately, it was the only game in town.

9

Despite the level of his fatigue when he finally fell asleep, Tom woke three hours later with the kind of throbbing headache usually reserved for the morning after a night of heavy drinking. His immediate thoughts were of Riena. Women weren't physically abused in South African jails and he knew she was basically healthy. But the day was going to be long and the news he had to give her would surely prove traumatic. There was no way to soften the things he had to tell her, nor was he sure she would want him to tell her anything but the bald truth.

Reluctantly, Tom dragged his body off his makeshift

bed and picked up his coffee cup; it looked the way his mouth felt. He grimaced at the thick brown rim that had congealed inside, threw what was left of the liquid over the edge of the *stoep* into the shrubbery, and absently lit a cigarette. He watched the brown liquid bounce from leaf to leaf until it reached the ground and told himself, as he inevitably did with the first puff of his first cigarette of the day, that it was time to stop smoking. Coffee. Tea. Shave. Then Riena, he said to himself, listing the mundane things as priorities in the hope that starting the day in as normal a manner as possible would make it turn out all right.

Tom's house overlooked the marshy water of a nameless *vlei* and he was close enough to the Indian Ocean to imagine its salty smell. One of the few advantages of being classified Coloured, he thought, for by no means the first time, was that he was not forced to live in an African township—damn crowded *locations* where no one had room to breathe.

The day had hardly begun but the mosquitoes were already attacking Tom's neck. It's going to be a hot one, he thought. In the pre-dawn light, he watched a dragonfly skim the brackish *vlei* water, the sapphire of its wings reflected in the rays of the rising sun. A *Piet-My-Vrou* called out to his mate from the other side of the marsh and, in the distance, the summer ocean awaited its daily hordes of sun-crazed vacationers. Indolence, Tom decided, was not all that unattractive a way of life. He balanced himself on the retaining wall of the porch and lit a second cigarette, promising himself it would be the last before he went inside. Since he wasn't going to quit that day, he thought, inhaling deeply, it didn't really matter.

He looked up at the pink clouds, drawing the sun into the sky, and wished himself on a fishing boat far out at sea. A day away from talk of bombs and politics and revolution would solve nothing. He knew that. But the idea was appealing. Hot and windy, he decided. A good day for flying kites. By the afternoon, the wind would drive Muizenberg's sun bathers away from the beaches, into the cafes with their juke boxes and slot machines. Now if he owned one of those, he'd be in good shape—though in good shape for what, he wasn't sure.

Having smoked his cigarette to the butt, Tom had no recourse but to start the business of the day. Kitchen first, he reminded himself, opening the screen door.

On his way past the bedroom door, Tom paused. Hearing movements, he changed his mind about the order of things. He knocked lightly before walking into the room.

Riena was standing at the window. She had angled the Venetian blinds and was staring at the traces of fog that hung in the air like slightly damp cotton balls.

"How're you doing?" Tom asked.

Riena turned around, as if she weren't quite sure why either of them were there.

"I'm confused," she said. "What time is it? Better yet, what day? The way my bladder feels, I must have slept for weeks."

"How's your arm?"

"That's another thing. Something keeps telling me I hurt my arm very recently but the scab looks like an old one."

"Don't you remember how you got hurt?"

"No. When I looked out there," she gestured toward the outdoors, "all I kept thinking was that I should be in prison. Not taking a holiday in the country. I think it's just the last few days that're mixed up. . . ."

". . . Do you remember having your baby?"

"Yes. But that was a month ago."

She made the statement with conviction. Nkolosi had done his work well. He had said nothing, however, about blocking out Riena's memory of the explosion, and Tom assumed that to be a natural result of trauma. For a moment, he debated triggering her memory of the explosion, thinking she might be better off not remembering, but he dismissed that as foolhardy. If she was to guard herself against the hazards to come, she had to know that she was an escapee. He walked over to her and led her back to the bed.

66

"Sit down for a minute, Riena," he said.

She did as she was told.

"You're not in jail because there was an explosion. It blew a hole in the wall of your cell and you walked away."

"When?"

"The night before last."

"Is that how I hurt my arm?" She had begun to sweat.

"Yes."

She bared her arm and showed him her wound. She was right. The scab looked well set and there was no sign of infection or inflammation.

"You must have given me mighty powerful medicine, Dr. Sibanda," she said. "By the way, I don't know what you used as a bandage; it smelled godawful. I turfed it into the corner over there. Now, if you don't mind, I'm going back to bed to think about all of this."

She was calm. Too calm, Tom thought. "Don't count on going back to bed, kiddo," Tom said gently. "I suggest you take a bath and get dressed. . . ."

". . . Do I smell that bad?"

Tom laughed. "No. But we do have a lot of talking to do. I'll hustle up some food and then help you bathe if you like."

"I could use some help," Riena said, swaying a little as she stood up.

She made no issue about his seeing her naked. They had swum together that way too often in the past for it to be a concern. December days in the *vlei*. Sharing the water with frogs and turtles and dragonflies, Tom thought.

"I'll run the water for you and make coffee," he said. "Can you make it to the bathroom by yourself?"

Ten minutes later, Tom was sitting on the steamy bathroom floor, watching Riena wolf down buttered toast as if it were spread with caviar. Then she lay back in the tub, staring at nothing. It had been a long time since Tom had last had sex. Riena's body was lean and firm, despite the slight stomach bulge which Nkolosi's ministrations had not completely eliminated. Embarrassed by the knowledge that her nakedness was arousing him, he stood up and turned his back on her to rummage in the closet under the sink.

"Time to get out," he said, a little too jovially. There was one large towel hanging over the sink and though it looked none too clean, he wrapped her in it to dry before she put his robe back on.

"I probably shouldn't look at myself," she said, removing part of the coating of steam and dirt from the bathroom mirror with the heel of her hand. She grimaced. "Could be worse I suppose." She saluted her image. "I'm still hungry," she said. "And where are my clothes?"

At the prison, Tom thought, wondering where they were going to find something for her to wear. "Let's worry about your stomach first. Riena, do you remember anything yet?"

"Leaving the prison came back to me while I was bathing but it was all vague and shadowy. Are the details important?"

Tom shook his head. It had suddenly occurred to him that if she didn't remember what had happened after the explosion, she also had no memory of having seen Alfred and the Negwenya.

"I probably should feel terrible but thanks to your magic healing powers, I don't."

Nkolosi's magic, Tom thought, realizing then that she had no memory of her encounter with the witchdoctor either.

"Lead me to the kitchen before I die of starvation."

"Eggs?"

"And more toast and coffee, please. I feel as if I've missed at least a week's worth of meals. How long did I sleep? I think I need some explanations, Tom."

"Food first, explanations later," Tom said, busying himself at the stove. "Incidentally, you do smell a lot better now than you did." He laughed, forcing himself to be casual.

"Was I really that ripe?"

"Well, let me put it this way; I'm not sorry I left the

68

bedroom window open."

"That bad, huh?" Riena laughed. "It is good to have old friends," she said, watching Tom move surely around his kitchen.

"And it's good to hear you laugh," Tom said, putting a plate of food down in front of her.

She attacked it with gusto. "I haven't done it for a long time," she said, her mouth half full.

"Done what?"

"Laughed."

Tom looked disappointed.

"That too," Riena said, laughing again as Tom joined her at the table.

He ate his toast slowly, surprised at how much pleasure he was deriving from her presence, despite the circumstances. It's almost like playing house again, he thought.

"I was thinking, while I soaked, that I'd like to try to see Ma and little Jake as soon as possible." Riena reached across the table, took one of Tom's cigarettes, and held it out for a light.

The time has come, Tom thought unhappily. But where to start? He looked at the expectant expression on Riena's face and, stalling for time, stood up and poured himself another cup of coffee.

"What's wrong, Tom?"

"Almost everything, I'm afraid," Tom said, sitting down again. "Almost everything."

"Talk," Riena said. "I'm listening."

Fully intending to stick with his decision and tell Riena the whole truth, Tom began to talk. He told her everything he knew about Nkolosi and about the history and goals of Africans for Independence.

"What does all of that have to do with me?" Riena asked.

"You've been inducted as a member. We both have."

"What?"

"I'm sorry, Riena."

She was looking at him as if she regretted ever having laid eyes on him, Tom thought. With all of her con-

69

tempt for the system, she was no more cut out to be a revolutionary than he was.

"Why on earth should I work for the AFI?" Riena said.

"Because if you don't, Nkolosi will kill your son. Or hand him over to the Negwenya. As for what he'll do to Ma. . . ."

". . . Is that what he told you?"

Tom nodded.

"And you believe him?"

"I don't know what to believe. I don't understand that bastard any better than you do."

"What is it I'm supposed to do?"

"Drive with me to Johannesburg and do a job for them," Tom said, finding himself unable to go into the specifics of what she had to do—or of what was to follow. There was no way, he thought, that he could tell her what he had to or about Nkolosi's final plan to poison everyone who bought milk from Johnson's Dairies. He would fill in the details on the way to Johannesburg, he decided.

"Where is Nkolosi now?" Riena's voice was low and calm. Too calm. But her eyes were burning with hatred.

"Damned if I know."

"Let's leave. We can get Ma and the baby and run away. . . ."

". . . Riena! Stop it. You know he'll find us."

"I could go along with the whole thing until we get to Johannesburg and then disappear."

"He'll make good his threats, Riena. You'll become an example for others who refuse to cooperate. And in the process, Ma and your. . . ."

". . . What about you, Tom? How do you feel about all of this? You've never believed that violence was the route to equality."

Riena sounded dispassionate and Tom found that disquieting. He'd expected her to shout. Argue.

"What's wrong, Tom? What did you expect from me? Tears? I suspect I've used them all up. Answer me. Please. Can you really convince yourself that violence i

70

an acceptable road to equality?"

"I'm not sure. I've argued on the side of passive resistance for a long time but the reality is that the sword is mightier than the pen."

"What good will it do us to be equal under the kind of government the Nkolosis and the Georges will impose on us?" Riena was formulating her words carefully, as if she was designing a final statement. "Do you really think our lot will be any easier under their rule than it is now? You tell me Nkolosi believes that he's using the Russians. What if they're really using him? We could end up like the East Berliners, or the Czechoslovakians, or the Poles."

"You may be right, Riena. I've thought about that too. But I think revolution, like everything else, is easier the second time around. If our people realize that, despite the revolution, change is impossible, they'll revolt again."

"It's hard to believe you're really that naive," Riena said.

"Nkolosi accused me of naiveté, too," Tom said. "I thought it was an insult at first but now I'm not so sure. Being considered an innocent isn't all that bad."

"If taking over is that easy, why didn't we do it long ago? There are over twenty million of us—twenty million, Tom. And a bare four million Europeans."

"Oh, for God's sake, Riena. Our people have been educated into servitude—and I didn't coin that phrase, so it's hardly naive. Most of them don't understand that change is possible."

"All right," Riena said. Patiently, now. As if she were addressing a child. "Assume for a moment that we are able to rid ourselves of all White domination. Who the hell is going to run this country? Or is our petrol going to flow from heaven into our gas tanks, the way the *kaffirs* in the *kraal* believe it does for the European now?"

Tom winced at the use of the derogatory word *kaffir*. "The purpose of the movement. . . ."

". . . Yes, Thomas. Tell me! Tell me their purpose." For the first time, Riena was raising her voice. "Justify

71

blowing up Black bodies; Coloured bodies. Tell me how Africans for Independence is going to shape a better world for my child. Tell me how burning our townships and schools and sabotaging our own trains is going to turn this country into Nirvana. Tell me! Go ahead, tell me!"

Cry, Tom thought. Please. But there were no tears. Empathizing with her anger and her sadness, Tom could readily understand why sentiment had no place in the business of revolution. "Riena, killing our own is the kind of sacrifice the world understands," he said gently, reaching out to take her hand.

"Maybe the end does justify the means sometimes, when the end itself makes sense," Riena said, pulling her hand away. "But what kind of end is it you're trying to justify to me, Tom? This country *is* changing. I know it's slow, but. . . ."

". . . do you really believe we could ever live together with the White South Africans, side by side in harmony . . . equal . . . ? Come on! I may have been a pacifist, but even I admitted, to myself at least, that the so-called Liberals who spout that kind of *mielie-pap* are worse than the Afrikaner who sleeps with a gun under his pillow and a Black woman at his side. I think it's too late for all of that slow, 'peaceful means' horse manure, Riena."

"How did they get to you so fast?" Riena said. "Don't you have any doubts? Or are you so terrified of the Negwenya and Nkolosi that you'll convince yourself of anything?"

"Of course I have doubts," Tom said, "and, yes, I'm terrified of the . . . her . . . and of Nkolosi. But I don't have a better solution, and I've had it with doing nothing. . . ."

"Will I have to kill?" Riena interrupted, standing up and wrapping Tom's trailing robe around her.

Tom shrugged. Riena stood for a moment, as if expecting reassurances. When they were not forthcoming, she said quietly: "When do we leave?"

"It's ten to six," Tom said, looking at his watch.

"We're supposed to be out of here in ten minutes."

"What about my clothes?"

The front door opened and shut and Tom stood up. "That's probably Simon with our papers," he said. "I'll check to see if he remembered to bring you something to wear."

"Oh, I'm sure he did," Riena said quietly, "your friends would hardly have forgotten that. They seem to have thought of everything else."

10

As the car carrying Tom and Riena sped through Belleville, dawn took over the city. Shift workers made their way back and forth to Cape Town's factories, bakery trucks barrelled down the highway, and milk bottles swayed in passing vans, clashing against each other in timpanic background to the car's easy purr. Tom, knowing that in every passionate cycle there had to be an hiatus, solidified his vision of heaven; it was, he decided, a place where everyone's moment of peace came at the same time. If cancer victims could renew their faith during remission and men doing battle could stop to breathe in the sunrise, he thought, it had to be possible for this thousand-mile journey to be a time of calm.

"I'm cold," Riena said. "Could you please close your window?"

"Enjoy the cold while you can," Tom said. He felt comfortable in his open-necked shirt, despite the morning air that caught the side of his neck through his half-open window. "You'll be grateful for the memory of this later, when we're driving through the Karroo."

Riena buttoned her sweater and glared at him. She was still angry at him and was not making the least effort to hide her displeasure.

"Truce?"

She said nothing.

"Come on, Riena. Fighting with each other isn't going to change anything."

"All right. I suppose staying angry is meaningless. I'll go along with a truce if you'll roll up that window a few inches."

"Sounds reasonable," Tom said, giving in to the extent of three inches in the interest of peace. "After this is all over. . . ."

". . . let's not talk about it till we get there, okay?" Riena interrupted.

"What would you like to talk about?"

"Damned if I know. I hardly know you anymore; I certainly have no idea what subject would interest you."

"How about screwing?" Tom said solemnly.

Riena tried to look offended but started to laugh instead.

"Well, it's a new subject, isn't it?" Tom said, laughing too.

Still smiling, Riena said: "You haven't changed all that much, have you, Tom? To tell you the truth, it's been so long since I made small talk with a man, I think I may have forgotten how." She sat silently for a moment, as if giving Tom's question serious consideration. "I haven't really felt much of anything since the day Alfred dragged me away from Jake. I can't say the thought of sex is entirely unappealing."

"Would you sleep with me?"

"Tom!"

"Don't act so shocked. I've probably wanted to go to bed with you since I first knew what it was for."

"It would be incestuous."

"In spirit, I suppose."

"Does the AFI approve of sex?"

"Sex, yes. Love, no."

"In that case, I'll give the matter my close attention." She shivered and moved closer to the warmth of his body. "Are there no women in your life, Tom?"

74

Tom grinned and looked down at her slim figure, enjoying the memory of the brief flashes he'd seen during the last few days.

"It's all academic fortunately," Riena said. "You did say you were under strict orders to drive straight through, didn't you?"

"Except for petrol and bathroom stops, yes."

"Then I'm safe." Riena laughed. "I'm getting much better at this, aren't I? Maybe if I get to be very good at this kind of bantering, I won't ever have to talk politics again in my life. There's a chance this trip won't be as bad as I anticipated."

"If you get much better at it, I'll have to arrange to run out of gas somewhere in the middle of Karroo."

For a while after their interchange nothing broke the silence except the whisper of wheels against highway. The car hugged the speed limit and the odometer lit up the passing miles.

"I'm hungry," Riena said, after they'd been on the road for an hour. "I always get hungry when there's nothing else to do."

"It's too early to eat. . . ."

". . . breakfast?"

"You've already eaten breakfast. Besides it's only seven o'clock; if we eat now, our food'll be gone too soon," Tom said.

"Can't we buy more?" Riena asked, eyeing the two brown shopping bags on the back seat. "If I don't do something I'll get car sick and vomit."

"Only potty and petrol stops remember?"

"When're we supposed to be there?"

"Tomorrow," Tom said.

"I really will get sick if I don't eat."

"If you could go to Europe, where would you want to go first?" Tom asked, hoping to distract her.

"Well, actually," Riena said, acknowledging his efforts, "I had such a good time last year in Monte Carlo. . . ."

". . . Oh, perhaps you were there at the same time as I," Tom said, laughing.

"Probably not," Riena went on, apparently enjoying the game. "I went in the off-season to avoid the crowds. I do so hate all of that ghastly pushing and shoving. . . ."

Tom was suddenly serious.

"In another life, Elizabeth Riena Parker Riess," he said quietly.

"Do you believe in reincarnation?" Riena asked in her normal voice, taking her cue from his change of mood.

"Do you?"

"I don't know. I've always wished. . . ."

". . . what? Would you want to be White the next time around?"

"I guess I haven't thought it out that carefully. I don't think so, though I'm not sure why. Funny, I think I'd want to come back just the way I am."

"Has your life been that great?"

"Not really. But I'm greedy; there are a lot of happy times I'd like to relive. . . ."

"With Jacob Prescott III?"

"Yes, with Jake. I really did . . . do . . . oh, shit, what's the difference. Dreaming about it isn't going to help."

"Do you dream in color?" Tom asked.

"That's a strange question. You're full of them, aren't you? I don't know what color I dream in."

"Have you ever dreamed you were White?"

"No. At least I don't think so. Have you?"

"Once," Tom said. "It was the most Godawful nightmare I've ever had."

"Wonder what Freud would make of that?" Riena spoke lightly, as if she sensed the tension that was building up in him.

"I asked a friend who was studying psychiatry. All he gave me was a bunch of double-talk mumbo jumbo."

"I'd probably react the same way, whether I dreamed I was White or Black," Riena said. "That's the trouble with us Coloureds. We're rejected by the Whites and we bitch about it, but we turn right around and reject the Blacks in the same way—no offense intended."

"No offense taken," Tom said, interested to find that she still didn't think of him as Coloured. "Will the whole world really be Coloured one day, d'you think?"

"God, I hope not!"

"I don't know," Tom said. "If all of the women looked like you, at least the world would be a beautiful place."

"Why, Thomas. Thank you."

Tom looked at her and grinned. He reached out and ruffled her hair and she caught his hand and held it.

"Want to eat?" he asked, sorry he had been so insistent upon waiting.

"Not too early anymore?"

Tom shook his head. "I was concerned about running out of food but we can always buy something on the road."

"I feel like I'm hearing a sound track in reverse," Riena said, laughing, "but I won't argue." She knelt on the seat and Tom balanced her with his left hand while she investigated the contents of the closed bag.

"Do they drive on the right or the left in Russia?" she asked, settling down with a thermos of coffee and a stack of egg and tomato sandwiches.

"What on earth inspired that question?" Tom held out his hand for a sandwich.

"I don't know. I suppose I was thinking about how unknowledgeable I am about things like that," she answered, her first sandwich already half eaten. "Coffee's not bad. Can you manage a cup while you're driving?"

"I'd like to try, otherwise I'll have to take a *Regmaker* later. I hate to rely on pills to keep me awake."

"You could let me do some of the driving," she said. Then she completed the maneuver with the coffee and grimaced because she had to use both arms. "Just remembered why I can't help with the driving."

"Arm hurting?"

"A little. It's not too bad."

"Why don't you try to get some sleep?"

"I just got up."

"Yes. I know. But sleep will help to complete the

healing process."

"All right, Doctor Sibanda," Riena said, "though how you managed to learn so much about medicine is beyond me. But first, did you happen to bring along anything sweet? I'm dying for a piece of chocolate."

"At this time of the morning? No. Sorry. I didn't think of it."

She disposed of the rest of her food, drank one more cup of coffee, and demanded a bathroom. Since her timing was perfect and there was a gas station a mile or so off the hightway, Tom detoured. Once they were back on the highway, she curled up and went to sleep. From then on she slept intermittently for twelve hours. Though the miles were broken up by occasional bouts of conversation, the next twelve hours had Tom thoroughly bored. Towns and hamlets sped by, one as faceless as the next. The arid landscape was relieved only by sand and stone and scrub; flat-topped koppies rose in the distance and infrequent thatched mud huts spoke of a part of humanity which chose to live in isolation.

"God it's hot," Riena said, fully awake at last. "It must be a hundred degrees out there."

"You slept through the worst of it. At least the dryness makes it tolerable. Wouldn't you like some of that cold air you rejected this morning?"

"Doesn't it ever rain here?" Riena said. "Cape Town's so lush and green. This all looks burnt out."

"You should see the Karroo after a summer rain," Tom said. "You'd never believe it. Masses of flowers, springing out of nowhere. . . ."

". . . and dying just as fast, I suppose."

Tom nodded, straining his eyes to fight the shimmering layer of heat that hovered over the highway. "We'll have to stop soon for petrol and water."

"Yes, I'm very thirsty."

Tom laughed. "Not for you. For the car. We can't afford to let the engine overheat."

"Where are we?"

"Near Beaufort West," Tom said, wishing he could

78

bypass that particular red-neck Afrikaner stronghold. He decelerated reluctantly at the dusty outskirts of town. "This must be how an American Black feels driving into a town in Mississippi," he said.

Riena took out a comb.

"Fixing your hair for the red-necks?" Tom asked sourly.

"Can it, Tom," Riena snapped. "I'm doing this for me and it's a long time since I cared to do anything for myself."

"Don't be so damn touchy," Tom said more gently. He slowed down for a large truck that was trying to pass him on the inside. "Listen, don't let the men in the lorry bother you. I'm going to let them pass us and they're sure to say something obscene.

He slowed down to a crawl, hoping to make the filling station up ahead without an incident. His hope was short lived.

"Out of the way, *Kaffir.*"

"Asshole," Tom said under his breath. The truck was parallel with them now and Tom could see the blood rush to Riena's cheeks as the driver leered at her and his companion gave Tom the finger.

"What you doin' wit' a *Kaffir,* Capie?" the driver yelled at Riena.

"If they stop, we'll have to keep going," Tom said, glancing at his gas gauge. It read empty, but he dared not stop while the truck stayed level with him.

Suddenly the truck driver lost interest. He veered his machine into the center of the highway, and roared out of sight.

"Let's fill up and get the hell out of here," Tom said, pleased by the anger he saw on Riena's face. A portion of good, healthy anger will make the next few weeks easier for her, he thought, leaning over to stroke her cheek in a gesture of friendship.

She covered his hand with her own and pressed it down on her face as if she needed to make physical contact with someone who was not an enemy. "It isn't a game, is it, Tom," she said, turning away . . . but not

79

before he had seen her tears. She had finally found a way to cry.

Sometime around dusk, which came late in that part of the Orange Free State, they passed Kimberley. The bushes at the side of the road stood out like stubble on a White man's cheek, and a welcome chill had returned to the air. Riena once again buttoned her sweater. By midnight, they had passed Vredefort and were nearing the Transvaal.

"It's difficult to believe that I was sweating a couple of hours ago," Riena said.

Tom had been trying to picture the Indian Ocean hundreds of miles to their right and the colder surf of the Atlantic to their left. It seemed hard for him to believe that the scrub at their side and the road ahead wasn't the entire world. "We'll have to slow down once we hit the Transvaal," he said. "Johannesburg's edges have spread and the early morning traffic's going to hold us up."

"I think we'd better find a bathroom or. . . ."

"Can you hold off for about ten minutes?" Tom interrupted. "I have a surprise for you."

"Anything to break the monotony," Riena said. "The Cape was magnificent, all those mountains and farms. . . ."

". . . and then came the Karroo."

Riena pulled a face. "Once you've seen one bush, you've seen them all."

"It's the first time you've seen the sky at night on the Karroo. I always feel as if the stars are so close, I could reach out and touch them if I really tried," Tom said.

"Ah! A romantic at heart," Riena teased.

Tom smiled.

"What's the surprise?" Riena asked.

"If I told you it wouldn't. . . ."

". . . be a surprise." He laughed. "I'd rather have something to look forward to, if it's all right with you."

"How does the idea of a bath grab you?"

"After all that dust and heat, it sounds like a miracle."

"In that case, one miracle coming up," Tom grinned.

"While you were asleep I remembered that an old friend of mine has a house about," he looked at the odometer, "ten miles from here. I'm sure he'd be delighted to see us and let us use his facilities."

"What about our orders?"

"He can be trusted to keep his mouth shut."

"I thought people like us weren't supposed to trust anyone." There was an unmistakable edge of bitterness in Riena's voice.

"Don't believe everything you read," Tom said. "Even fanatics occasionally trust someone."

"Are you sure Nkolosi won't find out?"

"Fuck Nkolosi."

"I'd rather not, if you don't mind. Is your friend a member of the AFI?"

"Not as far as I know. He's a storekeeper, part of the Black bourgeoisie. He'd much rather nothing changed; he rips people off for a fortune."

"What kind of store?"

"Groceries. We should be able to fill up those shopping bags we've emptied."

"Talking about empty. If that's the place up ahead, it looks like we're out of luck," Riena said. "A bath sounded incredible . . . and a toilet sounded even better. If I don't get to a bathroom soon, I'm going to burst."

"It's okay," Tom said, "I've got a key." He slowed down and parked in front of a house that stood isolated and in total darkness except for one lonely looking streetlamp at the end of a short driveway.

"So that's what this is all about," Riena was amused. "You knew we'd have the place to ourselves, didn't you? I'll bet you've been plotting this since dawn."

"I wish I could say yes, but it's not true. We've made such good time I just decided we could risk stopping for a while."

"Either way, I'm delighted," Riena said.

Tom unlocked the front door and they walked inside. He flipped on the light switches.

"Is that wise? Won't someone think we're burglars

and call the police?"

"Maybe. They're a bunch of Uncle Toms around here. I think I know where to find some candles though." He rummaged in a drawer and came up with two white candles and two copper holders. "Take one with you," he said, handing her one of the lit tapers. "The bathroom's over there. I'll make some fresh coffee."

"Make extra for the thermos," Riena reminded him, heading for the bathroom. "I want you to know," she said, opening the door, "I'm feeling better already."

11

For the second time in less than twenty four hours, Tom sat on a bathroom floor and watched Riena take delight in submerging her body in a tub of steaming water. This time, in a candle-lit bathroom in the middle of nowhere, he didn't look away; this time he enjoyed the arousal that had embarrassed him earlier. Not that he was anticipating any grand passion. Riena still had that reserved for his American competition. But then a grand passion would hardly fit the scheme of things right now, he thought.

"What tune was that you were whistling in the kitchen?" Riena asked, swishing her foot absently from one side of the tub to the other.

"Damned if I know," Tom said. "It was haunting me in the car while you were sleeping."

"Did you find any coffee out there?"

"Coffee, a couple of steaks and, would you believe, a relatively decent bottle of wine."

"Sounds tempting."

"Want me to wash your back?"

"Mm. That sounds even better," Riena said, handing

him a washcloth and a small bar of soap. "You used to do this for me all the time, remember?"

Tom took the soap, but ignored the washcloth. Starting at the base of her skull, he soaped her neck and shoulders, then worked his way down to her hips where the swell of her buttocks began.

When her entire back was covered in a slippery film, he leaned over and put down the soap.

Again, she handed him the washcloth; again he refused it.

"Do you still like to have your back massaged?" he asked.

"Doesn't everyone?"

Tom perched on the side of the tub and began to rub her shoulders, until she arched her back and sighed. "It's been a long time," she said quietly.

"You took a bath this morning," Tom said lightly.

"And this morning you ignored me."

"I thought that was what you wanted."

"I guess you're right; what I really wanted was food."

"And now?"

"I still think we should eat first," she teased.

Tom laughed, delighted at her openness. "You . . . don't have to . . . you know," he said, letting his fingers trail through her damp curls.

She turned and put her arms around him, as high as she could reach. Her gesture took him off guard and he rocked precariously over the water. She let go, smiling. "I have no other way to thank you," she said slowly.

Tom stood up, his hands dripping from having clutched at her to maintain his balance. "Thank me? For what?"

"If you hadn't come down to the docks. . . ."

". . . you might not be in this kind of trouble now."

"I might also be dead."

"I'm not one of your johns," Tom said harshly, turning his back to her and reaching for a towel.

"Tom?"

Her voice was soft and quiet. He turned around to find that she had stepped out of the tub and was standing, dripping, naked, vulnerable, a few inches from him. "I'm sorry. Let's not fight . . . I didn't mean to sound like . . . like. . . ."

"Forget it, Riena. Here, dry yourself, I'll get the food going." He tossed the towel at her and, angry and wounded, left the bathroom. He'd been a damn fool, he thought, to believe that after all these years she could begin to see him as a man. He slammed around the kitchen, trying to push away the image of her dark brown nipples, erect in the candlelight, inviting him to make love to her.

"Tom. Please listen," Riena said, coming into the kitchen carrying her taper. She put it on the table and sat down. "I really am sorry . . . and I do want to go to bed with you. It's just that it's been so long. I had myself convinced that sex was something I'd never want again. . . ."

". . . except with Jake, I suppose."

"Tom, I'm in love with Jake Prescott. Our son is little more than a month old. He won't ever know his father and I probably won't ever see him again, but. . . ."

Nkolosi really succeeded, Tom thought. It's only been two days, yet Riena believes she gave birth a month ago. He walked slowly over to her and half crouched at her side.

"I'm sorry, too, Riena. I don't think I'll ever understand how you could . . . can . . . love a European. But it doesn't matter. It's your life."

He stood up and lifted her gently out of the chair. Then, holding her close, he kissed the tears that were running freely down her cheeks.

"Please don't cry," he said. "I can't bear to see you cry. I couldn't stand it even when you were a kid."

She looked up, smiling tentatively, and he kissed her smile, gently at first, and then fiercely, as if he could stop them both from thinking about the past or the future.

Placing one arm around her waist, he picked up the candle from the table and led her to the bedroom. When they were lying together on the bed, she curled

84

tightly into the curve of his arm, and he let his fingertips play across her features, lightly, soothingly, certain she was most likely to respond if he was patient with her.

She was still only wrapped in a towel and he was fully dressed but he made no attempt to remove either her damp covering or his own clothes.

"Why don't you get undressed, Tom," Riena said after a while.

"Do you want me to? I'm quite content just holding you . . ."

". . . it's what I want."

Tom's body cast a towering silhouette in the candlelight. He took his time undressing and he could see Riena was pleased when he finally sat down on the edge of the bed and reached for her. His movements were without urgency, and by the time he lay down again it was clear that her need matched his. She pulled him closer and her body softened into his.

Sure of himself now, and of her, he timed his responses to hers, knowing that each was taking refuge in the other's expertise. Once, as she guided his hand to her breast, he thought he heard her murmur Jake, but by then it no longer mattered.

"You're very beautiful," he said, kneeling over her. "I'm not sure I can wait much longer."

Her eyes offered no resistance and her hands, caressing him gently, stopped moving and pressured his body toward hers. For a moment, when he entered her, he feared that he was causing her pain, that perhaps Nkolosi had only succeeded in convincing her mind and in stemming her flow of blood.

"Don't stop," she said.

She moved against him rhythmically, like a dancer responding to the steadily increasing excitement of a Bolero. Tom, forced to stop orchestrating, came with a fury that left him exhausted. He wanted desperately to sleep, but he took Riena in his arms and they lay for a while, neither of them willing to move, yet knowing that there was no time for sleep.

"I'm sorry we have to leave," Tom said finally.

"I am too. I don't mean to sound unromantic, but we are going to eat before we go, aren't we?"

"We can't. We've already been here for two hours," Tom said, struggling to his feet.

"You mean we have to resort to the rest of those boring sandwiches your friend Simon made? He doesn't have much imagination, does he?" Riena said, stretching languidly.

Tom, almost dressed, buttoned his shirt and smiled at her. The sight of her leaning against the pillow tempted him to take his shirt off again. Instead, he lit a cigarette, walked around to her side of the bed, and kissed the top of her head.

She reached out and took the cigarette from him.

"Sorry. Should have offered you one," he said, lighting another.

She leaned over to him and ruffled his hair. "It's wiry," she said.

"What did you expect? Silk?"

"I got used to J. . . ."

". . . it's all right, Riena," Tom said gently.

She looked away.

"What's the matter? You don't feel guilty, do you? About what's happened here, I mean. You couldn't."

"It's hard to feel guilty about betraying a phantom," she said slowly. "I know our child is tangible evidence of what existed between us . . . Jake and I . . . but I'm not sure our love can ever be recreated. As a living breathing thing, I mean."

"Things exist in their own space and time," Tom said. "There's no point in making judgments about the future and it's almost as foolish to try to relive the past."

"What about memories?"

"We embellish them to make life livable in the present, I suppose. I don't believe memories should serve as the starting point in a relationship though."

"Are you talking about us, you and me, or about my relationship with Jake? I think Jake and I would have to start all over again. I'm not the same now."

"It'll all be academic if we don't get moving," Tom

86

said. "You've got five minutes. Not a second longer."

"Give me six," Riena begged, swinging herself out of bed.

Less than ten minutes later, Tom was locking his friend's front door. Once they were in the car, he wasted no time. He released the handbrake before Riena had settled into her seat and put his foot on the gas. Nothing happened. The car moved no more than a few inches forward and stopped, almost as if he had parked badly and the curb was blocking his tires. He backed up and started again, pumping the accelerator pedal a little, in case there was an air bubble in the line.

He felt the same tug, and the engine cut out.

"What's wrong, Tom?" Riena sounded only mildly curious.

"Damn thing won't go forward," Tom said. "Maybe the aerial's caught in one of those mimosa branches."

"Want me to get out and check?"

"No. I'll do it." He sounded annoyed and slammed out of the car to check the antenna; it bounced freely at his touch. "I don't understand," he said, getting back in behind the wheel. "At this rate we'll never get to Jo'burg on schedule."

He started the car for a second time. It moved forward a few inches, and stopped.

"Maybe something's stuck under the wheels," Riena suggested.

Not hopeful, but willing to try anything, Tom slammed out of the car one more time. As he bent to look under its lowslung body, he smelled fire, and a thin curling wisp of smoke circled its way lazily toward him.

"Tom?" Riena said, leaning out of her open window. "What is it? You look scared half to death." She started to open the car door.

"Stay in there," Tom hissed. "Close your window and lock your door. And mine."

If he had followed his instincts, Tom would have taken his own advice and locked himself away from whatever lay underneath the car. But he was caught in the web of a powerful fascination. He knelt slowly on the rough curb and, holding on to the side of the car, followed the trail of smoke and peered underneath.

"I don't believe it," he said, grinning. He stood up and motioned to Riena to join him. "You're not going to believe this," he said.

Lying with her head against the wheel of his car was the ugliest, oldest, Black woman he'd ever seen.

"Drunk?" Riena said.

Tom tapped the woman's thigh with the point of his shoe. "Get up you fucker," he said, laughing. "I don't think she'd have noticed if I'd driven right over her." He bent down and shook the woman. "Move you old bugger," he said, helping the shapeless form to unfold itself as it pulled against him.

The old woman kept her head lowered. She held on tightly to an elaborately carved pipe, and she puffed at it every now and then, without changing the angle of her head. She moved slowly into the lamplight and didn't turn to face them until Tom and Riena were back in the car and pulling away from the curb.

Tom looked in his rear view mirror. He could see the old woman, the pipe between her teeth, staring intently at him.

"Oh, Jesus!" he said, flooring the accelerator.

"What is it, Tom?" Riena asked, putting out her hand to stop herself from falling against the dashboard. "You look as if you've seen the spirit of your dead grandmother."

"I've seen worse than that," Tom said hoarsely. He glanced in the rear view mirror, but the lamp post was too far away to tell if the figure still stood there.

"It was her eyes," he said slowly. "I recognized her eyes."

"Whose eyes? For godsakes, Tom. I haven't the vaguest idea what you're talking about. And I wish you'd slow down, or you'll kill us both."

"I'm sorry, Riena." Tom slowed down. Then he reached out and took her hand. "I'm not sure there is any way to explain—but I'll try. When the Negweny followed me, that day of the fire, what terrified me most was the look in her eyes. It was a combination of lust and affection. And something else I'd never seen before. Or since. Until just now. In that old hag's eyes."

"Do you think she was. . . ."

". . . I don't know what to think. Every time I try to think like a rational twentieth century adult, something like this happens and I'm scared shitless again."

"I wish I could think of some marvelous platitude," Riena said, moving closer to him.

Tom put his arm around her and hugged her. "Let's change the subject," he said quietly. "Are you hungry? I'm sorry we couldn't wait and eat that steak and open the wine. Now I owe you a decent meal."

"Instead of a meal, will you answer a question?"

"Riena Parker passes up food. That has to be a first."

"Maybe it's just my first act as Elizabeth Riess," Riena said. "That's the question, Tom. What exactly is it I'm supposed to do as Elizabeth Riess? What kind of woman is she supposed to be?"

"Tell you what," Tom said. "You get some sleep. I promise I'll wake you when the sun comes up and then I'll tell you as much as I can."

"Sounds fair enough," Riena said, pulling her legs up underneath her. Snuggling into his shoulder, she closed her eyes and fell into a sound sleep.

12

Tom focused on the distant outlines of the mine dumps that fringed the outer ring of Johannesburg's industrial areas. The dawn sunlight had begun to filter through the window and the traffic, even before five in the morning, had increased to a steady hum. He was still wondering how much to tell Riena; with her son and Ma's lives at stake, she would undoubtedly follow orders. Still, he was reluctant to tell her the full extent of her involvement.

"Riena," he said, shaking her gently. "Sun's up."

She sat up, disentangled herself from Tom, and stretched.

"There's coffee in the thermos. I filled it earlier, remember."

"I could use a toothbrush," Riena said, pouring herself a cup of coffee. "Ugh, it's lukewarm. Want a cup?"

"I wasn't concentrating when I made it," Tom said, grinning.

"It's better than nothing, I suppose," Riena grimaced, draining the cup. "Now, I believe you made me a promise."

"In a few hours," Tom said, between sips, "you'll become Michelle Barnard Cohn's housemaid. Does the name mean anything to you?"

"No."

"She's Piet Barnard's sister."

"Barnard?"

"The ex-warden of Roeland Street Gaol."

"Of course! Sorry . . . that sleep must have dulled my brain. Go on."

"She's also the wife of Arthur Cohn. You probably haven't heard of him but it appears he's a very powerful man. He's the head of the South African branch of OPI Overseas Press International."

"Hold it a minute. I've heard his name. It's coming back to me." She closed her eyes for a moment, straining to remember. "I remember now," she said. "I read an article about him in the prison library. Isn't he a liberal? The article said he goes to the UN every year. It's all coming back to me now. There was a whole section about his daughter. She made headlines demonstrating in some liberal cause."

"That's the family."

"What am I supposed to be doing there?"

"What are you supposed to be doing, or what are you *going* to do?"

"Both, I suppose."

"To begin with, you're going to help Mrs. Cohn with her household chores . . . set the table, dust, wash dishes, that sort of thing."

"I'm so pleased I went to Teachers' College," Riena said. "But don't you think I'm a little overqualified for the job?"

The car was winding its way past huge beige mounds of mine-dust; buildings and equipment were covered in a windspread layer of sand. Everything blended into the landscape like a new form of growth, the mutations of an industrial city.

"I'm sure the AFI didn't spare my life just so I could become a maid. What else do I have to do?" Riena insisted.

Tom realized there was no longer any way he could delay telling her the details. "About two days from now," he said slowly, "you are to take the Cohn family and whatever guests are in their home hostage."

"Just me? You've lost your mind, Tom Sibanda. You're as crazy as the rest of them."

"Simon will be around to help you. And at least one other man."

"What about you?"

Tom shook his head.

"That's all I have to do then," Riena said sarcastically. "This whole thing is getting crazier by the minute. I'm beginning to feel the rabbit hole would seem sane compared with this. Tom, listen to me. If even a small part of what I read in that article was true, Cohn is a good man to have on our side. He's a doer, not an armchair liberal. . . ." She stopped and looked at Tom's face. "There's more, isn't there?"

"That's all you need to know for the moment," Tom said, still unable to tell her anything more. She would learn about it all soon enough, he thought.

"Then answer my other question, Tom," Riena said, almost too calmly. "Why the Cohns?"

"Because they're important people. And because they'll be having a distinguished overnight guest."

91

"How do you know?"

"Nkolosi told me. There's a United Jewish Appeal Rally scheduled for Sunday. The Cohns are involved in it, and they always have the leading functionary as a houseguest the weekend before."

"Why won't you be there? Where will you be?"

"Hold it. One question at a time. I have other instructions, I can't tell you where I'll be, and to answer your next question before you ask it—there'll be about fifty other families involved in this."

"Just in Jo'burg?"

Tom shook his head. Riena said nothing more for several miles, so he concentrated on the hordes of Africans, trudging their way to work. Its being Saturday didn't seem to reduce the numbers. He wondered idly if there would be enough buses after the revolution, or if the roads would simply be more crowded with cars . . . if this ragged barefoot bunch learned how to drive. He glanced at Riena. She seemed to need time to assimilate the information he had given her and he was sure she was in no mood for idle speculation about the outcome of the revolution. For a moment he wondered why Nkolosi hadn't taken the easy route and tampered with her ideology. He had certainly been successful in changing the course of nature, so why not the other? The answer, as he saw it, had to lie in the witchdoctor's comment about the abuse of the power of magic. That and the man's sadistic pleasure when his power over people emanated from a fear he had created, or at least encouraged, in them. Or perhaps it was, at least in Riena's case, much simpler than that, Tom thought, remembering how quickly she had fallen asleep. The human body, even a young and relatively healthy one, had finite limitations, just as he supposed the mind had. Maybe Nkolosi had simply seen that Riena had reached the limits of both.

"How will I take them hostage?" Riena asked, as if there had been no break in the conversation.

"I've been given a gun for you."

"They could overpower me. Besides, I don't have the

vaguest idea how to use a gun."

"Make them believe you know how. By the time someone decides to test you, you'll have help. Listen, the whole idea is simply for you to detach their alarm system when they let you in on Monday to make their early morning tea. That way Simon will have no problem getting in. . . ."

". . . is it a big house?"

"Tremendous, apparently. There's a whole guest wing."

"Are you taking me there today?"

Tom nodded. "This afternoon."

"Where are you going? To set another explosion?"

She sounded bitter and disgusted, and Tom could hardly blame her.

"Did the explosion really help the cause, Tom, or are you and the rest of them just a bunch of madmen?" she asked. "And this new trouble you're planning. What makes you think the government will listen this time if they didn't before?"

"You keep lumping me in with 'them.' I didn't choose to be involved in this, any more than you did."

"That may be so, but you're doing a very good job of convincing yourself that what the AFI's doing is right."

"I don't know if their methods are right or wrong. All I do know is that even the Nationalists won't be able to ignore the climate of fear that's being created. Look, you won't have to hurt anyone, Riena. Simon and. . . ."

". . . You never told me where you'd be."

"I can't tell you."

"Will you be hurting people?"

Tom was silent.

"Will I be any less responsible if someone is hurt, Tom?"

"You wouldn't be here in the first place if you had a choice," Tom said. "All you can do is use Ma and your child as a defense against your conscience."

"Will I be able to contact you at all?"

"No. I'll contact you sometime before noon on

Monday."

Again Riena was silent, and though there were many things Tom would have liked to say to her, personal things, he said nothing. To do so seemed pointless. As they wound around the Wilds towards the Cohns' house, he put out his hand and took Riena's, hoping she would understand the gesture. He looked at the strelitzia and poinsettias that lined the edge of the rambling park, and at the golden shower that ignored the boundary and poured into the roadside, and he slowed down, stretching out the few moments that remained to them. Then the driver of the car behind him honked the horn of his maroon convertible impatiently and Tom pulled over to let him pass. He caught a glimpse of the man's face; he had seen it somewhere before.

"I'll drop you off at the bottom of the driveway," Tom said, struggling to remember why the man who'd passed him looked so familiar. It wasn't until they reached the Cohns' driveway and he saw the same car parked there that he remembered.

The driver was Piet Barnard. There'd been a newspaper lying in the kitchen of the house where he and Riena had stopped. Barnard's picture had made the front page because of his precipitate resignation. He'd meant to show Riena but since he hadn't, he decided to say nothing now; she was nervous enough already. There was something ironic, he thought, in the fact that Riena would soon be holding her jailer captive. Nkolosi would have said the gods were smiling on her. Since she'd never been up for parole, she'd probably never seen the warden who undoubtedly spent his time in his office pushing papers. Available for discipline or parole hearings, but otherwise having little contact with the prisoners.

"What do I do when it's all over?" Riena asked, turning to look at Tom. Her eyes were filled with fear.

"If anything goes wrong, our instructions are to try to get to Teyateyaneng. There are people there who will protect us."

"How will I find these . . . protectors? Will you be

with me?''

"Just go there. They'll find you.''

"Do I have to do this?''

"Yes, Riena, unless. . . .''

". . . now?''

Tom nodded. "Just say you're Emily's cousin from Cape Town and act surprised when they tell you Emily's gone.''

"How do you know they'll offer me her job?'' Riena asked.

"Because,'' Tom said, kissing her firmly on the mouth, "they need someone to make breakfast.''

13

Tom sat in the car and watched Riena move slowly toward the mulberry tree that marked the curve in the driveway. As she drew level with it, she stopped to look up into its branches. Then she turned to face him and waved, and he waved back, not aware that her gesture might be intended as a warning. By the time it occurred to him that he'd lingered too long, it was too late.

"What are you doing here, boy?'' Piet Barnard asked, peering through the open window at Tom.

"Just leaving, sir. Dropped Elizabeth off,'' Tom said, gesturing at Riena and, fortunately, remembering to call her by her new name.

"You got a pass?'' Barnard's voice was not unfriendly. If anything, he sounded bored, as if he were exchanging pleasantries with a neighbor to escape some undesirable weekend task.

Tom took out the pass Nkolosi had given him, and gave it to Barnard.

"Drive for Johnson's Dairies, do you?'' Barnard said, handing Tom back his pass.

Tom nodded, saying as little as possible because there was always the outside chance that something he said might remind the warden of their telephone conversation.

Piet Barnard straightened up and motioned Tom on. Wondering if the warden had ever been humiliated by having someone ask for his identification other than at a bank or some such institution, Tom turned the car around and drove back down the hill. He made a right at the first fork in the road and drove around the outskirts of some of Johannesburg's other prosperous European suburbs, checking a map every now and then to make sure he was heading in the right direction. He figured it would take him less than half an hour to reach his destination, and since his meeting wasn't for another hour, he had plenty of time.

He slowed down and detoured, thinking of Riena. She'd been dwarfed by the mulberry tree. When they were children, they'd stolen mulberry leaves regularly to feed their silkworms—miniscule black commas whose survival depended upon an inexhaustible supply of mulberry leaves. Those were perfect pets, he thought. A few strategically placed holes in a shoebox lid, courtesy of Ma's sewing shears, and there were no complaints. As long as they were fed, they stayed there. Blissfully happy. You could count on them to turn into fat white worms and on the inevitability of the next stage when they spun themselves into the center of silk cocoons. White. Yellow. Gold. There was no way to predict what color the silk would be until the first thread emerged. Then Riena sitting for hours, picking at her cocoons. One at a time. Finding the thread that could unravel it, so that she could wind the silk around cardboard hearts. Not so Tom, who left the cocoons intact, waiting for the moth and the eggs and the cycle to begin again.

Tom wondered if it had ever occurred to Riena to give him one of her silken hearts. He'd probably have thrown it away, he thought, embarrassed by the slightest hint that he was more than brother, playmate, confidante. He smiled, remembering Riena's face in the candlelight: high cheekbones flushed against her olive skin; full lips inherited from the "wrong" side of the family; hazel eyes, her other legacy and so like Piet Barnard's. He had to struggle to retain the image of her as a grown woman; it kept being supplanted by the petite adolescent. The one stealing mulberry leaves. The one who'd wanted so badly to be tall that she was willing to risk being caught in order to hang from a branch that left her feet dangling.

"Alfred said that Nkolosi said this makes you grow."

There were no trees in their own back yard. No matter what the attendant risks, it was an opportunity not to be missed. The same thing each time.

"Come on, Riena. They're gonna catch us."

"You go, Tom." Her armpits had to have been aching. "I have to try."

Tom thought of Riena. Now. Facing the Cohn household. She would have a rough time acting like a servant, even for a couple of days. That was one of the reasons she hadn't gone into service in the first place. She'd certainly had ample offers from Ma's customers, starting way back in their silkworm days. It was the same each time she was asked.

Ma: "It's steady work, Riena. We could use the extra money."

Riena: "I'm sorry, Ma. I won't do it. I can't." And to him: "They can't make me, can they, Tom? If I do that, I'll never leave."

She would feel uncomfortable in Houghton. In that house, Tom thought. It was solid, white, permanent. Upper middle class, White South Africa. It needed no papers to make it legitimate.

Tom was still daydreaming when he reached his destination, an abandoned mining compound that belonged to the De Waal Mining Company. He had known it would be deserted yet he found its air of desolation disquieting. Letting his eyes travel over the low-slung barracks, their corrugated roofs buckled by the sun, he peopled the compound. Filled it with Black men who spent their days in the belly of the earth and their nights on cement bunks, dreaming of families they might not have seen in months. Years. Wondering if their babies had become children and their children young men and women with families of their own. Some of the men had babies they'd never seen, wives who had taken lovers, parents who had died.

He rolled past the end of the barbed wire fence and turned off the road taking a narrow dirt track to a house that lay hidden behind bulges of sand that grew like silicone breasts out of the Transvaal dust. The unbroken quiet disturbed him enough that he found himself actually looking forward to his meeting with the AFI man and the Zulu mine worker who were supposed to be at the house. Usually, he thought, there are children around places like this, using the dumps as their personal playground. Here not even a stray dog or cat broke the silence.

Either he was early, Tom thought, or the other men were late. The key Nkolosi had given him slid in easily and he walked into the house alone. There was a table. A couple of chairs. A bed with a coir mattress. He went down to the cellar and found the rifles, wrapped in blankets and lying like corpses on the dank floor. He wandered aimlessly back upstairs, found a small transistor radio, and tuned it to Springbok Radio. He didn't want to think about Riena and the danger she was in. There was nothing he could do to help her now, though perhaps he should have warned her about the warden. What if the man recognized her? He dismissed that as unlikely. He certainly didn't want to examine his feelings for her. As for what he would do if no one showed up at the house and he were forced to handle tomorrow by himself, that subject was best left alone.

An early evening thunderstorm darkened the sky. Tom sat at the window and watched the dust divert the rain into channels that ran down the grimy window panes. Then he lay down on the cot, admitting to himself for the first time since leaving Cape Town that he was exhausted. The sound of the rain on the tin roof had a hypnotic effect and it didn't take long before he fell asleep. When he woke up, the sun was setting over the mine dumps and someone was knocking at the front door.

Tom, who had been dreaming of the smell of baking bread that sometimes masked the odor of poverty of his mother's kitchen, jumped off the bed. "If you didn't bring food," he called out, "you can't come in."

He was at the door before he realized how stupid he'd been to assume the knocking belonged to a friend and not an enemy. Pass or no pass, if anyone in authority found him trespassing they'd lock him in jail and throw away the key. They did that for far lesser offenses. He opened the door. The two men facing him were strangers.

"Thomas Sibanda?" the taller of the two men asked.

"Yes." His response tentative. He was still a novice at cloak and dagger.

"Let us in, man," the shorter man said. In the semi-darkness he looked like a White man but Tom reserved judgment.

"Turn on the light." The shorter man again. In command.

"Is that wise?" Tom asked. "If they. . . ."

". . . Don't worry. Not a fucking soul comes around here," the short man said, putting out his hand. "Johnson's the name. And you can stop looking at me like that. Yes, I'm White, and that's the name my parents gave me."

Tom turned to the other man. He was tall and stately, a Zulu judging by the circular cork discs embedded in his ear lobes.

"I am called David," the Zulu said. He made no move to shake hands.

"You're late," Tom said, fascinated by the man's distorted lobes which hung below the level of his jowls.

"I've got a bottle of Scotch in the car. I'll get it," the White man said, offering no explanation for having been late.

"Did you bring any food?"

99

"Bread and cheese, and some fruit."

He left the room and was back a moment later, carrying a brown paper bag. "Kitchen," he said, apparently not one to waste words.

There were only two chairs. Johnson took one of them and indicated to Tom that he should take the other. When Tom hesitated, Johnson said, "He prefers to stand."

David lounged against the wall, watching the two others. He refused both food and drink, and spoke only when he was directly addressed, which wasn't often.

"Tell me something about the De Waal Mining Company," Tom said, pouring himself a drink in a paper cup and tearing off a large chunk of bread.

"They pay their Africans well, by South African standards," Johnson said.

"How well?"

"Over three hundred Rands per year, per man. In exchange, they demand a contract for at least a year. Most of the time the man who signs the contract doesn't have the vaguest fucking idea what he's signing. He wants to get away from the *kraal;* he thinks he's going to get rich; or he's just plain afraid not to sign."

"And I suppose his wages are sent to his family?"

"Yes. It doesn't take even the *kaffir* long. . . ."

Tom looked over at David. His face was expressionless.

". . . to realize he's been had. He's exchanged being at the mercy of the crops for being at the mercy of the Company."

"Are the mine workers very unhappy?" Tom asked David.

"Not really," David said.

"I don't understand," Tom said. "Don't they live in a compound, eat off tin plates, sleep on cement bunks. . . ?"

"Yes on all counts. But they're peculiarly happy anyway. There's a fraternity, a brotherhood of laughter and music . . . " the White man said.

". . . and deprivation."

100

"Yes."

"Do you think that because they play the penny whistle, they're happy?"

"I don't know why they aren't miserable, Sibanda. But they aren't. Not until they get a gander at the city and the cars. . . ."

"What could you know about them?"

"Because I'm White? My heart's the same color as yours and his." He gestured at David. "The men in barracks 536 are Zulus. I'm not. Does that make me an inferior? Do you think it does, David?"

David moved gracefully away from the wall and changed his position. Before he could answer, Tom, embarrassed, said: "Forget it, Johnson. Why you're in this is your business."

Johnny Johnson grinned. "Damn right it is," was all the explanation he offered.

Tom looked at David. He was a man of innate elegance. It was hard for him to imagine the Zulu allowing himself to be turned into a performing bear, even at the command of the tourist bureau. He did not look like someone who would degrade himself for the entertainment of the Sunday visitors who showed up at the compound demanding just that. Entertainment. Relief from their weekend boredom. Expecting to see the Zulus reenact dances in which their people had taken pride for generations.

"Have you ever seen the Mine Dances?" Johnson asked, reading Tom's expression correctly.

"No."

"You'll see them tomorrow all right," the White man said, grinning again and displaying a gold tooth.

"I'd rather go canoeing," Tom said, feeling the effects of his second Scotch.

"Sundays are usually damn boring around here," Johnson said. "At least in the States the stores and the shows stay open. Goddamned Dutch Reform Church is antiquated."

"Have you been to America?"

The White man nodded.

"Why'd you come back?"

"The Americans can't make decent tea. As for thei[r] scones. . . ." He flashed his gold-toothed smile, the[n] grew serious. "Those war dances are something[,] Sibanda. Beads and feathers and paint. Assegais wavin[g,] terrifying that audience out of their minds for their Sun[-] day pleasure. I know one man who comes ever[y] week—says it's better than any horror show he's eve[r] seen. Tomorrow's Dingaan's Day, you know. It's mor[e] than a hundred years since Dingaan and his boys fucke[d] Piet Retief. . . ."

Johnson's voice trailed off. His eyes held a peculia[r] glaze; they reminded him of the way Riena had stared [at] the snake in Nkolosi's hand. That had to be it, To[m] thought. The man was under Nkolosi's spell. Why els[e] would a White man be working for the AFI?

"Tomorrow, Sibanda," Johnson said. "You'll be driv[-] ing one of my trucks into the mine."

"Your trucks?"

"I own Johnson's Dairies. You're supposed to be on[e] of my drivers, remember. Jesus. What rock did th[at] crazy black magician find you under?"

"I'm sorry, Johnson. Maybe if you gave me some ide[a] of why you're doing this. . . ."

". . . Not that it's any of your fucking business. Is i[t,] David?"

The Zulu didn't move.

"You're going to win, Sibanda," Johnson said. "It[']s[?] all really very simple; I just like being on the winnin[g] side."

"Why not leave South Africa? You could go to Ame[r]- ica. England. Australia. . . ."

". . . This is my country as much as yours." Johns[on] was angry now. "Why the hell should I leave?"

"What makes you believe we won't turn on you, to[o,] when we've finished using you?"

"It's a calculated risk. Look, there's no point in goin[g] on about it. Do you understand what you're suppose[d] to do tomorrow?"

Tom nodded.

"The milk delivery has to be there at six in the morning. On the dot. Not a minute earlier or later, or they won't let you in. Do you have an accurate watch?"

"Yes."

"Okay. The truck's parked around the back. We'll leave here in your car after we've helped you load the guns. I warn you, the milk's going to stink by morning. But there was no other way to do this."

"My car?"

"I'll be there tomorrow. In the audience. At a safe distance, I guarantee you. I'll drive your car there and leave it for you. I'll get home some other way."

"Who's going to drive the truck out of the compound?"

"David. He'll let you in and help you unload. He'll have an extra key. Make a fuss about the truck not starting and leave it near the kitchens. Tell them the mechanic will come out with the Monday delivery, then get the hell out of the compound until it's time for the dances to start."

"Do I have to stick around? Can't I just get into my car and. . . ."

". . . Your car won't be there until it's time for the dances. I can't get there much earlier, and I may be late. If I am, and you leave when I arrive, you'll look conspicuous leaving in the middle of everything. Watch, Sibanda, but stay out of the way, near the exit. That's far enough out of the direct path of David and his boys that you should be perfectly safe. When everyone else heads out, you do the same. And don't leave too soon; stay with the crowd.

"Do I come back here?"

"First you find a telephone and call this number," Johnson said, handing Tom a piece of paper. "Then you come back here."

Tom squinted at the scrap of paper, trying to read the number. The light from the house stopped at his feet and he had to kneel to see the writing. As he did so, a lizard, startled by his sudden movement, darted across the path of the light.

The number meant nothing to him.

"Whose telephone is this?" he asked, following the two men as they walked toward his car.

"Can't drive without a key," Johnson said, holding out his hand. He took it gingerly in two fingers, as if making physical contact with Tom once was all he could manage. "I don't know whose telephone number that is," he said quietly, "but I'll guarantee I know who'll answer the phone."

"Who?" Tom asked, sorry he'd asked in the first place.

David got in the car behind the wheel and Johnson opened the back door. "Meet my chauffeur," he grinned. "Might as well look legit."

Tom started to ask his question again but didn't. There really wasn't any need. He had no doubt at all that he'd be making his report directly to Nkolosi.

14

At six o'clock on Sunday morning, David let Tom unceremoniously through the service entrance of the De Waal Mining Company's working compound. It was a carbon copy of the deserted one, except that it was peopled by the men of Tom's imagination—the ones with whom he had populated the abandoned mine the day before. Inscrutable Black faces, hiding agonies the European would never understand. Not even the Johnny Johnsons who had cast their lot with them.

There was one thing Johnson had been right about, Tom thought. The contents of the milk truck smelled putrid. He could hardly wait to rid himself of the truck and its paradoxical contents; somehow milk and rifles made strange bedfellows. But then so did milk and poison.

Things went almost too smoothly. David had set up a relay line and by three minutes past six, Tom was unloading the bottles of sour milk. No one seemed to care when he mentioned, casually, that something appeared to have gone wrong with the refrigeration system, nor did they take the least bit of notice when he asked for a handful of men to help him push the truck out of the way. It took him several requests before he got the help he needed.

"The mechanic will come with tomorrow's delivery," he said, to no one in particular.

The truck was parked and he was ready to walk away but he felt that he couldn't leave without some acknowledgment of his having been there. He hung around for a few minutes, feeling like a prize fool.

"Go man."

It was David. He had stolen up quietly behind Tom and the words had not broken his long stride.

Putting his hands in his pockets, Tom strolled out of the same service gates he'd driven through only minutes before. He was astounded at the lack of security. He had expected to be stopped. Questioned. Asked to show the pass with which Nkolosi had provided him. He had the strange sensation that he didn't exist at all; that he was a figment of Nkolosi's imagination—not even his own. It was not so much a nightmare quality that he felt but a disembodiment, as if Tom the writer had nothing whatever to do with what was happening. Coffee, he thought, remembering having seen a small cafe down the road. He headed there. He would buy a magazine or newspaper. Eat a leisurely breakfast. Force his mind and body to fuse.

Tom stretched out the hours as best he could. He ate breakfast and went for a long walk. He leaned on a fence and watched two pigeons fight a third for possession of a hardened crust of bread. Finally, he returned to the cafe for more coffee, drinking cup after cup until he wondered if he had managed to consume the entire national product of Colombia.

When he got to the compound, there still weren't

many visitors around. Finding his way to the arena, he took a seat as close to the exit as possible and settled down to wait. It was hot in the sun and he grew sleepy, so sleepy in fact that he eventually closed his eyes and slept. He awoke to find himself in the midst of a close to capacity audience, and eyeball to eyeball with one of the few people in Johannesburg who knew his face—Piet Barnard.

Barnard nodded and walked on. Wide awake now, Tom looked at the people following the ex-warden. Right behind him was a tall woman in a pants suit, and behind her a man who was with her but seemed to be having difficulty keeping up with her long legged stride. He was shorter than she by several inches, white-haired and stocky. She stopped and waited for him, then linked her arm comfortably through his. When Barnard stopped and waited for them, Tom decided the couple had to be Arthur and Michelle Cohn.

Shifting his gaze a little, Tom tried to see if there were any other people who looked as if they belonged with the group. The two young women behind them, perhaps? He blinked and refocused, wanting to be wrong. Were it not for the difference in their complexions, one mulatto, the other merely tanned, they could have been sisters. Even twins. And one of them was unmistakably Riena.

Tom's first reaction was to turn his head away so that Riena would not see him but he quickly changed his mind. Barnard had seen him. The man had obviously recognized him as the person who had dropped Riena—Elizabeth—off the day before. He would think it peculiar if Tom didn't greet Riena. Damn the government and their inconsistencies, Tom thought. Why did this have to be one of the few events where mixed audiences were allowed. And damn the AFI. No personal involvement was all well and good as a general creed but he could hardly be expected to sit around and watch Riena be slaughtered. Besides, he rationalized, as if he were explaining to Nkolosi, she had a job to do. He would have to find a way to warn her.

He got up from his seat and walked quickly, so that he could catch up to her before she got lost in the milling crowd.

"Elizabeth!"

Not yet accustomed to her new name, Riena didn't respond. Then the woman with her apparently caught sight of Tom and said something to her, and Riena turned around. Her eyes widened, at first in delight and, seconds later, in horror. It had apparently dawned on her that Tom was not likely to be there without a purpose.

Excusing herself, Riena retraced her steps.

"For Christsake Riena, get the hell out of this place," Tom said.

"Tom. What're you doing here?"

"Listen to me, Riena. You have to go. Now."

"I can't. They wanted to do something nice for me. They're not bad people, Tom."

"Say you're sick. Anything."

"How do I get back to Houghton?"

Tom took out some money and gave it to her. "There are taxis out there. Take one."

"Are you. . . ."

". . . Go!"

Riena turned and half ran back to the woman she'd been with. Tom saw her talk and gesticulate. So did Piet Barnard. He walked toward the two young women and was soon escorting Riena to the exit.

Feeling an enormous sense of relief, Tom returned to his seat. Once his heart had regained its natural rhythm, he began to watch for Barnard's figure. When the announcements began and the man still hadn't returned, he decided that Barnard must have offered to drive Riena home. Wondering what reason she had given for wanting to leave, he settled back and tried to concentrate on the voice booming over the microphone.

"More than one hundred years ago," the announcer said, "a gang of Zulus viciously attacked and destroyed Piet Retief and his brave White followers. The war dances which preceded that bloody battle were to have been recreated for you later today.''

Were to have been? Something's gone wrong, Tom thought, wondering if he should make an immediate run for it or stay where he was.

"Since we have been warned that there is a strong possibility that rain will cut the dances short, we have decided to make a change in the program.''

Tom let out a long breath.

"The dance is frightening," the announcer continued. "It was designed to be. But remember, ladies and gentlemen, these are only simulations. No matter what may appear to be happening in front of you, you are perfectly safe.''

His car, Tom thought, as the audience burst into a round of spontaneous applause. He had not spotted Johnny Johnson out there. The man had said he might be late. What if he hadn't arrived yet? Reminding himself that panic was the last thing he needed at that moment, he listened to the clapping and wondered if it reached into the barracks where the Zulu warriors stood waiting to make their entrance.

Only they aren't warriors, he thought. They are urbanites whose ancestors once were warriors. Though he knew it shamed them to make a mockery of their tribal rituals, he knew, too, that there were those among them who didn't give a damn. And swelling those numbers were those who neither understood nor cared about the tenets of the AFI. Still there was one thing they all had in common, a single bond they all understood: revenge upon the White man whose laughter and contempt was the source of their greatest pain.

Tom pictured David, a giant who danced on eight foot stilts, taking out the knife he'd hidden in his belt; he conjured up feathered warriors, readying poison darts, secreting them in plumed headdresses. Somewhere in the deepest level of his gut, he sensed their assegais quivering with the scent of blood. By now, he thought, the arsenal he'd brought into the compound would have been distributed. Those who preferred the White man's weapon would be putting aside their knives and darts and assegais, preparing to use bullets in defense of their past—and their futures.

The minutes seemed to be ticking by like hours. The audience, waiting, shuffled in their seats. Get on with it, please, Tom thought.

And then the cry broke out, loud and clear from the entrance to the arena.

"Kill the Wizards!"

It was an ancient cry. Dingaan's. It rose again from Black throats, as it had risen over a century before.

The audience smiled, a trifle uncomfortable, reminding themselves that it was all a sham.

"Kill the Wizards and your women and children will bow before your spirits!"

The AFI have done their work well, Tom thought, staring transfixed. They looked deep into the Zulu heart and found there his ultimate fear, that his spirit not be revered. They had reminded each man down there that his happiness in the afterlife depended upon having lived his life with pride.

The dance began. Slowly. Each movement ordered by centuries of tradition. On the circumference of the arena, so close that had they reached out they might have caressed the cheeks of the audience, stood the chorus. Bodies glistening with oils and ungents, assegais held loosely, tapping the beat with the balls of unshod feet. And the beat itself, moving from legato to staccato in preordained rhythms being played by one lone drummer. All of it window dressing in support of the eight men gliding to and fro in the center of the circle—Dingaan's marshals reborn.

They were all tall men to begin with. In their feathered headdresses, bobbing and gyrating as they circled the musician, they appeared gigantic. As for David, elevated above the highest head in the crowd by his wooden stilts, he could see beyond the compound walls, almost to the plains that had once belonged to his father's father. To the cattle grazing at the edge of the Limpopo, Tom thought, and the bare-bosomed women singing as they walked the side of the hill.

109

Suddenly the rhythm picked up, and Tom's heartbeat with it. Wiping away the sweat that was pouring down his neck, he looked out into the sea of faces. Most of them were wearing plastic smiles. It can't be long now, he thought. Any moment those smiles will become death masks.

Thinking about escape, he looked across at the entrance to the arena. Two mining company guards caught his attention. He scanned the audience, wondering how many more of them were scattered around. Their presence was something he hadn't considered, or the guns that hung from their belts. He was sure, however, that the AFI had. There were probably as many Black guards as White ones. Once they realized what was happening, they would begin to shoot. . . .

He didn't have time to dwell on that thought, or any other.

"Kill the Wizards!"

The dancers were dancers no longer. Warriors now, they charged into the Sunday tourists, and the blood of Whites and Blacks soon mixed freely as it ran into the gutters around the arena.

Tom's mind took him out of the arena, out of the compound, to the safety of his car, but he could not move. He could not tear his eyes away from David, swaying above the crowd as he commanded his troops. Not until a guard's weapon found its mark and the Zulu, clutching his stomach, began to totter.

Miraculously, the shooting stopped and the crowd grew silent. For a moment, impossibly, the Zulu maintained his balance. Then, raising his hands in the air, he released the flow of blood. Like a telephone pole struck down by an electric storm, he came crashing to the ground.

The eerie hush that followed lasted no more than a fraction of a second. Though David must have died upon impact, Tom could have sworn he heard the dying giant say, as he lay face down in the gutter: "Their blood is the same as mine."

And mine is the same as theirs, Tom thought, as reality hit him. The crowd had resumed its frenetic rush toward the exits, pushing and shoving and trampling each other underfoot. They had but one simple desire—to escape with their lives.

Tom's body at last responded and he joined them. No less anxious than they to get out of the compound, he pushed as hard as the rest. For each step he took forward, it seemed to him that he was being pressed three in reverse, and he began to panic. He had waited too long, and he was locked between bodies, with no choice but to move as they did.

A massive shove from the right pushed Tom into the person on his left and, automatically, he turned his head to apologize for jabbing the man with his elbow.

"Sorry."

"It's all right man. Let's just get out of here alive," the man said. "Michelle? Are you okay?"

The woman's answer was lost to Tom. Arthur and Michelle Cohn, he thought. Surviving. Not knowing what the next day was going to bring them. Like Riena. Surviving, too, thanks to his warning. And for what? More of this?

With that, Tom found himself out of the arena. He followed the crowd to the parking area and had surprisingly little difficulty locating his car. Once he was inside, the next battle began. The stream of humanity around him chased in circles like cornered rats and precluded any but the slowest movement. Drivers started their cars and rushed ahead, not caring about direction as long as they were doing something; others made for the gates on foot, more than happy to abandon their cars if that meant a chance to get out faster. Women dragged screaming children; husbands searched for lost wives; families concentrated upon unit survival.

The wait to get out of the parking lot seemed endless. It took Tom almost an hour to get free of the traffic, bogged down now by ambulances and fire trucks whose sirens howled for the right of way. But finally he was clear of it all, cruising in an unfamiliar area where people who had not yet heard about the massacre were conducting themselves in normal fashion, chatting on street corners and taking Sunday strolls around the block.

Spotting a telephone booth up ahead, Tom parked the car and got out. With the scrap of paper Johnson had given him clutched in his hand, he shut himself inside. Grateful for the protection the glass door lent him from a world he was beginning to despise, he dialed long distance.

Someone picked up the phone at the other end at the second ring but said nothing.

"All that blood, damn you," Tom shouted. "All that blood and what are you going to have to show for it?"

"Calm yourself, Sibanda." Nkolosi's voice was soft. Soothing. A grandfather, healing the cut on his grandson's knee by gentle persuasion that he could kiss it and make it better.

"You weren't there, Nkolosi. You didn't see. . . ."

". . . Sibanda!"

The voice was harsher now. Demanding that Tom's hysteria be put aside.

"Will the government listen to our demands this time?"

" *Our* demands?" Amusement this time.

"Dammit Nkolosi. Stop playing games and answer me. Are they going to listen?"

"How do I know?"

"I thought you knew everything."

Laughter. Then silence.

"They aren't going to do anything, are they? You're probably not even going to try negotiation. You want this bloodbath to continue, don't you?"

"There will be talks with the Prime Minister tonight," Nkolosi said.

"Are you sure?"

"What is it you're doubting, Sibanda?"

"I'm doubting our progress." Tom knew he was saying too much but he felt compelled to keep talking, as if the sound of his own voice had become his last link with sanity.

"We must negotiate from strength instead of weakness," Nkolosi said.

The words sounded hollow to Tom. "What have we gained so far? Yes, I agree, we are successfully creating a climate of fear. The government will simply go on calling us fools and butchers for killing our own. They keep telling the world we're savages, and we're proving them right."

"We kill White men, too, Sibanda. Tomorrow our next plan goes into effect and. . . ."

". . . and what? What if they still don't listen?"

"We kill the fifty families we're holding. White families. Powerful families, man. They are the people who keep this country going—the rich White intellectuals who have the people convinced that a slow solution to this country's problems is still possible. What's wrong with you, Sibanda?" Nkolosi asked sharply. "Have you forgotten. . . ."

The AFI doesn't want to negotiate a damn thing, Tom thought, as Nkolosi's voice trailed off. "What happens after this next step? How many more steps will there have to be after that? What if we kill those people and the government still refuses to negotiate instant equality?"

"You know very well what happens next," Nkolosi said smoothly. "I suggest you drink your coffee black for a while."

Tom heard a laugh and then a click. A series of chills attacked his body and, for a while, it took enormous effort for him to stand upright. He waited until the feeling passed, almost wishing it wouldn't so that he could stay in the security of his glass house forever. But when the wave passed, he did move. Back to his car and back to the house in the abandoned compound.

Once there, Tom started to pace. He'd opened a window and the usual dusk shower streamed onto the sill. It gave him little satisfaction to know that the same rain, later than the announcer had anticipated but there all the same, was washing away the blood at the scene of the horror he'd helped to create. Lighting the fuse at

Roeland Street had been so much easier, he thought, acknowledging an urge to step into the rain and keep walking. "I have nowhere to go," he said out loud, staring at the mine dumps.

Conjuring up Nkolosi's uncompromising face, Tom tried to stir up the fear he needed for survival. Neither thoughts of the Negwenya nor of the police helped block out his desperate wish that he could wake up and find the whole thing had been just a gruesome nightmare.

Tired of pacing, Tom flipped on the radio. A well modulated voice had apparently informed the station's listeners that there had been an outbreak of violence at the De Waal Mining Company:

". . . That's as much as we know right now. We do know, however, that this is an isolated incident and there is no cause for alarm."

During the next bulletin, the head count on the dead and injured began. The numbers kept increasing and yet the announcer's voice remained calm, as if he were swallowing the political tranquilizers he was handing out, as an example for his listening public.

It was almost dark outside when one more confident pronouncement became one too many for Tom:

". . . The troublemakers, those still alive, have all been rounded up."

Taking the Voice of South Africa in his hands, Tom hurled it through the window. The world be damned, he thought. Nkolosi be damned. As for the Negwenya, she could do her worst. Anything had to be better than this.

**BOOK
TWO**

1

"I'm asking you to arrange for one passport for one woman, not start a revolution," Jake Prescott said.

The words, though sparked by months of frustration, sounded more plaintive than angry. Jake tried unsuccessfully to erase their inflection from his memory; he didn't like hearing himself beg any more than he liked asking a favor of Senator Philip Prescott, even if the man was his uncle. The real problem, Jake thought, was that he had never wanted to deal with negative emotions and so he had simply not equipped himself to do so. He simply ignored them. Pretended they didn't exist. Or he had done so in the past. Recently, however, he had become conscious of a whining undertone that colored his words with increasing frequency, and that pleased him even less than dealing with his own anger.

The truth was that Jake had spent thirty-three years in training as a nice guy. Emotions such as anger, contempt, even dislike, were fine for other people; they weren't good enough for him. Having never managed to outgrow childhood's need to be universally liked, he sublimated all of his negative visceral reactions in favor of patience and understanding. Worse yet, he had somehow appropriated from the chameleon an ability to protect himself from conflict by taking on the coloration of those around him. If, in the eyes of some, that made him dull, that was all right, too. What wasn't comfortable was the kind of contempt his attitude was earning him from men like Philip Prescott.

Whatever the reason for the changes that were taking place in his psyche, Jake was beginning to accept them and act upon them—much to his own surprise and everybody else's. Lately, when the conciliatory tone of his own words collided with his internal needs and he felt a burning sensation, as if he were trying to shed his reptilian skin, he found himself allowing his anger to seep through. Like right now. Acknowledging the instinct that was clenching his fist and moving it toward Senator Philip Prescott's even, white teeth, instead of pretending he was incapable of such base needs.

"It's not simply a question of arranging a passport," Philip Prescott said. "The woman's in jail. Thanks to you, she's guilty of a crime. . . ."

Jake started to say something but the Senator held up his hand and continued talking.

". . . The nature of the crime is unimportant. The fact is, either one of you could have arranged for a passport easily enough if you hadn't been caught at it. Maybe when she gets out, they'll give her one."

Jake shook his head. He'd tried that route. The South African authorities had laughed at him.

"All right, I believe you," Philip Prescott went on. "It doesn't change anything. Even if I could arrange for a passport and a visitor's visa, I still couldn't organize emigration papers."

"Can't? Or won't?"

The Senator played with his graying sideburn, a nervous habit impressionists were already using effectively, Jake thought. He was tempted to imitate it now, the way children with no other recourse mimicked their elders.

"If I help you, someone's bound to use it against me politically," the Senator said.

"Against you!" Jake was yelling now, showing his anger at last. "I thought liberation for the oppressed *was* your platform."

"Be rational, Jake," the Senator said, his tone inferring that he was addressing a willful child. "Getting Riena out of South Africa would be going directly against the laws of that country. It would be interfering in the affairs of a foreign government. My platform is equality at home." He leaned back easily in the worn leather chair that had been around for as long as Jake could remember. Despite the oriental rugs and parquet floor that gave the Senator's country study an air of the library of an Oxford Don, or perhaps because of that, Jake thought, the chair looked like it belonged.

"I've heard you say publicly that you abhor South Africa's racist policies," Jake said. He turned his back on his uncle and poured himself a brandy from a crystal decanter that stood, as it always did, next to a signed photograph of Lyndon B. Johnson. There was to be no passport; he'd really known that all along. Nine months had passed since he'd left South Africa. Left Riena. Since then, American troops had pulled out of Vietnam to the tune of the Watergate overture, the United Nations had been overpowered by emerging African States with unpronounceable names, and Ralph Nader had attacked Detroit. Less than a year since his sabbatical in Cape Town, he thought, and it felt more like a hundred. He'd gone there to research the influence of witchcraft on contemporary Africans. His findings not only fascinated him, they left him more than ever convinced that voodoo and power were synonymous in Africa. Back at Princeton, he'd given lectures, begun writing a book on his findings, and written long letters to Riena. Every one had been returned unopened, but he'd kept on writing them anyway. He'd appealed to his uncle for help, and to the bureaucracy in general, but it was a masturbatory enterprise, nothing more.

In almost a year of frustration and waning hope, all that had happened was that Jake's feelings of guilt had increased in direct proportion to the number of unanswered letters that lay in the top drawer of his mahogany desk. South Africa remained adamant in its policy of apartheid, the bureaucracy promised nothing and gave less, and his Uncle Philip was consistent in his refusal to help.

Just before Christmas, Jake had decided it was time to resume a semblance at least of a normal life. He'd started by calling his parents and offering to come home for Christmas. Home. Manchester, Vermont. Neat rows of manicured houses, well-bred parents offering him well-bred young women to induce him into taking his role of upper-middleclass son more seriously.

Coming home, Jake thought, had been an error. He lit the candle under the brandy warmer and wondered how much the ounce of Napoleon shining at the bottom of the snifter had cost his uncle. Then he sipped the tepid liquid and shuddered. Today's family cocktails would, he was sure, be like all the others in the round of holly and mistletoe parties he'd endured like a series of periodontia treatments. His mother was out there now, waiting, with yet another maiden in tow.

"It's too soon," Philip Prescott said. "The kind of power I have now doesn't allow me to change foreign policy. Once I'm in the White House. . . ."

Jake found his uncle's sensible tone disproportionately irritating. He was about to shout his rebuttal, to ask that he be treated like an adult and not like a petulant child, when the telephone rang. There had to be more to his uncle's unwillingness to help, he thought, turning around and leaning back against the liquor cabinet to watch the Senator.

"Who is this?" the Senator asked. He looked puzzled, then angry. "Who the devil are you?" Listening for a while, and then a different kind of anger. Controlled. "I'm listening."

Jake was fascinated. Unmoving. Trying to guess what might be causing the Senator to twist his sideburn with such viciousness around and around his finger. Though good breeding dictated that he leave the room, Jake stayed where he was.

"You'll have to do better than that," the Senator said. "Nobody gives a damn about things like that here. In fact, they'd probably give both of us medals."

By now Jake was so curious that nothing short of brute force could have dragged him from the room. He did grant his uncle some dubious privacy by averting his eyes to glance out of the window at the snow falling gently to the ground. Last year this time, he thought, he was on the beach in Cape Town, laughing at Bing Crosby's mellow pleas for a white Christmas.

"Listen, whatever the hell your name is. I know all

about Watergate. And Vietnam. Yes, preserving my good name will win me votes and the fact that a member of my family broke the laws of your country might lose me a few. In the long run it will all balance out. What I said before holds; you'll have to do better than that. . . ."

The Senator stopped talking and listened for what seemed to Jake to be an inordinately long time. The longer he listened, the more his erect posture gave way to round shouldered defeat. It was as if some unimaginably dread specter was turning him from his energetic and verbal persona into a carbon copy of his sister. Jake's mother. A quiet and delicate woman with a congenital heart disease that caused her family no end of concern. Even his pallor was the same as hers.

Sure that his uncle was about to have a heart attack, Jake moved toward the door to get help. The Senator signalled him to stay. Putting his hand over the mouthpiece, he said: "Pour me a brandy will you, Jake. And yourself as well. You're going to need another one."

By the time Jake had refilled both glasses and handed one to his uncle, unwarmed, the Senator was gently—too gently—replacing the telephone in its cradle. Though some of the color had returned to his face, he still looked ill. When Jake was spared the usual lecture about treating fine brandy the way you should treat women—warm them first—he knew there was a serious problem. To his additional surprise, his uncle circumvented tradition and drained the glass at once; there was no loving contemplation of the amber liquid, no swirling it around, no inhaling the aroma.

"Sit down, Jake," the Senator said, placing his empty glass carefully on his desk blotter. "I believe you're about to get what you want."

"Another glass of your excellent brandy?" Jake said, instantly wondering why he had chosen to be flippant. To his amazement, Philip Prescott burst out laughing.

"It wasn't that funny."

"You're right. It wasn't. I was laughing at something else—a private joke."

"Do you want to tell me what that conversation was about?" Jake asked, wondering if the strain of the campaign trail was beginning to take its toll.

"Oh yes. I want to talk to you, Jake. If I could, I'd wring your neck, but as second best, we'll talk." All traces of amusement were gone and the Senator's eyes were hard.

"What the hell's. . . ."

". . . you wanted to know about that phone call. You may wish you'd never asked. . . . My caller was a man who called himself by some foreign name. Sounded something like Nicholas, so for the purpose of this discussion, let's call him that."

"Foreign?"

"African, to be specific. South African."

"I don't know any. . . ."

". . . He appears to know you. Have you ever heard of an organization called Africans for Independence?"

Jake shook his head. "Never heard of it."

"Well I have. This man appears to be their leader."

"What does that have to do with me?"

"Patience. Hear me out. The AFI's a South African guerilla movement. It's ostensibly devoted to immediate equality. . . ."

". . . Ostensibly?"

"According to my sources, it's communist inspired."

"According to which sources?"

"It doesn't matter. What does is that your lady love has escaped from jail, thanks to the AFI. According to this Nicholas, she's about to give birth to your child. Or has already given birth—I'm not sure of the details.

"My child?"

"Yes. Your child. Don't look so shocked. Sex does have a way of producing by-products."

"My child," Jake repeated, clutching the arms of the Victorian armchair he was sitting on.

"Snap out of it, Jacob," the Senator said. "You're going to have to think clearly. Nicholas didn't call from South Africa just to make a birth announcement."

Jake stood up and began to pace nervously. "Go on,"

122

he said.

"I'll go on when you sit down. You're making me dizzy."

Jake sat down.

"The way this Nicholas explained it, Riena won't be turned in to the authorities, or the baby harmed, as long as she cooperates with the AFI."

"Mind if I pour myself another brandy?" Jake's voice was flat.

"Not if you pour me one too. While you do, I'm going to make a phone call." The Senator flipped through his Roladex, found what he was looking for, and punched the appropriate number of buttons.

"Mike? I'm calling from home. Will you check something out for me?" he said. "Were there any reports of violence in South Africa this morning? No? Yes, I know it's a weekday and I should still be in my office but we're having a family thing; early cocktails, you know." He paused, apparently listening to the response of the man he'd called Mike. "I know it's night in South Africa now, Mike," he said. "Are you trying to tell me they reserve violence for daylight hours? Check it out for me, be a good boy. No, I don't know anything you don't."

He looked up at Jake and covered the mouthpiece.

"Sometimes," he said, "it's useful to know the little people. The guy's an operator at OPI."

He uncovered the mouthpiece. "When?" he said. "Thank you, Mike. Appreciate it. You, too."

"It's true then," Jake said, seeing confirmation on his uncle's face.

"It just came through," the Senator said, replacing the receiver. "The AFI blew up the women's section of Roeland Street jail. It seems the authorities tried to call it a boiler accident to keep it from becoming international news. The AFI didn't like that, so they gave the Press a full report."

"Riena could be dead," Jake said, his voice hardly above a whisper.

"I don't think so, Jake. According to what I just heard, she's very much alive." Philip Prescott stood up and walked around his desk. He half-sat on the edge and appeared to be examining the shine on his Florsheims. Then he looked at his nephew and said: "I've changed my mind about helping you. I'll get you the papers you need, if you'll go back to Cape Town and handle some negotiations for me there."

"Negotiations?"

"That phone call you overheard was a threat. The caller said he intended to use your morality, or lack of it, to besmear the family's good name. That could really hurt me with the voters. . . ."

". . . You didn't take those threats seriously," Jake said, remembering the part of the conversation he heard. "What I did is hardly in the league of Watergate or Vietnam. As you said yourself, what I did may well gain you as many votes as you lose because of it."

"You broke the laws of a foreign country."

"Look, I'm delighted that there's a chance I'll get what I want. But I know you. You give nothing for nothing. If I'm going to negotiate something for you, I have to know what I'm doing."

The Senator sat for a moment without speaking. Watching his uncle's face, Jake saw the intensity of the man's emotions.

"All right Jake. I suppose if we're going to help each other, you do have a right to know what's going on. I don't have to tell you that politics is a dirty game or that I want to get to the White House badly. Very badly. There are men who are helping me get there. Powerful men to whom I'm obligated. Those men have a great deal of money tied up in South Africa, most of it in the De Waal Mining Company."

"In Johannesburg?"

Philip Prescott nodded.

"Do you have investments there, too?"

"One of the things I guaranteed when I accepted help from these men was that I wouldn't play politics in South Africa," the Senator went on, ignoring Jake's last question. "I guaranteed to protect their interests. . . ."

". . . How?"

124

"By preserving the status quo, if at all possible. By noninterference with the government's policies."

"So what I did has rocked your nice little boat. A member of your family breaking one of their fundamental laws and now wanting to marry a revolutionary. I don't buy it. There's something missing. Nobody's going to hold you responsible for my actions."

"I can't singlehandedly stop a revolution, Jake."

"So your alternate plan is to cooperate with a revolutionary regime," Jake said. His response was an intuitive one but it hit home.

"This Nicholas, I don't know how, is aware of my connection with De Waal. He said that when he and his people take over, everything will be nationalized. If I cooperate with him, he'll guarantee. . . ."

". . . Hold it a minute. Are you so sure his revolution's going to succeed?"

"No, of course I'm not, but I have to consider the possibility."

"What kind of cooperation is he asking?"

"My support, in secret, for his revolutionary government."

"Support?"

"Money, I suppose. That's what you would have to negotiate. He insisted on a personal emissary."

"You give him money. He buys guns and keeps quiet about your backers and takes care of you after the mines have been nationalized?"

"That's about the size of it."

"If the AFI is being supported by the Russians and this Nicholas turns out to be a pawn, you'll be supporting a communist regime. I can't believe you're willing to do that."

"I'm not."

He's still playing games with me, Jake thought. There's only one way he can get a monkey like that off his back.

"The elections are around the corner," the Senator said. "I want that man kept quiet until they're over."

"What he knows can hurt you as much once you're

125

in the White House as it can now," Jake said slowly. "There's only one way you're going to really rid yourself of him. . . . Negotiations won't solve anything. Not permanently. Nor will bribery. I'm not going to kill for you, dear uncle."

Philip Prescott laughed. "Do you really think I would send you to do a job like that? If I were going to have him killed, I'd hardly send an amateur. All I'm asking you to do is get him off my back. For now."

"For now?"

"It would take time to set up anything more . . . permanent."

"Yes, I suppose assassinations are delicate maneuvers," Jake said. He was amazed at his own reactions, his ability to discuss all of this rationally, as if nothing more passionate were at stake than winning or losing a game of chess. But then he knew his real reactions would come later, when he was alone.

"What if I won't do it?" he asked.

"You'll lose on all counts. I certainly won't get you the papers you want. And I'll send someone else over there. In that case I'll have to forego the initial steps. Listen to me carefully, Jake, before you make any rash decisions. If I have to send a stranger, I'll send a professional. He'll be instructed to use any means at his disposal to get to Nicholas."

"He'll have to find him first."

"That shouldn't be difficult. I'm sure Riena would know where to find him."

"She may not want to help."

"I'll send someone persuasive."

The threat in Philip Prescott's words was not even veiled. "You evil son of a bitch," Jake said, standing up. He towered over his uncle but the Senator didn't flinch.

"Your choice," he said. "Make it by the time today's party is over."

"Choice? What choice?" Jake looked at his uncle's face. It wore the look of a victor. "I could always go to the media. Spread the good word about the kind of bastard you really are."

126

"By all means. You do that," Philip Prescott said. "But if you do, I'll see to it that you never see your precious Riena again. I'll send someone over there, Jake. Even if my political career's a dead issue."

"God help America if you ever become President," Jake said.

"God help you if I don't," his uncle said, standing up. "I've never liked losing anymore than I've liked losers, Jake," he went on. "And I don't intend to change now."

2

Thanks to Philip Prescott's private pilot, Jake made it to New York in time to board that evening's ten o'clock flight to South Africa. By noon of the following day, five in the morning Vermont time, he was circling Johannesburg.

Delayed in a holding pattern, he took "Scenic South Africa" out of the pouch attached to the back of the seat in front of him and leafed through it for a second time. The Drakensberg towered over Paarl's vineyards; the Atlantic and Indian Oceans kissed at Cape Point and then parted in two curved fins that extended to the horizon; deserts surrounded diamond mines and Frank Lloyd Wright was enshrined behind gold dumps. Jake had met Afrikaners whose love of country was based on the conviction that South Africa was a mirror image of heaven. If physical beauty counted for anything, they probably weren't all that wrong, he thought. He pictured Plettenberg Bay, the way the river idled between rocky hills, caressing the shore as gently as a morning lover, fooling Sunday canoeists into believing that the Atlantic was myth and did not lie waiting beyond the next curve. That shapeless piece of German rock that lay on the banks of the Rhine was a pretender, he decided, feeling the 747 begin its descent. The real Lorelei was here.

Stepping off the plane onto South African soil, Jake shifted gear slightly and switched images. Though he hardly considered himself a returning hero, Odysseus approaching the temptress must, he thought, have felt much as he did now. He was afraid. Fascinated and repelled in one dichotomous surge of emotion.

At the ticket counter, waiting to reconfirm his connecting flight to Cape Town, Jake felt fatigue enfold him for the first time since he'd agreed to come back to South Africa. He noticed absently how the ticket agent's uniform buttons strained and then slid open when she leaned toward him to tell him his flight had been delayed for an hour. But he thought longingly of a hot shower and clean sheets. Not even the girl's obvious attributes placed anyone in the bed with him. A bed, he thought, that was his first hurdle.

To dull the disquieting thought that he'd made no provision for accommodations in Cape Town, Jake wandered off to find a cup of coffee, or better yet, a bourbon on the rocks. Somehow his search for a drink took him down a sterile passageway to a door marked CUSTOMS/DUANE. If finding a drink was that tough, he thought, trying to decide whether to walk back to the duty-free shop at the top of the corridor or knock on the door to ask directions, how on earth was he going to find a revolutionary whose name and address remained a mystery? He wasn't a private eye.

Jake's knuckles reached for the glass partition on the half-open door, but an angry voice stopped them in mid-air.

"Don't you dare tell us what to do. Just because your father's rich—fucking rich broads—his money's not going to help you, or your *kaffir-boetie* fiance. We know all about him. . . ."

". . . Do what you like." The reponse was weary but without fear. "Whatever you do, gentlemen, make it fast, will you? I'd like to get to New York in this lifetime."

Jake heard a strange sound, like a saw cutting through plasterboard. He stepped closer and looked inside the room.

A woman in her late twenties or early thirties sat on a straight-backed chair that was set against the far wall. She was surrounded by four uniformed men, customs officials by the looks of them. One of them was using a handsaw to cut his way clumsily through a plaster cast with little regard for the fact that it was still attached to a human foot.

"I was only damn well kidding when I said I had diamonds hidden in the cast. You knew that," the patient said, as the rigid cast fell to the floor and shattered.

The man holding the saw smiled. "Now we know for sure," he said. "We didn't before, *reg?*" He kicked a piece of the plaster of Paris debris with the tip of his boot; it bounced a few times and stopped. "You can go now."

The woman picked up a new leather suitcase and limped toward Jake.

"Something I can do for you?" Jake said. He had to raise his voice to be heard above the hilarity inside. By the sounds of things, the men were well pleased with themselves. "Can I buy you a cup of coffee or something?"

"Preferably something."

"You'll have to lead the way. I'm lost."

The woman nodded and moved ahead, taking over ownership of the drab corridor despite her limp and lending it color by her passage through it. Jake followed, intrigued.

Both the bar and the coffee shop were around the next corner. The woman hesitated, glanced at Jake, and headed for the latter. It was a little cleaner than most and less congested, but the familiar smell of goodbyes that hung in the air gave it entree into the sorority of airport restaurants. Jake ordered two coffees which appeared instantaneously in china cups, along with a small jug of steaming milk. One sip reassured him that the brew was no less putrid than the papercup variety at

129

American airports. The clatter of a wagon making frequent trips up and down the aisles for dirty dishes reverberated in his head, and for the first time since he'd become aware of conservation, he thought fondly of paper products.

Jake looked over at the woman and was about to speak, but she seemed disinclined to do anything other than concentrate on the 747 on the runway outside. He added more sugar to his coffee and tried not to be caught staring. Not that the woman was traditionally beautiful; her features were too irregular for that, her cheekbones not high enough. It was more the way she held her head that drew him, the way her green eyes sloped slightly down instead of up, the way her sun-streaked hair poised on her head in a gravity defying twist that demanded to be released over her shoulders. Thirty, Jake decided. She had to be thirty . . . probably one of those women whose looks would keep. It had been a long time since he'd been inclined to apply the word elegant to anyone, but it was the right word to use now. Jeans, madras shirt open to a place between prude and loose, gold Mogen David resting easily against a tanned neck. . . .

"Star, sir?"

Jake jumped as a rolled-up newspaper attacked his waist. He turned slightly, looked down at the two sepia eyes, and connected them with a grubby little hand extended palm upward. The newspaper now lay across his lap. He dug in his pocket for a coin and realized, embarrassed, that he had not exchanged any currency. He not only couldn't buy the newspaper, he wouldn't be able to pay for the coffee he'd offered with such apparent chivalry.

Seeing his embarrassment, the woman opened her purse. The child grabbed the newspaper from Jake's lap and moved to the other side of the table. When he had left, the woman handed Jake the paper and stood up. She hadn't touched her coffee except to add milk.

"Would you mind watching my suitcase while I make a phone call?" she said. "I'm going to have to drag myself back to Cape Town to have my foot checked; I might as well make sure someone'll be at the airport to pick me up."

"Why don't you have a new cast put on here? In Johannesburg?"

"The thing was about due to be removed anyway. Maybe it won't need to be replaced. Frankly, I never thought my foot was broken in the first place and it's certainly not hurting. It just feels a little stiff. Besides, I was going to New York to speak at a convention. No point in rushing there now; it's too late to make my session. Damn AFI. . . ."

She walked away before Jake could say anything more.

While she was gone, Jake examined the vagaries of the fates that had connived to have the first person he met on his return in some way linked with the AFI. It was too much to hope that this woman, to whom he had not yet even introduced himself, could lead him directly to his quarry. Still, if he played his cards right, she could probably lead him to someone who could. . . .

". . . I'm back."

"Jake Prescott," the American said, standing up and holding out his hand before the woman sat down.

"Deanna Rosen." Her handshake was firm. "Did you say Jake Prescott?"

"Yes."

Deanna sat down, took a sip of her cold coffee and pulled a face. "I feel as if I've heard the name before."

"I have an uncle who's running for President. . . ."

". . . that must be it." She didn't look convinced.

"Did you say something about the AFI before you left?"

Jake hadn't meant to blurt out the question in quite that manner, or that soon. Deanna stiffened, and he was instantly sorry he had.

"Are you a newsman?"

"No." Jake smiled, hoping to relieve the tension. He was gratified to see Deanna's shoulders lower a few degrees. "Look," he went on, "I didn't mean to annoy

131

you. It's just that I heard about the bombing before I left the States, and I was curious."

"I'm sorry," Deanna said. She leaned back in her chair and smiled at Jake. "I didn't mean to jump on you, so we're even. I'm a little touchy, that's all."

"Forget I asked."

"It's okay. Actually, that's what that whole fiasco you witnessed back there was all about. Ivan, my fiance—or ex-fiance I suppose—was a member. He left for Botswana a couple of weeks ago and hasn't come back. The idiots assume just because he was involved, I must be too."

"Are you?"

"No." Deanna had stiffened again. "But it's really none of your business, Mr. Prescott."

"Jake. Please. And once again, I apologize," Jake said.

"Accepted . . . Jake," Deanna said, looking at her watch. "I presume you're hanging around the airport waiting for a connection? Where're you going?"

"I'm taking the one o'clock flight to Cape Town."

"Since it's now twenty to two, you might have a problem making your flight."

Jake laughed. "The flight was delayed. It's leaving at two o'clock."

"In that case," Deanna said, "we might as well leave together. That's the flight I'm on. I booked it before I called home." She picked up the check and stood up.

"You must've gathered before that I didn't change any money," Jake said. "Could I owe you a cup of coffee?"

"Deal. Where're you staying, so I can be sure to collect?"

"I don't know. I didn't make reservations."

"In the middle of the season!" Her tone suggested that he was a moron. "You don't have a snowball's hope in hell of finding anything decent." She hesitated, then said: "Listen. I've temporarily moved back in with my parents. They have tons of room, and they love Americans. . . ."

". . . I couldn't. . . ."

". . . I'd welcome the diversion of showing you around."

"What about your trip to the States?"

"Next vacation."

That was a sudden decision, Jake thought, flattered, but reminding himself that he had come to South Africa with a purpose. Then, rationalizing Deanna's connection with the AFI as a reason for acceptance of her invitation, he nodded. If she could lead him to Nicholas. . . . "All right. Thank you. But just for a couple of days until I find something." Perhaps, he thought, watching Deanna again as, her limp already almost imperceptible, she moved surely ahead of him, his luck really had changed.

The flight from Johannesburg to Cape Town took less than two hours. Deanna curled against the window and was asleep before the seat belt sign was turned off. Jake avoided serious thought by doing much the same thing. He woke long enough to accept a platter of fresh fruit and cheese from a rolling cart, drank a glass of South African wine that rivaled any California burgundy he'd tasted, then settled back to sleep. When they arrived in Cape Town, he was groggy and grateful that Deanna apparently felt no need to make small talk.

They were met at the airport by a tall, elderly Black man. Deanna hugged him; much to the disgust of those Whites who happened to be watching. He was introduced simply as Johan.

Sitting in the back seat of a green Anglia, Jake concentrated on trying to shake free of a heavy mantle of fatigue. He credited it to avoidance—not physical, since there was little he could have done till now to change things—but mental avoidance. He had consciously played Scarlett O'Hara since leaving Vermont, telling himself nothing would change if he didn't think about things until tomorrow. Every now and then he had tried to conjure up Riena's face. He couldn't. There was a nightmare quality to his efforts, a feeling that he was hyperventilating in an effort to wake up, though he wasn't asleep in the first place. He had no difficulty picturing her body; he remembered in the minutest of detail their lovemaking, their quarrels and their promises. It was as if a sculptor had fashioned a slab of marble into flesh and limbs and movement and then, tiring of it, had left the face untouched.

"Almost there," Deanna said, twisting her head to look over her shoulder at Jake. "Look for a shocking pink double-story."

"Pink?"

"My little sister had it painted to match her toe nails while our parents were away on holiday. They almost killed her. There it is. . . ."

"I'm impressed," Jake said. It was hard not to be, despite the house's vivid exterior. There were high granadilla hedges burdened with blue and white flowers; fig trees, their branches loaded with purple fruit; prize pink chrysanthemums growing halfway up the newly varnished front door, which was where Johan deposited them.

Behind a bay window, an ecru-aproned maid polished silver on a bed of newspaper. The yapping of a small dog turned frenzied, and the maid looked up. Within seconds, the door flew open, and they were being ushered into the house.

"Are you hungry, Miss Dee?" the old lady asked, ignoring Jake while she welcomed her surrogate daughter back into the fold, accepting her early return without question.

"Starving, Alice. Where's everybody?"

"Mrs. Rosen's still at her bridge club. It's too early for the master to be home, and Miss Susan's upstairs doing her homework."

"No I'm not," a skinny girl of about twelve said, balancing precariously on the bannister. "What the hell're you doing here, Deanna? Thought I was rid of you for a while, fer Chrissakes."

"Miss Susan!"

"Aren't you used to her mouth yet, Alice?" Deanna could barely repress a smile. This was apparently a familiar scene.

134

Susan stuck her tongue out at her sister, winked broadly, wiggled her hot pink toes at them all, and disappeared.

"As you've probably gathered," Deanna said, "that was my sister, Susan. If anyone ever tells you menopause babies are a good idea, beat him to death with a large stick. Now, if that didn't take care of your appetite, let's have a bite to eat. Dinner isn't served until rather late around here on a Friday. My parents go to Temple first, and services aren't over until eight."

She led the way into the dining room, pointed to a chair at the opposite end of the table, and tugged at a cord that dangled to the right of a stinkwood sideboard. Jake wondered how the silver Alice had been polishing had so quickly been replaced by white linen and crystal.

"Why you come home from America so fast?" Johan said, rushing to answer the call of the bell-pull. He was grinning a toothless grin and trying to adjust a wide pink bandanna that crossed diagonally from one white jacketed shoulder to his waist.

Deanna held up her foot. "I didn't go to America after all," she said.

Johan's bushy eyebrows flew toward his hairline, and Jake and Deanna laughed.

"Bring the food will you please," Deanna said. "You'll hear all about it later on, while you serve dinner."

Johan left and quickly returned with a silver serving platter piled high with cold cuts and cheeses, butter and honey. Behind him, Alice carried hot bread and a pot of coffee on a twin tray.

"Don't stand on ceremony," Deanna said, piling roast beef and cold chicken on her plate. "Are there any tomatoes, Johan? Bring some, will you?" She attacked her food and was reaching over to refill her plate when Johan returned with a plate of sliced tomatoes.

Jake, surprised at his own hunger, took several slices. Neither of them said a word until their first hunger pangs were satisfied. Then, lathering a slice of bread

135

thickly with butter, Deanna sat back against the solidity of the carved oak chair and looked at Jake expectantly. He knew small talk was expected of him, but he couldn't think of anything intelligent to say.

Deanna leaned forward again and dripped honey onto the slice of bread.

"Listen. I have an idea. There's nothing much I can do about my foot right now, so why don't we go for a dip? I can't really swim until I have it checked, but I can dunk myself . . . or would you rather sleep?"

"I didn't bring a swimsuit," Jake said. He was sorry. He'd like to have seen Deanna in a swimsuit.

"No problem. I'm sure I can find you a pair of trunks somewhere around the house. I'd offer to take you skinny dipping, but the only place you can do that is Graaf's Pool and that's 'men only.'"

"Yes, I've been to Graaf's Pool," Jake said. "And Saunders' Rocks. Clifton, too."

"How about Hout Baai?"

Jake shook his head.

"Then that's where we'll go. It's only five-thirty. We have plenty of time to get there and back by dinner. You'll have to drive though. Johan has things to do around this time, and I suppose I shouldn't drive until I've had my foot checked."

Jake nodded. He'd driven on the left before with little difficulty.

By the time they reached Hout Baai, the sun had begun to fight the horizon. The semi-circular barrier of rocks that protected the beach from the open sea looked like papier-mache, and the sand was bathed in an apricot glow. The Atlantic, Jake thought, looked different now than it did then . . . the last time he'd seen it . . . the morning of Riena's arrest. They'd needed a break from sweat-stained sheets and lovemaking, so she'd decided to go into town for her usual Saturday meeting with Tom Sibanda, her adopted brother. He'd sat around the shanty until, afflicted with a solid case of cabin fever, he'd left too, angry that the government's asinine policies precluded their having walked into town together.

Christmas decorations, wilted but still gay, had festooned the streets; the air was filled with the echoes of Christmas carols, and here and there, a discarded gift box littered the sidewalk, despite the fact that New Year's Day had already come and gone.

Without checking its destination, he'd jumped onto a bus. It wound around a mountain road, rising high above the white beaches, crowded with long-limbed, taupe bodies.

When the signs said Clifton, Jake left the bus. He'd stood on a ramp high up on the road overlooking the Atlantic and wondered at the logic of a people who baked in the sun to take on the color of the people they despised. It was obscene, he thought, remembering the blue-jeaned schoolgirl who'd sauntered past him and winked, the movement of her eye a shutter that disposed of the scene below and replaced it with a transparency of Riena's olive body.

He'd followed her into the Clifton Hotel Terrace Bar.

"Hurry up," Deanna called out. "I'm almost ready to get out. It's freezing in here."

Jake didn't stop to wonder whether it was memory or the residual heat of the day that was causing the sweat to run down his neck and trickle from his armpits to his waist. He stripped quickly and dove into the water. It dealt him a physical blow. When he surfaced, he seemed to be staring straight into the eyes of the bronze leopard that kept watch over the area from the side of the mountain.

"It can't be more than forty degrees in here," he said, startled.

Deanna laughed. "It's not quite that bad, but it never goes above sixty," she said. "If you want warm water, you'll have to swim in the Indian Ocean. It's really worth it after you get out, though." She climbed a little awkwardly onto a rock and dried herself.

"It sure isn't Miami," Jake said, getting as near as he could to where he'd left his towel. As he straightened himself up, his body began to prickle, then a warm flush drove its way from his toes to his scalp.

"You won't have any trouble sleeping tonight," Deanna said, watching him. She was dressed and ready to go.

Jake thought he heard her add that it was almost as good as making love. "The other beaches were crowded," he said. "Why's this one so empty?" He could see one figure, crouched in the shadow of a large rock at the other end of the beach, near their car. Other than that, the shoreline was deserted.

"Shark," Deanna said.

"What?"

"No need to shout. You weren't attacked, were you?"

"No, but. . . ."

". . . but nothing. It's all a bunch of baloney. Some kid reported a sighting to the newspapers about a week ago, and now no one will come here. Not that I mind. I love it when it's like this."

Jake, his heart pounding, looked around. The crouching figure stood up and padded toward them, then veered away out of sight.

"Let's go," Deanna said.

Back to the hot-pink house, Jake thought, and away from sharks. The house had probably faded to rose in the dusk he thought, almost fondly, having to move fast to keep up with Deanna who was already approaching the rock where he'd seen the man crouching a few moments before.

Suddenly Deanna stopped in her tracks and knelt down in the sand.

"Take a look at this."

Breathing heavily from the unaccustomed pressure his movement through the soft sand had created on his muscles, Jake reached Deanna and squatted next to her.

"What's that?" he asked, watching her finger trace a strange, fluted pattern in the sand. "Maybe someone was trying to draw the leopard up there." He looked up. In the glow of the sunset, the sculpture seemed to be made of lava.

"No," Deanna said quietly. "Look closely."

Jake examined the jagged outlines, and a form started to take shape, a curling tail, pointed ears, a shell shard eye.

"Fascinating, isn't she?" Deanna said, slowly erasing the figure.

As the sand painting disappeared, Jake felt a chill touching his spine as the sun lost its battle with the horizon.

"Unless I'm very much mistaken," Deanna said, "that was the Negwenya."

"Negwenya?"

She ignored Jake's implicit question and stared into the sky, then at the other end of the beach where a lone man stood silhouetted against the twilight. Shaking her head as if to clear it, she took Jake's arm and led him to the car.

They were passing Clifton when she spoke again.

"Sorry I acted so strangely," she said. "It's just that every time I think he's been around, it spooks me."

"He?"

Deanna laughed. "You must really think I'm crazy. The Negwenya's a dragon . . . I'll tell you about her sometime if you're interested. The 'he' who gives me the creeps is Nkolosi."

3

"Did you say Nicholas?"

"That would be the Anglicized version, I suppose. Actually, it's a Zulu name. You pronounce it Inklawzi, but Nicholas is pretty close if you're not used to the other sounds."

"Does he have anything to do with the AFI?"

Deanna looked at Jake curiously. "How would you

know that?"

"Do you mind if we stop for a drink?" Jake said, seeing that they were about to pass the Clifton Hotel. "I can cash a traveler's check." He braked a little too suddenly and turned into the parking lot before Deanna had a chance to answer.

When they were seated at a table on the terrace, Jake said: "Do you know that there's probably no beach in the world that rivals this one? Even Copacabana's dirty and crowded . . . Those cottages on the cliff, do people live in them all year round?"

"Yes, people live here all the time, and yes, I know we're fortunate that we have no seaweed, no bluebottles stinging the soles of our feet. But you didn't almost kill us both turning in here to babble non sequiturs about the scenery. You are babbling, you know."

Jake watched the changing expression in Deanna's eyes as she waited for him to explain. She smells of salt and Nivea Cream and Chanel, he thought, not knowing how to begin and wishing he'd kept driving along High Level Road.

"When we met at the airport," he said, "I asked you about the AFI. . . ."

". . . Jake Prescott. Now I know why the name sounded so familiar," Deanna said. "She only mentioned it once, so it took me a while to make the connection. You're Riena's lover, aren't you?"

Jake was too shocked to react.

"Her mother's been my mother's dressmaker since the year dot. Through a strange set of coincidences, although lately I'm not sure I believe in coincidence, I was around right after Riena gave birth to her . . . your . . . son."

"Where are they?"

"I have no idea where Riena is. The baby's with Riena's mother . . . adopted mother. I took him there before I took Riena back to the docks. Johan and I went down there this morning on the way to the airport to see how she was doing but she was gone."

"Back up. I feel like I'm lost in a maze."

140

"You're right," Deanna said. "If you get me a drink I promise to start at the beginning."

Jake waved over a cocktail waitress and ordered. Then he listened, fascinated. He had an urge to rush out and call Margaret Mead, whom he'd met once, briefly, at a conference. Dragons. Witchdoctors. A revolutionary movement unified by a collective unconscious. His natural pragmatism discarded the whole thing as outrageous, while years of anthropological study told him that anything the mind conceived was possible.

"I had no idea Riena was even pregnant until yesterday," Jake said finally.

"Are you still in love with her?"

"I don't know. It's sometimes impossible to isolate feelings. I loved her then. I feel a sense of responsibility for her . . . and the baby."

"Jake, if you're not in love with Riena, it might be fairer if you left her alone. Her life is complicated enough."

"Can you take me to Maria? Tell me where to find Nkolosi?"

"To answer your first question, I can but I won't. I'll lend you my car and tell you how to get to her house. Nkolosi? I don't have the foggiest. I sometimes see him hanging around the campus but other than that. . . ."

"I need another drink. What about you?"

Deanna shook her head. "It's getting pretty late. I think we should go back to the house."

"I'll drop you off and head straight for Maria's, if that's all right with you."

"Come in for a moment first so I can show you your room and give you a key. That way if you get in late, you won't have to disturb anyone."

"I feel I'm taking advantage. . . ."

". . . no problem. You can meet my parents in the morning. Breakfast's at eight on Saturdays, outside on the veranda. I may still be asleep, but make yourself at home. Tell you what, if you don't have anything planned for tomorrow, why don't you meet me at the university around lunchtime?"

"I thought you were on vacation."

"I am, but I have a few things I'd like to take care of, including a visit to the doctor. We can do some touristy things in the afternoon, maybe take a cable car up Table Mountain or go to Kirstenbosch. . . ."

"I'd like that."

"Good. Be at my office between twelve and one, and we'll take off from there."

Shortly before eight, Jake drew on his last reserves of energy and, map in hand, returned to Deanna's car. Following her simple directions, he found himself in Observatory before he was ready to face Maria, so he drove along Main Street, trying to organize his thoughts. The stores had long since closed for the day; occasionally a delivery boy rode by at a lethargic pace or a woman emerged flushed from a late beauty parlor appointment, but the usual type of Main Street shoppers were absent, and it was too early for Friday night drunks. He stopped at a traffic light and looked at a travel agency, its door disguised by a poster of a pointing bobby. Next year, maybe, he thought. Then his eye was caught by a teenager who was examining him from a perch on the corner mailbox.

The boy angled the tip of his orange satin Carnival hat, almost as if in greeting.

Jake looked more closely. "Denis?"

The boy tipped his hat again.

In the time it took Jake to park and get out of the car, he heard again the whip-like rhythm of the canvas tent that had been the foreshore's alarm clock those last few mornings with Riena. He'd wanted so badly to take her to the circus, but that had been another of those incomprehensible verbotens. After arguing about it with her and losing, he'd agreed to meet Denis at the foreshore and take him. He was, after all, Maria's latest orphan . . . then. Now she had a new mouth to feed. Flashes of Barnum and Bailey delight mingled with anger at the memory of the way the audience had been sectioned off. We must look like Oreo cookies to those aerialists, he'd thought, glancing down at the "pass for White"

142

child next to him. He'd asked Riena later why the circus had no freak show, and she'd laughed and said: "This whole country's a freak show, isn't it?"

"Still want to be an elephant trainer?" Jake said, leaning out of the window.

The boy nodded. His neon hat incongruously topped patched blue jeans and a T-shirt whose faded letters read: "The answer's still no, but don't stop asking."

"Want a ride home?"

"Hokay."

Jake was struck by Denis' lack of surprise at seeing him, as if their trip to the circus had been yesterday.

Climbing off his perch, Denis made sure his hat was on firmly and followed Jake to the car. He hugged a corner of the seat and looked straight ahead.

"Say something," Jake said, unnerved by the silence from a boy whose constant chatter less than a year ago had been the most characteristic thing about him.

"Hokay," Dennis said. "Fuck you, Whitey." He turned his back on the American and stared out of the window until the car pulled up in front of his home. Before Jake could say another word, Denis had disappeared.

Conscious of boldly curious eyes trained on his spine, Jake knocked nervously at Maria's door. He heard the whirring of a sewing machine and a hollow chronic sounding cough. Out of nowhere, whispering Friday night groups began to form in the street behind him, people grateful for any diversion from poverty and beer.

Jake knocked again and waited. The whirring continued. He looked around for Denis but the boy, his "fuck you" message delivered, was nowhere to be seen. Gingerly, he tried the doorknob; the door opened to his touch.

"May I come in?"

The machine sound didn't stop. He advanced a little further into the room. It smelled of poverty, and felt like a sauna.

"I'll be right out, Madam. I'm just finishing off the

hem." The voice was weary and old, and the rhythm of the machine never faltered.

Jake accepted the delay and retreated to the porch. He sat down on a rickety chair, watching the watchers on the street—groups of adults who leaned against the fences and each other, their bodies questioning his right to be there. Even the children, up too late, found him more interesting than their games. He felt a compulsion to stand up and scream that he had business with the seamstress and stretched out his hand as if to ward off an attacker.

"Yes?"

His chair crashed over onto its side as Jake shot out of it, his body reacting as if in self-defense.

"Did Mrs. Petersen send you for her dress?"

"No."

"Should I know you?" Maria's face registered nothing, not even curiosity.

"May I please come in?"

"Why?"

"I'd like to talk to you about Riena."

"She's not here."

As though there was nothing more to say, Maria turned back to her machine. Jake followed her inside and watched her pick up a heap of satin from a bed of newspapers on the floor. Even in the dim light, the reds and yellows leaped out at him like strobes.

Maria coughed and fondled the fabric. In the far corner of the room, an infant whimpered and the woman moved toward the sound.

"Riena's not here," she said again.

"Where is she?"

"Dead for all I know—or care." She moved over to the cradle and rocked it gently. "This is her baby. The father was an American. A White man. . . ."

"Maria," Jake said, feeling as if Tennessee Williams had taken charge of the script, "I'm Jake Prescott, the child's father."

"So what? I told you, Riena's not here. Or are you planning to seduce me in her absence?" She smiled gro-

144

tesquely, in an agonizing caricature of prostitution.

Bile rose in Jake's throat, and he wanted to vomit. "Please," he said, holding out his hand. "I know nothing can change what's happened, but I need to talk to you."

"You can't stay long," Maria said, indifferent again. "I have work to do."

"Should I close the front door?"

"It's cooler if everything stays closed."

Jake could hardly breathe, but he shut the door.

"Could I see the child?"

The brown statue eyed him with distrust.

"You mean your son?"

The seamstress picked the baby up and held him out. Jake eyed the papoose, wrapped in a hand-stitched square of red satin like a leftover Carnival fragment. He took the sweet-sour bundle into his arms, and it immediately began to cry.

"Men!" Maria said. She reclaimed the baby and placing him across her shoulder, rubbed its back with a gentle circular motion. "Don't cry little Jacob, don't cry," she whispered, each word corresponding with the three hundred and sixty degree movement of her hand.

"Jacob?"

The crying had stopped, but the hand continued describing its circle. "Yes, Jacob," she said, laying the baby in its cradle.

"We must talk," Jake said.

"Talk quickly then. I have work to do." She stood with her back to the cradle, protecting it. "If you've come to tell me that my daughter's dead, you would be bringing good news."

"I bring news that she's alive."

Maria's face didn't change expression. "You've told me," she said. "Now get out." She sat down on the chair that faced her sewing machine. Jake raised his voice as the whirring started up. "We have to talk," he said again.

"Haven't you gone yet? My lady'll be here any minute; I can't afford to lose her, she's a good customer,"

145

Maria said. "Look. If you want to wait while I finish this, I'll talk to you. Otherwise, get out."

Jake removed a bolt of satin from a chair and sat down, fingering the soft fabric. As if he were reading Braille, the music came back to him, and the sight of minstrels weaving through the streets, drunk on dancing and laughter. Cape Town. Carnival time. The police closing their eyes; boozers and wife-beaters throwing bottles and belts into the limbo of three days of celebration. It would soon be a year, Jake thought. The Carnival was due to return, but he wouldn't be there to see it. Not without Riena.

"People aren't arrested during Mardi Gras are they?" she'd said, insisting that they go together. Openly. Pretenders to love in the sunshine. ". . . banners, home-made instruments, singing and dancing through the streets . . . the cops like our music," was her answer to his pragmatism. That and dreamy talk of penny pinching to buy the satins. Coloured tailors and dress-makers working dawn hours to make costumes for their friends and relatives; ceremonial parades and competitions taking the city hostage.

And so they'd walked the streets together hand in hand, blending into the parrot jungle that had sent its stars to invade the city. Flashes of color decorated buses and bicycles; marching banjo troupes sang double-entendre theme songs that set White feet tapping and won trophies for the beat and the sound while the words comforted the singers.

On the third day, he'd asked what happens when it's all over.

"What usually happens when the party's over?" She sounded matter-of-fact, like a mother warning her child that dark circles came in the wake of a late night.

He remembered the aftermath: garden boys shading their heads with the battered remnants of minstrel hats; servants using satin dust rags; bathroom curtains glowing in the January breeze. And the little girls, he thought. The only winners, wearing satin dresses to play jacks in the gutter. He looked at the trophy in Ma-

ia's corner, gathering dust, and reminded himself that
ust as surely, booze and belts were drawn out of limbo.

"Done," Maria said, hollowing her back as she
stretched.

"You won't need as many customers after today,"
Jake said, pulling his wallet out of his pocket. Without
considering the consequences of his actions, he
counted out five thousand dollars in travelers checks.
"I want to take the baby to the United States," he went
on, signing his name over and over in a kind of glorious
frenzy.

"Why don't you just go back to America and leave us
alone," Maria said. "I'll take care of the baby."

"How? You can hardly feed yourself," Jake said. He
gathered up the signed checks that were scattered
across the cheap formica table, tapped them into a neat
stack and held them out to the rigid woman standing at
the other end of the room.

She made no move toward him.

"Take these to the bank," Jake said. "They'll give you
over four thousand Rand. That's more than you could
earn in five or six years of dressmaking."

"We manage," Maria said, shaking her head.

"It's a lot of money." Jake was determined not to be
ejected. "You and your family can move out of this
place, maybe to the country. You could have your own
bedroom, your own workroom. . . ."

He was interrupted by a keening, made up of the pur-
est tragedy. The sound came from the woman's gut,
through closed lips. Her head swayed like an adder,
rhythmically, from side to side.

Jake walked over to her and folded her hand around
the wad of paper. "Take it," he said. "I'll be back for
the baby." He moved to the cradle and bent over his
son. He had broken from his wrapping, and his hands
and feet were experimenting with freedom.

"Maria, listen to me," Jake said, turning to face the
woman. Her hands were caressing the wheel of her sewing machine; her head was still in motion. "This baby
will have everything in America—good food, warm

clothes, an excellent education. . . ."

The whirring began again, like background music signalling the end of a scene. He stopped talking and let the curtain come down.

It wasn't until he was almost in Sea Point that he allowed himself to face what he had done. Not only had he bought his own baby, a son he neither wanted nor knew how to raise, he'd used Philip Prescott's down payment to Nkolosi to make the purchase. He contemplated the nearest cliff as his only recourse, but good sense and Scarlett O'Hara prevailed. In the morning, he thought. I'll think about it in the morning.

4

A buzzer in the next room woke Jake on Saturday. Disoriented, he stared at the newspaper that lay on the chintz coverlet he'd neglected to remove the night before. Courtesy of a guest who'd neglected to throw away Thursday's late edition, he was faced with a display of mutilated bodies, littering the front page with the abandon of a Superman comic strip. Only, Jake thought, there was no Clark Kent to come to the rescue.

Now fully awake, Jake walked to the window and pushed the curtains aside. Below him, Johan leaned against Deanna's Anglia and watched the passing cars. The sea was barely visible at the edge of the horizon. He tried to think through the realities of his visit to Maria. It was all very well to have said that he would take his son to America. He could deal with that actuality later. His more immediate problem was finding a way to replace the money intended for Nkolosi, money which, in a roundabout manner, would have bought passports for Riena and the baby.

Ignoring his stubble and sleep-rumpled clothes, Jake opened his door and tiptoed down the hallway. He le himself quietly out of the house and walked toward the sea, turning left off High Level Road onto a street that ed to Saunders Rocks. He stood on the Promenade, ifty feet above the sand. Leaning on the guard rail, he wondered about the guests who stayed at the President across the street. He'd been told that the hotel reserved a certain percentage of suites for visiting Black dignitaries.

Turning around, Jake looked at the smaller and more attractive hotel next to the so-called "International" one. There, he knew, they made no such provisions. Plateglass windows displayed a few diners breakfasting early on starched white tablecloths. He could see Black waiters and waitresses lolling against center-poles and empty chairs, waiting for their resident guests to give them a sense of purpose and he realized that he was very hungry. He glanced at his watch. It was still only seven o'clock and breakfast at the Rosens wasn't until eight.

A man in a swimsuit stepped out of the smaller hotel. Remembering the chill of the ocean, Jake shivered so visibly that the man noticed and smiled as he jogged down the concrete steps that led to the beach. On an impulse, Jake followed him across the sand and onto the rocks. Their surface was slippery; shallow overnight pools barely hid their residue of mussels, and starfish and silver dollars clung to the rocks like Madeira trim on a peasant skirt.

The grey-haired swimmer poised in an attitude of prayer and cut expertly into the water. His elbow moved regularly in and out of the sea and Jake watched, mesmerized.

Towelling himself briskly less than three minutes later, the man smiled again and called out: "You should try it."

"It's cold enough after the sun's beaten down on the water all day," Jake said.

The man moved surely over the rocks toward the steps and stopped for a moment to lean against the "Whites Only" sign buried deep in the concrete. "You don't know what you're missing," he said, brushing his feet and slipping into a pair of brown sandals.

Time to start up the hill, Jake thought. He climbed the steps and stood for a moment next to a bench obscenely scarred by a matching "Whites Only" sign to the one down on the beach.

Telling himself that he was hiding its ugliness by accepting the hospitality of its sun-warmed slats, Jake sat down. Only one thing was clear, he thought. He would have to find five thousand dollars to replace the travelers checks he'd given Maria. He took out a cigarette and lit it. The taste of burnt paper filled his nostrils and he coughed, ground it out, and started back to the house. Five thousand dollars, he thought again, picturing his non-existent bank balance. It might as well have been a million but he'd have to raise it somehow. Without the money, it would take a miracle to rid his uncle of Nkolosi and get Riena and the baby out of the country.

Deanna let Jake into the house. She was wearing a utilitarian blue bathrobe and her hair hung loose around her shoulders.

"Excuse the way I look," Jake said. "I went for a walk first. Didn't want to wake up the household."

"It's all right. Saturdays are pretty informal around here. I'm going to get dressed but why don't you have breakfast right away."

Once again Jake ran his hand across his stubble. He hesitated but the aroma of breakfast won out. It wafted from the dining room where Johan, his bandana scarcely in place, offered a world of crisp linen, gleaming crystal and an English breakfast. A mahogany sideboard, its wood glowing with the labor of lemon oil, carried an array of silver-covered dishes. Tomato juice in goblets complimented a single red rose that set off the whiteness of Irish linen and a perfect basket of fresh fruit, its contents polished to a high waxen gloss crowned the center of the table.

"Food's ready, *Baas*," Johan said. "Everybody sleep too late today. You like melon first? I can bring some from the kitchen."

He started to raise the lids along the sideboard. Jake looked at the first one and frowned.

"*Mabela*," Johan said, pointing to what looked like steaming chocolate pudding. "You eat with milk and sugar. Also butter, maybe." He picked up a large cereal bowl and a soup ladle but Jake moved to the next dish, and on down the line: scrambled eggs, fried chicken livers, and lamb chops. If Saturday breakfasts were informal, he could hardly imagine what the other mornings brought to the table.

Johan dipped into the *Mabela*. "Just try, *Baas*," he said, placing the bowl on the table in front of Jake. It smelled delicious. Feeling like a child stealing last night's dessert, he reached for a Waterford milk jug and poured rivers of white around the chocolate mound. Then he sprinkled the peak with sugar and watched it dissolve.

"Deanna says she'll be right down."

Jake jumped as Susan whirled into the room and sat down, her pants straining at the seams. "How can you eat that vile stuff?" she said, gulping down a glass of juice and sliding a slice of toast under a heap of butter. "Ugh! Cocoa Farina. Disgusting. 'Bye." As quickly as she had appeared, she was gone.

Johan, standing by, whipped away Jake's bowl as soon as it was empty and placed a plate piled high with eggs and an assortment of meat in front of him. He was toying with the idea of forcing himself to eat one too many chicken livers when Johan stiffened.

"Morning, Master."

"'ning. Usual, please."

Jake followed Johan's gaze. An older man stood in the doorway, looking him over. Jake rose and extended his hand.

"Who're you?" the man said, not responding.

"Prescott. Jake. Friend of Deanna's," Jake said, automatically imitating the man's barracks style.

"Sit down!" It was a command. "Thought Deanna was in the States by now."

"You can't get rid of me that easily," Deanna said,

coming into the room.

'What the hell's going on around here?" Her father sounded totally unamused.

Deanna sat down to breakfast and explanations with no sign of temerity. The passage of her fork to her mouth was no less constant than the tapping of her father's foot on the Oriental design beneath his shoe.

"Thank you for your help, Prescott," Martin Rosen said, after listening to his daughter's recounting. A heavily pulsating vein in his neck looked at bursting point. "Anything I can do for you while you're here . . . welcome to stay of course . . . see you later." He slammed his napkin into his unfinished toast. "As for you. . . ." He was talking to Deanna. ". . . go to the doctor."

Martin Rosen stomped out of the room and Johan relaxed his antique spine. Jake lit a cigarette from a pack of Peter Stuyvesants he'd picked up at the Clifton Bar. "Does your father always speak in phrases?" he said.

"I won't apologize for him. He's a rude old bugger. . . ."

". . . Miss Dee!" Johan said.

"Still love him, Johan?" Deanna said. "You and mom. That's two more than most people can count on."

"Deanna! Are you all right? What happened? Did you miss your plane? Where's your cast? Usual please Johan." Mrs. Shirley Rosen came into the room, sat down, asked four questions, and gave Johan an order, in one continuous and surprisingly graceful series of movements.

"I love you," Deanna said, getting up to hug her "even if you are a Jewish mother. I'm fine and this is Jake Prescott."

Shirley Rosen looked down with satisfaction at her Melba toast, apple and cup of tea. Her expression told Jake she was grateful that it was her usual breakfast and not some new concoction designed to add to her confusion. She was an attractive older version of Deanna. Her pale morning suit opened to show a shantung blouse; her small ears were perfectly complimented by pearl studs that matched the string around her neck and her hands displayed only a narrow gold wedding band and a small prewealth solitaire. Her nails were short and unpainted.

"I can fly to New York any one of a dozen ways," Deanna said, answering something Jake had missed during his inspection of her mother.

"The direct flight, you promised, Dee. Uncle Arthur will be waiting at Idlewild. . . ."

". . . Kennedy. And I can take care of. . . ." Deanna stopped and laughed. "This argument's been going on for three months," she said to Jake. "If I delay my trip till Easter, it probably won't stop till then. There's only one direct flight a week from Cape Town to New York but if you leave Cape Town early enough in the morning you can make a connection out of Jo'burg any day. . . ."

". . . a milk train that makes five stops," Mrs. Rosen interrupted, "and you'd have to stop in Dakar, Monrovia, Accra, Lagos, Kinshasa. . . ."

"Would you have to debark each time?" Jake asked.

"Hard to say. Those African states have no hard and fast regulations. Generally they let you stay on board but sometimes they insist that everyone get off," Deanna said.

"Why?"

"If they suspect a South African on board of having some relevance to their cause; if they need tourists at the airport store; if they're bored. . . ." Deanna paused just long enough for her mother to take over.

"The airports aren't exactly modern and they're not air-conditioned. You know how hot it can get there, Dee," she said.

Jake pictured himself on the blazing tarmac of a primitive airfield, his arms full of baby while savage guerillas held a planeload of passengers at gunpoint. He could almost smell his sweat mingling with the sharp, sour odor of urine and see it spreading its amber glow across his shirtsleeve.

"Any friend of Dee's is welcome to stay here, young man," Mrs. Rosen said, as if suddenly remembering her manners. "Stay as long as you like."

"Thank you, Mrs. Rosen," Jake said. "I'm not quite sure of my plans but I'll move to a hotel some time today."

"Nonsense. It'll only cost you a lot of money and it won't be half as nice as here, will it, Dee? Besides, we're having a party tomorrow. You'll stay for that, won't you?"

"I'd like that," Jake said. "By the way, I apologize for my appearance. I don't always look this scruffy. I took a walk early this morning. . . ."

". . . I don't blame you. This is such a beautiful place to be, isn't it? I can't imagine wanting to live anywhere else." She looked out of the window at her rose garden, smiled and stood up. "I'd better cut some roses for the table before it gets too hot out there," she said, "if you two children will excuse me. Dee, why don't you and your friend take your coffee out onto the porch? It's lovely out there now. Pity it was too breezy to breakfast there this morning. Perhaps tomorrow. You may clear now, Johan."

She pecked her daughter's cheek and dismissed the morning meal.

"In case you didn't notice, she makes up for my father's brevity," Deanna said, pouring two more cups of coffee. "She's right about going outside, though."

Balancing their cups, Jake and Deanna settled themselves into two identical basket chairs that faced Lion's Head. The mountain was still buried in purple shadows and each bush and scrub emerged slowly from the contours of its craggy bed.

"Do snakes come down?" Jake said.

"Not often. Jake, if there's anything I can do to help, say so. Dad may sound like a grouch but he does know a lot of influential people around this *dorp*."

Jake laughed. "Those customs men are going to find themselves in trouble then," he said.

"Not really. They can pretty much do as they please. People have smuggled out diamonds in stranger places than casts. *Dagga* too."

154

"Dagga?"

"It's a potent form of marijuana. Between that and *Skokiaan.* . . ."

". . . What?"

"*Skokiaan.* Your Moonshine would be the closest thing to it, I suppose. The Africans ferment the stuff under the ground. I know Johan brews it somewhere in our garden. It's pure alcohol. They generally drink it through a straw while it's still buried. They don't want to waste any time turning themselves blind."

"Literally?"

"Yes."

"Is *Sko* . . . *Skokiaan* legal?"

Deanna laughed. "Is Moonshine? Bastards have a hard enough time getting beer brewing permits in the *locations.* For someone who lived in Cape Town for nearly a year. . . ."

". . . Guess I moved in the wrong circles."

"I suppose so, or we might have met the first time around. Jake, I don't mean to sound like I'm prying but what are you going to do? Nkolosi isn't an ordinary man. If he leads you to Riena, he'll want payment. . . ."

Jake didn't say anything. He had told Deanna very little about his reasons for wanting to find Nkolosi. Five thousand dollars was, he knew, several years' wages to most Africans but he was beginning to wonder if it would have sufficed for this one.

"I get the feeling you need to make contact with someone in a position of power in the White community, a Member of Parliament or a top newsman," Deanna said.

"Know anyone like that?"

"I did have a friend who was a photographer with "Drum" but he took pictures at the Sharpeville riots. He got the negatives out of the country but he made the mistake of hanging on to a set of prints. Someone found them and turned them in."

"Is he in jail?"

"No. He's in Paris as a matter of fact. His friends were being pulled out of bed and thrown in jail for lesser of-

155

fenses so he left. Rapidly."

"Was he Black?"

"No. There is one other man. . . . My father has an old friend who's an M.P. He's an intelligent Nationalist, which let me tell you is a rare and wondrous combination. Van Der Merwe. Daniel. I don't know if he could do anything for you, or if he would, but he certainly has clout."

A police siren wailed down High Level Road. Deanna stopped talking till the sound had died away. "I feel like a paranoid but you really never know about stray eyes and ears," she said. "Listen, I think Van's coming to our brunch tomorrow. Why don't you just wait until then before you do anything. I could give you a ride into town on my way to the University. You could go shopping or something."

"You going to drive?"

Deanna nodded. "My foot's fine. Those buggers may have done me a favor. I'd still be lugging that thing around."

"Maybe I'll walk into town. I have thinking to do and walking might stimulate my brain cells. I'll make my way to UCT later."

"Whatever you like," Deanna said, standing up, "but if I don't go now, I might as well not bother. I won't be leaving for ten minutes, so if you change your mind. . . ."

Jake shook his head. He knew that if he accepted her offer he'd have a hard time resisting the temptation to tell her what he'd done. He desperately needed to talk about it. But he said nothing and watched her leave. It had been an impulsive gesture and instinct told him Deanna would be disapproving, not of the gesture itself but of the lack of planning behind it. Somehow it was important to him that she not think of him with disapproval. If, indeed, she thought of him at all.

5

After a hot shower and a shave, Jake began his five-mile trek into Cape Town. Striped sun umbrellas scattered the lawns on either side of the Rosens' house and neat borders of asters and pansies turned their faces to Lion's Head. It towered over the suburban residences, turning Sea Point into an MGM set. The streets were free of debris. They reminded Jake of the boulevards in East Berlin, like Unter den Linden which was kept spotless by groups of senior citizens who emerged after dark with brooms and rakes and water pails. He'd seen few strollers there; the locals walked with a sense of urgency that affected even the tourists. This, Jake thought, was like a spring Sunday in Manchester, Vermont. Here the people in the streets took time to stroll . . . the Whites because they belonged and the non-Whites because they had learned that hurrying changed nothing.

As a double-decker "Plumstead" bus lumbered into sight, Jake wondered why he'd always summarily rejected the idea of living an uncomplicated New England life. He started for the bus stop, then changed his mind and wandered down High Level Road to Main Street and on down Regent Street toward the ocean. He passed a restaurant being readied for its "morning tea" customers, an expensive dress shop, an antique cellar which would normally have tempted him inside.

But he kept walking toward Beach Road, where the rolling greens began. They separated him from the ocean promenade. Nannies sprawled beside carriages in the sun and a child in checkered gingham jumped rope, her spindly arms and bare feet in perfect harmony. Nothing else moved, as if the world were holding its breath to the tune of "Strawberry Shortcake, Huckleberry Pie."

The chant followed Jake down the road until, out of earshot, he was forced to face the thought that was causing him the most pain. Still, no matter how hard he tried, he could not conjure up Riena's face. He could see her skin, feel her warmth, picture the stiffening of her shoulders whenever he'd mentioned a life together. But her eyes, her mouth, the curve of her nose, were lost to him. He strained to put the fragments together, angry that his subconscious had placed her in his past instead of his present and future.

"Shit!" Jake clutched his left shin. It had connected with the corner of a bench where an elderly couple sat hand in wrinkled hand. With apologies, he turned toward the beach. He almost welcomed the interruption of physical pain. Below, on the sand, two teenage lovers browned in the segregated sun of a "Whites Only" beach. He watched them enviously. When he continued along the promenade, he found himself glancing down at his fly like an adolescent.

He increased his pace.

The opposite side of Beach Road was decorated by a series of modern, glass-fronted apartment buildings; moving toward him was the Mouille Point lighthouse. Circular. Red and white. Its foghorn punctuating traffic and leading customers to the Doll's House around the corner. There a young man in a peaked cap waited hopefully for his usual Sunday influx of drive-in-and-eat diners, his stance a flagrant imitation of American Graffiti's heroes. The censored version of course, Jake thought.

At the next island, he turned away from the beach. The route to the main road took him past manicured bowling greens where retired businessmen in white ducks stood in easy groups, then past apartments growing less elegant, store windows grimier and passers-by less leisurely. He was approaching a Coloured section of town whose dividing line seemed to be the sports stadium up ahead. That and the fire and police depart-

158

ments just beyond. He quickened his pace, trying not to fill the stadium with colored satins and banjos and voices raised in song. His efforts were useless. The ghosts of tapping feet and clapping hands ushered him into an area of shabby houses and shops that were dingy and dark. The streets were filled with a preponderance of Coloureds who stared at him curiously. Jake, his feet beginning to ache and his back wet with exertion, wondered what they saw—a good looking tourist taking in the sights or a distraught Odysseus. Horns honked around him; half remembered scents of a rumpled bed mixed with the Chanel of shoppers, and the strain of trying to evoke Riena's features in every face he saw metamorphosed into the acceptable pain of hot and tired feet.

And then he was out of it, back in the world of department stores and fashionably dressed women, parking meters and cafés where Café au Lait was out and Expresso was in.

Thirsty, Jake felt in his pockets for a coin. The gesture reminded him of a more pressing problem. Money. The only rational thing to do was to call his parents and ask them to wire five thousand dollars to him care of American Express, whose sturdy double-doors happened to be glaring at him from the other side of Adderley Street.

Foregoing the coffee, he crossed the street and went inside.

"Over there, Sir. Miss Cramer should be able to assist you in making the necessary arrangements." The young woman's smile was well-rehearsed and comforting.

Miss Cramer sat exectantly at her desk, hands folded on a small stack of papers. "Good morning, *goeie môre. Can I help you, kan ek U help?*"

She's a miracle of modern technology, Jake thought. A bilingual recording in reasonably attractive female form. "If I call the States and have money wired here, will there be any problem collecting it?" he said.

"Not as long as you have proper identification," Miss Cramer said, holding out her hand.

Jake took out his wallet and handed it over.

159

"Thank you, Mr. Prescott. I'll be right back," Miss Cramer said. She and his wallet disappeared, her high heels fighting with the beige institutional carpeting so that her progress across the room made her look more like a manikin than ever.

Jake lit a cigarette. It was half an hour before the lady, for whom he was beginning to feel an attachment that was not unrelated to her possession of his wallet, reappeared.

"Mr. Dunn says there's no problem," she said, displaying his credit cards. "Show these when you return for your money."

"Where would I go to make a call to the United States?" Jake asked, hoping she would tell him he could use her telephone. "It'll be collect."

"Can't let you use the phone. Regulations, you know," she said. "The G.P.O.'s just around the corner. Up the street, two blocks. On your left. You can't miss it." She sat down, folded her hands and replaced them carefully on her papers. "Goodbye, Mr. Prescott. *Totsiens Meneer Prescott.*"

At the glass double-doors, about to step out onto the sidewalk, Jake put his hand on Miss Cramer's reflection and paused. He half expected her to scream rape and was almost disappointed when she didn't move. Then he stepped into the throng of busy shoppers.

The tall grey stone of the General Post Office blocked out the sun. Its cold marble interior denied the existence of anything not directly ordained by a universal bureaucracy of postal authorities and Jake felt a kind of helplessness descend upon him. He felt the same way in banks, immigration offices, standing in line for the rides at Disneyland. Overorganized. As if the red tape obscured his thought processes.

He stood in front of a counter marked TELE-GRAMS/*TELEGRAMME*. When he became aware of the murmur of a restless queue at his back, he composed a cable to his parents. Before handing it over, he glanced at his watch. It was cocktail hour in Vermont. A collect call home, he thought, really would be a far

160

more intelligent move. He pictured his parents, about to sit down in the dining room that his mother insisted on using for every meal, she and his father dressed for company as they were every night. Thirty years together and they still dined formally, by candlelight, carefully keeping their Lord and Lady of the Manor affect intact.

"You going to just stand there?" the postal clerk said, spurred on by the audibly shuffling line at Jake's heels.

Mumbling an apology, Jake wedged himself into a phone booth and, using a ten-cent piece, dialed the overseas operator. To his amazement, there was less than two minutes' delay between his placing the call and the sharp ringing of the telephone.

"Hello? Dad?"

"Jake?"

"Sorry I had to call collect," Jake said.

"Never mind that. Are you all right?" His father's voice was clear but there was enough of a delay between each word that Jake felt as if he were hearing an echo, instead of the words themselves.

His mother picked up the extension in the study. "Are you all right, Jake? Honestly?"

"I'm fine, Mother. Dad, are you still there?"

Jake Prescott Senior cleared his throat. It was a sound that had guided his son safely through crowded baseball stadiums, department stores and supermarkets.

"I'm here, son. Do you need money? Is that why you called?"

Suddenly Jake realized how much he resented having to ask his father for money. Again. Not that five thousand dollars would so much as cause a ripple in his father's bank account. He waited for his mother to remind him that he was welcome to any mount of money he wanted but why on earth didn't he learn to save. He started to say yes . . . it's a loan . . . you'll get every penny back. Instead, he said: "No. Thanks. Just wanted to make contact."

"Jake, if you're in trouble say so," his mother said.

"I'm fine, honestly, Mom."

161

"How much do you need? Never mind, will a few thousand dollars see you through?" his father said.

"No. Thank you," Jake said. He swallowed hard.

"When will you be back? Mary asked.

Mary. His mother's last holiday offering. "I'll write as soon as I know more about my timing," Jake said.

"Where are you staying?" Katherine Prescott asked.

"With a friend right now but I'll be moving tomorrow."

"Make sure you find a decent place."

Jake laughed. Ph.D., veteran, it made no difference. He would always remain Katherine Prescott's little boy. "I'm going to hang up now," he said. "Take care of yourselves." She'll keep him up all night, Jake thought. Asking for assurances. And he'll give them to her. His father knew all about Riena but he'd asked Jake not to tell his mother, hoping, Jake supposed, that a Mary or an Ann would come along and his sweet Kate would never have to know.

Drifting into introspection, Jake almost missed his parents' goodbyes. "I'll send a cable if I leave in less than a week," he said.

"Right. Goodbye son. . . ."

". . . Goodbye," his mother interrupted.

"Goodbye Mother, Dad, see you soon."

Purposely walking to the far end of the building to avoid the sunless alley where he had entered, Jake stepped out into Castle Street. Magically, the sun was shining, as if the Post Office had been designed to confine its gloom to the back entrance. Across the busy street, the City Hall clock chimed its 11:45 a.m. message across the gingerbread walls of the early Dutch fortress that lent authenticity to the street named in its honor. Dusty World War II documents had replaced the sailors who'd once stopped within its walls en route to the treasures of India but the structure itself was intact.

It was too early to start for the University. Hoping to find some distraction, Jake wandered toward the O.K. Bazaars. Its window displays beckoned him inside. He spotted a fresh fruit-drink stand at the far end of the store and bought a guava juice, letting its thick pulpy sweetness trace an icy path down his throat. Ordering a second one, he held the paper cup in his hand and contemplated the juice's appealing salmon color. Then he sipped it, slowly this time, savoring its grainy texture on his tongue.

All around him, people crowded at bargain counters. Bright-eyed shopgirls, many of them Coloured, rang their registers with practiced skill; children peered over candy counters; babies dug their noses into soft ice cream cones. Jake leaned against the wall with his twenty-cent cup of juice, watching the scenario. It was not unpleasant to be anonymous, he thought, hearing friends greet each other, chat for a moment, and strain to find a polite mechanism that would allow them to continue their shopping.

Throwing his empty cup into a metal waste-basket, Jake headed back to the street. The exit he used led him directly into the flower market, a narrow alleyway where awnings sheltered him from the sun and flower sellers competed volubly for his attention. Offers came from all directions as an army went into combat, their weapons botanical, their enemy the passers-by.

"Lovely roses, Mister. Take them home to your Missus."

"Mine're cheaper, Mister. They'll last longer, too. The buds're tighter."

They were a mother and daughter team, working the street in matching rags.

"How much?" Jake asked the older woman who had placed herself firmly in his path, her arms filled with dozens of red and yellow rosebuds.

The young girl started to respond but her mother gave her a "this one's mine, don't waste any more time on him" look. "Only seventy-five cents a dozen, Sir . . . or you can take three dozen for one Rand eighty. I'll be losing money. . . ."

The daughter replaced her armload in a water-filled barrel.

Jake thought about buying roses for Deanna. For

Shirley Rosen. It was a foolish thought. The Rosens' garden was filled with prize specimens. He gave the woman seventy-five cents, took one rose for his buttonhole and smiling at her shock when he refused change, started toward the bus stop.

Dodging an enormous newspaper truck, Jake crossed to the Grand Parade grounds, unknowingly reversing Riena's route on the day he'd last see her. Once there, he was again besieged, this time by fruit and vegetable vendors. Different weapons, same war, he thought.

"Tamaties, lemoene, waatlemoen."

"Hé jou lekker ding, come buy some *tamaties."*

"Tamaties en uie. Tomatoes and onions. How much you want, *ou Gamat?* They's reely fresh. You don't know what youse missing. How's about it?"

Jake grinned at the bad English, probably worse Afrikaans and comic strip American slang that made up the dialect peculiar to the uneducated Cape Coloureds.

"Are the bottom ones still rotten, Lumme?" a woman with a shopping bag asked.

Lumme concentrated on unwrapping a stick of gum. He pushed it well back in his mouth, chewed it three times with a contented expression, then took it delicately out of his mouth and aimed it at a garbage can a yard away. When the entire operation had been completed, he looked at his customer and said: "Could I afford to chew three times and throw it away if I sold rotten *tamaties?* Would I, *Mevrou?"*

The woman laughed and applauded. Satisfied, she filled a bag with tomatoes. The show had been part of what she'd come to expect for the price of the produce.

"Argie-lay! Argie-lay!"

Jake jumped. The sound had come from his knees, from the mouth of a child who was weaving a path from knee to knee through the Grand Parade. His dwindling supply of the midday Argus Late was attached by a string to a wobbly red skate board which trailed him past the produce stands, through tables covered with vases and pot-plants, around second-hand book stalls and under auction tables groaning with knick-knacks. Soon, Jake thought, the Parade would be deserted. It was getting hot and Capetonians would head for the beaches. The stores would close for the weekend and he'd have to fight shopgirls and servants for a seat on the bus.

As if in confirmation, the City Hall clock struck noon and an auctioneer up ahead announced the last bargain of the day.

Jake moved closer.

"Going, going, gone to the lady in the yellow skirt," the auctioneer bellowed, holding some useless object at arm's length.

An elderly Coloured woman elbowed her way through the crowd shouting: "I'm the lady, mister. I'm the lady." She pulled out a scrappy looking purse and counted out the pennies she needed for her purchase.

She's paying to be called a lady, Jake thought, watching the auctioneer lick the point of his pencil and take the woman's particulars with all the skill of a slow first grader. Then he hailed a bus that would take him most of the way to the University, asked the conductor to tell him when he had reached the closest stop, and promptly fell asleep.

For no reason he could define, Jake woke refreshed and even optimistic. It was a long uphill climb from the Rosebank stop to the University but he hardly noticed until he reached the old windmill that was his landmark for a left turn onto De Waal Drive. It was a public monument, another relic of Dutch Colonialism. He had explored it once, with a friend from the University. They had spent most of the time inside arguing about the Zulus and their relationship to contemporary living. His friend, a South African anthropologist, had insisted it would take many more decades before the Zulu's subconscious had fully accepted the White man's culture as his own. Jake had argued that he was not at all convinced that was a good idea in the first place.

"If the Zulu wants to live and work under our system, he'd better learn its rules," his friend had said, with not so much as a hint of indecision.

Jake had ultimately capitulated. The Zulu, they'd agreed, would have to adapt. Like the Japanese and Indian Americans. The Zulu man who was called a woman and considered that sufficient cause for mortal combat had no place in urban Africa, Jake thought. He remembered an Afrikaner worker telling him he'd eaten his lunch while watching just such a fight to the death. Now there, he decided, was a species that warranted anthropological investigation.

Passing the old mill, Jake turned onto De Waal Drive. It curved its way through Cape Town's heart, flanked mainly by large open spaces where buck ran free in full view of passing motorists. Every now and then, the fields were interrupted by pine forests whose wild mushroom smell hung almost tangibly in the air, or by a dirt road that started at the edge of the tarmac and disappeared into the woods. One of the few major roads led to Groote Schuur Hospital and Christian Barnard, another to Cape Town University. The campus snuggled into the bosom of the mountain like a nursing infant, its newer buildings designed to blend with the older ones and all of them seeming to grow out of the rock.

With far less effort than he'd anticipated given the spread of the campus, Jake found the reception desk of the Civil Engineering Department. The ozone of Academe had long been his natural habitat, and he felt immediately at home.

"Jake Prescott," he said, surprised to find the receptionist at her desk on a Saturday. "Dr. Rosen's expecting me."

"Oh yes, Dr. Prescott," the girl said. She smiled and handed him an envelope with his name printed on it. "Dr. Rosen will be back shortly. She left this for you."

Disappointed, Jake opened the envelope and took out the note inside. The handwriting was as neat and firm as he'd have predicted, though slightly smaller than Deanna's self-assurance might have led him to expect.

"Jake, I'll be back around one thirty."

He looked at his watch. It was only one o'clock.

"I saw Nkolosi on campus when I arrived this morning. Decided to take a chance and tell him you wanted to see him. He said he'd wait for you in the woods near the playing fields. Be careful.

Deanna"

Jake crumpled up the note and with a soft: "Tell Dr. Rosen I'll be back," he retraced his steps to the University gates. He had no idea what he could say that might induce Nkolosi to tell him where to find Riena. Or to leave Philip Prescott alone. He did know that he had to speak to the man, and now was as good a time as any.

Picking up a pine cone from the ground, Jake veered off to the right towards the woods. It wasn't until he saw the crouched figure of a man that he dropped the cone and examined the curiously familiar ridged pattern on his palm.

"Nkolosi?" he said, praying for inspiration and scratching the inside of his hand which had begun to itch, "I'm Jake Prescott."

6

Nkolosi raised his head and began to uncoil his body. Slowly. Responding to Jake's voice as if to a snake charmer's flute. "I know who you are," he said, standing up.

Jake examined the sand at the witchdoctor's feet. There were a few acorns, a salamander dozing in a renegade sunbeam that had managed to filter through the trees, the pine cone he'd dropped. Nothing else.

Certainly no scalloped silhouette of a dragon.

"Did you lose something, Mr. Prescott?"

Nkolosi's tone was polite, that of one gentleman exchanging pleasantries with another across a conference table before addressing the real business of the day. If Jake had anticipated an accent, it was not this one. Sibilant. Formal. Almost Oxford in its precision.

"You look as if you were expecting a baboon," Nkolosi said.

"Actually, I was expecting to see the Negwenya."

The witchdoctor roared with laughter. "She is for those who believe in her, Mr. Prescott. Or are you perhaps a believer? It would be quite unusual if you were."

Strangely, Jake felt himself relaxing. He grinned and shook his head. "I suppose I'm a voodoo agnostic," he said. "I find it almost as hard not to believe."

"Was the money you gave Maria your uncle's entire message to me or was there more?" Nkolosi sounded casual, one old friend asking another about a mutual acquaintance.

"How did you. . . ."

". . . you will learn that there is not much I don't know, Mr. Prescott," Nkolosi said.

"Then you must also know that my uncle wants you off his back," Jake said, trying to maintain the atmosphere of easy gossip. "And that I wish to find Riena."

"Easily done."

"Where is she?"

"I said easily done. Not that I would do it. As for your suggestion that I 'get off your uncle's back' as you so charmingly put it. . . ."

The witchdoctor's tone had changed. There was a new, guttural quality. Jake tensed.

"Yes, Mr. Prescott," Nkolosi said. "You're right, of course. Now that the amentities have been disposed of, the bargaining must begin."

"Your English," Jake said. "It's. . . ."

". . .Oxford. Your ear did not deceive you. I've been back here for a decade, so it's no longer natural to me, but I'm able to dredge it up when I need it; it has obvious shock value, don't you think?"

"You were educated there?"

"No. I was educated here, by my father and his father. Oxford was only what I believe you would call 'the frosting on the cake.' "

"Nkolosi . . . am I pronouncing that correctly?"

"Yes. Surprisingly."

"Is that what they called you at Oxford?"

"No. Nicholas. Nicholas Ngoma."

"Ngoma?"

"It means dance and drum. Many of our words have double meanings. Mr. Prescott, this conversation is most pleasant but it's solving neither your problems nor mine. Shall we get down to business?"

Jake tried to gauge Nkolosi's thoughts from the expression in his eyes. It was impossible. They were no more revealing than a swirl of brown acrylic on a palette knife. Impersonal. Like his blue jeans and Levis shirt.

"I see you're looking at my American affectation. I would prefer to wear a leopard skin sarong; it would be a good deal more comfortable. Unfortunately, where I live the mosquitoes would feast on me."

"Where do you live?"

Nkolosi laughed. "There are men who would pay a fortune for that information."

"Speaking of payment, Mr. Ngoma . . . Nkolosi. As you already know, I. . . ."

"Yes. I know. If it serves to make you feel any better, the five thousand dollars would have bought you very little other than what I'm prepared to give anyway."

"Give? Just like that?"

"No. Not 'just like that.' 'There are no free lunches.' Isn't that what they say in your country?"

Despite his growing nervousness, Jake smiled.

"I am pleased my Americanisms amuse you, Mr. Prescott," Nkolosi said, his eyes hooded. Deadly. Almost imperceptibly, he had begun to sway, an adder in motion. "The way I see it," he said, "there are two separate issues to consider. Your uncle's problem and your

169

need to find Riena."

"Yes."

"As far as the Senator is concerned. . . ."

"I'll replace the money if you'll leave the Senator alone. The five thousand was only a down payment. Tell me how much it will take to keep you quiet."

"I don't need money."

"Not even to buy guns for your revolution?" Jake asked, hating himself for doing so.

"I'm a wealthy man, Mr. Prescott. And I have even wealthier supporters."

"If you're so damn rich, why don't you give some of your money to those of your people who aren't?"

"You want me to build swimming pools in the *locations?*"

"No. Buy food."

"It's better for the revolution if they stay hungry. Contentment has a way of breeding apathy."

"If you're not willing to deal with my uncle, why did you tell him to send someone to negotiate with you?"

"Because I knew he would send you," Nkolosi said. "I will deal with your uncle later, when I am ready."

"You already know what it is that I want," Jake said, beginning to tire of the game. "Since you don't want to talk about my uncle, will you discuss that? You have information that I want. You won't take money in exchange for silence, so I must assume that you won't take it for information either. There must be some form of payment that will satisfy you."

"Yes," Nkolosi said. The word was a hiss and his eyes were immutable. "There most assuredly is."

"What form of payment. . . ."

". . . Patience, Mr. Prescott. Your American system provides you with many commodities. Patience is not one of them. I believe Dr. Rosen has mentioned to you one Daniel Van Der Merwe."

Jake nodded.

"On Monday a dozen or more prominent South Africans will be detained by the AFI. Daniel Van Der Merwe is to be one of those."

"Detained?"

"A euphemism our government uses freely to describe the process of imprisoning people in their own homes."

"Why're you telling me this? I could warn the authorities. . . ."

". . . You won't. Not if you want to see Riena and your child again. Healthy," Nkolosi said.

The adder strikes, Jake thought, watching Nkolosi lean against the rough surface of the trunk of a pine tree. He seemed to merge into the bark. All but his smile.

"Mr. Van Der Merwe swims every morning. Early. Once you've spent some time with him, as you will be doing tomorrow, I believe, it should be an easy matter to join him for a swim. It's a short step from that to changing in his flat. While you are there, my man will come to the door. You will let him in."

Out of old Aristotelian habit, Jake pursued the conversation through to its conclusion. "Will I be held too?"

"No." Nkolosi's definitive response was reassuring. "You'll be free to go."

"Where?"

"Where good sense dictates. I suggest you return to the Rosens' and stay there for two or three days. Then take a train north to the village of Teyateyaneng. Riena will come there, too."

"Will Van Der Merwe be killed?"

"No. That is not our intent. Particularly with Van Der Merwe. The AFI needs him."

"If you've no intention of hurting your victims, they'll eventually be freed. They'll turn in descriptions of their captors; the police'll catch up with you . . . and me. When they do. . . ."

". . . Your part in the whole thing will be considered naiveté, Mr. Prescott. No White South African would be stupid enough to open the door to an unidentified voice. An American, on the other hand, might well do so."

"Unless he happens to be from New York or Chicago," Jake said. "One other thing," he went on. "You said something about the AFI 'needing' Van Der Merwe. Isn't he clearly on the other side?"

Nkolosi shrugged and Jake, certain no explanation was forthcoming, said: "Where's Riena now?"

"On her way to Johannesburg. She'll be holding the Cohn household."

Jake must have looked puzzled because Nkolosi said: "Arthur Cohn is a newsman. A liberal."

"If he's a liberal, why antagonize him?"

"Quite simply, because it's too late for the kind of slow progress he advocates. The South African definition of a liberal differs somewhat from the American one; it generally refers to a White South African who believes equality is possible . . . sometime."

"What happens if I do everything you want?"

"You'll see Riena and the baby again. If you don't . . . I meant what I said earlier."

"What guarantee do I have that you won't harm them anyway?"

"None. You'll simply have to trust me, Mr. Prescott."

The way he'd trust a puff adder not to strike, Jake thought.

"You've already met Van Der Merwe," Nkolosi said, "though not formally."

"I don't think so," Jake began. He stopped when Nkolosi held up his hand in an imperative demand for silence.

It wasn't the hand but the look on the African's face that kept Jake from continuing. They sat in silence for several minutes, until Jake's untrained ears finally heard what the witchdoctor's trained ones had detected measurably sooner. A dog growled; footsteps crackled through the underbrush, and he could hear the low pitched murmur of men's voices.

Jake turned his head for a split second; it was long enough for Nkolosi to fade into the trees.

"Fucking troublemaker. Thought we had him this time. Hey, man. You see a queer looking *kaffir* hanging around?''

The uniformed man who spoke to Jake sounded more irritated than anything else. Jake shook his head.

"C'mon. You're just wasting time. You want to spend your whole bloody Saturday on a wild goose . . . *kaffir* chase?" the second man said. "If he was still around, our friend here wouldn't be so quiet. Right, Addie?"

He tugged at the leash of a large German Shepherd and bent down to pet it. The dog bared its fangs in a less than amiable snarl and snapped at the hand that was stroking him. Apparently, Jake thought, the guard dog had not yet been properly taught to correlate white with good and black with evil.

The threesome left.

Jake sat down heavily and leaned against a tree trunk. He picked up a pine cone and began to remove its scales. Systematically. As if he might find answers beneath them, instead of pine nuts. Answers to questions like how men such as Van Der Merwe and Cohn could be persuaded to support the AFI; how Nkolosi had come by his Oxford education and his wealth. At least, Jake thought, he had nothing to fear from Nkolosi's Mata Hari, not as long as he retained his skepticism. As for what Philip Prescott's reaction would be when he learned that Jake had failed in his mission—it was a subject Jake preferred not to examine. Not yet. Not until he had found an alternative to the help the Senator had promised. When there was still the question of replacing the money. . . .

"Loves me, loves me not," Jake said aloud, pulling the last two scales off the cone's husk. Then he looked at his watch. Although he felt as if hours had passed, it still wasn't time to meet Deanna. Perhaps Nkolosi would come back before one thirty, he thought.

Using the end of the denuded pine cone, Jake began to doodle in the sand. It wasn't until he got up to leave that he realized he was leaving behind a delicate tracing of a dragon in repose.

7

Jake brushed himself off and left the woods. There no longer seemed any point in waiting; one thirty had come and gone and there was no sign of Nkolosi. He found Deanna sitting in the sun, on the steps of the engineering building.

"Did you find him?" she said, standing up and walking toward him.

"Yes," Jake said. "Thank you for setting it up."

"Did it do any good?"

"I'll tell you if you'll point us in the direction of a cup of coffee," Jake said. "Unless you still have work to do. Have you seen the doctor yet, by the way?"

"As a matter of fact, that's that I had to rush off for."

"And?"

"He's pronounced me sound—at least in body."

"What about the work you wanted to do here?"

"It's always a disaster preparing for a new semester, let alone a new year. The paperwork is . . . actually, I'd be delighted to close up shop for the day." She slung a white patent leather purse over her shoulder. "Where would you like to go?"

"To tell you the truth, I don't care," Jake said, "as long as there's a minimum of walking involved."

"Can your poor weary body make it to my car, or do I have to carry you there?" Deanna said.

Jake laughed and followed her to the Anglia. He let the sunbaked warmth of the upholstery enfold him like an eiderdown as he sorted, sifted. When he emerged from his introspection, he noted with pleasure Deanna's composure behind the wheel.

"You drive like a man," he said.

"Chauvinist."

"A little."

"That's like being a little bit pregnant, Jake."

"In the United States not many women drive stick shifts," Jake said.

"Well here most of us do. We're spoiled in so many other ways, that's probably our last ditch pioneer stand." She smiled at him without taking her eyes off the road. Apparently aware that she was being appraised, she said: "Ask any questions you like. I don't have to answer them."

"Late twenties, Virgo, high I.Q. And extremely attractive," Jake said, liking Deanna all the more for not demanding an immediate dissection of his meeting with Nkolosi.

"Close," Deanna said. "Virgo, early thirties, intelligent, attractive and modest."

They were winding up an oak-lined street, climbing steeply. Cape Town looked like Rio or Haifa or any other city that lay wedged between mountain and ocean.

"This is Signal Hill," Deanna said. "The teenagers come here to neck. At night you can see the lights of Cape Town. . . ."

". . . If you're looking," Jake said, watching the contours of Deanna's face and ignoring the scenery. He pictured himself making love to her high above the city and promptly felt foolish. His life was complicated enough without the intrusion of adolescent fantasies. As Deanna turned off the road onto a red sand clearing, he tried again to conjure up Riena's face. He was no more successful than he'd been earlier.

"We're here," Deanna said.

"Where?" Jake's ears were blocked from the altitude and he was almost too tired to move. All he could see was an ugly flatroofed cement building at the far edge of the clearing. It wasn't until he was inside the structure and saw the heavy cables reaching into the sky from iron tracks on the floor that he realized where he was. The building was a three-walled fortress. Small. Compact. Its missing fourth wall an opening that waited to swallow the creaking cage of the cable-car he'd seen in the distance from Riena's shanty. It would take them to the top of Table Mountain. He generally tended to stay away from the normal tourist attractions, Jake thought, so it wasn't all that surprising that he'd missed this one.

"We'll have it all to ourselves, I think," Deanna said, climbing into the still-swaying cage the instant its iron gate opened.

"I know this is the tourist season. Maybe it's empty because they know something we don't know. It's a long way up." He looked at a bulletin board filled with snapshots of happy groups and wondered if the pictures were taken before or after their ascent. He'd always been something of a physical coward, preferring the lodge to the ski slopes. "Has it ever. . . ."

". . . Broken down? Hurtled bodies to the bottom of the mountain? No. It's been known to get stuck half-way, though."

"I suppose if that's the worst that can happen," Jake said.

Deanna laughed. "Take a chance, Jake," she said. "It's empty because it's late on a Saturday and people are getting ready for the evening. You'll love it at the top. You'll get coffee, and with luck, I'll get something to eat and a rundown on your confrontation with our local witchdoctor."

Jake had little choice but to acquiesce. He was unprepared for what was to come; the ride up dwarfed all of his Vermont memories.

"It almost forces you to believe in miracles, doesn't it?" Deanna said, leaning precariously over the side.

Jake looked down. Proteas grew out of granite, wisps of clouds pillowed crevasses, and Cape Town swayed beneath them like a Lilliputian fantasy.

"Is there any other way down?" he asked.

"You can climb. By the way of Kirstenbosch. It's a glorious walk—if you're fit."

Jake winced.

"You could always soak your feet in Lady Barnard's Bath when we got there," Deanna said, waving at a full load of passengers in the downward-bound car.

"Last big group of the day," the driver said. "You two going to walk back?"

"I don't think the Lady's handmaidens would object if you paddle instead of pitching pennies like the rest of the common folk," Deanna said. "Want to try walking down, Jake?"

"Another time," Jake said. "How do we make sure the driver waits around for us?"

"I'll be there," the driver said, jerking the cable-car to a halt near a narrow pathway.

"I'm counting on it," Jake said.

He and Deanna followed the path through the rocks. It led to a large cafe which sat squarely on top of the mountain. The place was deserted.

"The service is putrid," Deanna said, sitting down at a window table, "but their tea and scones more than compensate. The view speaks for itself."

She was right on all three counts. Although they were the waiter's only customers, he felt duty-bound to uphold the reputation of the place; it took him thirty minutes to fill their simple orders.

"They haven't heard of anti-trust laws up here I'm afraid," Deanna said lavishing her hot scone with butter, apricot jam and whipped cream. After she'd bitten into it, she poured two cups of tea from a cheap porcelain teapot. "At least tea bags haven't reached the summit," she said, happily contemplating the steaming dark brew that flowed from the chipped spout. "Good thing you also decided to have tea; two different beverages might have held up our order until morning."

"How much is this Olympian feast going to cost me?" Jake said.

"About one Rand fifty. Including tip."

"That's less than two dollars. At those prices I could really be king of the mountain."

Deanna swished the tea leaves around in the bottom of her cup with the last drop of tea. "Just think," she said. "If you did live here, you'd instantly become a superior being." It was a flat statement.

177

"You can't really mean that."

"Of course not. It's just that one Rand fifty doesn't include the price of conscience. That's the additional cost of living White South Africa doesn't acknowledge when it talks about 'how good things are.' It isn't on the tax forms, so it doesn't really exist."

"Why stay here if you feel that way?"

"Lethargy, I guess."

"Are you politically active?"

"God, no. I have enough trouble coping with my own life, let alone telling other people how to live. Does that sound horribly selfish?"

"Realistic."

Deanna toyed with a sugar cube, taking tiny nibbles at it until it was gone. She doesn't have an ounce of fat on her, Jake thought. Her dieting friends must hate her.

"I've often thought about leaving South Africa," Deanna said. "The truth is, I love it here." She reached for another sugar cube, thought better of it, and took out a cigarette from a navy-blue and white pack. Jake lit it for her and shook one out for himself. "Everyone I know talks about leaving," she went on, tapping the edge of the ashtray with the tip of her Tothmans, "but it's mostly talk. They put their suburban homes up for sale at well above market value. Then they sit back and say: 'See. I'm trying to leave but I can't sell my house.' That way, they can rationalize staying on to their friends. And to themselves."

Jake could detect no rancor in her voice.

"I have a friend whose house has been on the market for six years. Every time values go up and a sale looks possible, he increases the asking price."

"You don't have a house and with your qualifications you could make it anywhere," Jake said. "I don't think I met any female Ph.Ds when I was here the last time. Are there really very few, or. . . ."

". . . This is both an elitist and a chauvinistic society. It takes money to go to the University and most people here still believe women only go to College to find husbands . . . My parents never thought I'd stick it out they just wanted me to meet a nice Jewish doctor or engineer and settle down."

"Was your. . . ."

". . . Ivan's a lawyer." Deanna laughed. "That was close enough for them until they found out about his liberal leanings. That frightened them."

"Do you miss him?"

"Ivan? Of course I do. He's a very special person. We understand each other's needs. Not too many South African men believe in independence for women—or equality."

"Are you in love with him?"

"We're good for each other."

"That doesn't really answer my question," Jake said.

"It wasn't meant to."

"Why don't you join him?"

"Someday. Maybe. Right now he has other priorities. So do I. I like my work and he's so caught up with. . . ."

". . . The AFI?"

"Yes. Which reminds me. You haven't filled me in on Nkolosi. Did he tell you where to find Riena?"

After Deanna's declaration of non-involvement in politics, Jake had decided to tell her as little as possible. Talking, he'd thought, would at best provide him with a temporary catharsis, at worst, it could cause the kind of complications she, by self-admission, preferred to avoid. That she had helped Riena appeared to be a philanthropic act, rather than a poilitical one. Yet it was hard to believe that she was apathetic.

"He told me to go to Teyateyaneng," Jake said, knowing he had to say something.

"And?"

Fortunately for Jake, the waiter chose that moment to amble over to them. "The clouds're coming down," he said. "You want to pay now? Last car will be leaving soon."

"It's not even six o'clock," Deanna said, pulling her sweater around her shoulders as if mention of a change in the weather had chilled her. "The last car doesn't usually leave until it's almost dark."

"Pity we'll have to miss the sunset. It must be quite something from here," Jake said, delighted with the change in topic. He had expected to have to field questions about tactics he'd used to extract information from Nkolosi and whether or not he was taking off for Teyateyaneng. He paid the bill and they left the cafe for the cable station, Deanna clambering expertly over the rocks while he chose a more conservative approach.

"It's going to be foggy tonight," she said. "I love the fog." She climbed to the edge of the shelf on which the restaurant was built and pointed at the bay. "Would you leave that?"

It was a rhetorical question. Jake kept walking and Deanna joined him. "Where to now?" he asked, boarding the cablecar.

"Ever been to Rhodes Memorial?"

Jack nodded. It was one of the few tourist attractions that had interested him enough to balance his aversion to crowds.

"When I was a child we lived in a house within sight of Cecil Rhodes' statue. I used to fantasize about him on rainy days; I thought he dismounted and took shelter and I never quite stopped hoping that one day he'd choose our house. The cafe there serves great crumpets." She stopped abruptly. "I'm talking too much," she said. "It's not like me. I must miss Ivan more than I realized."

Jake smiled and shook his head. Then he looked out at the bay, drawn by the encroaching fog. It diffused the sun into a pink and orange glow, creating a channel across the water that could as easily have been lava flowing through an obsidian bed as what it was—a triangular copper shadow.

The cable-car clanged into its three-sided home and settled into its iron bedstead. "We could watch the sunset from Signal Hill, if you like," Deanna said.

Jake was pleased. There was little more he could do about anything, except dwell on his problems. Watching the sunset with Deanna was an infinitely more pleas-

180

ant prospect. They exchanged banalities as they drove down the steepest part of the same winding streets they had traversed earlier. After they turned into the parking area, Deanna edged the car close to the precipice, pulled up the emergency brake with both hands and fiddled with the knob on the radio.

"Cigarette?" Jake lit two and handed one to Deanna. He wanted to stretch across the dividing line of the hand-brake and take her fingers in his. Grip them tightly in his own. Instead, he crushed his cigarette in the ashtray and instantly lit another.

The top ten hits of the week ushered in the darkness. Once it began it came swiftly, the way Jake remembered its arrival in Santa Cruz during his summer there as a teaching assistant. He watched the lights of Cape Town giving birth to mirror images of themselves in the Atlantic, turning the shoreline into a belated Christmas celebration. Strange, he thought, how impersonal they look from this vantage point. Cold. Their narcissistic quality removed by distance. He had walked on the promenade at night, moving between Beach Road and its necklace of colored lights that danced in the sea breeze and the susurrous of the ocean. Up close, the lights in the water winked lewdly at the strollers who turned the promenade into a gaudy Easter Parade. Lovers and dog walkers, pimps and politicians, equalized by Italian ices flavored with the salt of the ocean, replaced the sunshine jump-rope children; motorcycles replaced baby carriages. Outdoor cafés served Capuccino brimming with steamed milk. The coffee had a bitter edge but then few ordered it to drink it; it had become a Jet Set rite to time the passage of sugar through the thick froth, watching it slowly dampen and brown. It was all a parody of the Riviera: the outdoor cafés with Cinzano ashtrays; the beaded curtains and crepes suzettes. If they served *boerewors* and *bredie* on the *stoeps* of Dutch Colonials, Jake thought, they'd have no need to steal an identity; if they played *boeremusik* instead of rock, and penny whistles instead of electric guitars other cultures might begin to borrow from them.

181

"Sometimes my orderly nature gets the better of me and I want to rearrange the stars in symmetrical patterns," Deanna said, after a long but comfortable silence.

Jake had expected her to question him further about Nkolosi. She did not. In a strange way, his relief was tempered by disappointment, as if curiosity would have been akin to caring.

"I was so busy looking at the lights, I forgot that there were stars, too," Jake said. "It must be pretty late."

"Almost eight."

"Hungry?"

"A little."

"How about dinner and a movie?"

"It's too late for the films. Besides, people book ahead on Saturdays. You should remember that. Dinner will have to be simple for pretty much the same reasons."

"A sandwich would be fine," Jake said. "I'm sorry about the movies though. I'm fascinated by what your censors do. I saw *South Pacific* here and it was an hour shorter than the original; they cut out everything that smacked of interracial romance."

"Talking about romance," Deanna began.

Damn, Jake thought, having inadvertently provided Deanna with a new entrée into the one topic he wanted to avoid.

"I'm going to a wedding tomorrow. Malay friends of mine. Why don't you come? They were expecting me to bring Ivan. Call it anthropological research if you need an excuse," Deanna went on.

"Love to come," Jake said, relieved but once again experiencing the same fine edge of disappointment he'd felt earlier. He reached across and took her hand, this time not resisting the impulse. He felt her stiffen but he leaned across anyway and kissed her. Gently. Not demanding anything.

"I think we should go," Deanna said, disengaging her hand, but smiling. "The moonlight does it every time. How I wish everything in life were as predictable."

"Want me to drive?" Jake said, assuming the same

182

light tone. "I'll come around to your side and escort you around so the bogeyman doesn't get you."

Deanna laughed. "I don't think I'll be attacked if I walk around by myself," she said.

Jake opened his door. The sound of its opening coincided with a second, louder click.

He pulled back and waited, saying nothing.

"I heard it too," Deanna said. "Lock your door, Jake."

"What was it?"

"Probably just. . . ."

". . . You're White. What about the woman?"

The voice that interrupted Deanna was low and guttural, disembodied by the flashlight that blinded Jake. The man had wrenched the door open so fast that Jake, whose fingers still gripped the door handle, felt his armpit stretch. In a gesture that was more automatic reflex than protective, he flung his hand toward the white light. His knuckles connected with metal, then with flesh as he was pulled from the car and flung against it.

"Don't give me no shit," the voice said, still disembodied. "Now turn around. Slowly."

"It's the police, Jake. Do what he tells you," Deanna called out.

"She's right," the man said. Still holding onto Jake, although less roughly, he pushed the American toward the car's open door. "Woman's White too," he said to a second man who materialized out of the darkness.

"Why are you harassing us?" Jake was amazed at his capacity for remaining civil. There was more New England left in him than he liked to admit; he thought.

"Just doing my job," the policeman said. He released his hold on Jake. "Why don't you take the lady home and fuck her in bed, man. You're too old for cars and you'd be a lot safer. Stick around here and if the *tsotsis* don't get you, the rape artists will."

Or the police, Jake thought. Shaking, he got back into the Anglia. He listened as the police car, its lights out, started its engine and rolled away.

"If I'd been Coloured, they'd have arrested me,"

Deanna said.

"And if *I* hadn't been White?"

"A non-European man with a White girl? I don'
know. Things are changing but. . . ."

". . . Would they have beaten me up?"

"For starters."

Jake took Deanna's hand. This time she didn't pul
away; she needed comfort as much as he.

"We'd better go," Deanna said after a few minutes
"Are you all right?"

"I'm fine. My shoulder joint's aching, but I don'
think he did any real damage. I can still drive if you
want me to."

"No. Thanks." Deanna started up the engine and re
leased the brake. "If you don't mind, let's go straigh
home. Somehow I've lost my appetite." She backed the
car out of the parking lot and began the last part of the
descent to High Level Road.

Jake's fingers probed his bruised shoulder muscles
They were knotting up. Neither he nor Deanna spoke
but the silence was not a companionable one; it was
rather, a void. A vacuum which, for Jake, was beginning
to be filled with an insidious sense of disbelief.

8

"Sure you don't want a sandwich?" Deanna said.

"No. Thanks anyway." Jake could hear the low mur
mur of voices from the living room, the Rosens playing
bridge. He wanted to avoid them and anyone else to
whom he might have to be formally polite.

Since at that moment all Jake wanted was to give in to
fatigue, he said a restrained goodnight to Deanna at the
bottom of the stairs. The brunch was only a few hour
away and he had serious thinking to do before he me

Van Der Merwe. He lay down on the covers in the guest room, knowing he had to shower but too tired to undress. As he began to define his approach to the politician, he admitted to himself for the first time that he was going to do everything Nkolosi had demanded of him. It was motivation that was troubling him. Not Nkolosi's. That was clear enough. But his own. His feelings for Riena were more confused than ever. He felt a mixture of memories and guilt and he knew it made no sense to construct a future based on either. And what about Deanna? How heavily were his ties with her, tenuous at best, participating in his confusion? Without having met her, he might by now have been longingly anticipating his reunion with Riena.

He was a true Scorpio, Jake thought. Life never quite lived up to his fantasies. Unfortunately, while his never-never world did succeed in dulling the worst of reality, it also often blinded him to much that was good.

That self-admission notwithstanding, Jake began an imaginary dialogue with Daniel Van Der Merwe, one in which the politician quickly agreed to provide the Ameican with passports for Riena and the baby. Jake's thank yous merged with his first dreams of the night, dreams in which he told Philip Prescott—graphically—what he could do with his help.

Sunday began much as Saturday had done: the same buzzer and quiet curse from the next room; the sun shining through chintz; Johan, in baggy pants, drinking coffee in the garden below, stealing time before he had to don his pink bandana.

Jake watched the old man, in gardener's disguise, weeding a bed of phlox and crooning to himself as he crouched bareheaded in the morning sunlight. It was the same melody Johan had sung the morning before. The Rosen Sonata, Jake thought. To be completed later when Martin's grunts and Susan's complaints were added, with Shirley playing counterpoint to them all. And Deanna? Was she part of the orchestration?

Tentatively, Jake examined his bruises, remembering the strange opera of the night before. Down the hall, a bathroom door opened and slammed shut.

"Move it, Susan," Martin Rosen said. "You know your mother's waiting for the bathroom."

"How come just because Dee decided to come back home, I'm thrown out of the other bathroom?"

"She's older than you are."

It was a litany no more exclusively South African than American, a universal wail of Western teenagers, like telephones and make-up. Worse in South Africa because so many homes, at least those Jake had seen, had only two inside bathrooms; the third was outside for the servants.

Still fingering his bruises, Jake tried to put the previous day into perspective. He was grateful for the distraction of renewed arguing in the hallway, this time not about bathrooms.

"Why, Dad? I don't understand you for Godsakes," Susan yelled.

"That's exactly it. For the sake of God we will not change our name to Rose. We are Jews first and last, even if a Pogrom comes and even if you do marry a Goy one day. Although who would be *meshuggah* enough to marry you. . . ?"

They moved out of earshot and Jake was forced to resume thinking. He tried to feel the full responsibility of what he had done to Riena and face what it was he intended to do about it. All he could see was Deanna standing on Table Mountain; Deanna in control behind the wheel of the car; Deanna in his arms.

Jake focused his attention on the garden. He could see Susan greeting two pig-tailed friends. Three teenage Lolitas, plotting the downfall of the adult world, Jake thought. Susan looked up, caught his eye and grinned, as if in confirmation. Then she and her friends moved under the fig tree and put their heads together.

"Don't be an idiot, Renee," Jake heard Susan say. "He's only a guest. He can't interfere with us."

The three girls giggled and moved their heads out of its shamrock design. They stood up casually, innocently, and started toward Johan. As if on impulse, one

186

of them leaped high over a series of rose bushes. The other two cheered and did the same thing.

"Morning, Johan," Susan sang out, closing in on the grizzled head as if she were about to leapfrog over it.

Johan straightened up, then bowed gravely as she sailed over him.

"Those're my new friends, Renee and Lynn," Susan said, walking back to Johan. "They just moved in down the road."

"Pleased to meet you, Miss Renee. Miss Lynn."

"Pleased to meet you, Johan," the girls chanted, subtly parroting his tone.

Any moment Scarlett will float across the lawn, Jake thought. He imagined Johan guarding Susan's baby carriage; grinning at her as she took her first step across his manicured lawn. He had surely brown-bagged her baby clothes home to his grandchildren who were being raised old-style in the *kraal,* had probably loved her the way he might have loved them, had his loving not been confined to semi-annual visits.

"Watch us, Johan," Susan said.

Pig-tails flying, she and her friends executed a second series of leaps over the rose bushes. Jake watched the old man; his face showed pride in one who, as far as he was concerned, could do no wrong.

"Careful, Miss Susan. Don't hurt yourself," he said.

Susan clicked her tongue at him. "I'm not a baby, Johan," she said. Taking a running leap, she sailed over a late-blossoming azalea whose remaining bloom paid tribute to Johan's green thumb.

"Can you do that?" Susan said. Her two friends had stopped jumping and were sitting on the grass, watching with the air of Romans waiting for the gladiator to appear.

"I still very strong, Miss Susan," Johan said.

"Then do it."

Susan's words were goading. Her face pleading. Her body commanding. Johan, old and tired, looked torn. He's probably never refused her anything, Jake thought, as the old man placed his gardening tool down carefully on the pathway, stood up and wiped his hands on his trouser legs.

"Okay, Miss Susan," he said. "Here I come."

Lumbering up to the new bushes, he raised himself awkwardly off the ground. He cleared them with ease and smiled when Susan and her friends applauded enthusiastically.

"Now that one. The azalea. Oh, Johan, please," Susan said.

Taking a longer run this time, Johan approached the shrub. He cleared it without difficulty. Grinning happily, he resumed his weeding.

"Wait, Johan!"

Now Susan's tone was clearly imperative. She pointed to a three foot high loquat tree, a sapling planted where its pointed leaves would not have to share the sun with other fruit trees.

"Bet you can't jump over that one."

Johan scratched his head as if in doubt but his expression was confident; he appeared to be enjoying himself. He stiffened his shoulders and sucked in his old man's belly. "You really want me to jump it?" he said.

"Bet you can't do it, Johan," Susan said.

The elderly Basuto made his way to the opposite end of the garden. "Here I come, Miss Susan," he shouted. His feet were apparently obeying some residual memory of youthful vigor. His approach became stronger. Surer.

"You did it, you did it." Susan, glancing at her friends who were giggling openly, looked so much like a racehorse trainer that Jake expected to see a whip and stopwatch appear in her hands. "Now that one," she said, pointing to the fig tree.

It has to be at least six feet high, Jake thought, measuring the tree with his eyes. Confident that the game had come to an end, he lit a cigarette and inhaled deeply. When he looked out again, Johan was rolling up his sleeves and pant legs while the three girls rolled on the lawn in helpless convulsions.

Johan took a long sip of coffee and began to run. Once around the house. Twice. Three times before beginning his final approach.

Dear God, he's serious, Jake thought suddenly. He flung open his window and yelled: "Johan don't," knowing it was too late. The old body had gathered momentum and nothing could stop it now, not even its heaving chest or creeping rheumatism. Least of all, Jake's warning or the gasping laughter of the girls on the lawn. He'll bounce off the trunk like Wily Coyote, Jake told himself hopefully, as Johan connected with the tree. Arms outstretched.

The body sagged to the ground and crumbled like a parachute silk.

"Help him for Chrissake," Jake shouted, struggling into his shirt and jeans. Berating himself for not having predicted the results at the beginning of the game, he flew down the stairs.

"Is he alive?" Jake said, running toward the fig tree. No one answered him. He stopped in his tracks; Johan was sitting up, leaning against the victorious tree trunk. Tears were streaming down his wrinkled face.

"Are you hurt, Johan? I'll get a doctor. An ambulance. I didn't mean for you to get hurt." Susan had her arms around Johan's neck. She was crying bitterly.

"I'm all right, little Miss. Really. Just a stupid old *kaffir*. You mustn't cry for me." He disentangled her arms gently with one hand and rubbed his battered face with the other.

Renee and Lynn were gone.

"You thoughtless young. . . ." Jake stopped. Johan was glaring at him; Susan was still sobbing, her head against the Basuto's chest. Jake didn't know how to deal with that kind of love. Symbiotic. Rooted in quicksand but rooted nonetheless. He turned away.

"Miss Susan. Telephone," Alice said, walking out of the kitchen.

Susan didn't move.

"Go, Miss Susan. I'm fine," Johan said.

"He's been hurt," Jake said. "Please, Alice, make sure he's all right. Hasn't broken anything. He might have internal damage."

189

"He's a stupid old *bok,*" Alice said. "I saw the whole thing. Serves him right for showing off. Come on, Susan. See you later, Tarzan."

Susan followed Alice into the house. She looked back several times before she disappeared.

"That child should be punished for what she did," Jake said, kneeling next to Johan who had collapsed on the grass the instant Susan was out of sight.

"No, Master Prescott," Johan said. He sat up and leaned against the tree that had almost destroyed him. "She didn't mean it. She's a good girl."

"My name's Jake. And she's a walking disaster. Spoiled brat!"

"Please Master . . . *Baas.* Leave her alone. I don't want to make her trouble."

Johan looked distressed. For the first time, he looked as if he were in pain.

"Can I take you to a doctor?" Jake said.

"No thank you, *Bass* Jake. A little *Skokiaan* will fix me good."

"At this hour?"

"Any hour, *Baas.*"

"Tell me something, Johan," Jake said. "What made you think you could jump over that tree? You're not superman. Or Tarzan."

Johan grinnned. "*Skokiaan* for breakfast makes a man a little crazy," he said.

"I saw you drinking coffee. Was that. . . ."

". . . the best coffee, Master Prescott," Johan said. "I wanted to make Susan happy."

"You really love her, don't you?"

"She my child."

"What will you do when the revolution comes, Johan?"

"It won't come," Johan said.

"You sound very sure of that. What about the AFI? They believe it will."

Slowly, his movements dignified, Johan stood up. With a look of pure disgust on his face, he spat at the base of the tree. "Those are evil people," he said. "How

they think I could hurt the Master. The Missus. Or Miss
Dee and my baby?"

"You may have no choice," Jake said.

"This my home."

"What about the people who live next door? Could
you kill them?" Jake asked.

Johan looked across the garden, taking Jake literally.
"Good people that side," he said, pointing to the right.
"Other side. . . . Master doesn't like them. If the revo-
lution comes . . ." He grinned. "I go finish my coffee."

"Go, Johan. If you're certain you're okay," Jake said.

The old man ambled off, limping slightly.

Jake watched him drain the contents of his coffee
cup. You'll get rid of the neighbors on the left, Jake
thought. Another man will take care of the ones on the
right. And you can be damn sure that someone, another
family's Johan, or the son or daughter of Johan, will see
to it that the Rosens get theirs.

As he started back toward the house, Jake found himself haunted by snatches of pacifist cafeteria talk. Hy-
pothesis: Two men move across the trenches toward
you. Bayonets raised. The enemy. One of them was
once your friend. Solution: Defend yourself against the
stranger; don't think about the fact that the man next to
you will take care of your buddy. Q.E.D.: There's no
way to be a little bit involved in revolution. That, too, is
like being a little bit pregnant.

9

The incident with Johan left a sticky sweat on Jake's
skin and he had to scrub himself twice in the shower.
While he was doing so, he tried to imagine what Van
Der Merwe would look like: tall, broad-shouldered,
crew-cut. A nose like that of an oveworked pugilist's. In

the past Jake had found it helpful to form a picture of his adversaries and he saw no reason why this time should be any different. He thought briefly about why he was defining the M.P. as his enemy, then discarded that line of thought as unproductive. He turned, instead, to rehearsing the parts of his story he intended to tell: his affair with Riena; her arrest; his attempts to get a passport for her. He also had no choice but to admit knowledge of her pregnancy, since he was going to ask for two passports. He decided that the simplest thing to do would be to say that he had no idea whether or not Riena had given birth or survived the explosion at the jail. He would tell a sad story but keep the level of self-pity at a minimum, Jake thought. From what he'd heard about the politician, that was his best shot at enlisting the man's sympathy—that and hints of collusion with the American government.

The trick, Jake thought, would be to enlist the politician's help and then satisfy Nkolosi's demands without being suspect. If he could do that, he wouldn't need his uncle. Once she and the child were out of South Africa, the Senator's threats to Riena's safety would become meaningless.

He towelled himself dry vigorously, having fairly well convinced himself that doing what was expedient was also serving the best ends. The witchdoctor had assured him that the politician would come to no harm and that he, Jake, would not be suspect. Certainly his own motives were impeccable.

By the time Jake reached the French doors that led to the porch he felt better than he had in a long time. Adjusting the tie he'd been asked to wear, he stood and watched Johan and Alice prepare a long table for the brunch. The brightly colored linen they were using suited his new mood of optimism and it was even appropriate that the two servants were bustling around as if nothing untoward had happened earlier. He wondered if he could possibly have imagined the whole thing.

"Morning, Jake. Would you like a cup of coffee?"

Jake turned around, his transient well-being shattered by Deanna's voice which reminded him of the one fact he'd been avoiding: he wanted to take her home to Vermont. Not Riena.

"Recovered from last night?"

"No scars," Jake said. "You?"

"I'm fine." She moved past him onto the porch. "Alice. Could we have some coffee out here please. And a couple of slices of toast."

She sat down at the far end of the porch next to a small, white wrought iron table and Jake joined her. Again, her lack of requirement for idle chatter pleased him. There was none of the pressure that usually kept him from being a house guest in a foreign country, no interminable questions about what it was like to live in America or what he thought about the political situation, here or there.

The Rosens' first guests arrived promptly at eleven o'clock. Introductions had no sooner been completed when a booming *"Goeie môre, mense"* brought with it a man whose easy and practiced manner singled him out as Daniel Van Der Merwe. He was nothing like Jake had pictured. Lanky, spare, he had the look of a professional athlete rather than a politician.

"So glad you could make it, Van," Shirley Rosen said, raising her cheek to be kissed.

Van Der Merwe sniffed exaggeratedly. "Wouldn't miss one of your meals for anything, Shirl, you know that. Kippers 'n eggs?"

"Yes." Mrs. Rosen looked pleased. "Martin, give Van a drink."

"Shandy?" her husband said. "Perhaps you'd like one, too, Jake? Or haven't you developed a taste for our national drink?"

"Love one," Jake said, watching Deanna's father top off half a glass of warm beer with what South Africans called lemonade. He knew it better as Seven-Up.

"Van, this is Jacob Prescott," Deanna said, taking a glass from her father and handing it to Van Der Merwe.

The politician held up his glass, said: "Cheers," and

took a healthy sip. "You're the young man at the beach, aren't you?"

"I'm sorry, Sir, I don't remember having met you before," Jake said.

"Yesterday morning. At the beach. But don't worry . . . Jake, is it? I had an advantage even then. I'd seen you on a newsreel with a man who's campaigning for the Presidency. A Senator from Vermont?"

"My uncle," Jake said.

"Is he going to win?"

"We certainly hope so."

The politician laughed and held out his glass for a refill. His hostess was beaming.

"You can't possibly know what you've done for my mother," Deanna said to Jake. "She's a devout namedropper and to have the nephew of. . . ."

". . . She's right," Shirley Rosen interrupted, taking Van's glass from him. Before she had a chance to refill it, Johan appeared in full regalia.

"Brunch is ready," he said.

"Thank you, Johan. Let's sit down everybody. Still want a refill, Van? We are having wine," Mrs. Rosen said, moving toward the table.

"Maybe later," the politican said. "Any particular seat?"

His hostess shook her head. "No. I said informal and I meant it."

"What, Shirl, no place-cards?" Van Der Merwe teased. "Watch out, Martin. Next thing you know, she'll tell you she wants to be liberated."

He sat down and Jake made for the chair next to him, then thought better of it. The man was patently the center of attention and any chance of a private conversation would have to come later anyway. He sat down between Deanna and a stout, middle-aged woman who looked as if she'd already indulged in too many extraneous meals. Either that, or she had deliberately chosen her apricot linen suit in a size too small, Jake thought.

Despite the perfection of the food and the service, Jake found himself scarcely aware of either. It was as though the table talk was reaching him through the impediment of a mosquito netting; each time he was addressed, he had to strain before the buzz became words and the sentences took on meaning.

"Sharpeville was no different than Kent State, was it, Mr. Prescott?" the woman next to Jake said.

"Come on, Gertie. Sharpeville was over a decade ago. Mr. Prescott was probably much more concerned with his next date and his University grades than with what was happening six thousand miles away," her husband said.

"Both Kent State and Sharpeville were the result of police inexperience, wouldn't you say, Jake?" Deanna said.

Jake tried to remember the details of the South African racial incident that had made headlines around the beginning of the sixties. Or was it the end of the fifties? He wasn't sure. He seemed to remember something about a rally in a *location,* a town meeting taken over by Black insurgents.

"We all know the police panicked," Martin Rosen said. "One man got so hysterical they had to lock him away afterwards. Started babbling about dragons and other equally outrageous things."

"Let me refresh your memory, Jake," Mr. Porter said. "The police were sent in purely as a preventive measure. Some young hooligans started to rock a tank. . . ."

A tank at a town meeting, Jake thought, the whole incident coming back to him.

". . . Some policeman had been brutalized in Durban the night before," Martin Rosen was saying. "You can't really blame those youngsters for having felt edgy."

"Edgy is one thing, trigger-happy's another," the woman next to Jake said. He was surprised; by the tone of her original question, he'd have expected her to defend the behaviour of the police.

Suddenly Jake remembered. Headlines and photographs flashed across his memory. "Women and children," he said involuntarily. The fringes of the meeting had been ringed by women, many of them with babies strapped to their backs to free their hands for older children. Most of the bullets had entered spines.

"What I really want to know," the woman said, "is how we can assign individual guilt in cases like Kent State or Sharpeville."

"Mob psychology precludes that, Mrs. um. . . ."

". . . Porter."

"Mrs. Porter. When the mores of the individual break down, they are replaced—at least in a mob situation—by a different set of standards."

"You mean some kind of mob psychology takes over and different things become acceptable?"

"Yes. Massacre becomes an acceptable way of behavior. . . ." Jake stopped. "I'm sorry," he said, "I sound like I'm lecturing."

"No. Go on," Van Der Merwe said.

"Well . . . I was going to say that its comparative is the 'I'm only following orders' syndrome of the Nazis. . . ."

". . . Martyrs," someone said at the other end of the table. "That's what Sharpeville was really all about. Somebody, some group, was trying to create martyrs!"

The far end of the table took over the discussion and Jake replaced his protective gauze. He didn't really listen again until Tom M'boya's name filtered through to him.

"It was incredible," Martin Rosen said. "Thousands of natives marching into the center of Jo'burg, and not one of them saying a word. Spookiest thing I've ever seen, I tell you. M'boya had sworn it was going to be a peaceful demonstration and that no one was carrying weapons. . . ."

". . . Sort of like your Martin Luther King thing," someone added for Jake's benefit. He winced. He happened to have been present at "the Martin Luther King thing" and any such casual reference to the tragedy felt like an assault upon his person.

"Except that nothing happened," Shirley Rosen said, taking over the conversation. "They marched into the middle of town and stopped. Right, Marty?"

"Thanks to one *gatis* policeman," someone said.

"*Gatis?*" The word was new to Jake and his mispronunciation of the guttural "g" caused a ripple of amusement.

"Afrikaans," Martin Rosen said, resuming the story-telling. "He just decided he'd had enough. Handed his gun to a friend and walked into the crowd, waving his baton and shouting at them in Sasuto to go home . . . with a few suitably chosen four letter words thrown in."

"And?" Jake asked.

"And nothing," Martin said. "They turned around and went home like a bunch of bloody sheep."

"Why?"

"Who the hell knows," Mr. Porter said. "There's no way to understand that mentality. I mean, if they thought like human beings they wouldn't grow wool on their heads, now would they?"

Van Der Merwe, who had been sitting quietly during the interchange, put his fork down firmly on his plate. The look on his face was one of control. "They respect courage," he said. "And, Jake, I'm afraid they tend not to understand what this 'rights' business is all about. *Their* bellies are full, while their friends on the outside are dying of starvation and trying like hell to get across our borders; here we provide schools, housing, jobs. . . ."

"But they have no. . . ."

". . . Vote? You're right. And they're discriminated against; and they have little or no voice in the government of the country. The sad truth is that they couldn't give a damn . . . excuse me, Shirley . . . about those things."

"Can't they have full bellies and a say in what happens to them?"

"Not yet. It's too soon for that, no matter what the world says."

And the great game of separate development continues, Jake thought. South African Monopoly. A monster perpetuating itself in the armchairs of the upper middle class.

"How many teas and how many coffees?" Shirley Rosen tried to change the subject; judging by her expression, she expected it to be a losing battle. She was right.

". . . Let me tell one more story for the benefit of our American friend," Van Der Merwe said. "Bear with me, those of you who've heard it.

"About fifteen years ago I was having dinner with an old chicken farmer. He lived by himself on the outskirts of Jo'burg and every once in a while. . . . Never mind. That's not relevant. Anyway, during dinner we heard noises outside. All the old bugger could care about was protecting his livestock, so he picked up a shotgun . . . a rusty, useless relic . . . and rushed outside."

Van Der Merwe paused to sip his wine.

"It was dusk," he continued, "but still light enough to see a huge mob of Black men coming toward the house. I'd followed him outside and damned if I didn't stand there and watch him walk right into them yelling: '*Voetsak. Gaan voetsak. Ek sal skiet.*' He looked at Jake. "That means go away or I'll shoot."

"What happened?" Jake asked, feeling as if the question were required of him.

"Well, to cut a long story short, they turned and walked back where they had come from. Seems a gang of mine workers had decided to revolt but all it took was one crazy old man with a rusty. . . ."

". . . Could their reaction have been the result of all of those years of education into servitude?" Jake said. "The human race readily learns to take orders, as I said before."

To his surprise, the politician nodded. "An intelligent evaluation," he said, "but I have to worry about the present . . . deal with the results of those generations of 'education for servitude' as you call it. They're palpably unready for freedom."

"I'm going to drink my coffee in the lounge," Shirley Rosen said. "Anyone who wants to be less serious is welcome to join me." She stood up and her guests, all but Jake and Daniel Van Der Merwe, followed her inside.

The two men moved closer to each other and prepared to continue their discussion. The older man reached over and emptied the remainder of a bottle of Johannisberger Riesling into his glass; Jake took out his pack of cigarettes.

"I'm glad that's not one of my vices," Van Der Merwe said, watching Jake light up and inhale.

"I think it's time for me to stop telling myself I'm going to quit," Jake said. "Maybe being honest with myself about it will make it feel less like a vice."

"There are worse things." The politician reached for a mint and lifted his wine glass. "You see two of mine," he said.

Judging by the man's trim body, Jake thought, he didn't indulge his vices any too often.

"You seemed very preoccupied during the meal," Van Der Merwe said.

Plunge in, Jake thought. "I was . . . trying to figure a way to enlist your help with a personal matter," he said.

"Well, go ahead. You have my undivided attention. And, I might add, my curiosity. Anyone who can eat Shirley's food with that kind of disinterest has to be burdened with massive problems."

"I don't know how much trouble I'm getting into by telling you this," Jake began. Then, as simply as possible, consciously striving for a tone devoid of self-pity, he told the M.P. about Riena. "There may be a child," he said finally, as if he didn't know for sure. "If there is, and if Riena survived the explosion, I'll need two passports." He made no mention of the AFI or Nkolosi.

"Tell me something, Prescott," Van Der Merwe said. "Why don't you just get on the next plane to the States and forget the whole thing?"

Jake shrugged.

"You aren't the first man to make that kind of . . . mistake. You do realize that?"

"I did leave. I went home for almost a year."

"Are you still in love with the girl?"

199

"Love? I don't know. I thought I was. . . ."

". . . And now you think you're in love with Deanna?"

Jake felt more than a little ridiculous at having been so transparent. He must have looked the part because Van Der Merwe laughed. "How will your parents feel about having a Coloured daughter-in-law?" he asked. "Or haven't you told them about Riena?"

"Only my father. I thought, we both thought, presenting my mother with a *fait accompli* would be easier all around."

"What if the girl died in the explosion?"

"If there's a child I still want to take it back with me to the States."

"You're crazy."

"Probably. I can't imagine raising a child on my own. But that doesn't mean it can't be done."

"Anything can be done; it's a question of whether or not it can be done well. And whether or not it's worth the pain. If the girl, Riena, is dead and you ever decide you want to marry someone else, she'll have to be quite something to take on another woman's half-breed child."

"I really don't feel I have a choice," Jake said. "If I fathered a child, at least half of the responsibility for raising it is mine. I can try to ensure that it has a shot at freedom . . . equality."

"If Riena gave birth in prison, the chances are the child was handed over to her closest relative."

"I think I know who would have it," Jake said.

"Why not simply leave as much money as you can spare with that person?"

"No. I couldn't live with myself." Jake realized how virtuous he was sounding but he could see no reaction on the older man's face.

"You're either a fool or a masochist," the politician said. "I shouldn't even have listened to you but now that I have, I'll think about it. And I will try to find out for you if Riena's alive, though I suspect that's a hopeless task. The dead weren't properly identified. About the passports . . . I don't know. It would be easy enough to get them for you; it's the intrinsic commitment I'm unsure of."

Van Der Merwe seemed almost to have forgotten Jake's presence; it was as if he were talking to himself, continuing a debate that was by no means a new one.

"It would be like an admission of failing faith in a system I've supported, publicly and privately, all of my life. If I'm going to use my power to make changes, I should use it less lightly," the older man said.

Lightly, Jake thought, unable to imagine that the politician did anything without much careful consideration. He swam every day, summer and winter; he socialized only with people he'd know for most of his life; he'd been a trusted member of the Nationalist Party for twenty-five years.

"The United States Senate could be very helpful to me," Van Der Merwe went on, this time addressing Jake directly.

"It might be the White House," Jake said, ignoring the voice reminding him that, having failed to bribe Nkolosi, the only way he could exert any influence over his uncle was to blackmail him, the way Nkolosi was doing.

"I'll have to think this through very carefully," Van Der Merwe said.

"When can you let me have your decision?"

"Why don't you join me for a swim tomorrow morning? I'm not sure I'll have an answer for you but the swim will do you good anyway."

Jake hoped his relief wasn't visible. It apparently was not, because Van Der Merwe patted him awkwardly on the back and said: "Try not to worry too much, son." He stood and moved toward the French doors. "Time to join the others, I think." When Jake had caught up with him he said: "Why didn't your uncle help you?"

"He. . . ."

"Never mind. I understand; it's an election year."

Jake wasn't sure but he thought he could detect a note of bitterness in the politician's voice, as if he felt he, too, had often made compromises of which he was not particularly proud. For a moment he felt guilt about using Van Der Merwe. Then he put the thought aside and followed the older man indoors.

10

For the next few hours Jake responded as politely as he could to the Rosens' guests. Since they had never met him before, he thought, they would dismiss his air of distraction, believing it to be his normal behaviour. Besides, chances were he wouldn't see any of them again, except Van Der Merwe, and he understood the reason Jake seemed only partially there. Or at least the politician thought he did.

With one ear turned to the conversation around him, Jake tried to analyze his feelings. One part of him wanted to warn Van Der Merwe about the AFI's plans and enlist his full help in rescuing Riena. He liked the man and he was rarely comfortable with deceit. But each time Jake so much as contemplated making a confession, he was bombarded by strange images. They diverted his thoughts. Supplanted them. There was a man with a stretched belly, his face grotesquely distorted with pain, his mouth open in a scream. An infant in the arms of a clawed creature. Jake squinted, as if to see more clearly, and a new picture formed. A dragon, its wings intricately patterned, each scallop etched in exquisite detail. Its gaze was knowing, intimate, the sparkle in its eyes more real than the questioning expression in those of the woman talking to him.

"Are you ill, Mr. Prescott?" Mrs. Porter said. "You look awful."

"Stop fussing," her husband said, putting out his hand to pat Jake on the shoulder. "He's probably no used to drinking during the day."

At the man's touch, Jake recoiled. Mr. Porter looked puzzled at the American's reaction but his, "Hope we meet again sometime," sounded genuine enough. Jake tried to smile but he had the sensation that all he was doing was baring his teeth. Even that took effort. He kept reminding himself that the man was not Nkolosi, despite the fact that his features kept dissolving and re-forming to shape the witchdoctor's mirthless grin.

"Is something wrong, Jake?" Deanna asked. "You really don't have to come with me this afternoon. If you'd prefer to rest. . . ?"

Jake frowned. "Did we have plans?"

"The wedding. Remember? We talked about it yesterday."

"Oh yes. Of course." Jake felt foolish. "I'd love to come."

"In that case, we have to leave soon."

Jake watched the retreating Porters. His head had cleared and he felt fine. "Dinner afterwards?"

"We could stop on the way back for prawns piripiri. Or don't you like spicy food?" Deanna's voice was normal but she was looking at Jake with concern. "Better yet," she went on, "let's come back here. I can make Monkey Gland Steak. It's quick and easy. . . ."

". . . Monkey Gland?"

"You're getting pale again," Deanna said, laughing. "It's just a fancy name for rump steak."

"That's a relief," Jake said, laughing with her.

"If you're coming. . . ." Deanna picked up her handbag and dangled her keys.

"Delightful party, Mrs. Rosen," Jake said. He made a point of saying a friendly but formal farewell to Van Der Merwe, then followed Deanna to her Anglia. Being outside in the sunshine seemed to complete his cure and he felt positively cheerful as he climbed into the passenger side of the car.

"Do I look respectable enough?" he asked.

"Perfect," Deanna said, backing out of the driveway. "Where are we actually going?"

"Wynberg."

"A church?"

"No. The wedding's at the groom's house."

"Are we going to be late?"

"For what?"

"For the beginning of the ceremony."

"It started about three days ago but no, we won't be late."

"I'm not sure I understand," Jake said, taking out a cigarette.

"I keep forgetting you're a foreigner," Deanna said. "A Malay wedding can last for anything up to five days, depending on the affluence of the groom's family. They're the ones who pay for it. With two daughters, my father thinks that's a marvelous custom."

"You mean they've been partying for three days?"

"Yes. And the bride and groom don't meet till it's all over."

"You mean they've never met?"

Deanna nodded.

"An arranged marriage? In the seventies?"

"You're sure it's all that bad an idea?"

"Don't tell me you approve?"

"From what I've seen, those marriages often turn out rather well; can you say the same about the other kind?" Deanna curved the car onto De Waal Drive. "The majority of Africans still believe in it, too, and it seems to work for them."

"How did you meet this Malay family?" Jake asked.

"Old man Patel, the groom's grandfather, owned a greengrocery next door to my grandparents' store."

"And you were allowed to socialize with them?"

"Pre Immorality Act. Actually, I was sort of a go-between for Joe Patel, the groom's father, and Maria. . . ."

". . . Maria?"

"The same. My grandparents had a yardgoods store. Oma took in dressmaking and Opa covered buttons and listened to the customers' problems. Maria was Oma's apprentice."

204

"I'm a little confused."

"I used to go into the store on Saturdays to make buttons. I loved seeing those scraps of material and metal shells turn into neat little round buttons. Anyway, Maria and Joe had a crush on each other. Everytime I went next door . . . the Patels also sold ice-cream so I was there a lot . . . Joe gave me peaches or loquats or lichees for Maria. And she used to mend his shirts."

"Why didn't they get married?"

"She already had a husband and two sons—one of her own and her husband's child from another marriage. From what I gathered, her husband wasn't around much, so it wasn't too much of a loss for her when the Immorality Act separated them. He was a Zulu."

"Riena told me Maria found her wandering around the streets and took her in."

"Yes, but that was after Maria went into business for herself. She couldn't find anyone to take care of the children when her mother died, and the boys were too young to be left alone."

"Who's getting married?"

"Joe's son. The old man put Joe through law school. . . ."

". . . A lawyer's son who sticks with the old traditions?"

"It's not all that surprising, Jake," Deanna said. "The family's a matriarchy. Old Mrs. Patel still rules the household and what she says goes."

"Are you sure the groom's never managed to sneak a look at his bride?"

"Of course I'm not. Maybe he did before the wedding. Once that gets going, it's almost impossible. All of the males in the bridal party celebrate in one room, the females in another. . . ."

". . . Does that mean we'll have to separate?"

Deanna speeded up and swerved to pass an open vegetable truck before she answered. "No," she said, slowing down. "The guests all join the women."

"Sounds like a mighty expensive way to have a wedding," Jake said.

"It is. The women wear matching outfits and change completely several times a day. I've often wondered what happens to all those clothes once the wedding's over."

They had entered a busy little side street. It was directly at right angles to the local railroad station and Jake could see a passenger train moving by at a leisurely pace.

"This was my grandfather's store," Deanna said, slowing down as they passed a small, dingy looking storefront. The door was shut but a Coloured man sat leaning against it, a sheaf of papers in his hand. Though his seat was an upturned orange crate, he wore a pin striped suit and sported an enormous pair of dark sunglasses.

Jake watched as a far less elegantly clothed man handed "Pin Stripe" money. He was quickly pushed aside by a woman anxious to do the same. "Must be a bookie," Jake said.

"You're not far off," Deanna said. "He's one of the Chinaman's more successful runners. He's got things set up so he doesn't have to run; his customers come to him."

"What's he doing?"

"Those people handing him money are playing *Fafi*. . . ."

". . . That's some kind of gambling game, isn't it?"

"Yes. It's a primitive numbers racket. The Chinaman sends out a list of numbers and odds every day. Supposedly, he dreams of a number once a night. The locals bet on which one it's going to be; whoever has the right number is paid out."

"Is the Chinaman honest?"

"Jake! You must be joking."

"But the people keep playing?"

"They do the same thing in Las Vegas."

"That's closely controlled. Some people do leave winners."

"There are winners at this, too. Otherwise no one would play. The questions is, how many winners. . . ."

". . . And at what odds? I can't imagine you with grandparents in this neighborhood," Jake said. The area had the air of Petticoat Lane after hours. Being a Sunday, everything was closed, courtesy of the Dutch Reformed Church which considered it a sin to trade on the Lord's day, or to do much of anything else for that matter, except perhaps go to church, get married, die and, Jake assumed, have sex. With the proviso, of course, that no classification lines were crossed.

"My grandparents left Berlin in '35 with the Nazis at their heels. They were thrilled to find a way to make a living—in any neighborhood. Besides, it was different here when I was a child. Or it seemed different. . . ."

She parked the car, backing between a battered Studebaker and a bakery van. "We're here," she said. "Be sure to lock the car, please."

"That Studebaker's a collector's item. Who'd bother to steal your car with that around?"

"Any thief around here. New and shiny they understand; it's doubtful they'd know that was a collector's item."

As they made their way down the street and into the Patels' garden, Jake had the sensation that he and Deanna were being closely observed. The kind of surveillance he felt was not simply a territorial one, that of a White man invading a nonWhite world. What he felt was something different, an indefinable discomfort that brought back a vestige of the edge of dementia that had attacked him earlier. Fortunately, the feeling was short-lived. In the time it took to reach the Patels' front door, it was gone.

"Dee. Welcome. I wasn't sure you would come. You look wonderful."

A woman, elderly and engulfed in powder blue chiffon, opened the door before Deanna had time to ring the bell. She encircled the younger woman in ample arms and kissed her warmly on both cheeks. Before Jake had been introduced, she turned to him and said: "Welcome to you, too, young man."

Linking her arm through Deanna's, she propelled her

207

into the house. "Still taking the money your Opa gives you and putting it in your Oma's apron pocket?" she asked. Twisting around to look at Jake, she said: "Some lady you have here. Her grandfather was the most generous man in the world; even when he had nothing, he used to slip Dee half-a-crown on Saturday. She didn't want to hurt him by refusing so. . . ."

Someone called to Mrs. Patel and she disengaged herself from Deanna.

"Back on duty," she said. "You two make yourselves at home."

"She thinks you're my fiancé," Deanna whispered to Jake. "I hope you don't mind; it's easier not to go into complicated explanations."

The only part I mind is that it's not true. Jake thought, as the other female members of the bridal party walked into the room and filled it with what seemed like bales of powder blue chiffon.

He and Deanna walked behind them into a large room. They were assigned to one of six long, beflowered tables where they found themselves seated with the only other non-Malays that he could see. Deanna, perfectly at home, sipped sugary dark tea from a tiny cup. She nibbled on a confection that looked a petit four, but which Jake soon discovered had a strange, scented fragrance, like the rolls of pastel candies his neighbors had handed out at Halloween.

An hour went by. Deanna talked animatedly to the man at her right while Jake, half asleep in the dim light, waited for something to happen. Nothing did. He might as well, he thought, have been at one of his mother's sedate tea parties. The only difference was the bridal party, sitting in a cloud of chiffon on what Deanna had called a *kaross*. It was the Malay name, she'd said, for a rather substantial blanket.

"Have you noticed the absence of children?" Deanna said at last.

"Is that why it's so quiet?" Jake said.

Deanna smiled and stood up. Taking Jake's hand she led him through the guests, between tables and out onto the porch.

A dozen or more small, flat rattan baskets stood neatly lined up against the wall but Jake could see nothing unusual enough to be responsible for the look of anticipation on Deanna's face. He started to ask her a question but was stopped by the appearance of the women of the bridal party. Slippered and veiled, they flowed onto the porch. Each woman picked up a basket, slung it around her wrist, and descended two or three steps into the garden.

Suddenly, as if appearing out of nowhere, a group of children began to gather. Some of them were, judging by their Sunday clothes, the offspring of guests; others were ragamuffins, urchins, the children of the streets of Wynberg.

Mystified, Jake turned to question Deanna. The look on her face stopped him; there was no way he could break her mood of enchantment. He shifted his gaze back to the woman closest to him.

Slowly, teasing the children, she slid her hand into her basket. She paused, then smiled and, in one smooth movement, withdrew her hand and scattered a fistful of minute, shiny objects into the gamins. As the other women followed suit the children, who had a moment before decorated the garden like an unexpected crop of Spring blossoms, turned into a flurry of lizards. Involuntarily, Jake stepped back, the way he had once in Antigua when, on a solitary walk up one of the most beautiful hills in creation, his feet had disturbed a nest of lizards.

"They keep what they _find_," Deanna said.

Her voice penetrated but Jake didn't comment. He was having difficulty brushing away the dragon which thoughts of lizards had conjured up. The same dragon that had so distressed him earlier.

"They've been waiting around all day for this," Deanna said, looking at the children and, therefore, unaware of Jake's distress. "It's the equivalent of throwing rice . . . there's one."

Jake forced himself back to reality. Deanna was point-

209

ing at the littlest child, encouraging him to pick up the coin before someone else got to it. When he did so and held it high over his head in the gesture of an Olympic medal winner, she applauded.

It took no more than three minutes before the ceremony was over. When the children had dispersed, the women returned to their guests and Deanna, still smiling, said: "Do you want to leave now?"

Jake hesitated. He certainly did not want to go back inside the house, nor did he wish to be impolite. To his relief, Deanna suggested he wait for her while she said goodbye for both of them. Grateful for her sensitivity, he settled down on the porch step. He could see several children squatting at the edge of the garden, counting their spoils in the protection of a mulberry bush. The youngest one, the one Deanna had helped, slouched against a rose-covered archway. His urchin's cap was cocked over one eye and his legs were crossed at the ankles. All he needs to be a veritable Frank Sinatra is a trenchcoat, Jake thought, feeling so much better that he was beginning to wonder why he had felt such distress in the first place.

Something glinted and Jake leaned over to pick it up.

"Did you find a tickey?" Deanna said behind him. "I haven't seen too many of them around lately."

Jake stood up and handed her the predecimalization threepenny bit.

"Keep it," Deanna said, handing it back. "Who knows, maybe it is magic, the way the children believe; maybe it'll bring you luck."

They walked in silence to the car.

"Hungry?" Deanna asked, starting the motor and sliding easily out of the parking space.

"Not particularly."

"I don't have a watch on," Deanna said flipping on the car radio. "I hope it isn't six o'clock yet."

"My watch stopped this morning and I didn't reset it," Jake said. "What's special about six o'clock?"

"The cricket matches end. I don't want to get caught in the Newlands traffic. Anything you'd like to do before. . . ."

The rest of Deanna's sentence was lost as the impact of what was being said on the radio commanded attention:

> "For those of you who have not been listening to the wireless," the announcer said, "there was an unprecedented outbreak of violence today at the De Waal Mining Company. During a reenactment of the Dingaan's battle against Piet Retief, Zulu dancers attacked members of the audience. The names of those killed and injured are still being withheld to protect the families but those Zulus involved and still alive have been apprehended. We have been assured that this is an isolated incident and that the compound is now peaceful. The *Trammers* will be at work at dawn as usual. New Boer Boys have been put in charge of the compound and the police are listening to a delegation from the mine . . ."

"Have you ever heard of the Zulu poet Vilakazi?" Deanna said, her voice very quiet. Without waiting for Jake's answer, she went on. "He wrote a poem a long time ago that . . . would you like to hear it? It's stayed with me for years."

Stunned by the announcement, Jake merely nodded.

In a monotone that served to emphasize the drama of the Black poet's cry, Deanna said:

> The earth will swallow us who burrow
> And, if I die there, underground
> What does it matter? Who am I?
> Dear Lord? All around me, every day,
> I see men stumble, fall and die.

"Those poor bastards," she said.

"The people who died?"

"Yes. The dead and the wounded—and the other less obvious casualties, like the families of those Zulus who'll probably never understand why it happened. If

211

anyone bothers to let them know that their relatives are dead and they should mourn. And think of the harm this will do to the people who're trying to find a peaceful solution. . . ."

Jake could think of no adequate response. In the silence that followed Vilakazi's poem and Deanna's questioning of the system, they listened again to the radio:

". . . The Minister of Bantu Administration has issued the following message to those in the outside world who might be assigning blame: 'The malnutrition you see amongst the Blacks in our country is a result of wrong eating habits . . .' "

"Dear God!" Deanna exploded.

". . . I, for one, feel as if I am living under glass. I only wish there were some way to show the world that in Sophiatown and Windermere and the other townships, life is going on as usual."

"Damn right it is," Deanna said, turning off the radio. "Nothing ever stops the pennywhistle . . . but then nothing stops the *Tsotsis* either. It's all symptomatic of the same disease. Last week Alice stopped on her way home to listen to her son play the pennywhistle on a streetcorner in the *location*. A gang of *Tsotsis* attacked her with knitting needles. Knitting needles, Jake. They took her week's wages. . . ."

Again, Jake listened but did not respond. Nothing he could say would make any sense, he thought. How could it when it was all so far beyond his comprehension. It would be sheer idiocy to offer an opinion on anything this complex when his own life was in such a mess.

Out of nowhere, like the precurser of a migraine, Jake saw again what he had seen before—an infant in the arms of a clawed creature. His infant. Nkolosi's creature.

"Where to?" Deanna asked.

It took Jake a moment to answer. "Are we anywhere near Maria's house?" he said. "I'd like to see my child."

11

"We're close in miles but God knows how long it's going to take to get out of this," Deanna said, weaving in and out of a tangle of traffic that had come upon them like a well planned invasion. This, Jake assumed, was the Newlands jam she had hoped to avoid.

"You drive like a New York cabbie," Jake said, admiring the consummate skill with which she made forward progress while the rest of the cars seemed destined to be stuck with inching their way along.

"Is that a compliment?" Deanna sounded amused.

"Yes."

"In that case, I'd better not neglect my job." She nodded her head to the right. "We are now passing the Rondebosch common. If you look closely, you might catch a glimpse of a fox hunt."

"Shades of Colonial days," Jake said, watching the nannies chatting around their sandbox charges.

"Actually, for some reason the hunt never made it to South Africa," Deanna said, slowing down to make the turn off the main thoroughfare onto Brook Road.

It took Jake a moment to recognize the street as Maria's. He'd always approached it from the other end. And there was something else that was different; the street was deserted. No beer drinking groups hid the cracks in the concrete sidewalk, covering its ugliness; just matchbox houses guarding miniature gardens.

"I'll drive around for a while. I really don't feel like coming inside. How long do you need?"

"Twenty minutes should do it," Jake said, wondering

213

what "it" was, since he had no idea what compulsion was driving him to Maria's house. "Why don't you go down to the brook?"

"Brook?"

"This is Brook Road, isn't it?"

Deanna laughed. "There is no brook," she said. "I'm not sure but I think it was diverted by town planners."

A siren, voice of an unseen authority, accompanied Jake out of the car. He could feel eyes peering at him from behind closed shutters and, as he had in Wynberg, he felt physically uncomfortable. Oppressed. He pulled at his collar as if it were choking him, then remembered that he'd already taken off his tie and opened the top buttons of his shirt. Tempted to forget the whole thing, he measured the distance to the front door. It's only a few short strides, he thought, stepping carefully over a crack that looked as if it were about to open up. Would it, he wondered, reveal a Mephistophilian world. More likely, the mysterious brook ran beneath and he would fall through and drown. Not, he thought, an altogether unappealing alternative to the confrontation he was inviting simply by being there.

Once at the door, Jake knocked softly. He was reluctant to awaken the child. After a moment, he knocked again. Louder. Then more loudly still.

"Maria?"

There was no response. He knocked one more time. Stopped. Listened. He could hear nothing, not even the drone of the sewing machine. He tried the door, his hand so slippery with sweat that it had difficulty gripping the handle. When he used two hands, the knob turned. The door opened easily and he stepped into darkness.

"Maria!"

Jake's only response was the sticky silence of a house that had been abandoned, its character removed along with the furnishings.

Although Jake's eyes had not yet adjusted to the darkness, he could see a faint tracing of light along the edges of the window. Interesting how people abandon curtains as if they were part of the house. Jake thought ir-relevantly. He moved toward the rectangle and pulled the fabric aside. Below still, a black cord hung from a plug in the wall. Dangling. Useless. Sentinel over an empty room in an empty house.

As if the substance of the brick could fill the void forming at the pit of his stomach, Jake walked around the room touching each of the walls. Stepping carefully over the bleached rectangle where the sewing machine had stood, he knelt to unplug the cord from its socket because, somehow, its functionless existence offended him. Mechanically, he picked up one of the scraps of paper that lay on the floor, then one more and yet another. The pieces were small but recognizable. Travel-er's checks. The ones he had given Maria.

Carefully, deliberately, Jake set about piling them at this feet, concentrating as he built an altar to American Express.

"They can be replaced."

Nkolosi's voice bounced off the walls with the timbre of a priest performing last rites.

Jake tried to stand up but a numbness attacked his legs and he was forced to crouch. "Did you tear them up?" he said. Or thought he did. He wasn't sure.

"No. Maria did that before we got here."

"We?"

"The Negwenya and I."

"Where are they . . . Maria and the baby?"

"Safe. In Teya. . . ."

". . . Why Nkolosi? You said if I cooperated you'd leave them alone."

"Think back, Mr. Prescott. That's not exactly what I said, is it?"

"You said they wouldn't be harmed."

"Nor will they be. Not unless you tell Van Der Merwe about me. You were contemplating doing that earlier this afternoon."

"How do you know?"

"Would you believe me if I said I specialize in under-standing human nature? That I believe in insurance?"

"It's as if you have the ability to crawl into people's brains," Jake said.

Nkolosi's smile didn't reach his eyes. "Were you seeing images of. . . ."

". . . Your face," Jake interrupted, remembering Nkolosi's features superimposed on the unsuspecting Mr. Porter's.

"And dragons perhaps?"

"For godsake how?" Jane whispered. Inside his head, the words had been a scream.

"Don't try to understand. It is enough that you are beginning to accept. The Negwenya and I are part of something beyond your European consciousness."

"Where is she?"

"She?"

"The Negwenya."

"Here. There. Making sure our . . . guests . . . are comfortable. She considers herself the child's surrogate mother, you know. I, for one, could think of no better guardian."

The vision of a baby in the arms of a clawed creature, Jake thought. It had been no figment of trauma. "Surrogate mother?"

"In our tradition no child has only one mother," Nkolosi said. "Your baby was born at the same instant in time as the Negwenya's. Even then she wanted to take it but I managed to dissuade her. . . ."

The rest of the witchdoctor's words were drowned in a surge of nausea as Jake stumbled to the window, unlatched it and pushed it open. Though the air was still warm, a dusk breeze touched the sweat on his neck and his temples and cooled him. He pictured his child. Their child. His and Riena's. Round and smooth and olive. No changling that, he thought. The witchdoctor is mad. Stark, raving mad.

"What good will it do you to hurt Maria and the baby?" Jake said, turning to face Nkolosi.

The witchdoctor didn't answer. He was sitting crosslegged in the center of the room, staring at the paper pyre that Jake had constructed.

Jake kicked aside the cord that he had dropped at the first sound of Nkolosi's voice and began to move around the brown Buddha.

"Stop!"

Trying to ignore the imperative, Jake told himself to keep moving. He couldn't. The best he could do was sway in the direction of the door.

"Don't you like magic, Mr. Prescott?" Nkolosi sounded amused now. Condescending.

Jake followed the direction of the African's gaze.

A gently moving almost whimsical finger of flame was stroking the edges of the paper. Curling the scraps. Browning them. Directing them one by one to form an eye. A scalloped wing.

Jake stared. There was nothing random about the familiar form being sculpted. The Negwenya stared back at him, her eye fluttering slightly. Seductively. Winking as the ashes settled to the floor, then still quiet, moving only when the edge of Nkolosi's breath reached out and touched it.

"Jake?"

Released from whatever enchantment had been holding him, Jake faced the door.

"It's been over half an hour," Deanna said. "I was getting worried. Is everything all right?"

"Nk. . . ." Jake stopped. There was no point in saying anything. He would only look like a fool, fixated by something incomprehensible. Yet he might have gone on, had Nkolosi been there. Now. Not vanished as if he had existed only as a figment of Jake's imagination. He stretched out his foot to erase the Negwenya but there was no need. The ashes were . . . ashes.

"Didn't you know they were leaving?"

Jake shook his head, knowing she meant Maria and the child because she had not been there to see what he had seen.

"Damn," Deanna said, walking up to the remains of the fire. "Maria lived with a Zulu too long. Why they insist on making fires in the middle of a room is beyond me. The asphyxiation rate. . . ."

". . . Can we get out of here?" Jake thought his voice sounded odd but didn't seem to notice.

"Are you going to try to find them? It won't be easy, you know."

Mad. Stark raving mad, Jake thought again. He shrugged. "I wouldn't know where to begin," he said.

"I'd be eternally grateful if we could begin with dinner," Deanna said.

Thank you for your ability to know when not to ask questions, Jake thought, grateful for Deanna's flippant response. His experience of only minutes ago had to be written on his face. Grooved into his voice. Yet there was no way he could have coped with a serious discussion right then.

"Dinner," he said, adopting Deanna's casual tone. "Why not? Why the hell not?"

12

The drive back to Sea Point was long enough to give Jake a chance to regain at least part of his equilibrium. This time Deanna knew, by some instinct, that neither silence nor questions were called for. She chatted about inconsequentials: why *snoek* was better than whitefish and why she loved Cole Porter and hated acid rock. She pointed out every tourist sight.

"I'll get started in the kitchen while you fix us a couple of drinks. Bar's in the cabinet in the study," she said finally, unlocking the front door of the house.

Jake, who had hardly said two words since they'd left Observatory, poured two good sized Scotches and measured his recuperative powers by the steadiness of his hand. Not bad, considering, he thought, carrying the glasses into the kitchen. Leaning against the wall, he watched Deanna move around the large, old-fashioned

218

room.

"Don't fool yourself," she said. "I may look as if I'm enjoying this domesticity but I'm a confirmed Sunday cook. Once a week is more than enough." She put a checkered cloth over the table, placed a tall, white taper in the center, and stood back to survey her handiwork. "I do love this room. You don't mind eating in here, do you?"

"Why should I?"

"Sorry. I'm used to the South African penchant for formality. You certainly don't need to stand around in here while I'm cooking. Why don't you go to the study. Put on some music. Relax."

"I'd rather watch you. Do you mind?"

"I'm flattered. But I'll probably put you to work."

Jake smiled and sat down. Deanna leaned against the sink and looked at him.

"You look as if you want to say something," he said.

"I do. Shut me up if you feel it's none of my business. I know you feel sorry for Riena but it seems to me you're also feeling mighty sorry for yourself."

"I feel guilty."

"Why?"

"Isn't the answer obvious?"

"Not really. I keep wondering if the underlying reason for your guilt is that you loved a Coloured woman in the first place."

"That's only a mortal sin in this country."

"I gather it's not too highly thought of in New England either."

"I have a responsibility to Riena and the baby. . . ."

". . . You're doing everything you can, Jake. At some point you may have to give up. Go back to Princeton. Put the whole thing in the past."

"Is that what you're doing about Ivan? I've seen the way you jump every time the phone rings. Aren't you still hanging on?"

"Touché."

"Then you do still want to marry Ivan? Have a couple of kids? Live happily ever after." While he, Jake thought, would be lucky to be assigned a place in her scrapbook.

"If you'll open a bottle of wine, we can eat," Deanna said, shutting off further discussion.

Jake was not unhappy that she'd changed the subject. He opened a bottle of South African burgundy and they sat down to the promised Monkey Gland Steak. After *pflaumentorte* with large helpings of whipped cream, Deanna suggested brandy.

"Just coffee, I think," Jake said. "My head's spinning already."

"You shouldn't pass up a chance to drink KWV."

"Never heard of it."

"It's made by the trade for the trade. We get a bottle a year through a friend."

"All right. You pour this time and I'll do the dishes."

"No need. Pile them in the sink and Alice can do them in the morning." She was slurring her words slightly.

"Don't you have a dishwasher?"

Deanna laughed. "What for? Alice would think we were trying to replace her. She was scared half to death when we got the washing machine and vacuum; kept insisting washboards and rug beaters were the natural order of things."

Small wonder the Nkolosis get away with intimidation, Jake thought, his alcoholic blur serving to soften the memory of how much he had been affected by the man's tricks. His latest encounter with the African had become a part of a separate reality; it belonged to a different Jake Prescott, not to the sophisticated man drinking cognac with a woman he had every intention of seducing.

"Let's go into the study," Deanna said. "I'l like to listen to some music. The cornier the better."

"Corny?"

"Irving Berlin. Cole Porter. Gerschwin, maybe."

After she had decided on Cole Porter and the room was filled with his unmistakable brand of sentimentality, Deanna sat down in a plush, wing easy chair and kicked off her shoes. "Isn't this about the time I'm supposed to suggest changing into something more comfortable," she said.

For a moment Jake thought she might be as bent on seduction as he, but her smile and the words that followed quickly disillusioned him.

"I spoke to Ivan last night."

"Where was he calling from?"

"I'm not sure. He must still be in this country because he couldn't speak freely. Or for long. He just wanted to let me know he was in one piece. I do miss him, Jake."

For the first time, she looked vulnerable. Her defenses are breaking down, Jake thought. He wondered briefly if the pleasure of making love to her would be dulled because a permanent relationship with her was unlikely.

The last notes of "Night and Day" coincided with the jarring sound of the telephone. Deanna pushed herself out of the chair and Jake glanced at his watch, wondering who would call late on a Sunday evening. To his surprise, it was not even ten o'clock.

"Van? Yes. I am a little bombed. It's good for the soul." She paused, listening and nodding. "Stop worrying. I'm a big girl, remember. You want to speak to him?" She covered the mouthpiece with her hand. "It's Van."

"For me?" Jake stood up a little unsteadily and took the receiver from her. "Mr. Van Der Merwe?"

The politician sounded strange, off-key, almost somnambulant.

"Thank you. Yes. I'll be there," Jake said. "Sorry to hear. . . ." He stopped. The phone was buzzing in his ear.

"What was all that about?" Deanna asked. She had sat down, on the sofa this time, and was curled up in the corner.

"I'm not sure," Jake said. He sat down slowly next to her. She shifted position and flexed her foot. Jake found his eyes focusing on her toenails. They were the color of fresh blood.

"Maybe the old boy's going senile," Deanna said.

"That's what his opposition's been saying for a long time. You two certainly talked for long enough this afternoon; did you ask him to help you? Jake? Jake, are you still here?" She leaned toward him. "What is it?"

Jake blinked and refocused. "Nothing," he said. "Too much to drink, I guess." That must be it, he thought, forcing himself to look away from the odious sight of talons protruding from Deanna's feet.

Deanna reached out and stroked Jake's cheek. "I shouldn't drink," she said. "It makes me horny."

Apparently I shouldn't either, Jake thought, forcing himself to look back at Deanna's toes to reassure himself that they were perfectly normal. As, indeed, they were. Having done that, he took her hand and held it against his face. He felt awkward, shy, a sophomore who knew little more than how to talk a good game.

"I'm over twenty-one and at least as lonely as you are," Deanna said, misreading Jake's hesitation as a gentlemanly reluctance to appear pushy. She moved closer and kissed him firmly on the mouth. "Would you like to go upstairs?"

Drunk or sober, Jake thought, the lady knows what she wants. "I can't think of anything I'd rather do," he said. But he didn't move. "Deanna, have you considered the fact that maybe you've just had too much. . . ."

". . . What is it, Jake? A sudden attack of morality? Or does the role reversal bother you?"

"I'm sorry. I don't know. . . ."

". . . Van says you think you're in love with me." She stood up and walked over to the window. "You don't even know me. Not really."

"What business did Van have. . . ?"

". . . Come on, Jake. Stop taking yourself so seriously. Van tends to try to protect me from my baser instincts, that's all." She laughed. "He knows that when I drink I have visions of bubble baths and Dior lingerie. I'm not sure why."

That's the second time tonight she's admitted being unsure of herself, Jake thought. She had sat down again, this time on the window seat. The antique satin drapes were the same shade as her dress and she blended into their folds.

"When I was little, I used to hide inside this window seat. I remember. . . ." Deanna stood up and adjusted the volume of the music. Ignoring Jake, she started to dance, moving slowly and sinuously at first, then faster and faster until, as abruptly as she had begun, she stopped. "Sometimes, when I was in there," she went on as if there had been no interruption, "I listened to my father and his friends talking politics. Sitting on their fat arses, getting fatter and doing nothing. They never really gave a damn about anything except the stock market."

The tempo of the music changed and she started dancing again, following the strong drumbeat with her feet and her shoulders.

"Join me, Jake."

Jake shook his head. "You have me outclassed," he said. "You're very good."

"I have a lot of hidden talents," Deanna said. Shimmying slowly up and down, she winked at him and held out her hand.

Desire for her supplanting caution, Jake pushed himself up and moved toward her. She smiled again. Suddenly he could see only the Negwenya's face, her eye winking at him in an obscene invitation to the dance.

"Jake?"

There was no time for explanations. Sweating profusely, Jake ran for the stairs. Even taking them two at a time, he barely reached the toilet before his stomach convulsed and he vomited.

When he finally flushed the last vestiges of his dinner into the sewage system, Jake wanted nothing more than to flush himself down with it.

Knowing there was no way he could go back downstairs smelling the way he did, he opened a window and turned on the water in the shower. He could hardly wait to step inside the stall, approaching it almost as if the water were going to peform some kind of baptismal rite and he would emerge without the fragmentation he'd been experiencing since his encounter with Nkolosi.

By the time Jake turned off the water, his skin was crinkling. He had scrubbed himself with masochistic pleasure, relishing the sting of soap in his eyes and letting the water flow over his head until he had to struggle to breathe. And he did feel better. Much better.

Wrapping himself in a bath sheet, he looked around to make sure he had done an adequate job of cleaning up. When he was satisfied, he turned off the light and went down the hallway to the guest room. He opened the door softly, afraid that any loud sound or abrupt movement would disturb his fragile balance. Someone had turned on a night light; its glow muted the shadows and created the kind of nursery atmosphere he needed. He had closed the door and was leaning against it before he realized that he wasn't alone.

"You all right?" Deanna said. Without waiting for an answer, she lifted her hand and began to play with the long shadows her fingers were creating on the wall. "Watch, ladies and gentlemen," she said. "Before your very eyes this cute little bunny rabbit will become . . . a snake. And now . . . an elephant. See the trunk swaying." Then two hands. Working at it. Failing at first, until: "I knew I'd remember. See Jake. That damn African's not so clever after all. He's not the only one who can manufacture dragons. Ladies and gentlemen: Now you see it; now you don't." The image appearing, disappearing, appearing again.

Jake's laugh sounded more like a bark but he dropped his towel and walked toward the bed. "You want me, dragon lady," he said. "You can have me."

Deanna stopped playing with shadows. "Shower didn't help much, did it," she said. "You're still weaving."

"You talk too much," Jake said, lying down next to her.

"Sorry. My seduction techniques need refining."

Jake took her in his arms and kissed her, tentatively at

224

first, then more firmly out of a larger need. This was what he had wanted from the moment he'd met Deanna; not simply that she should be his lover but his healer, too.

"Relax, Jake," Deanna said, moving away slightly. "We have all night. Or do you have a secret date waiting for you at dawn? If all you want is to get this over with. . . ."

All of the tension that had been draining out of Jake's body returned at the mention of morning. Suddenly every movement caused him pain.

"Lie on your stomach," Deanna said.

"What?"

"Nothing perverted, I promise you. I like my sex straight."

Jake rolled over.

"I learned this from a Japanese friend," she said, massaging his shoulders and down, paralleling his spine, she played him like a violin until he felt himself drifting into an opiate half sleep. When she stopped, he took her in his arms naturally at last. And then astride her, still with a strange detachment but without pain. His hands moving of their own volition, hers clinging to the small of his back. Moving. Up. Down. Her body in rhythm with his, his hands stroking her, responding to the smooth flesh and the rising nipples against his chest.

She was sweating now, her breath short, her hands moving faster. He wanted to tell her how beautiful she was, that he wanted to love her, not fuck her, but he was the actor, not the director. A Fellini player, waiting for the next sequence in a script that had been kept from him, losing enjoyment of the present because of a shadowy knowledge that the scene to come was not one he wished to play.

Deanna arched her body and raised her palms. Jake could feel the tips of her nails tracing a duplicate pattern up his spine to his shoulders and down again. Gently, at first, the digging. Deeper. Gouging.

Jake screamed.

"God, Jake! What is it?"

In one swift movement, Deanna pushed him off, rolled over and stood up, her nightgown ravelled around her hips. She pulled it down and automatically ironed out the wrinkles with her hand before she reached the light switch.

"Your nails!" Jake moaned, feeling his face contort with pain. Slowly, moving only centimeters at a time, he turned so that Deanna could see his back; it felt ripped open in a hundred places. "The bed. Get a towel before the blood. . . ."

". . . There is no blood, Jake."

"I can feel it oozing."

Deanna touched his flesh lightly with her fingertips. "There's nothing there," she said, holding her hands up to the light. "Do you see any blood?"

Jake shook his head and lay down, staring at the ceiling as the pain faded. Sitting down on the bed, Deanna began to stroke his forehead. She was looking at him as if he were a child with a fever, Jake thought.

"I'm sorry," he said. "You're a very beautiful woman."

The pain that he had felt was gone and he no longer felt detached. Suddenly the only thing that mattered was making love to Deanna but the desire in her eyes had been replaced by curiosity and pity.

"What was it, Jake?" What happened?"

"I felt her claws ripping me open."

"I don't understand."

"The Negwenya. She was here, in bed with me. . . ."

". . . Oh, come on. You were in bed with me. Not some African dragon that only exists inside the heads of people who believe in her. You must have been dropping off . . . not much of a compliment to me, is it?" She smiled. "I must be more out of practice that I thought."

"I'm the one who's out of practice," Jake said, reaching for her.

"You don't have to, you know," she said, lying down next to him.

"I know that," Jake said, taking her into his arms.

"It's what I want, more than anything in the world."

It was true, he thought, looking at her. Ivan was her past and probably her future, but he needed her now.

13

It was only after Deanna had fallen asleep that Jake once again began to chase circular thoughts. They moved around him in ever-diminishing circles until, choking, he got up. Sitting at the desk, he tried listing those issues most urgently in need of solution. It was simple enough to list the problems but his answer sheet remained singularly blank; even a paper solution eluded him.

Moving to the armchair, Jake stared at Deanna. She stirred restlessly, as if he were penetrating her dreams. If all went well, he thought, looking away, he would have two or three days before he'd have to leave for Teyateyaneng. If not. . . . Standing up, Jake gathered his belongings together and stuffed them carelessly into his duffle bag, like a man convinced he would be unpacking momentarily. He had scattered his clothes around the room like a man who'd intended to stay forever, he thought. If all did not go well, he told himself again, he'd find a cab as rapidly as possible and come back to the Rosens' to collect his things. If something went wrong he would have to get to Riena as quickly as possible. Warn her. Do what he could to help her. There would be no time for farewells here, tender or otherwise.

"What're you doing?" Deanna mumbled. She raised herself slightly and glanced at the bedside clock. "Fuck'em and run. Is that it?"

Jake stopped packing and walked over to the bed. He sat down on the edge and stroked her hair, wanting more than anything to get back into the bed with her.

227

"When I can't sleep, I have fits of tidiness. Go back to sleep. I'm going for a walk."

"It's five o'clock in the morning."

"I know. I probably should have been a milkman. I like early mornings," Jake said hearing the clatter of bottles outside the window and the milkman's whistle as he moved toward the house. Jake imagined the man's face, a dark blur against the dawn, and his uniform—luminescent as his product. He looked over at the desk, at the note he had prepared in case he had to rush back to the house with only enough time to collect his bag. It took every bit of self discipline he could muster to stay silent about his appointment with Van Der Merwe. With luck, he thought, all would go as planned. Deanna would still be in bed when he returned and he would join her. Make love to her again.

"You're definitely crazy," Deanna said, digging herself deeper into the bedclothes. "See you later. Goodnight."

Giving up all hope of sleep, Jake stood at the window and watched the shadows harden into trees and flowers. He comforted himself with the thought that, for him, a totally sleepless night brought in its wake a kind of transient euphoria which would see him through the early part of the day.

At five thirty, when the servants began their kitchen chatter, he pulled on the swimsuit Deanna had loaned him, then his blue jeans and a windbreaker. Deanna was once again sleeping soundly but he paused briefly before leaving the room and went back to the bed to kiss her lightly. She didn't stir as, without giving himself time to deliberate any further, he left the room . . . and the house.

"Up too early, Baas," Johan said. He was standing at the end of the driveway, dunking something into his outsized mug of coffee. He held up the cup and grinned his toothless grin. "Is coffee, Baas."

Impulsively, Jake put his hand in his pocket and took out a five rand note. "Buy yourself something," he said putting the money into the old man's hand.

Johan backed away and bowed. "I not need it," he said gravely. "You a nice man, M . . . Mr. Prescott."

Jake didn't argue. "No more jumping over trees?"

"Never more. This old body tell me never more to do that," Johan said. Shyly, he put out his gnarled hand. Jake gripped it firmly. He felt a strong impulse to hug the old man but he just smiled and walked away.

The purpose of Van Der Merwe's call the night before had been to ask Jake if he'd mind coming to the apartment first before they went swimming. He was to be there at six o'clock. Sharp. The route to Surfcrest, where Van Der Merwe was a permanent resident, was the same as the one Jake would have taken to Saunders Rocks. He got to his destination ten minutes early. Since he had not quite enough time to walk on the beach and yet was too early to knock on the politician's door, he decided to indulge himself. A boyhood trip to New York City had left him with a fascination for fire escapes; he felt about them much the same way steam engine afficionados felt about old trains. He walked around the back of Surfcrest, past the kitchen crew taking their first coffee break of the day, and climbed the fire escape.

Leaning against the iron balustrade on the third floor, Van Der Merwe's level, Jake examined the sky. For the first time since his arrival, it was cloudy. The sun was struggling for supremacy, scattering its rays in random, sharp white lines, and the railing was cold to his touch. Perhaps, Jake thought, Van Der Merwe intended to forego his morning swim. If so, Nkolosi's plan would have to be rewritten. Without the necessity for a shower, Jake would not be left alone to open the door for the AFI agent. Somehow, he had to come up with an alternate plan, and it had to be one that would not point to his complicity.

There was a sudden creak behind him, as if a cat or a dog had missed a stair and landed too heavily on the next. He turned around but there was nothing within sight. Natural expansion of metal, he decided, stepping closer to where the sound had come from. As he did so,

229

a crumpled beer can joined another at his feet. He moved closer and peered upward at the sole of a large shoe and the dog eared corner of a Superman comic book. Both apparently belonged to the Black man who lay dozing, his body contorted between step and wall, his right hand wearing his jacket pocket like a mitten.

Jake's stare was enough to make the man stir. He opened his eyes, straightened up, and turned up the collar of his jacket with his free hand. The other remained where it had been.

Repositioning himself, the man grinned at Jake. "Boring out here," he said, apparently feeling called upon to say something.

Jake nodded and looked at his watch. He had managed to kill five minutes more than he had intended and was five minutes late for his appointment. He went as quickly as he could down the stairs and around the building to the front entrance, tidied his reflection in the glass doors, and went inside.

The door of Van Der Merwe's small bachelor apartment opened at Jake's first knock.

"Come in. You're late." Van Der Merwe looked tired. He led Jake into a simply furnished living room and gestured at one of the chairs. "Be right with you," he said. "I don't remember locking the door. Can't be too careful."

Jake's heartbeat picked up. He would have to find some way to unlock that door if they weren't going swimming. And it looked as if they weren't; Van Der Merwe wasn't wearing a swimsuit.

"Aren't we going to swim?" he asked, the suspense more than he could bear.

"For the first time in years, I don't feel much like it," Van Der Merwe said returning from his security check. "Today is one of those rare days that I wish I had a wife. A child. Something more than my electorate. . . ." He ran his hand over his chin, as if he couldn't quite remember whether or not he had shaved. "I think I'm getting old."

Fortunately for Jake, the euphoria he had anticipated

was balancing his inclination to panic. He told himself that he would have no trouble making an opportunity to unlatch the door and that Nkolosi's emissary, whoever he was, would have the good sense to try the handle before he knocked and took the chance of alerting the politician.

"I thought you'd be pleased. You seemed none too keen to try the water the other morning," Van Der Merwe said. "Besides, you might not feel like doing much of anything after we've talked."

"If it's bad news, I might want to drown myself," Jake said. He tried to include a measure of relief, disappointment and anticipation in his facial expression and tone while attempting to remember exactly how much he had told the politician. Rearranging his features to what he hoped showed anxiety tempered with hope, he said: "Is she . . . dead?"

"They think so."

"They *think* so?" A method actor by nature, Jake was quickly caught up in the role he'd assumed. His venom against the anonymous authority was real.

"I warned you earlier that they probably hadn't done too efficient a job of identifying remains. I asked what questions I could but with the warden having quit, they had nowhere to turn for answers. I could have asked him directly but he's gone to Johannesburg. I couldn't even find out if Riena gave birth before the explosion. The daily log was destroyed in the fire."

Act shocked, Jake thought. Sad. Angry. Again he felt his features rearranging themselves. "You said you had good news, too," he said after what he hoped was a suitable period of silence.

"Yes, You said you thought you knew who would have the child if there is one. Check it out. If you're right, I'll help you get your progeny out of the country. I'll need a photograph and birth certificate. . . ."

". . . Birth certificate? Where do I look for that?"

"If the child was born in prison, its guardian will have been given the birth certificate. I don't understand the difficulty, Prescott." He sounded a little annoyed at

231

Jake's apparent stupidity but softened at the look on the American's face. "I'm sorry, Jake. You're understandably distracted," he said.

Jake was having trouble concentrating on anything other than the door handle. "Should I bring everything to you here?" he asked, forcing himself to continue the game.

"No. I don't want you coming here again. Post the birth certificate and photograph to me. I'll get the papers to you somehow." He paused. "Now listen to me carefully, son. Once you have everything you need, I want you out of this country on the next plane. Do you understand that?"

Jake was watching the handle again. Expecting it to turn and not knowing whether what he felt was desire to get the whole farce over with or hope that it wouldn't happen at all.

"How can I leave without knowing whether Riena's dead or alive?" he asked.

"You won't have any choice. Once I've made arrangements for the child—assuming there is one, of course—that's it."

Jake nodded. Somehow he had to get the politician out of the room. "I really don't feel very well," he said. "Could I trouble you for a cup of coffee?"

"You do look like hell," Van Der Merwe said standing up. "But then you did when you walked in. What did you do, spend the night with the devil? I'll get you coffee but you'll have to wait a few minutes; I don't keep instant. I was going to ask you to have breakfast with me downstairs in our restaurant but you don't look . . . would you like a slice of toast? I eat most of my meals down there but I do keep emergency rations around."

Van Der Merwe was talking to cover his discomfort, Jake thought, but the ephemeral loneliness he had sensed in the politician earlier was gone. The politician's hospitality was unconvincing, as if he hoped Jake would choose to leave now that business had been taken care of.

Though food was the last thing the American wanted,

232

the offer provided him with the chance of a few extra minutes alone. It was all he needed. He nodded his thanks.

"I won't be long. Make yourself at home."

The words were the right ones but they lacked sincerity. Jake heard them from the window where he was watching the early Monday morning traffic snake down Beach Road toward Cape Town. Everything was being made too easy for him, he thought, listening to the clatter of a coffee cup being placed a little too firmly on its saucer. He had gone over to the window to give himself time to invent a story in case he was interrupted while unlocking the door. But even that posed no real problem. He would say he had dropped his pen in the foyer and was going out to retrieve it. Simple. Believable. And unnecessary. No one interfered with him. He had unlatched the door and was ensconced in an easy chair, reading a magazine, by the time the politician returned.

"How complicated is all of this you're doing for me?" Jake asked, picking up the coffee cup Van Der Merwe had placed next to him and eyeing the toast with distaste.

"It isn't. One becomes practiced at circumventing red tape."

You and my uncle and all the other power players, Jake thought, forcing his eyes to stay away from the door. You control it all, don't you. All the little men and women, thinking their lives are running in self-prescribed circles when they've really relinquished control. He knew he was trying to turn Van Der Merwe into an ogre. It was the only means he had of justifying what was about to happen. His euphoria was dissipating and his body had begun to ache from lack of sleep; a steady doubt was building in his mind, destroying the illusion that every time he heard his child crying in America, it would be the voice of forgiveness. The infant was no priest, nor would its nursery serve as a confessional.

"Why did you decide to help me?"

It was not until the question emerged that Jake realized how much he needed to hear the answer.

"In a way, I suppose I'm covering all bases. In case I'm found lacking on Judgment Day."

"Damn classification system."

"I'm fully aware of its failings," Van Der Merwe said. "But as an anthropologist you must know that hegemony isn't unique to this country. Post-Alexandrian Greece, for example. . . ."

". . . Government sponsored bigotry curtails the rights of all people. I mean, how can you justify classifying the Japanese 'honorary Whites' while the Chinese are treated as Coloureds? Can you imagine what it must feel like to have to prove that you're not Chinese to get into a movie? And who makes that judgment if you've forgotten your I.D.? A ticket taker?"

"The world is run by petty clerks, Jake."

"Can someone be reclassified?"

"Yes. Sometimes. If you know which strings to pull, whose palms to grease."

"Is that what you're doing for me?"

The politician nodded.

"Have you ever done it before?"

"Once. I had an Indian reclassified so that he could stay with his Coloured wife; so that his teenage daughter wouldn't become an ex post facto bastard."

Van Der Merwe paused to refill the coffee cups and Jake's attention was again diverted to the door. Almost imperceptibly, the handle was moving. He put his hand in his pocket ostensibly to take out his cigarettes but really to hide the fact that it had begun to shake. Before he had time to withdraw it, the door flew open and was instantly kicked shut. As if to prove that he was the same man Jake had seen on the fire escape, the intruder crumpled a beer can and dropped it onto the tiled hallway floor. It ricocheted against an old copper spittoon and clattered to a halt. Deliberately, the man at the door flattened it heavily underfoot.

"That's what'll happen to your heads if either of you move," he said. Then, recognizing Jake: "Got tired of freezing my arse off out there."

"You two appear to be acquainted," Van Der Merwe

234

said quietly. Too calmly. As if he had expected the intrusion. Welcomed it. As if he could see the structures around which he had built his life crumbling and to ignore the self preservation techniques that had worked for him in the past. His attitude, Jake thought, went along with having acknowledged his loneliness, offering to help Jake, giving up the morning swim that was as much a part of his daily routine as shaving.

"I wondered what you were doing fiddling with the front door but I figured I'd find out soon enough," the politician said, in confirmation of Jake's thoughts.

"Shut up and get me a drink," the intruder said, levelling his gun at Van Der Merwe's head. He held the weapon easily, as if it were an extension of his hand.

Van Der Merwe stared at the silencer, his expression contemptuous. He didn't move. Jake sat in the chair as if chained into it, knowing any thought of escape was no more than foolish fantasy.

"Fuck you. I'll get it myself," the man said. He strode over to the liquor cabinet and tore it open, his movements jerky, almost spastic. His gun was kept carefully angled at Van Der Merwe's head. Without turning his back, he took out a bottle. It was KWV Brandy. Unopened. Clenching the top in his teeth, the man twisted the bottle with his free hand. It came off quite easily. Holding the bottle up in an insolent gesture that reminded Jake of the child in the garden at the wedding he'd gone to with Deanna, the man spat the bottle top across the room at the politician and took a long swallow.

"Sit down you old fart," he said, looking at Van Der Merwe. When the politician didn't move, the man fingered his gun with loving strokes. "You deaf, asshole? I said sit down!"

"What do you want? Both of you?" Van Der Merwe said. He sounded old and weary but still he did not move.

"Fucking good stuff," the man said drinking again and holding the bottle up to the light to check the level of its contents. It was half empty.

235

Van Der Merwe took a step toward him. "You couldn't drink something else, I suppose," he said holding out his hand.

The man laughed derisively. "Too good for me, is it?" Lifting the bottle to shoulder level, he dribbled the remaining amber liquid over his shoe and into the carpet. "Now sit down!"

Deliberately, his face showing no emotion, Van Der Merwe moved toward his oppressor. "I don't know what you want and I don't really care," he said. "Get out of here or shoot me but I will not obey you. Do you hear me? I will not. . . ."

Though his brain had to have been befuddled by alcohol, the man understood what was happening. Slowly, taking careful aim, he raised his gun and shot Van Der Merwe through the head. Grinning. Deriving maximum pleasure from the sound of the bullet penetrating the politician's skull. Doubtless, Jake thought, his normal reactions dulled in a split second of disbelief, the man was no longer bored.

"You're next if you don't do what you're told," the man said, pointing his gun at Jake.

The sound of his voice destroyed the suspension of disbelief and, for the second time in less than twenty four hours, Jake vomited.

"You have ten seconds, mister, or you're going to look like him."

Jake was still gagging. Heaving. The man was fiddling with his silencer. When he was satisfied, he took out a single key and threw it at Jake.

"There's a milk truck in the lot. Unlock the back, then bring it around to the fire escape. I'll slide inside."

With concentrated effort, Jake kept his eyes away from what used to be Daniel Van Der Merwe. He couldn't believe his luck. There was nothing to stop him driving away. Nothing.

"In case you're thinking of leaving without me, don't."

"What's going to stop me?"

The man's eyes were beginning to glaze over with the

236

effects of the beer and brandy he'd drunk. He was swaying slightly and was leaning his hip against a chair for support.

"I'll find you, Whitey," he said. "Now get going, before I get bored again." The hand that held the gun dropped two or three inches, as if it were getting heavy.

No, Jake thought. He couldn't live with yet another threat. There had to be something he could do. Some way he could distract the man. Take his gun. Though what he'd do with it once he had it, he didn't know. Shoot him? Jake discarded the idea at once as absurd. That could be murder. It was bad enough to be an accessory to all of this but he was incapable of killing. What he needed to be able to do was incapacitate the man somehow.

Jake's eyes came to rest on the brandy bottle. It lay within a foot of where he stood, near Van Der Merwe's stiffening hand and speckled with spots whose origin he had no wish to examine. In the movies, he thought, the hero would pick up the bottle, attack his captor, and emerge victorious. But this was no movie; there were no distractions. . . .

As if on cue, the telephone rang. The man's head jerked around involuntarily and that was all the time Jake needed. He stooped and picked up the bottle. He was taller than the Black man. Stronger. Caught off guard and more than a little drunk, Nkolosi's man was no match for Jake who played the scene like a Saturday matinee. Swinging the bottle above his head, he brought it down hard on the Black man's skull and, with a look of astonishment in his eyes, the AFI agent crumpled to the floor.

Moving in slow motion, Jake picked up the key he had dropped when he'd lunged for the bottle. Then he looked down at his clothes, made certain they were unstained, and dropped the key into the tangle of bodies. Stepping carefully around them, he left the apartment for the taxi rank next door at the President Hotel. With a little bit of luck, he thought, he could pick up his things without disturbing Deanna and make the next plane to Johannesburg. He had checked and they left once an hour. He thought about the note he'd written for Deanna, one she'd never have had a chance to read if the morning had gone as planned. Knowing that if she read the note at all, he'd be on his way to Johannesburg and Riena, he'd told her he loved her. Simply. Without embellishment. He'd said nothing about his destination, only that he was leaving to find Riena and the child. If she remembered their conversation on Table Mountain, she'd assume he was taking a train to Teyateyaneng. If she didn't she would have no idea where he'd gone. Since he'd never mentioned Johannesburg, there would be no reason for her to think of it.

Having given the taxi driver the Rosens' address, Jake returned to his introspection. That he was no longer in love with Riena was both a fact and irrelevant, he thought. He owed her his help and he had a responsibility to the child. He was also an accessory to murder; that, too, was an unalterable fact. He would see no way that his life was ever going to return to normal. Not without some kind of miracle. Certainly, he had no right to Deanna's love. He found himself suddenly grateful that she was so obviously still in love with Ivan. Had she loved him. . . .

The taxi pulled up at the end of the Rosens' driveway.

"Wait for me here, please," Jake said. "I won't be long. When I get back, I have to go to D. F. Malan Airport."

The taxi drive lay back and closed his eyes, happy to leave the meter ticking and catch up with his sleep at the same time.

Johan greeted Jake as he started toward the house. "Miss Dee waiting for you, Mr. Prescott."

"Yes, I'm waiting for you," Deanna said, walking toward them. She was dressed in an old pair of jeans and her hair was tied back in a makeshift bun. Without make-up, she looked young and vulnerable.

"How long have you been waiting out here?"

"Long enough. I read your note, Jake. Are you still leaving?"

238

"There's a taxi waiting for me."

"Tell him to go. I'll drive you to the station."

So she did believe he was going to Teyateyaneng, Jake thought. "I don't think so, Deanna, but thank you. I hate long goodbyes."

"Will I see you again?" Her voice was quiet. Almost emotionless. As if there were things she wanted to say but elected not to until she'd heard the answer to her question.

Jake wanted to take her in his arms and tell her he'd be back. Remembering the last time he'd made promises he couldn't keep, he held his arms at his sides. "I don't have the right to come back," he said.

"I think I could love you, Jacob," Deanna said. She stretched and kissed him lightly. Then she turned and walked into the garden.

"I'll carry that with me," Jake said, too softly for her to hear. "Goodbye, Deanna Rosen."

BOOK
THREE

1

For every mile of the almost one thousand she and Tom had traveled since leaving Cape Town, Riena had kept hoping that something would alter the course of events prescribed by Nkolosi. Now, listening to Tom tell her to go to Teyateyaneng if things went wrong, she had to accept the fact that no miracle was going to intervene. One of the questions left unresolved in her mind was Tom's certainty that the Cohns would instantly offer her Emily's job—assuming Emily had been disposed of by Nkolosi.

"How do you know they'll offer me her job?" she asked.

Tom smiled. "Because," he said, kissing her firmly on the mouth, "they need someone to make breakfast."

Riena clung to him for a moment, looking over his shoulder at the Cohns' house. When she pulled away she started to speak but stopped. There was nothing left to say; it was time to go.

It was no more than a few yards from the car to the mulberry tree that marked the bend in the Cohns' driveway, yet it took sheer force of will for Riena to get to it without looking back. Once there, she paused to reassure herself by playing the word Teyateyaneng in her thoughts like a musical instrument.

One of the tree's branches hung close to Riena's head. She reached up and touched it. Climb the tree, she thought. Climb to the top and stay there, where it's safe. Resisting, she knelt to watch the progress of an earthworm which had appeared from a tiny hole, emerging slowly to survey the territory above-ground before daring to begin its journey across the grass to parts unknown. It had made barely any progress when a

Mossie, small, sandy-grey, swooped down out of the tree. It landed on the ground and waited quietly, watching the earthworm for a moment before taking it in its beak.

Riena shivered and stood up. The bird, startled, lifted its head, its pinpoint eyes examining the human that was invading its domain. Then it raised its wings and darted out of sight. Which are you, Tom, predator or prey, she asked, directing the question toward the car which still hadn't moved. Whichever he was, she wanted to run to him and beg him not to leave her.

Knowing it was too late, she watched as a White man walked across her line of vision. He glanced at her and took a step in her direction. Then apparently changing his mind, he sauntered toward Tom. Riena waved at the car, hoping Tom would see her, notice the man and drive on. He waved back and she listened for the car's engine; nothing disturbed the silence except crickets and birds and the rustling of leaves overhead. Steady, Tom, she said softly as the White man reached his target and leaned against the window frame. Keep cool. Don't think about now, think about Teyateyaneng.

The word rippled like windchimes and this time Riena remembered. Helpless to do anything for Tom, she sat down on the grass and allowed the memory to enfold her.

It was a long time since she'd thought about her natural mother. She'd spent so many years trying to believe that Ma and Tom and Alfred were her real family, that her own mother's face had become shadowy and vague. But not her voice. Forgetting that was as impossible as imagining she'd never heard Debussy. No matter what other music she'd grown to love since, Debussy had been her introduction to a world outside of the top ten hits of the week. No one would ever quite compare.

She could not have been more than eight, Riena thought, when her mother told her about Teyateyaneng. . . .

"What are we, Mamma? Am I a Coloured brat?"

"Your ancestors lived in the village of Teyateyaneng,

in the shadow of Thaba Bosigo—the Mountain of the Night."

"Is it a big mountain, Mamma?"

"Some people say it's only a hill."

"Have you seen it, Mamma?"

"Yes, I've seen it, child."

"Is it a mountain?"

"Our ancestors fought in its shadow. They stood with Moshesh against the great Matabele leader Mosilekatse and founded our Basuto nation there. To me it's a mountain. Besides, I only saw it in the sunlight. It was at night that they said the witchdoctors turned it into a great big mountain to protect our warriors against the enemy."

"Then I'm Basuto?"

"You are—at least as much as you are White."

Riena remembered having thought about her mother's words for a long time. She'd wanted to ask about her White father but hadn't found the courage. One night weeks later, after she'd been picked on by bullies in the alley next to their house, she'd returned to the conversation. . . .

"Could we find a witchdoctor to make me big?" she'd asked, as her mother comforted her. "I'm so tired of being little."

Riena picked a blade of the Cohns' grass and chewed the end, reliving the anger she'd felt at always being smaller than the others. For years, she'd kept hoping a witchdoctor would decide to make her big, too, like the mountain, so that she could punish her enemies. Later, after Sharpeville, she'd control her life. She'd become practical in all things but most especially in that which related to survival. Looking up into the branches of the mulberry tree, she grinned. How angry Tom had been at her for dangling from every branch of every tree in the hopes that it would stretch her body, she thought.

Remembering how, in their silkworm collecting stage, she'd risked discovery by staying too long in the White man's garden so that she could hang from the branches of his tree, she stood up. Nothing had really changed, she thought. She still felt small and insignificant—and she was still staying too long in the White man's garden.

Though she knew she was continuing to linger when she should have been inside the house by now, Riena began to explore. It was hard not to be impressed: the mulberry tree shaded a white tiled swimming pool; the scent of roses mingled with mimosa in full bloom; and the house itself looked as if it had been planted there, as if a gardener had meant to grow a sunflower and the house had grown in its place—turning its face to the sunshine as it grew, the way the flower would have done. Even the convertible in the driveway belonged, she thought, recognizing the car that had followed them around the Wilds.

Playing for time, Riena walked around the mulberry tree toward a fig tree. She let the ripest fig drop into her hand and ate it, waiting for the sting on her tongue that would tell her the ants agreed with her choice of fruit. It came. Peppery. Like chewing on a nasturtium leaf. Once long ago, in a past life perhaps, she thought, she must have been a farmer's daughter. She headed toward a grape vine, its tendrils curling lazily around its support, like a child clinging to its mother's pinkie.

The grapes felt warm and smooth to the touch. She picked one and held the long, yellow-green oval between her fingers, peeling it carefully to expose its transparent flesh. Delaying deliberately to draw out her anticipation, she placed it in the middle of her tongue and held it against her palate while she peeled another. When the second Hannepoort was ready, she pressed down on the first and swallowed.

"You'll get appendicitis from eating all those pips." Alfred's voice. Always the prophet of doom. Disturbing the flow of his grapes from fingers to mouth to spit out the hard brown seeds. Tom saying nothing. Not caring enough to agree or disagree. Grinning when he was asked to mediate and calling them idiots for fighting over something so trivial.

"Can I help you?"

Riena pulled her hand off the vine and whirled around.

"It's all right," the man said. "I'm sorry I startled you."

It was the man who'd spoken to Tom. Riena automatically glanced through the trees toward the spot where the car had stood.

"I'm the one who should apologize," she said. "I have no right . . . I shouldn't have been taking your. . . ."

". . . Eat them. They'll rot on the vine if you don't." The man had a strained expression on his face, as if he were struggling to remember something. As if, Riena thought, he felt he'd seen her before and was trying to recapture the memory of where and when.

"I'm Elizabeth Riess," she said. "I've come to visit Emily. I'm her cousin."

"I'm Mr. Barnard—Emily's madam's brother," the man laughed. "That does sound complicated, doesn't it?"

Riena tried to smile. She hadn't recognized the warden immediately because she'd only seen him a few times, and always at a distance. She might not have recognized him at all had it not been for the newspaper article that Tom had hidden, obviously thinking it would remind her of the explosion and upset her. She'd let him believe she hadn't seen it. . . .

"I . . . I don't think so, Sir."

Riena was shocked to find that her words sounded reasonably normal. She felt as if all of the blood had drained out of her head—as if at any moment she would faint at the feet of her former jailer. Tom had said something about a distinguished guest and she'd assumed a diplomat. A foreigner. He'd surely have told her if he'd known Pieter Barnard was going to be there, too.

"I must look like someone you know," she said, knowing she must respond to Barnard's comment.

"Probably." Barnard sounded unconvinced. "Look, why don't you come inside. Emily's probably making

247

breakfast. I'm sure my sister won't mind if you keep her company."

Riena followed him through the trees and up the path to the front door, wondering briefly why he wasn't taking her around to the servants' entrance. He started to ring the doorbell, changed his mind, and took a single key from his pocket. "Damn precautions," he said struggling to turn the key. "Can't even walk in the garden. . . ."

The key finally turned and he led her into a large cool foyer. It was an extention of the garden: strelitzias grew out of copper vases and maiden-hair ferns trailed around antique tables. Riena thought of Ma's Brook Street house. Three generations sleeping in one room no larger than this entrance hall; a sewing machine instead of an antique table. Nothing much else. Except the smell of poverty and despair in place of the scent of flowers.

"Come, Elizabeth. Do they call you Bessie, by the way? I'll take you to Emily. I'm thirsty as the devil; don't know where she was with morning tea, that cousin of yours." He peered at her. "You look as if you could do with a cup of something yourself, young lady. Probably something to eat, too. You're too thin by a long shot."

The man's kindness served to increase Riena's sense of discomfort. She was an intruder, an imposter, and with Barnard around she was sure to be discovered. According to Tom, Nkolosi had prearranged everything. Emily was to have been gone when she, Riena—Elizabeth Riess—arrived. She couldn't see why the Cohns would ask her to be her "cousin's" replacement if Emily was still around. What if Nkolosi's plan had misfired and Emily *was* fine? What would she say when she was introduced to a total stranger purporting to be a relative?

"Move, girl," Barnard said, prodding her to walk ahead of him. "My brother-in-law won't thank either of us if our conversation wakes him. This is the one day he gets to sleep late."

248

Riena took a few steps forward and stopped. Oh God, she thought, what if Nkolosi has "taken care of" Emily? What would they find in the kitchen? She glanced over her shoulder at Barnard and again found him staring at her, frowning deeply as if he were trying to trigger some response that was just barely out of reach. He looked pained and Riena found herself feeling sorry for him. She had to subdue an urge to confess.

"Piet? That you?"

The voice was a woman's.

"Yes, Mickey."

"I could have sworn I heard you talking to someone. Is Art up?"

"I was talking to a friend of Emily's—a cousin."

"Another cousin?" The owner of the voice walked into the passageway. She wore a ceremonial silk kimono and her hair was carelessly knotted in the nape of her neck. "Thanks to Emily, I overslept," she said. "I can't imagine what happened to my morning tea. Did you get yours?"

"No. And I'm thirsty as. . . ."

"Not surprising, given the amount of alcohol you consumed last night, brother. Sorry about the tea; Emily's been acting most peculiarly of late. She was never overly efficient but she was always reliable."

She rambled on, taking no notice whatsoever of Riena.

"I suppose a constant run of cousins is better than the funerals we had to accept from our last girl," she said. "I haven't heard her this morning at all. Dammit, there were things I wanted to do early. . . ."

". . . Mickey, this is Elizabeth." Barnard, tired of waiting for a pause, interrupted his sister's patter.

"How d'you do, Elizabeth. Would you like to go outside, Piet—never mind. I'd better do it myself. Bessie, why don't you wait in the kitchen. I'll see if I can find your 'cousin.' Better than another male 'cousin' I suppose. That last one, the Zulu boy who's been hanging around, made me nervous. I don't think he was doing Emily any good. . . ."

Still jabbering, Michelle Cohn disappeared. Riena, not quite knowing what to say in her wake, followed Barnard into the kitchen. It was empty.

"She means well," Barnard said. He was referring, Riena supposed, to his garrulous and not overly tactful sister.

"How would you like to make tea, Bessie?" Barnard asked, pleasantly enough. "I'll show you where to find everything."

"Certainly, Master Barnard."

"Good. But for heaven's sake don't call me 'Master.' I've had enough of that to last me a lifetime. And listen, if you'd rather not be called Bessie, say so. My sister tends to make assumptions."

"It doesn't matter," Riena said, filling the kettle. Barnard picked up the tray that had been prepared the night before to ease the serving of early morning tea. He removed a beadtrimmed doily from the sugar bowl and the tea-cosy from the teapot.

"Wait. You haven't warmed the pot," Riena said as he started to spoon tea leaves into the silver urn. The entire set was solid silver and embossed with a crest.

Barnard laughed. "I'm not too good at this domestic stuff," he said, taking three cups and saucers from one cupboard and adding two mugs from another.

The servants' cups, Riena thought, wondering what breed of germs the family expected to inherit from their staff. She swirled hot water inside the teapot and started to spoon in the tea.

"Piet! For godsake wake Arthur and get him out here."

Michelle Cohn sounded near hysteria. Riena jumped and the tea leaves spilled onto the counter and the floor. She looked around for a sponge, determined to stop herself from shaking before Barnard noticed.

"What is it, Mickey? Calm down and tell me what's wrong."

"Just get Arthur, will you. It's Emily. Oh, God. . . ." Her voice rose several decibels. "I don't know what's wrong with her but whatever it is . . . Maybe you can help. You're one of her kind."

It took Riena a moment to realize that Barnard had left the room. Since she was the only one left there, Mrs. Cohn had to be speaking to her.

"Come with me."

Under normal circumstances, Riena would surely have resented the woman's imperious tone and implied insult. Now, she followed her outdoors to the servants' quarters with only one thought in mind—whatever it was that had happened to Emily, it was Nkolosi's doing. She felt fear and a sense of responsibility but overriding any of that was a detached admiration for the witch-doctor's power. Rather a friend than an enemy, she thought. Or at least ally, since only the Negwenya could be Nkolosi's playmate.

Suddenly Riena heard a shrill sound, so like a high pitched whistle that she turned around to go back to the kitchen and remove the kettle from the stove, assuming she had forgotten to turn it off in her haste to do as she'd been told.

"Come on, girl," Michelle Cohn commanded.

"The kettle. . . ."

". . . That's not the kettle. It's coming from there." She pointed at a small concrete building that faced the garden. "The door's on the other side. . . ."

It came again, thin and sharp, a stiletto transformed into sound. Mortally afraid of what she would find but equally terrified of not looking, Riena increased her pace. "Damn you, Nkolosi," she said, approaching the open door of the small building. "Damn you to hell."

2

"Well, what are you waiting for? Go inside." Michelle Cohn sounded annoyed. She was standing in the middle of the cement area that separated the main house from the servants' quarters, her hands on her hips and a look of exasperation on her face. "Let's find out what's going on."

Riena took a step into the room. She breathed in and gagged. The smell attacked her as if it were a physical entity. It was putrid. Rotten. Like the strange bandage she'd pulled off her arm that first morning in Tom's house and tossed into the corner.

"Aaiee . . . Aaiee . . . Aaiee."

The cadence came from a shapeless, swaying form that huddled in the center of the one-room house. The light from the open doorway was not enough to combat the darkness inside. Riena had to wait for her eyes to adjust from the strong sunlight.

"Emily?"

"Aaiee . . . Aaiee . . . Aaiee."

The genuflecting shape swayed back and forth in rhythmic patterns before two yellow candle eyes that burned low to the ground. Whether or not the form was female was impossible to tell. To say that it was human was pure assumption. There was a blanket draped where it's head and shoulders should have been, apparently stripped from the mattress that stood propped against the window to shut out the daylight. What little furniture there was had been stacked against the walls, leaving the floor clear but for the creature, its fire, and a circular kneeling pad. Now that Riena's eyes had made the necessary adjustment, she could see that the woven straw mat was disfigured by ugly dark stains.

Tentatively, not at all confident that she wasn't in any physical danger, Riena edged around the figure toward the mattress. She struggled with it, wondering how Emily had managed to lift it on her own; it was coir and far too heavy for one woman to move. She must have had help, Riena thought. But from whom? Nkolosi? The Negwenya? She glanced at the strange shadows being cast by the candles and looked quickly away, although not so quickly that she failed to notice that the figure had stopped swaying.

Setting her shoulder against the mattress, Riena heaved. The mattress moved enough to allow a beam of light to shine on the figure that crouched for an instant longer and then sprang. Like a huge cat. Reaching out its nails and clawing at Riena—the intruder. Catching Riena's cheek before it landed and preparing to spring again.

Riena, who had fallen back against the mattress, tried to regain her balance. Before she could do so, she and Emily were grappling again. Or at least Emily was grappling. Hard as she tried, there was no way Riena seemed able to get a handhold on her attacker. The woman kept slipping away under her grasp.

But Emily's best weapon, the one that finally defeated Riena, was her odor. It seemed to cut off her breathing and she had no choice but to back away. As she did so, she saw why it had been so difficult to defend herself; Emily was stark naked except for a coil of beadwork around her neck. The smell that had so sickened Riena had come from the series of rust colored streaks that crusted Emily's body. Even her head had been shaved and it, too, was covered by the same dark blotches. Dried blood, Riena thought, wanting instinctively to look for an animal carcass but afraid to take her eyes off Emily for even an instant.

"Emily! Stop!" Riena, panting from the exertion, rested her back against the far wall of the room. "I want to help you."

Emily was on her hands and knees now, scrambling across the floor, stopping intermittently to scan the room. Then, still crawling, she moved to a corner and retrieved an object that was hidden behind the open door.

Whatever it was, Emily clutched it to her breast and huddled in the corner, pressing herself against it as if she were trying to become part of the wall. Looking up at Riena, her eyes like a wounded Springbok, she began to sway as she had done before.

Watching her, waiting for the keening to begin again, Riena saw herself after the explosion at the jail, stripped of her prison clothes and huddled naked in the corner of her cell. She had felt as if all dignity had been removed from her, too. Picking up the blanket that had fallen from Emily's shoulders and no longer afraid, she wrapped it around the woman. Emily didn't resist; her eyes were unseeing and her body was dripping with a mixture of her own sweat and the muck with which she had covered herself. Again, Riena saw herself in that cell, surrounded by the dead and the dying. Now she was wrapped in a grey woolen prison blanket, staring at the hole that had been blown in the outer wall of her cell—trying to care enough about living to walk out of that hole and away from the prison. Pregnant. Feeling the child move inside her and, for a moment, caring so much that she had to leave. Stumbling over a body and pieces of bodies in her haste to leave before she was tempted to kneel and examine the stiffening corpse of a friend. Pausing neither for mourning or goodbyes, she'd stepped over it, the cement floor rough against her bare feet. . . .

"Aaiee . . . Aaiee . . . Aaiee."

Gently, the woman placed the object she'd been holding against her own cheek, patting and stroking it. Riena, still kneeling in front of her after having wrapped her in the blanket, at last recognized the object—or what was left of it. It was split wide open, and most of its rainbow beading was gone, but the object Emily was fondling was a Sotho wedding doll. The kind young Sotho brides carried to their marriage ceremony in place of bouquets.

254

Riena tried to picture Emily the maiden, on her wedding day. She looked at the remains of the cone shaped doll, held together by the pressure of Emily's fingers. Though it had started out legless and armless, as tradition demanded, it had been lovingly beaded by the bride's mother. Her wishes for her daughter's future spelled out in the number of beads and the sequence of colors. And the doll had once had a head . . . and two copper earrings. . . .

"What's all this flap about?"

A man Riena hadn't seen before stood in the doorway. He wore a dressing gown and slippers, and his greying hair was unkempt. Though he looked half asleep, his voice was well controlled and there was an air about him of a man who was used to dealing with emergencies. Arthur Cohn, newsman, Riena thought.

"Jesus," he said. "This room smells like the bottom of a bloody parrot's cage—a dead parrot. Girl—whatever your name is—open the windows."

Riena, still squatting on the floor near Emily, struggled to her feet.

"Emily? Emily, can you hear me?" Cohn said.

The young Sotho woman rocked on her heels. "Aaiee . . . Aaiee . . . Aaiee."

"Stop that caterwauling and come out here." The words were tough but his tone lacked anger.

Emily enclosed the doll in her arms aand rocked it like an infant.

"I think you'd better call an ambulance, Sir," Riena said, walking toward him. He stood aside to let her out of the house.

"What's your name, girl?"

"Bessie," Michelle Cohn said. "She's Emily's cousin."

"Elizabeth," Riena said. "Elizabeth Riess."

"What's the matter with your cousin, Elizabeth? Has she been swilling *skokiaan?*"

"I don't think so, Sir."

"Then what the hell *is* wrong with her?"

Riena shrugged. There was no way on earth that she could explain, she thought. How could she tell this placid White man that her "cousin" was acting like a lunatic because the mutilated cone-shaped object in her arms symbolized a child, Emily's child. That somewhere, in a world apart from servants and morning tea, the doll had been her wedding bouquet? That the doll had a name and that Emily's firstborn bore that name? They probably didn't even know that she was married, these Europeans. Why should they care that she was separated from her child, the way Riena was from her son? Well, you see, Master Cohn, she imagined herself saying. That doll Emily's holding reflects the state of health of her own child. As it is mutilated, so Nkolosi has . . . Nkolosi? Oh, he's the witchdoctor who's done this to her. To her child. Or maybe the child's been adopted by the Negwenya. Who's that? That's easy too. She's a dragon, folks. Nkolosi's Mata Hari. You see, that's why I'm here. I'm not really Emily's cousin. They've threatened my child, too, so I've come to. . . .

"Call an ambulance," Cohn said to his brother-in-law. "This girl obviously doesn't know any more about this than we do."

"Why not," Barnard said. "I'm getting to be an expert at calling ambulances. Twice in one damn week. Want me to call the police too?"

"Do that, Piet," his sister said. "And you, Bessie. Elizabeth. Would you be kind enough to try to get some clothes on that creature in there. You should probably hose her down first. Hose down the room while you're about it and take everything that belongs to her and bundle it all up in one of her blankets. I don't want them to leave anything behind when they take her away. *All* I need is for her to come back here. . . ."

". . . She's probably harmless, Mickey," her husband said.

"Harmless? Look at the scratches on this girl's face. Did she do that to you?"

Riena touched her cheek. It felt ridged and her hand came away bloody.

"It's nothing, Madam," she said. "Could I ask. . . . Where will they take her?"

"Aaiee . . . Aaiee . . . Aaiee."

"I have no idea. What do you think, Art? Art? Where did he go?"

"In there," Riena said, pointing in Emily's direction.

"He mustn't touch her. Don't let him touch her. Get him out of there," she said, pushing Riena toward the door.

Reluctantly, Riena went back inside. Arthur Cohn was kneeling in front of Emily, much as she herself had done earlier. The woman hadn't changed position. She was still clutching the doll to her breast. Rocking and keening. Her eyes no more aware than they had been.

"Emily? It's Master Cohn. Let me help you, please." He put his hands on her upper arms and very gently began to raise her off the floor.

"Don't touch her, Arthur," his wife screamed. "They'll blame you. . . ."

Her husband's look silenced her. Emily increased her pitch. "Aaiee . . . Aaiee . . . Aaiee." Louder. And then louder still. Struggling now to free herself from the hands that were interrupting the rhythm of her movements.

Cohn released her. Her body folded into its original position and her "Aaiee . . . Aaiee . . . Aaiee" slowly decreased in volume.

"Did you see her eyes?" Cohn pleaded, turning to Riena. "They look . . . dead. And what's she smeared herself with? It looks like caked. . . ."

". . . Blood, Sir."

Cohn paled. "Whose blood?"

"Do you think she could have been raped?" his wife asked. "The new garden boy . . . or that Zulu . . . John. I knew I didn't like the looks of him."

Let them believe Emily had been raped, Riena thought. What difference could it make—unless they directly accused the Zulu. The idea of a Zulu committing rape was preposterous. His pride would never allow it—and a Zulu's pride was more valuable to him than his life.

"Whose blood?" Cohn repeated.

"Some animal, Sir."

"But why, in God's name?"

"You know, Arthur, I don't think it was rape," Michelle Cohn said slowly.

"Why?"

"It's something that's been coming on for a while. You wouldn't have noticed, you've been so busy since you came back from the U.N., but she hasn't been herself for days."

"Why didn't you say anything?"

"I thought it would pass. I don't understand these people anyway."

"Is she right, Elizabeth?" Cohn asked, looking embarrassed, as if the question were sheer foolishness.

"I . . . don't know, Sir."

"What about the blood? Why would she do something like that?"

"Some . . . people . . . believe it protects them."

"From what? Evil spirits?" He paused. "Dear God, I don't believe I'm even asking these questions. All I can say is I'm glad our guest changed his mind about staying with us. Coming to South Africa for a UJA Rally is one thing; getting involved in this kind of thing is another. I can just see Moshe Dayan waiting around for some attention while I. . . ."

". . . Why did he change his mind, Art?" his wife asked.

"I'm not sure. Something about security." He glanced at Riena as if he didn't want to say any more in front of her.

Could a rumor about the AFI plot have leaked out, she wondered, dismissing the idea at once as impossible. If Nkolosi had enough control to reach out across a thousand miles and do what he had done to Emily, he could surely discern a traitor in the ranks. So Moshe Dayan had been the distinguished guest of whom Tom had spoken, she thought, wondering how Nkolosi would take the news that the Israeli had changed his mind about staying with the Cohns. It was comforting to know that there were things over which Nkolosi had no control.

"Let's go outside," Cohn said to Riena. "I can't bear this smell a moment longer. She'll be all right alone for the time being."

Riena followed him out. Barnard had returned from making his telephone call.

"Are they coming?" Cohn asked.

"They said they'd be here in a few minutes," his brother-in-law said.

"The police too?"

"I asked for a police ambulance."

"They're usually pretty efficient around here," Cohn said. "How did you discover her, Mickey?"

"She didn't bring morning tea, did she, Piet? I went to look for her and. . . ."

"I feel like a hex," Barnard said. He looked at Riena and she thought she saw him pale and start to say something. To her intense relief, a siren coming up the hill precluded further conversation. It had been less than five minutes since Barnard had called them; he had to have used the right buzz words to get them to move that fast, she thought.

"I told them to come around the back of the house," Barnard said, seeing his brother-in-law walk toward the gate that separated the front and back gardens.

"I might as well show them the way," Cohn said, disappearing from sight. In a moment he reappeared, followed by a policeman and two Black ambulance attendants who were carrying a stretcher.

"In there," Cohn said, pointing at the little house.

The policeman followed them inside.

"Aaiee . . . Aaiee . . . Aaiagh."

The cries rang out one more time, the last one dying in Emily's throat. It wasn't long before the two Black men were carrying her out, strapped to the stretcher. One of them turned his head and spat. "*Nkau,*" he said. "Monkey!" He was holding his neck with his free hand.

"She attacked me, so I had to knock her out," he said.

"You did the right thing," Michelle Cohn said. Neither her husband nor her brother said anything.

Riena was relieved to see that Emily had been covered by a sheet. She wanted to ask if the doll was underneath it but she dared not draw attention to herself while the policeman was around. What if she were asked to show her papers? What if there was something wrong and he asked her to come along to headquarters? The Cohns would find someone else to take Emily's place and . . . With a great deal of effort, she kept herself from moving forward to look beneath the sheet.

"I blew out the candles," the Afrikaner policeman said, coming out of the room. "The place stinks; you'll have to air it out, Sir." The other two men stopped and put down the stretcher. "Go on. Move it," the policeman said. "We haven't got all day." They moved on and he turned to Arthur Cohn. "You'd better get yourself a new girl."

"She'll be all right, won't she?" Michelle Cohn said.

"No, Mrs. Cohn."

"Where will you take her?"

"To their hospital. They'll keep her for a while and then send her back to the *kraal*."

"Who'll look after her there?"

"Her family. Maybe. Or maybe they'll just let her starve to death."

"Are you sure she won't recover?"

"We see this kind of thing all the time," the policeman said.

"*Dagga?*"

"Not *dagga* . . . or liquor."

"What then?" Cohn asked, ignoring his wife's "I told you so" look.

"You might not believe this, Sir. Ask her if you don't believe me." He nodded in Riena's direction. "It's witchcraft, Sir. Voodoo—if you know what I mean."

"Why would anyone want to use voodoo on our Emily?" Mrs. Cohn asked.

"Michelle!" Arthur Cohn looked astonished. "You can't possibly believe that there's any truth in that nonsense."

"It's true. *Wraggies*—really," the man assured him. "Doesn't take much to make them revert, Mr. Cohn, Sir. See this?" He reached into his pocket and pulled out Emily's wedding doll. MIchelle Cohn took a step backwards.

"What's that?"

The policeman grinned. "I believe this is how they punish their wives for adultery, Mrs. Cohn," he said, looking as if he felt very important now that he was center stage. He included Arthur Cohn in a conspiratorial wink that incorporated a special union of all of the husbands of the world. "Looks like her husband found out. Instead of beating her up like I'd do to my *vrou,* he takes it out on their kid. I suppose when they have so many, one more or less doesn't matter."

Riena was amazed that the man had recognized the doll as anything more than a piece of trash. Now if he'll return it to Emily, she thought, it won't matter that he has the story wrong.

"You don't mind if I take this with me, do you?" the man said, shattering Riena's hopes. Without the doll in her possession, there was indeed no chance for Emily.

"Take it, the ugly thing," Mrs. Cohn said.

"Why would you want it?" her husband asked.

"Good way to keep my wife in line, Sir. Kid, too. Better get going now."

"Thank you for getting here so fast," Arthur Cohn called out to his retreating figure.

"You're very welcome, Sir. Glad to help," the policeman said, his hand on the gate.

"Arthur, tell him to let us know how she is," Michelle Cohn said. "If they send her home, we can give her some money, I wouldn't want them to let her die."

"I'll keep track of her," her husband said.

Riena heard the clanging of a metal door and an engine starting up. Not knowing what else to do, she followed the Cohns and Piet Barnard into the kitchen. The tea tray was standing where she'd left it.

"How would you like a job?" Mrs. Cohn asked. She refilled the kettle and put it on the stove. "Or are you

261

working for someone else? We'll pay you more. . . ."

". . . I'd like to work for you, Madam," Riena said.

"Good. I suppose you have references?"

Riena handed over the letters that Tom had given her; they identified her as Elizabeth Riess.

"These look fine." Michelle Cohn expressed no surprise that Riena had the references handy. "Let's see, I think that should do it. You're Coloured so you don't need a Pass."

"You can use Emily's clothes for now but her uniforms might not fit you properly—you're such a skinny little thing. Still, I suppose they'll do until I can get you your own. Let's see, Emily's were blue but I think black and white for you."

She stood back and examined the merchandise she'd acquired and Riena almost expected to be asked to show her teeth.

"Yes, black and white. Where are your things, by the way?"

"My friend, the one who brought me here, has them in his car, Madam."

"Was he supposed to come for you later?"

"Yes, Madam," Riena said. When Tom didn't show up later, Mrs. Cohn would have little difficulty believing that he had simply let her down.

"Well, I suppose that's that, then, Elizabeth. Welcome to the family." Mrs. Cohn looked pleased with herself, and Riena hoped she was displaying the right amount of gratitude. "Now be a good girl. Slip into one of Emily's uniforms and help me with breakfast," she went on, "and don't forget to wash your hands."

3

Every now and then, while they prepared breakfast, Mrs. Cohn stepped back to look at Riena and smile. It was as if she had bought a new mix master at a bargain price and had to keep reassuring herself that she'd been as astute as she remembered. When her husband wandered into the kitchen to see how the meal was progressing, she said: "Elizabeth's going to stay and work for us. Isn't she pretty, Art?"

"She reminds me of Shari," Cohn said.

"You can't mean our Shari? Our daughter?"

"That's exactly who I mean."

"But Elizabeth's. . . ."

". . . Coloured. Yes, I know. All the same, there's something about her. Bone structure, maybe. Don't worry," he said, seeing the look of consternation on his wife's face. "I really don't think those old stories about your father are true. . . ."

He jumped out of the way as his wife pretended to attack him with a spoon.

"There's been quite enough violence around here for one day," he said, backing out of the room.

"Have you been attacking my brother-in-law again," Barnard said, walking in as Cohn departed.

"Can you imagine. He thinks Elizabeth here looks like Shari. *Our* Shari.

"He's bringing up those old stories about Daddy. . . ."

". . . Come on, Mickey. He's just teasing you. Then again, maybe that's why I keep thinking I've seen the girl somewhere before." He began counting off on his fingers and his sister lunged at him. He dodged out of the way. "Elizabeth. What's your mother's name?"

"Maria, Sir."

"Oh. That's not the name I had in mind."

"That's my adoptive mother," Riena said, trying not to mind what was going on. "My natural mother's name was Sarah."

Barnard looked almost disappointed. "That's that, then," he said. "Wait a minute." He appeared to be doing a calculation in his head. "Your grandmother. What was her name?"

"Evvy."

"Mickey. Remember that nanny we had on the farm when I was about ten. . . ."

". . . Hand me a couple more eggs, will you, Piet. I don't think I scrambled quite enough of them and they need to sit in the fridge for a while before we cook them," his sister said. Her eyes told him there was no way she would continue the discussion about their father.

"What do you think, Mickey?" Barnard said, ignoring her signals.

By the looks of his sister, Riena thought, Pieter Barnard was extremely fortunate that at that moment, the doorbell rang.

"Answer it, girl," Mrs. Cohn said.

Answer it yourself, Riena thought. But she did as she was told. Before she had a chance to actually open the door, a woman's voice called out: "Hurry up, will you. It's Anne."

"Sorry, Madam. I was in the kitchen," Riena said, opening the door.

Without a second glance, the woman strode inside. "Where's my husband?" She sounded thoroughly infuriated.

"Anne! What are you doing here? Piet's around somewhere." Michelle hugged the woman, her expression hovering between surprise and pleasure. Her husband, behind her, looked shocked.

"He'd better be around. I have a few things I want to say to him."

"Anne?" Piet Barnard walked into the foyer which

264

despite its generous size, was beginning to feel crowded. "What are you doing here?"

"I didn't think a note from you was a quite adequate farewell after twenty years so I spent a sleepless night and then decided to follow you here. Pay the taxi will you, Art. He's waiting outside; I left Cape Town without cashing a check."

"I'll go," Barnard said.

He looked like an animal who couldn't wait to be released from his cage, Riena thought. As for Mrs. Barnard, she looked amazingly well groomed for a woman who hadn't slept and had been traveling for hours.

"No you don't," Anne Barnard said, putting a hand on her husband's arm to stop him leaving. "You're likely to drive off with him."

"Anne!" her sister-in-law reprimanded. "Calm down." Then, noticing that Riena was still there, "Elizabeth. Make some fresh tea, would you please."

"Where's Emily?"

"It's a long story, Anne," Michelle said, taking her arm. "Come into the lounge. Have a cup of tea. . . ."

". . . You and your infernal cups of tea, Michelle. Get me a brandy."

"Isn't it a bit early in the day?" her husband said.

"That isn't any of your business anymore, is it? You left me," Anne Barnard said. Taking her sister-in-law's arm, she stalked off.

"I didn't leave you, Anne. All I did was. . . ." Barnard stopped. His wife and sister were out of sight.

Riena retreated to the kitchen and filled the kettle one more time. Though she didn't know for sure why Barnard's wife was so furious with him, she suspected it was far more complex than his having left to visit his sister and brother-in-law without asking her to go with him. Tom had told her about the warden's preemptory resignation and about the empathy he'd felt in the man. While she'd been in jail, she'd heard rumors about him. Talk that he sometimes ignored small infractions of the rules, that he felt sympathy for the underdog, that he

265

took prisoner requests seriously. One of her cell mates had once returned from a parole hearing and told her that she and the warden had shared an elevator. Her friend had boldly straddled the corner under the 'Whites Only' sign, defying the warden to complain and send her to a non-European elevator. He'd noticed all right but he hadn't complained.

"If I came here all the way from Barchester Towers, you can bloody well listen to me," she heard Anne Barnard yelling.

"Quiet, Anne. Do you want the whole world to. . . ."

". . . To what? Hear your wife call you a *kaffir boetie?* I don't give a damn who hears. Watch me, I'll tell the whole world."

Anne Barnard strode through the kitchen with her husband trailing after her. She slammed out of the back door. He opened it quietly and followed. She'd called him *kaffir boetie,* Riena thought. *Kaffir* brother. Friend of the Black man.

"I felt responsible so I resigned," Barnard said. The kitchen window was wide open and Riena could hear the conversation clearly. "You were furious, so I came here to give us both time to get over it."

"*You* felt responsible?" Anne was speaking slowly now, enunciating her words carefully, as if her husband were hard of hearing. Her Afrikaans accent became more pronounced. "Why on earth did you let it bother you, Piet? I don't understand," she went on.

"Not understanding is one thing. Throwing things around in a drunken rage is another."

"Were you mad because I broke your precious Mommy's Cheval Mirror," Anne said, "or does my drinking embarrass you?"

"Yes, it embarrasses me."

"Well what you did embarrassed me, Piet. I like my status as your wife. And I don't believe you resigned because a few *kaffirs* got blown up. That had nothing to do with you. Why did you really have the guilts, Piet?" She paused. "Were you fucking one of your little Col-

266

oured inmates? Is that it? You and your Daddy—two of a kind. Or did you have something to do with the explosion? Did you light the bloody fuse yourself to get rid of some dirty evidence?''

There was a prolonged silence.

"Answer me," Anne Barnard screamed. "I asked if you lit that bloody fuse yourself?"

She's really rolling now, Riena thought, feeling extremely sorry for Pieter Barnard.

"I always suspected those stories about your father were true," the woman yelled.

"Anne. Why don't you get some rest? You're tired. Can't we talk about this later. When you're more rational."

Her husband's sensible tone apparently enraged Anne still further. "Now," she screamed. "I want to know now. Are you going to apologize—to me and to your bosses—and go back to your job? Because if you aren't. . . ."

"Elizabeth. I think you should go and clean out that room now," Michelle Cohn said, walking into the kitchen.

"You make me sick, Piet," Anne Barnard shouted.

Mrs. Cohn strode over to the window. "Hey, you two. They can hear you across the valley." She pointed in the direction of the outlying suburbs.

"Shut up, Mickey," Anne said.

Michelle closed the window. "The breakfast's ruined," she said, as if everything were normal. "I guess it's going to have to be each man for himself. By the way, will fifty Rands a month be satisfactory?"

Riena nodded. She was tempted to make a counter offer to see how high Michelle Cohn was prepared to go but she stopped herself. Fifty Rands, she thought. She remembered asking Jake what full-time servants were paid in America and being astounded at his answer. What Mrs. Cohn was offering her was the equivalent of sixty dollars a month—less than the amount an American housekeeper earned in a week.

"What else would you like me to do today, Madam?"

"Let's see—the house is in fairly good shape. Why don't you clean up the kitchen, do the beds and run over the bathrooms. It'll take you the rest of the day to scrub down Emily's room. Your room now."

Riena looked at the clock on the wall. It was already noon.

"Where were you going after your visit with poor Emily?" Mrs. Cohn asked.

"My friend was going to pick me up here. We were going. . . ."

". . . Why don't you go with him when he comes," Mrs. Cohn said. "It is Saturday, after all. I'm sure we'll be going out, too." She looked out of the window. "I think we'll be going out."

"What about tomorrow, Madam?"

"I'll need you to make morning tea at eight. You can stay for breakfast and then take off again. We'll start a proper routine on Monday—morning tea at six and a full day. Thursday will be your regular day off during the week."

Since Nkolosi's plans weren't going into effect until Monday, why couldn't he have allowed her to arrive at the Cohns' one day later, Riena thought. Emily would have had an extra day of sanity and she'd have had one more day with Tom. Now she was going to have all of those hours with nothing to do; she hadn't brought so much as a book.

"Could I borrow something to read, please, Madam?"

"There are some magazines in the bathroom. I've finished with them."

"May I borrow a book, please?"

"A book?" Mrs. Cohn looked as if she had asked for a bottle of gin. "A book—of course. Take anything you like. We don't have too much light reading around but you'll find something."

"Thank you, Madam."

"I think you're going to work out just fine, Elizabeth," Michelle Cohn said. "Let me know if there's anything you need. Help yourself to a sandwich for lunch; there's servants' meat in the freezer if you're around at

268

suppertime."

An hour later, Riena was ready to tackle Emily's quarters. She closed the kitchen door behind her, glad that the Barnards had gone inside to do their fighting in private. Emily's quarters weren't all that bad, she thought. Though it was only a nine by twelve concrete room, the building was close enough to the laundry and the servants' bathroom to have made Emily's winter mornings bearable, on those days when the Transvaal cold made straight for one's marrow. But the best thing about her temporary home, Riena thought, was that the door faced away from the main house. Should Tom decide to visit her after all . . . she stopped herself. There was no point in thinking about it; he was not going to come. She was going to have to see this one through alone.

4

After Riena had hosed down Emily's quarters, she washed everything she could find. By the time she was finished, she was exhausted. Because she knew it was going to be a long day and an even longer night, she tried to look upon the whole process as occupational therapy, but that did not stop her being pleased when she was done. She was standing back surveying the results when Michelle Cohn came out to tell her that they were, after all, going out for dinner; she brought with her a radio and a plate of leftover sandwiches.

"I'll leave the laundry and bathroom unlocked for you. You'll find clean sheets and blankets in there," she said. "The rest of the house will be locked. We need you, Elizabeth, so eat these sandwiches, will you." She looked around. "You've done a terrific job. Terrific."

When she'd gone, Riena lay down on the bed. She left the door open so that she could watch Johannesburg's daily summer thunderstorm pulling the clouds together. There was something satisfying about the certainty of knowing that for ten minutes the rain would pour down and then it would all be over. The sun would come out again and the smell of clean grass and trees would enter the room to dilute the Dettol that she'd used as disinfectant.

Slowly at first, and then so fast that Riena hardly knew it had happened, it grew dark outside. Down in the valley, the suburban lights came on, warming the darkness. Soon, she slept. When she woke, it was seven o'clock on Sunday morning. She groaned and turned over. She was disoriented and hungry, but not quite hungry enough to reach for the plate of food Mrs. Cohn had given her; it lay shrivelled and untouched, the edges of the bread dry and curling away from the bologna filling that had hardened overnight.

Time for morning tea, Riena thought, forcing herself out of bed. The one good thing about her old dissipated life, she thought, had been the hours she'd kept—late nights and early mornings. That had definitely suited her better than this. She tried to figure out how she could walk across the yard and shower before dressing. There was no robe around and no coat she could use as a substitute. And she needed a shower. Badly. Compromising, she grabbed underwear, slipped on a uniform, and went across as quickly as she could.

She felt better when she was clean and dressed. She'd been told that summer breakfasts at the Cohns were generally served on the terrace at the side of the house, so she strolled over there before knocking at the kitchen door. One end of the terrace had the same view as the front of Emily's quarters: Johannesburg spread itself across the valley and a cloudless sky gave promise of a perfect day. The rolling lawns, spread out directly below her, were the Transvaal's testimony to its daily summer showers and to the gardener's efficiency. She pictured a cutglass vase of yellow roses centering the breakfast table and wondered if she'd get into trouble for picking them without permission. She grinned. As long as she was going to play servant, she thought, she might as well do the job properly.

"There's nothing like an electric storm to clear the air, is there?"

Riena turned around. "Good morning, Mr. Barnard," she said.

"Good morning, Elizabeth." He walked up to her and stood beside her. He looked, she thought, as if he hadn't slept much.

"I used to be very scared of thunderstorms when I was little," Riena said.

"I lived on a farm," Barnard said. "If you think they sounded frightening in the city, you should have heard them out there in the country. I miss them all the same."

"Where do you live now, Sir?" Riena asked, playing the game.

"In Cape Town. We have Southeasters there but it's not the same."

"I'd better go inside and make tea," Riena said.

Barnard nodded. "I left the door unlocked. I'll have mine out here, please."

It took Riena no time at all to prepare the tea tray; by the time the water was boiling, Michelle Cohn had joined her.

"Good morning, Em . . . Elizabeth. I'm glad you didn't oversleep, I'm dying for my tea."

"Good morning, Madam. What time would you like breakfast?" Riena said, wondering if her enthusiasm sounded as phony to Michelle Cohn as it did to her.

"Not before half past nine," Mrs. Cohn said. She opened a new package of Marie Biscuits and nibbled at the edges of a cookie. "Meals are a little haphazard around here on Sundays. Are you going to visit Emily in the hospital later?"

Riena thought quickly. "I'm afraid of hospitals, Madam," she said, hoping the excuse sounded believable.

"Well, I did say you could have the day off. . . ."

Taking the cue, Riena offered to stay and help out.

271

"You're sure?"

Riena nodded.

"We don't usually entertain on Sundays but we're having a special guest to dinner. If you could stay . . . you're sure you don't mind?"

"I'm sure, Madam."

"Our guest is Moshe Dayan. Do you know who he is?"

"Yes, Madam." The guest Tom had mentioned was to have been Moshe Dayan, Riena thought, impressed. "He fights for the Jews," she said.

"I suppose that's as good a description as any," Mrs. Cohn said, looking surprised that Riena knew the name. "Now don't be frightened by the guards who come with him. He's a very important man. . . ."

The doorbell rang.

"Who on earth would that be at this hour of the morning?" Mrs. Cohn said.

Riena started for the door.

"Don't bother. I'll get it." There was another ring and a moment's silence. "Shari. Pussycat. Is anything wrong? What are you doing here at this hour? Come in, come in. I'll wake your father."

"Don't, Mom. I'll stay for a while . . . if you'll give me a cup of coffee."

"Tea's ready."

"You and your tea, Mother! I drink coffee, remember?"

"Too much of it, if you ask me," her mother said. "And you're smoking again."

"Mother!"

"I'm sorry. It's so good to see you, darling."

They walked into the kitchen hand in hand, the mother tall and lanky, the daughter petite and built more like her father who was a half a head shorter than his wife. She looked no more than in her early twenties, Riena thought, taking in this new member of the family. Her hair was drawn back and tied with a light green scarf that was almost the color of her eyes, and her hiphugging jeans looked European and expensive. The skin revealed by her midriff top was deeply tanned.

"Where's Emily?" the young woman asked.

"This is Elizabeth. I'll tell you about Emily later."

"Hello, Elizabeth. I'm Shari." Her smile was genuine.

"*Miss* Shari's my daughter," Michelle Cohn said.

"It's Shari, and you remind me of someone, Elizabeth."

So this was Shari, Riena thought, looking more closely at the shape of the girl's face, at the slight build and narrow wrists and ankles. They were right, she decided, mentally superimposing her own high cheekbones on Shari's face. Were it not for that particular legacy from her own mother, she thought, the two of them might well have been sisters—or cousins at least.

"We're picking up Dayan later to take him to the Mine Dances. And your Aunt Anne and Uncle Piet are here," Mrs. Cohn said.

"Dayan? *The* Dayan?"

"*The* Dayan."

"You're being very casual about it, aren't you? But then I don't know why I'm surprised; you and Daddy are always picking up famous strays."

"Come with us, Shari. Your father would be so pleased."

Shari hesitated and looked at Riena. "Tell you what," she said slowly. "If we can take Elizabeth with us, I'll come."

"Shari!" Her mother looked thoroughly exasperated. "Do you always have to start something? Why would Elizabeth want to come?"

"For the same reason we want to go—to see the Dances. What you really mean is that you'd prefer it if she stays here in the kitchen."

"It's all right," Riena said. "I don't. . . ."

". . . You'll come with us." Mrs. Cohn's tone brooked no argument.

Shari smiled at Riena, as if they were co-conspirators. Afraid that she might upset Mrs. Cohn, Riena only half returned the smile.

"Tea ready?" Piet Barnard asked, walking into the un-

273

comfortable silence. He seemed genuinely pleased to see Shari. "My favorite niece," he said, kissing her. "What an unexpected pleasure." He stood back and looked from her to Riena. "I was right, wasn't I, Mickey? Now that I see the two of them together, I know I'm right."

"I don't want to hear any more of that nonsense. Are you coming with us to the Mine Dances?"

"If Anne wants to go."

"She has a headache."

"Well, maybe I'll come anyway. I do want to visit Dad this afternoon. I could take my own car and go straight from there to the farm."

"I saw the old bugger last weekend. He's as difficult as ever."

"Is he really that bad?"

"I've been married to Arthur for a quarter of a century and Dad still talks about the problems of being married to a Jew as if . . . oh what's the use. He's too old to change."

"I wonder why he never remarried?"

"He was never the most agreeable man in the world, Piet. Since Mom died, he's been impossible," his sister said. "Hand me that dish, will you, Elizabeth."

"You know something, much as I disagree with Grandpa and his damn views, he's tough. He'll survive. I'm not sure we will—we're too spoiled. When the time comes to pay for all this . . ." Her voice trailed off while her gesture took in Riena, the manicured garden and the terrace beyond, with its Mediterranean air of casual elegance.

"Does that mean you want to come with me to see you Grandfather this afternoon?" Barnard laughed at the expression on Shari's face.

"No, Uncle Piet. I love him but I don't want to come. I'm not in the mood for one of our battles."

Barnard yawned and stretched. "I'm ready to go back to bed. When do we have to leave?"

"Not for a few hours," Michelle said. "Oh and by the way, it's a good idea to take two cars. We'll need the

274

room; Elizabeth's coming along.''

''Shari's idea?''

''My idea,'' Shari said. ''Can't you tell?''

''Little Annie Sunshine,'' Barnard said. ''I should have known.'' He turned away, mumbling something that sounded to Riena like an old Swahili proverb about *Kucha,* the sunrise, following *Mvua,* the rain. That he knew any Swahili at all was surprising, she thought; the language wasn't heard much in South Africa. She'd picked it up in prison from a cellmate who'd come from Nairobi with a White family. Out of boredom more than anything else, she and the girl had come to an arrangement—she would teach her Afrikaans in exchange for Swahili lessons.

''How did Daddy do at the U.N. this time?'' Shari asked her mother.

''Why don't you ask me?'' her father said, coming into the room. Shari ran to her father and hugged him. ''Dad. I thought I'd have to wait hours for you to get up.''

''Since we are all up now, except Anne who'll probably stay asleep, you might as well start breakfast, Elizabeth,'' Mrs. Cohn said.

''What was it you wanted to know about the U.N.?'' Cohn asked his daughter.

''How'd it go? Are you going back next year?''

''Badly, and I don't think so.''

''Chicken.''

''Why travel all of that way to be maligned when I can be bad-mouthed right here at home?''

''Who's maligning you? All I did was call you chicken.''

''I wonder how Emily's doing,'' Michelle Cohn said. 'I really would like to help her if I can. If they send her back to the *kraal,* let's make sure we post her some food and clothes and money.''

''Why?'' her husband asked.

''I'm not sure. A gesture, I suppose. . . .''

''. . . After what I saw and heard in New York,'' Arthur Cohn interrupted, ''I'm not certain I want our family to make any more gestures. Sons-of-bitches. . . ."

". . . Arthur!"

"I mean it, Mickey. I don't think I will go there again. Not unless that Senator—what's his name, Prescott—makes it into the White House. He'll keep the bastards in line."

Riena had to struggle not to drop the plate she was holding. Jake had mentioned his uncle to her; he had never gone into any details about his uncle's views.

"If their attitude keeps you at home," Michelle Cohn said to her husband, "I'm glad they made you angry."

"What infuriated you so, Art?" Barnard asked.

"The general attitude of the so-called 'emerging Black nations.' They curse and swear at South Africa and at America . . . they're rude and arrogant and nobody seems to give a damn."

"Anyone who denounces our attitude is called a communist supporter; if they support us, they're called bigots. America's in a tough spot, Art," Barnard said.

"Come on, Piet. America's economic commitment to this country is enormous," Cohn said. "That's proof of where they really stand."

"None of it's the way you make it sound, Dad," Shari said. "Lately America's State Department's been walking on eggs. They can't afford to make a commitment either way, not right now."

"I've heard talk of African shuttle diplomacy," Michelle said.

"Won't do any good until Rhodesia settles down. . . . Enough," Cohn said. "It's Sunday morning and no time for such seriousness. Shari, are you staying for dinner tonight?"

"I don't know. There's a meeting. . . ."

". . . Saving the world again?"

"Yes."

"When are you going to stop all of this fooling around and take up something serious. Like cricket, maybe?" her father joked. He looked lovingly at his daughter.

"You look very nice today," her mother said.

"You always approve of my Sunday morning scrubbed look," Shari said, kissing her mother.

"Why don't you let your skin breathe more than once a week? Then you wouldn't need all that make-up in the first place."

"That's why I like Sunday mornings around here," Shari said. "We've gone from Dayan to America's involvement in Africa to my pores in less than five minutes."

Her father patted her rear. "Seriously, why don't you do something useful," he said. "Forget the journalism stuff and become a lawyer. Defend the black buggers if you like, but journalism does no one any good."

"I want to follow in your footsteps at OPI. Imagine. Daughter follows father as head of South Africa's Overseas Press International." She laughed.

"Don't laugh. OPI's protected your hide more than once."

"Mom says you're having Moshe Dayan—*the* Moshe Dayan—for dinner tonight. Is he here for the UJA Rally?"

"Yes."

"How much of UJA's contribution comes from South African Jews d'you think?"

"I don't know exactly but we contribute the same proportion as the Americans."

"Why did the Nats let all of that money out of the country after the Yom Kippur War? I mean, they must have known not all of it was going to Israel. That some of it was being siphoned into private Swiss accounts?"

"I suppose they've never been able to prove anything," Barnard said.

Riena, serving breakfast, took in snatches of the conversation. She'd been told to take some breakfast for herself and, surprised at not being offered the usual servants' *mielie pap*, ate scrambled eggs and kippers—making sure that she used the metal plate and special cutlery set aside for the help.

After she'd cleared the verandah and washed the dishes, she asked if there was anything else she could do.

"You could make the beds and wipe over the bathrooms, if you don't mind. Perhaps a little dusting—this is your day off. Then let's set the table for dinner. Our guest asked us to keep things simple; this will be his only chance to be informal."

"What are we making for dinner, Madam?"

"We're having cold chicken and salads. We'll be picking up everything at the delicatessen this afternoon, so no cooking."

"What about sweets?"

"I baked a cake. It's in the freezer."

When everything was done, Riena went to her room to change out of her uniform. She had washed her own clothes, Nkolosi's clothes, the night before and hung them out to dry. She took them off the line and decided they had to be ironed. Standing in the laundry room with the ironing board out, she wondered if a massive hangover was keeping Anne Barnard quiet. Compared with yesterday, she thought, the household seemed unnaturally calm.

"We have to leave in five minutes," Shari said, wandering into the laundry room. She perched on a high, backless stool and watched Riena put the finishing touches to her skirt and blouse.

When they were all ready to leave, Anne Barnard still had not stirred.

"We can all go together after all," Cohn said. "Anne's staying here and I just spoke to Dayan. He sends his apologies; he's not feeling well."

"Will he be coming tonight?"

"I don't think so, Mickey."

Michelle Cohn looked disappointed. "I so much wanted to meet him."

"You will—at the Rally."

"That's not the same. Art, if Dayan's not coming, why are we going to the Mine Dances?"

"Can you think of anything else you'd rather do?"

"I suppose not."

"Then let's go. We haven't been in a long time."

278

"We could certainly fit in one car."

"I'd still rather take my own car," Piet Barnard said. "If I go to see Dad afterwards, I won't have to backtrack."

Arthur nodded.

"Besides," Shari said, "we promised to take Elizabeth. We can't. . . ."

". . . I don't mind," Riena began.

"I think it will do us all good to get out," Cohn said. "I'll go with Piet; Mickey, you follow us with Shari and Elizabeth."

Wishing they had changed their minds, Riena followed the women out of the house. The mother and daughter sat in the front of the car chatting. Riena, sitting in the back, couldn't hear their conversation, nor was she expected to make a contribution. Michelle Cohn was a careless driver and Riena was soon feeling nauseous and counting the minutes to De Waal Mining Company. She tried to concentrate on Barnard's car which his sister tailgated most of the way.

When they got to the parking lot, they were still right behind Barnard. They parked next to him and Michelle was soon walking ahead of the two younger women, her arm linked through her husband's. Barnard, walking alone with his hands in his pockets, passed the couple, and was the first one inside the arena.

"I think I heard someone call you," Shari said, when they were almost at their seats. She stopped walking. "There. I heard it again."

This time Riena heard her name being called out. It probably hadn't registered the first time because she wasn't used to being called Elizabeth, she thought. Turning around, she searched the faces of the audience for Tom who was the only other person who knew her as Elizabeth.

"I won't be a moment," she said to Shari.

It wasn't until she drew closer to him that she realized that Tom wasn't smiling. Nor did he look in the least bit pleased to see her.

"For Christsake, Riena," he said, "get the hell out of

this place.''

"Tom. What are you doing here?''

"Listen to me, Riena.'' She could see that he was really upset. Scared. "You have to go. Now.''

"I can't,'' Riena said, torn between wanting to please Tom and not wishing to cause a scene with the Cohns. "They wanted to do something nice for me. They're not bad people. . . .''

". . . Say you're sick. Anything.''

"How do I get back to Houghton?''

Tom took out some money and gave it to her. She took it. "There are taxis out there,'' he said. "Take one.''

"Are you. . . .''

". . . Go!''

Half running, Riena returned to where Shari was waiting for her.

"What's wrong?'' the young woman asked. "You look ill.''

"I just got some bad news. I don't feel very well. Do you think everyone would understand if I went back to the house?''

"Of course they'd understand,'' Shari said. "If you like, I'll take my mother's car and drive you home. I'm sure Uncle Piet wouldn't mind taking the others home under the circumstances.''

"Is anything wrong?'' Barnard asked, walking up to them.

Shari repeated what Riena had told her.

"I'll drive you,'' Barnard said. "I don't really feel like staying.''

"That's not necessary, Sir. There must be a taxi outside.''

"Nonsense. Shari, tell your parents what happened, would you, please. I'll see all of you later.''

He and Riena left the arena and were soon standing next to Barnard's car. She really did feel sick, Riena thought, watching Barnard unlock the car doors. What was it that Tom was so afraid of? What was going to happen out there?

"More than one hundred years ago," she heard an announcer say over a PA system, "a band of Zulu warriors viciously attacked and destroyed. . . ."

Barnard started the engine and the rest of the sentence was drowned out as they roared away from the De Waal Mining Company onto the open road.

5

"How do you feel?" Barnard asked, once they had left the mine area behind them.

"Much better, thank you, Mr. Barnard," Riena had to shout to be heard above the noise of the car engine. "I got a shock, and I don't like crowds to begin with."

They stopped at a traffic light. Barnard glanced at her and smiled. "You do seem better," he said. "Tell you what. If you think you can manage without going back to the house, how would you feel about driving out with me to my father's farm? We're part of the way there—unless you want me to take you somewhere else. Does the family emergency require your presence?"

Riena was taken aback. If they were stopped for any reason, Barnard could be harassed for having her in the car—particularly since she was sitting in the front with him. She couldn't imagine why he would take that kind of risk just to save himself half an hour.

"I'll drive you to the house first," he said, apparently taking her silence for reluctance.

"I'd be happy to come to the farm, Mr. Bernard."

She meant it. Going back to the empty house was not going to help her and if Barnard was willing to take the risk, she was, too. After all, it was broad daylight and not as if they were parked somewhere. . . .

"As far as anyone's concerned, my sister's 'lending' you to her father for the day and I'm transporting you there.''

"Wouldn't it be better if I sat in the back seat?''

Barnard's answer was to let out the throttle.

Riena had never ridden in a convertible before. She liked the feel of the wind in her hair and the heightened sensation of speed that came from being low to the ground. Giving in to the sensory stimuli, she watched the landscape until they passed a sign to Krugersdorp and Barnard turned West. Then she relaxed against the seat and closed her eyes. It was a damn sight more fun than taking trains and buses, she thought. Though it was bumpier than she'd have imagined, almost as rough a ride as the truck that had taken her from Johannesburg to Cape Town after Sharpeville.

She thought about that drive—wedged between a woman who smelled as if she'd never heard of bathing and a man who sepnt more time with his hand on the bottle than on the wheel. Still she'd been grateful to them; she'd spent two days wandering aimlessly around the location after her mother was shot. Her grandmother long since dead and no one around to care what she did. Every now and then someone would feed her but people had too many troubles of their own to take much notice of one more rootless child. Nobody wanted to take her in; no one could afford one more mouth to feed.

Then one night she'd crept into her mother's Aunt's house to sleep on the floor. The next thing she knew, she was on her way to Cape Town. She supposed the aunt and her husband—or boyfriend—had really meant to take care of her when they got to the Cape. But the jobs they'd expected hadn't materialized and they'd had enough of a hard time taking care of themselves. So she'd found herself out on the street again; wandering around the Coloured section of Observatory.

As she had so many times in the past, Riena wondered what might have happened to her had Ma not taken her in. Picturing Maria with little Jake, she tried to feel maternal; instead, she felt detached, as if she were thinking about a nephew whom she had seen only once. It happened every time she thought about her son—an almost tangible fog descended upon her, as if she hadn't experienced a birth trauma at all but had given birth intellectually. She knew she should have been longing to hold her child but there was an emptiness where the emotion ought to have been.

"Damn."

Barnard stopped short and Riena opened her eyes. Two old Black men were shepherding a goat across the road. The goat was unwilling and the men, showing no concern for the high speed traffic, were apparently determined that it would do as they wished. They begged, cajoled and cursed it, all to no account. When it became as obvious to them as it was to Riena that the animal was not going to move forward under its own steam, one man grabbed its head and the other its rear and they dragged it across the highway.

By now, Barnard was grinning. He had started out by yelling at them to *"Hamba! Hamba Sukawena,"* a not very polite way of telling them to get the hell out of the road. But when they stood triumphantly at the other side of the highway, waving at him and bowing like two sheiks granting him right-of-way, Barnard called out to them to *"Hamba gahle.* Go in peace."

"Hamba Morena," one of them responded. "Go Master."

Laughing, Barnard took off again. "We're almost there," he said.

"Where?"

"Klipfontein."

"How far are we from Houghton?"

"About thirty miles or so," Barnard said.

The houses had grown increasingly sparse, at least those that could be seen from the road. They had reached the beginning of the real farmlands, where homesteads were large and hidden from the road. It was easy to believe that South Africa's true wealth lay in her land, Riena thought, rubbing her hip where it had caught the door handle when they'd stopped short. She had automatically reached for the hanging strap, she remembered, as if she were on the bus—the one she'd taken on so many Saturdays from Cape Town to Ma's house in Observatory. She'd sworn every week to leave before the crowds deserted the parade and Capetonians headed for the beaches, but each week saw her caught again in the crush of homeward bound shopgirls and servants. So the ten minute ride to Ma's house had meant clinging to the overhead strap which she could barely reach, or lunging for it whenever the bus stopped short. She must have had to do that more often than she'd realized, she thought, if it had become such second nature to her.

"Here we are," Barnard said, slowing down the car.

He turned onto a dirt road and stopped in front of a heavy pair of farm gates. "There are still about two miles of potholes to come," he said, getting out of the car to open the gates.

"Should I close the gates behind you?" Riena asked.

Barnard nodded. "I suppose so, thanks. The old boy'd kill me if I left them open."

After the two promised miles of winding dirt road, they rounded one more bend and the farmhouse was upon them. Barnard braked and got out of the car. He stood with his hand on the door, looking around. When the dust they had raised settled back onto the rust colored surface of the road, Riena got out and joined him.

The beauty of the place took her breath away. Agapanthus bloomed higher than the living room window, two fig trees offered their bounty across the porch railing, and nasturtiums and geraniums intertwined in their eagerness to flow in the path of all who approached the front door.

"My father's probably in the garden somewhere," Barnard said. "Let's find him."

Riena hesitated.

"After I introduce you to him, you can wander around. You seemed to enjoy my sister's garden; this one is wilder but I think you'll like it."

They found Mr. Barnard Sr. walking around the neglected surface of a tennis court that may once have provided the family with daily enjoyment, Riena thought, but was now unusable. Bougainvillea streamed over the fenced path that led to the court, agapanthus grew wild and purple where shining wrought iron tables might once have welcomed Sunday visitors and miniature wild sweet-peas filled the morning with a fresh young scent. Like an infant, newly bathed and dusted with talcum powder.

Barnard picked two lupins and two nasturtium leaves and handed one of each to Riena. She bit into the fiery pepper of the leaf first and then into the opaque stem of the lupin; as always, its astringency made her pucker.

"What're you doing here, son?" the old man asked, when he finally looked in their direction and recognized Piet.

"Visiting you, Dad," Piet said, walking toward him. "This is Elizabeth Riess. She's. . . ."

Barnard Sr. nodded cursorily. "Where's Anne?"

"Asleep at Michelle's."

Looking at Riena, Barnard Sr. raised a white eyebrow. "Don't you work anymore, Pieter? I thought you were down in Cape Town, making a living."

In the space of less than a minute, Riena thought, the old man had succeeded in embarrassing her and in making his son look like a schoolboy truant. Somehow, she felt in him an enormous sense of power, as if he were a man who was used to getting his way and not someone to be crossed. Not lightly. He was of the Nkolosis, she thought. A controller and manipulator. Given the power and training of a Nkolosi, he could have been a dangerous man instead of merely an Afrikaner patriarch ruling a small territory.

"I suppose you want something," the father was saying.

"Only to see you."

The old man's face softened momentarily. "Let's see if those buggers in the kitchen can get us some coffee," he said, pointing to the house. He linked arms with his son and leaned on him slightly. "I'm getting old, Piet," he said. "I feel tired."

285

"Make yourself at home, Elizabeth," Piet Barnard said. "I'll tell them inside to give me an extra cup for you. Why don't you come around to the porch in a while."

Riena watched them, father and son, move toward the house, the younger man holding back to give the older one the feeling that he was creating the pace. It was a reminder to her that even the most powerful of men had mortal bodies. Eventually, they had to relinquish control to the next generation. Nkolosi, too, was mortal, she thought, wondering if he had chosen his successor or if that decision was being left to the gods. Perhaps the Negwenya would make that choice. Decide for herself to whom she would next lend her skills, using them for good or evil according to the dictates of her new Master. Or did Nkolosi have a son? Was some young boy already being taught how to hold the reins that had been handed down to Nkolosi by his father?

Wandering around the garden, Riena let almost half an hour slip by before she began making her way back to the house. She was thirsty, she thought. A cup of coffee would go down well. As she approached the porch, she found a patch of clover. There was no way she could resist, so she knelt to search for one with four leaves, remembering how her mother used to call them *Buloy'i*—magic. She could use some good magic, she thought.

"Whatever happened to Evvy?"

Piet Barnard's question floated out to her.

Riena stood up and walked firmly toward the porch, meaning to show herself. But when she came within sight of the two men and realized that, though she could see old man Barnard dunking his dark brown rusk unashamedly in his coffee mug, she was out of his line of vision, curiosity outweighed propriety.

"Evvy?"

"The nanny we had when I was nine or ten—the one whose eyes looked like a Keane painting. I remember her getting pregnant and then she wasn't around anymore."

"She left," Piet's father said brusquely.

"Why?"

"How should I know? Went off to have her baby I suppose."

"Why didn't she come back? They usually did, even if it was just to visit."

At first the old man didn't answer, as if the topic were not important enough to pursue. Then, apparently changing his mind, he said: "Servants came and went, Pieter. I never took any notice. If your mother were still alive she'd probably know what happened to what's her name . . . Evvy. She was the one who supported the servants' old age and derelictions."

"I remember," Piet said. Riena wondered at the hurt in his voice. "She used to say *'Hulle is ook mense, man'*—'They're people too, husband'—as she thought they were almost like us."

"They're happy, Piet," his father said. "You don't have to worry about them. I treat them well. Listen. John's out there now, singing. They smile all the time . . . they don't want things to change."

"See John run," the son said. The old man didn't react. "I think Mother actually believed hearty portions of servants' meat and *mielie pap* could hold back change," the younger man went on.

The old man shrugged. Apparently disinterested.

As he had done in his sister's kitchen, Piet Barnard counted on his fingers. "The child Evvy was carrying would be around forty by now," he said. "If it was a girl, she could have a child who's nearing thirty—Evvy could have a grandchild Shari's age or older.

"That would mean Evvy's daughter—if that's what she had—would have to have given birth when she was fourteen. . . ."

". . . Which happens all the time, as we both know."

"What are you driving at, Piet?" The old man sounded more weary than annoyed, yet the stiffening of his shoulders told Riena that he wasn't altogether pleased with the turn the conversation had taken.

Evvy's daughter was Sarah, Riena wanted to shout,

knowing suddenly that what Piet Barnard suspected was true. Sarah had given birth to a daughter right before her fourteenth birthday—a little more than nine months after she'd been raped by four *Tsotsis* in the location. Evvy hadn't come back to the farm because she'd been too proud—and because she'd had to take care of her daughter. And later, her granddaughter Riena. Evvy had never told Sarah the name of her father, nor had she spoken about her job with the Barnards. Just the mention of a farm every now and again, a farm Riena had assumed to be in Basutoland. By the time Evvy died, of something no one understood, Sarah had learned to take care of her own child. It was Evvy who had instilled in Sarah pride in her ancestors. Her Black ancestors. . . .

"Things were a lot simpler when I was a child, weren't they, Dad?" Piet Barnard said.

"That's because the *verdamme* Commies weren't around then," his father growled. "Interfering in things that are none of their business!"

"What're Commies, Dad?"

"You listen to me. I'm nearly seventy-five years old and I know what I'm talking about. Do you think these bloody *kaffirs* care about things like voting? And dignity?" He spat over the porch railing. "They have food and clothes and hospitals and schools. Fat lot they care about human rights."

He enunciated the last two words as if he were quoting from a dirty book, Riena thought.

"What rights do we have that are so important," he went on. "The Blacks in the rest of Africa are starving to death—our *kaffirs* are a damn sight better off than they are. *Jy's mal*, Pieter. You're crazy."

"Seems to me we can't live with them or without them, Dad," Barnard said quietly.

The old man didn't answer him. As if the effort of his diatribe had exhausted him, he put his head back and fell asleep in the afternoon sun.

Riena retreated a few steps and realigned her approach, making noises to indicate that she was just arriving.

"There you are," Piet Barnard said. "I was wondering if you got lost in the woods."

"Did I take too long, Mr. Barnard? I'm sorry."

"No. Not at all. But the coffee is cold. Why don't you ask them to heat. . . ."

". . . Cold will be fine."

"Good." He pointed at the mug that stood on a tray at his side. "Help yourself. Are you hungry? There are some biscuits. . . ."

". . . No thank you. I am thirsty though."

"We'll be leaving in about an hour." He nodded at his father. "I haven't the heart to wake him."

"Wake him. Wake who?" The old man sat up and reached for his cup. "I was tired of the discussion, that's all—an old man's privilege."

"Want to come to Houghton with us, Dad?"

Barnard Sr. looked at Riena, examining her carefully.

"Shari's going to be there for supper. There was supposed to be another guest. . . ."

". . . Michelle told me. That Dayan man. . . ."

The younger man looked exasperated but he didn't comment.

"If Shari's going to be there, I'll come. I never see that child anymore. What happened to that Dayan man? Michelle not good enough for him because she isn't. . . ."

". . . Dad!"

"I still think Michelle should have married one of us."

His son turned away without acknowledging his father's remark. "Why don't you plan to stay overnight?" he said. "Someone can drive you home tomorrow."

"What did you say your name was?" Barnard Sr. asked, looking at Riena as if he were seeing her for the first time.

"Elizabeth Riess, Sir."

"Do I know you?"

Riena shook her head.

"What are you doing here?"

"I think we should leave soon," Piet Barnard said. "If

289

you're coming with us, Dad. . . ."

"Yes. All right. But I know that girl. . . ."

Still mumbling, the old man went inside. Riena expected to have to wait around for a while but in a surprisingly short time they were in the car, headed toward Houghton. The car was basically built for two, and since Riena was relegated to the narrow back seat, the ride was not nearly as much fun as it had been on the way to the farm. The old man fell asleep instantly but conversation was impossible. Riena concentrated on protecting herself against the bumps in the road; it seemed to her that by the time they turned into the Cohn driveway, they had covered twice the distance they'd traveled on the way to the farm.

"They're back, too," Piet Barnard said, turning off the ignition and pointing at his sister's car. He looked at Riena. "Elizabeth, since Dayan's not coming and today should be your day off, why don't you rest? We can all pitch in for supper; it won't kill us."

"I am tired, Mr. Barnard," Riena said. "What time is it, Sir?"

"Four o'clock," Barnard Sr. said, stretching. He turned around to look at Riena. "You're a pretty girl. In my younger days. . . ."

". . . Let's go inside," his son said quickly.

The younger man looked defeated, Riena thought, climbing out of the car. "Thank you for taking me along, Mr. Barnard," she said, making an effort to smile because the sins of the fathers should not be visited upon the sons and wondering why that should be true for him when it didn't seem to be true for anyone else. Certainly not for her—or for her son.

Glad to be back in her room, Riena kicked off her shoes and lay down on the bed. Idly, she turned on the radio.

"For those of you who have not been listening to the wireless, there has been an unprecedented outbreak of violence today. . . ."

"Oh, shit," Riena said, turning the dial to try to find some music.

". . . Zulu dancers attacked members of the audience."

It was a different station, another voice, but obviously part of the same announcement. Riena sat up and listened.

"The name of those killed and injured are still being withheld to protect their families but those Zulus who were involved and are alive have been apprehended."

Zulu dancers, Riena thought, forcing herself to face the subject she'd been avoiding for hours; unless there had been a festival somewhere, a special event about which she knew nothing, Zulu dancers could mean only one thing—the De Waal Mining Company. Trouble there would explain Tom's urgency. The way he'd commanded her to leave. His reluctance to explain his mission in Johannesburg.

"De Waal Mining Company officials have indicated

that they have already begun a full scale investigation. . . ."

The announcer's words left little room for doubt. Please let Tom be safe, Riena prayed. And the Cohns? Had they been injured? Would Piet Barnard suspect her motives for wanting to leave the Dances? Would he think she'd known what was going to happen and. . . . She stopped herself. The last thing she needed to do was panic. In her anguish, she had missed most of the details but she knew the station would keep rebroadcasting them, adding to them for the rest of the day. She did catch the end of a message from the Minister of Bantu Administration who reassured the outside world that: ". . . the malnutrition you see amongst the Blacks in our country is a result of wrong eating habits," as if that absolved his government of all responsibility for the unhappiness the world might see as the base for violence such as today's.

Slowly, Riena put on her shoes. She crossed the concrete divider between her temporary quarters and the main house and tried the kitchen door. It was locked so she tapped lightly. She could see figures gathered in the kitchen.

Shari let her in. "Yes," she said, the friendliness gone from her voice. "What do you want?"

Deciding to act as if she knew nothing about what had happened. Riena asked if she could make herself a cup of coffee and a sandwich.

"Go ahead," Michelle Cohn said, "but be quick about it." Then turning to her husband and daughter, she suggested they join the others in the lounge.

"Thank God they can't blame the Jews for this one," Cohn said heavily, following his wife out of the room.

"Can't they?" Michelle said. "Someone will, you know."

"Grandpa will, if he doesn't blame the Communists," Shari said.

"Do you think Israel could use a couple of old farts like us?" Riena heard Cohn ask his wife. "My patience with South Africa has about run out."

They had stopped in the hallway.

"You'd leave everything behind?" Shari asked.

"It's only money," her father said. "I have a friend who says if he can't take it with him, he refuses to die," he went on, in what sounded like a brave attempt at alleviating the sober atmosphere, "but I'm not so sure."

"I'm sure Israel would welcome you, Dad," Shari said.

"And me?" her mother asked.

"There are non-Jews in Israel too, Mother."

Michelle Cohn laughed. "I suppose you're right."

"I've made a decision," Cohn said.

"So have I, Art. I'm too tired to stand out here. . . ."

". . . Seriously, Mickey. I'm taking you and Shari and anyone else who wants to go to the Carlton Hotel."

"Why, in God's name?"

"I have a feeling—call it an old newsman's instinct —that we've only seen the prelude to what's coming. I'd feel happier knowing you were safely deposited at a hotel."

"I agree with you, Art," his brother-in-law said, apparently coming out of the lounge to join the others in the hallway. "I don't think it's an isolated incident either. Where's Dad, by the way?"

"In the garden with Anne," his sister said.

"Shouldn't they be inside?"

"I don't think the danger's all that immediate," Cohn said. "It'll probably take a day or two. . . ."

". . . What makes you so sure, Dad?"

"Can't you see what's happening? There's an acceleration of violence that has to be deliberate. It has the smell of a highly organized plot. . . ."

". . . A plot to do what? I haven't heard of any demands being made."

"Someone's creating a climate of fear. . . ."

293

". . . Surely OPI must know what's going on," Piet Barnard interrupted. "Don't you claim to have eyes and ears everywhere?"

"Yes, we do. And I'm about to find out what the hell this is all about," the newsman said. "I'm going to the office."

"May I come along?" his brother-in-law asked.

"I think they need one young man to stay around here," Cohn said.

"Young? Flatterer."

"Young compared with Dad," Michelle said.

"I wonder if I can arrange for a security guard for a while," Cohn said. "Now I'm really sorry Dayan isn't staying with us; we'd have been well protected."

Riena jumped. If they arranged for guards, Nkolosi's plan would be foiled before it began. For a moment she wished it would happen but then fear of failure and its results took precedence over everything else.

"I don't want to go to the Carlton, nor do I want guards snooping around. This is our home, not a jail," Mrs. Cohn said.

Her husband didn't argue. Perhaps, Riena thought, he'd already decided to go ahead. As long as the security people remained hidden, his wife would never know. "Okay, Mickey," she heard him say, "but if I find anything in that maze of ticker tapes down at OPI, you'll have to go along with me. . . ."

". . . You two men can stand out here if you like, we're going inside," Michelle said.

Riena heard the click of heels on the polished parquet as Mrs. Cohn and her daughter left the hallway.

"There's something I have to tell you," Barnard said. There was hesitation in his voice. "It might help you establish that pattern you're looking for."

"Does it have anything to do with why you resigned as warden?" Cohn asked. "I shouldn't have to tell you that I won't judge you, no matter what you've done."

"Thank you," Barnard said quietly, "and yes, it is

about my resignation. To cut a long and probably boring tale short, before the explosion at the jail I had started to doubt. . . ."

They moved out of earshot. On the pretext of going inside to collect any teacups that might be lying around, Riena took a tray and walked down the hallway. As she passed the library, she could see the two men in earnest conversation. Hoping to catch a part of their discussion, she slowed down.

". . . I watched her leave the jail, Art," Piet Barnard said. "I could have stopped her but I didn't."

Riena walked on in a daze. It was impossible, she thought. He could not have recognized her; the night had been dark and filled with tumult. Her face had been shrouded by the blanket and the night, except for those brief moments when she'd stopped to speak to the guard in the glare of the strobes.

Having come too far to turn back to the kitchen, she went into the lounge. One look around told her Michelle Cohn had not abandoned her habit of serving tea in a crisis. She was sitting on the sofa next to her sister-in-law, with an array of teacups in front of her on a glass-topped ball-and-claw table.

"May I clear the table, Madam?"

"Do you know what your people have done to us?" Anne Barnard said, before Mrs. Cohn could answer Riena.

"Aunt Anne!" Shari was indignant, the momentary chilliness she'd displayed toward Riena in the kitchen gone. "You can hardly blame. . . ."

". . . It's all right, Miss Shari," Riena interrupted. "I've heard about what happened, Madam. I'm very sorry."

"Sorry! Sorry doesn't buy back lives."

"Neither White nor Black ones," Shari said.

Riena loaded her tray and retreated to the kitchen. She washed the tea things and made herself a sandwich and a cup of coffee to take to her quarters. When she left the kitchen, she made certain she locked the outside door securely behind her, thinking how foolish it was to protect people one day and become their enemy the next.

Resisting the temptation to turn on the radio, she choked down her sandwich. Then, with nothing left to do except think or sleep, she lay down on Emily's bed. She had left the door open so that she could watch the sunset, but it was not yet six o'clock and the sunshine was as bright as ever outside her confining quarters. Strange, she thought, how the room felt so small to her; the house she'd shared with her mother and various and sundry transients had been no larger, and it had included a kitchen area and bathroom within the same space. Her prison cell had been smaller yet.

After tossing around on the bed for a while, Riena faced the fact that she was not going to fall asleep. She was not by nature a pacer but she got up and started to walk up and down the nine-by-twelve room, moving faster and faster until her head was spinning. In prison, she remembered, her cellmates had habitually prowled their shared quarters, like veld jackals who'd been captured and put in the zoo. Not joining them had been her defense against total conditioning. Now, into the sunset hours, she paced and prowled, feeling more locked in than she had ever done at Roeland Street. Several times, she headed for the door, determined to walk out of the room and off the property and not come back. But she had nowhere to go. Once, she went outside and stared at the night sky, envying its stillness and half expecting the moon to drop into her lap or the stars to begin chasing each other in reaction to her mounting tension.

Lying down again, Riena looked around the stark room and tried to feel the presence of the young woman who'd lived there before her, examining Emily's few remaining possessions not in the blanket bundle under the bed. Finally, unable to resist any longer, she reached across the bedside table to the transistor radio, disturbing a white lace doily that covered the cigarette burns on top of the old piece of furniture. More than anything, she needed a voice to distract her from the shadows that had invaded the room, strange moving shapes created by the trees and the moon and the clouds but transmuted by her mind into everything she wanted to forget; a swaying branch became an undulating tail; jagged leaves turned into scales; oddly shaped clouds transformed into an infant's head, distorted by a blow.

". . . Heading the news today is the chaos at De Waal Mining Company. For those of you who've not yet heard, there's been an unprecedented outbreak of violence by Zulu dancers who attacked their audience with spears, assegais and poison darts. They were joined by well-armed Bantu infiltrators. Mine officials have told us categorically that there is no need for widespread alarm. This was an isolated incident, badly organized and unrelated to any other violent outburst of the recent past. Again, there is not yet a list of the dead and injured but judging by the rough count of Bantu dead, indications are. . . ."

Again, Riena turned off the radio. It was impossible to decide which was worse—the bloody signature of the AFI or the attitude of the South African government which expected people to swallow whatever pablum was fed them. And the people did, she thought. Picturing Tom bleeding to death alone somewhere, she felt suddenly cold and pulled her blankets tightly around her.

Huddled like that, Riena fell into a twilight sleep. She never ceased to be aware that she was tossing on her bed and sweating into the blanket, yet she couldn't wake up enough to rid herself of the shapes and sounds that haunted her night. She heard metal tearing into human bone and saw warriors in warpaint attacking a faceless enemy, tall Black men with feathers on their

297

heads and beads around their wrists and ankles, beading that came loose, until each wrist and ankle looked like Emily's wedding doll. And hovering overhead, she saw the Negwenya. A smiling demon whose shadow kept moving, swaying, across her warriors below.

She turned over heavily and heard herself groan. Now she was lying on the ground in Zeekoevlei, a red-bellied Lightning Bird hovering over her, an earthworm struggling in its deformed beak. It dropped the worm on her bare stomach. She felt it wriggle across her. The bird swooped. Missed. Gouged her flesh, coming dangerously near to her eyes. A tap, tap, tapping began. The sound of a blind man's cane, and she knew the man had been blinded by the talons of the creature that hovered over her face.

It circled again, lower this time. Riena lashed out.

She was awake now, reaching for the lamp and staring at the centipede she had brushed off her stomach and onto the floor, when the tapping came again.

"Riena, it's Tom. Let me in."

She walked around the centipede and opened the door she didn't remember having closed and locked. "I thought you were a blind man and that the Lightning Bird. . . ."

Tom stepped inside and shut the door quickly behind him.

". . . Thank God you came. I was worried. Frightened. I thought you were dead. Sit down. Are you all right?"

"Hey. Slow down," Tom said, taking her in his arms and pulling her toward the bed. "I'm not supposed to be here but I needed to see you. I'm in one piece, Riena."

"For a moment I thought you'd come to talk," Riena said.

"I'd rather talk lying down, if we can straighten up this mess you've made of the bed. What on earth were you doing?"

"Fighting monsters."

They lay on the bed, and while he told her what he had done at the mining compound, she stroked him as if he were a child in need of comfort.

"I've been listening to the wireless," she said, when he stopped talking. "They're trying hard to convince the people that what happened at De Waal is 'an isolated incident' and that the European triumphed."

"I'm not sure who triumphed," Tom said. "I know I didn't. That damn Nkolosi's the devil incarnate, Riena. I spoke to him afterwards. . . . I can't tell you what that man's voice does to me. I hear it and I feel like a little boy, deathly afraid of the dark. . . ."

Riena kissed him. At first it was like kissing someone who wasn't fully conscious but he soon began to respond.

"We can't do this. There's no time," he said, sitting up. "I shouldn't be here at all. If anyone sees me. . . ."

". . . Nkolosi's spies?" Riena was not entirely joking.

"Or the Cohns. How're things going?"

"What about the other families who are going to be held hostage? Are they all being held by reluctant revolutionaries like us?"

"I don't think so. Most of them are very much involved with the AFI and believe in its goals. Every now and then something goes wrong and they have to induct people like us; or the opportunity presents itself and so the AFI uses it—Nkolosi uses it."

"Tom, what about Emily? What happened to her and why? Was she just an innocent in all of this?"

"Nkolosi tried to get her to do what you're going to do. He told her he had her child and wanted her to be his 'inside man.' She had to make a choice between her child and the people she'd been with for years. I don't know if she made that choice or if she didn't believe Nkolosi would carry through his threats."

"Do you think he's really hurt . . . killed . . . her child?"

"I don't know. Either way, he's got you scared enough to cooperate, so he's achieved his purpose."

Riena thought of her baby being mutilated and drew Tom down onto the bed to gain comfort from the warmth of his body. "How long are we supposed to hold the people?" she asked.

"Ostensibly until talks with the government lead to something positive. Actually, I believe, until talks break down."

"How will we know when that's happened?"

"The wireless. Simon has instructions to keep it on. when talks break down—or succeed—you and the others doing the same thing are supposed to come to Teyateyaneng."

"If that happens, Nkolosi will have surrounded himself with an army of revolutionaries. You know the legend of Thaba Bosigo, don't you? Do you think Nkolosi sees himself as another Moshesh?"

"As long as he's not Moselikatse going down to defeat."

"Assume for a moment that he is, Tom. Do you think there's a Moshesh around, ready to take over?"

Tom didn't answer.

"There has to be a better way," Riena said. "Something people like us can do to bring about change without violence." Without, she thought, Nkolosi and his Mata Hari controlling our minds.

Still Tom was silent.

"Tom?"

"I don't know," he said, taking her in his arms and touching her face. Gently. Like a man who knew he was going blind imprinting a face in his memory for a time when he'd no longer be able to see it. "Riena, I love you. I wasn't going to say anything. It seemed futile. . . ."

". . . What if Nkolosi hears you?" Riena asked. "Or your jealous dragon-lover?"

"Right now I don't care," Tom said.

300

"Then nor do I."

She took off her shirt and leaned against him, guiding his hands to her breasts. But she didn't say she loved him—not even when he was making love to her and her body, arched under his, told her it was so. There was Jake. The baby. This was no time to profess anything except a passing need.

Riena was asleep when Tom left. A real sleep. When the alarm rang at five o'clock, she wasn't sure whether or not she had dreamed that he'd come to her. The only thing that was inarguable was the ringing at the other side of the room. It came from a clock that stood on top of a shabby wooden dresser and as she groped to put it off, she tried to remember setting it and putting it there. She couldn't. She pressed the button to cut off the noise. Then it was the quiet that scared her—that and the knowledge that it was morning. Monday morning.

7

Shortly before six o'clock, Riena presented herself at the kitchen entrance and knocked on the door. She knew that whoever let her in would have to detach the burglar alarm system first, so she waited patiently rather than knocking a second time. She had adjusted her uniform and was making sure her cap was on straight when the door was opened for her.

"Good morning, Elizabeth. You're right on time," Mrs. Cohn said, smiling pleasantly.

"Good morning, Madam."

"I couldn't sleep, so I've already had my tea. You'll have to prepare separate trays for my brother and his wife and remember, breakfast has to be ready on time."

"How many do I set for?" Riena asked, her eyes on the door. She could still leave, she thought. It wasn't too late.

"Set for six," Mrs. Cohn said. "Shari stayed here last night and so did my father. Mrs. Barnard may want breakfast in bed but set a place for her just in case. Put cereal on the table and make a pot of oatmeal . . . and at least six slices of toast to begin with. Oh, and we like fruit for breakfast; cut up grapefruit. . . ."

". . . What about eggs, Madam?" Riena asked, accepting the fact that it was too late to escape.

"I'm not sure. We'll tell you later and you can make them while we eat our fruit." She started out of the kitchen. "If you need me for anything, I'll be in the garden cutting flowers for the house. It's best to do it while. . . ."

She disappeared out of earshot.

Simon was probably out there, waiting in the bushes, Riena thought. He would have to bring Mrs. Cohn in with him. As she moved efficiently around the kitchen preparing the tea trays, she wondered how Michelle Cohn would react. Would she become hysterical, or would some hidden reserve of courage see her through? She had known the Cohns for only a short while, she thought, yet she was not eager to see their faces when they recognized her treachery. Piet Barnard was the former warden of the jail that had held her captive but there was a quality in him, a warmth that drew her. His father, Barnard Sr., was her grandfather; it should have been easy for her to hate him. Yet she did not. If there was a rationale for what she was about to do, it was not based in hatred of these White people, but rather in her fear of what Nkolosi might do to Maria and to her son. She tried to tell herself that she had an obligation to her race and that she was acting out of the right set of loyalties, but some inner voice kept insisting that the world she was helping to create for the new generation would be no better than the one it was replacing.

Survival. That was the answer, she told herself, picking up Piet Barnard's tray. That was what it was really all about. Only survival was of the essence. She rattled the tray at Barnard's door and put it down on the floor as she'd been instructed to do.

"Tea, Mr. Barnard," she said.

She heard him moan and wondered how much of the previous night had been spent doing battle with his wife. His father? His sister? He seemed to be out of step with all of them. They had probably all drunk too many Scotches, Riena thought, and exchanged too many unkind words in the masturbatory political word games that inevitably followed an outbreak of violence. That they were her relatives, all of them, was not a particularly attractive thought.

The former warden had turned on the early morning news. A rehash of what was being called "the incident at the mines" seeped under the door, and not for the first time since her alarm had woken her, Riena tried to separate dream from reality. Had Tom come to her during the night to tell her he loved her, or had that only been a comforting dream, created by her to offset the nightmares? She had found no trace of his visit this morning, other than her own certainty that his visit had been real.

Michelle Cohn had not reappeared by the time the family began to trickle into the dining room and Riena had to assume that the woman was being held by Simon who was waiting for the rest of the family to gather before he made his entrance. How well Nkolosi knew their habits, she thought, to have planned the timing so precisely.

"Where's my mother?" Shari asked, summoning Riena to the table by ringing the small crystal bell that stood next to Mrs. Cohn's place setting. "I've checked her bedroom and she's not there. She's usually the first at the table."

"She's in the garden, cutting flowers."

"It's not like her to be late for breakfast. Maybe I should make sure she's okay, Dad?"

"I'll go," her father said, standing up.

"I should have gone home last night," Mr. Barnard Sr. grumbled.

"Me too," Shari said. "I'll take you home right after

breakfast, Grandpa.''

"Start eating," Cohn said. "I'll be right back."

The doorbell rang. "That must be the Madam," Riena said, her heart pounding. "I'll get it; she must have locked herself out."

Cohn sat down. "Women," he said, indulgently.

Seconds later, knowing the drama was about to begin and helpless to stop it, Riena opened the front door. She recognized Simon instantly as the man she'd seen in Tom's house the night of the explosion. He held a revolver in one hand and Mrs. Cohn with the other, his large hand fitting easily around the back of her neck.

"Lock and bolt the door behind me," he said, pushing the woman into the foyer ahead of him.

Riena did as she was told.

"Where's your weapon?"

Riena shook her head. The weapon Tom had given her was hidden under Emily's mattress.

"Take the gun out of my pocket. And use it if you have to."

Riena didn't move.

"Do what I told you. Take it. Then make sure all of the doors are locked and close all of the curtains. Is everyone in the dining room?"

"Everyone except her sister-in-law," Riena said. She reached out gingerly and took the gun from Simon's pocket. She didn't have the faintest idea what kind of gun it was or what to do with it, nor did she have any intention of ever using it.

"That's better. Now get the other woman into the dining room. I've cut the phone lines but I want them all in one room."

"What about the gardener?" Riena asked.

"He doesn't come on Mondays," Simon said.

Once again, Riena was astounded at the data that had been collected from such a vast distance.

Simon pushed Michelle Cohn toward the dining room. "Get that other woman," he said over his shoulder to Riena who was staring, terrified, at the weapon in her hand. "And stop holding that thing as if it were covered with shit."

She'd be most likely to kill herself with it if she tried to use it, Riena thought, trying to hold the gun more firmly. When she got to Anne's door, she hesitated and knocked.

"I'm afraid you'll have to get up, Mrs. Barnard," she said, walking into the room. The woman was staring at the ceiling in an almost catatonic manner, as if she had no intention of ever moving.

"Mrs. Barnard. . . ."

". . . What is it? What are you doing in this room?"

Her recovery rate from whatever it was that had ailed her was phenomenal, Riena thought. "I'm sorry. You'll have to get up now and come with me," she said. She picked up the dressing gown that lay on the floor and tossed it onto the bed. The woman didn't move. "Now!" Riena ordered, leveling the gun at her.

Anne Barnard sat bolt upright in bed. "What is that . . . is that what I think it is?" She sounded far more outraged than frightened.

"Come," Riena said, hardput not to smile at the woman's indignance.

Slowly, Anne Barnard obeyed, but the insulted expression never left her face.

"Walk ahead of me into the dining room."

"May I brush my hair first, or is that *verboten?*"

Taken aback, Riena nodded. "As long as you can do it in thirty seconds," she said.

Anne Barnard picked up her brush and began deliberately stroking her hair. Then, suddenly, she whirled around and threw the brush at Riena who surprised herself by moving neatly aside. The woman's got spunk, she thought.

"Are you ready now, Madam?" Riena asked, unable to keep the sarcasm from creeping into her voice.

"You disgust me," Anne Barnard said. She walked in front of Riena, holding her head high, a priestess walking proudly to the sacrificial altar.

Rejoining the others in the dining room, Riena told Anne quietly to sit down. She did so without saying another word.

"Now listen to me, all of you," Simon said, "I have no intention of hurting you as long as you cooperate."

And she couldn't hurt them even if they didn't cooperate, Riena thought, standing with her back against the wall to stop her shaking from becoming visible.

"Did you close all of the curtains?" Simon asked her.

"Won't that look suspicious? I think they're usually kept open."

"We'll have to take that chance."

Riena started out of the room.

"What do you want?" Cohn asked.

She turned around to look at him. At all of them. Cohn looked amazingly calm, she thought, as if he'd known all along that this was going to happen. Michelle was looking at him and Shari was drumming her nails on the table top. Her grandfather's face registered the same contempt that Riena had seen earlier on Anne's face—Anne, who was reaching for her husband's hand, pulling it away from holding his temples and covering his face.

"If it's money you're after," Arthur Cohn continued, "take whatever you can find and get the hell out of here. Both of you. I'll even show you where to find the jewelry."

"I think you know that money and jewelry have nothing to do with this," Simon said. "Just do as you're told and no one will get hurt."

"How long do you intend to hold us like this?" Michelle Cohn asked softly. She appeared to have recovered from her earlier shocked state.

As long as we need to. Look, it's going to be a long day. I suggest you act as normally as you can. Eat breakfast for one thing."

"I'll make some eggs," Shari said, standing up. Riena saw the look in her eyes.

Simon had seen it too. "No, you don't. No one's going anywhere without one of us along. You, Elizabeth, escort this woman into the kitchen. That one, too." He nodded at Mrs. Cohn. "I'm sure you'll enjoy watching them make breakfast. It'll be a switch. And make sure they cook enough for us as well."

When Riena had taken care of the curtains, she returned to the dining room to get the two women. They stood up.

"Who are you, really?" Michelle Cohn said, looking first at Riena and then at her own daughter. "Art, I don't understand what's going on."

"Since we're all gathered together like one big happy family," he said. "there's something Dad wants to tell us. Isn't there, Dad? You'll tell Mickey who Elizabeth really is, won't you?"

"Daddy?"

Michelle Cohn's voice had become childlike; Riena found it far less irritating than her usual arrogance.

"Art?"

Her husband leaned toward her and put his arm around her shoulders.

"Evvy," the old man said flatly. When he stood up, not even Simon made a move to stop him. "This girl, Elizabeth, or whatever her name is, is my . . . grand-daughter. Her grandmother, Evvy. . . ."

"Oh God." Michelle collapsed onto the table, knocking her crystal bell to the floor where it shattered.

For a moment, the old man stood straight and tall. He looked at Riena and tried to smile. "You're very pretty," he said. Then he crumpled into his chair, the youth he'd regained for that instant in time gone. An old man burying an old sin.

"Is that why you've done this?" Arthur Cohn asked Riena.

She shook her head.

Michelle Cohn stared at Riena. She started to speak but stopped, and Riena wondered what she was thinking as a lifetime of feeling superior came to an end.

"Like I said, you people might as well eat. Two of you women get moving, I don't care which two," Simon said.

You people, Riena thought. There it was again, that ugly phrase. It sounded no less crass coming from Si-

307

mon than it had from Anne Barnard. He was no better than she was. No less angry or prejudiced.

"Go with them," Simon ordered.

Riena did as she'd been ordered. With the revolver growing heavy in her hand, she stood guard in the kitchen while mother and daughter prepared breakfast. Later, she and Simon watched as the family ate. Seeing them consume the food with amazingly hearty appetites given the circumstances, Riena realized that she, too, was hungry. She couldn't recall when she'd last eaten a decent meal.

"When do you think this will be over?" she asked Simon in broken Swahili.

"After the morning milk delivery," he said, answering in the same tongue.

"What do you mean?"

Simon looked at the family. They were trying to act as if everything were normal, eating and exchanging small talk. They were like sailors discussing the weather while out of the corners of their eyes they kept watching the pirates who were preparing the plank they'd shortly be required to walk, Riena thought. She looked at her watch, the one that had been supplied her along with her clothes. To her astonishment, it was nearing ten o'clock. On the one hand, it seemed impossible that almost two hours had passed since Simon's entrance into the Cohn household; on the other, it felt as if she'd been holding the revolver forever. For a pacifist, she thought, she was acquiring quite an arsenal.

Simon yawned and Riena wondered if he was tired or merely bored. "What did you mean?" she asked again, still in Swahili. "What does the milk delivery have to do with all of this?"

"Today the AFI talks to the Nats. Again. Tomorrow they'll find out what happens when talks fail."

"*When* talks fail?"

Simon nodded. Though he did not express surprise that she understood Swahili, he was apparently assuming that he was safe as long as he stayed away from any other language. Since so few South Africans spoke Swahili, Riena thought, it was a reasonable assumption.

"We have infiltrated the major dairy system," he said, without mentioning the name of the actual dairy chain to which he was referring. "Their milk deliveries tomorrow will be poisoned. No one who drinks their milk will live."

"Blacks, Whites, men, women, children? The innocent and the guilty? I don't believe it," Riena said, switching to English and watching Piet Barnard who was expending enormous energy on buttering his toast. She had the feeling that he'd been listening to her dialogue with Simon and that he'd understood. Tell them for me, her eyes said to him. Survive and tell them. If he didn't, she thought, she would have to; there were some trades her conscience couldn't make and this was one of them.

"Believe it, lady," Simon said.

No wonder Tom hadn't told her what else was to come, Riena thought, feeling sick to her stomach. "That's all you need to know for the moment," he'd said, when she'd asked if there was more.

"You should be pleased," Simon went on, in English this time. "Our plan will convince them without guns or explosives."

"Will that make them any less dead?" she asked in Swahili, finding the right words with difficulty.

Simon shrugged. This was once a man with feelings, Riena thought, wondering what kind of bargain he'd made with Nkolosi—and with himself. And then she remembered. Tom had told her; refuge and an engineering degree in exchange for loyalty to the AFI. Perhaps that was how it had started, she thought, but now he was convinced that this was the only way. Convinced because it was too late to develop a conscience.

Nkolosi wants it to happen, doesn't he?" she said. "He doesn't want those talks to succeed."

Simon didn't answer.

"Every major dairy?" she asked, in Swahili again. Saying "milk place" because she couldn't remember the word for dairy.

He nodded.

"But our people drink that milk, too."

"So what? Our survivors will outnumber theirs by far; at most, a couple of Africans will die with every European family."

Riena tried unsuccessfully to ignore a memory that was pushing its way into her consciousness: a little girl watching her mother scrub floors in a White woman's house. The mother grateful that the White Madam allowed her to bring the child along, the child bored, her only duty to bring in the milk bottles . . .

"Mamma, what if someone poisoned the milk?"

"Hush, child."

"Would you poison your Madam's milk, Mamma?"

The mother slaps the child hard across the face. The child puts her hand to the stinging but she doesn't cry. There is one more question she wants to ask first: would you poison the Madam's neighbor?

Later, much later, when the girl's mother is less angry with her and angrier with the White Madam, the child asks the question. Her mother tells her it couldn't work.

"You," Simon said, pointing at Shari. "Is there a portable around?"

"I'll get one," Shari said, standing up.

"Go with her." He nodded at Riena.

Shari sat down again. "There's one in the guest room," she said.

"Get it!"

"Get it yourself."

Simon leveled his gun at her, the way Riena had done to Anne Barnard.

"Get it, Shari," Arthur Cohn said. His daughter obeyed, with Riena trailing behind her.

"Is this really the way?" Shari asked, when they were in the guest room.

"The wireless," Riena said. She wanted to tell this young woman whom she so resembled that this method was not of her design but she said nothing.

Back in the dining room, Shari put the radio in the middle of the table.

"Find Springbok Radio," Simon ordered.

This time, Shari did as she was told without arguing.

". . . We have to interrupt this ten thirty newscast for a tragic announcement. Mr. Daniel Van Der Merwe, respected Nationalist Member of Parliament, was found shot to death early this morning in his Cape Town flat. His body was discovered by a Miss Deanna Rosen, a family friend who went to see him this morning to seek advice on a personal matter."

"Was that part of the plan?" Riena asked in Swahili.

"Did your people do that?" Cohn asked her. Without waiting for her answer, he turned to his brother-in-law. "Remember what I told you yesterday, Piet? I expected more of the same."

Suddenly, Riena remembered the conversation she'd overheard the day before—and one sentence in particular: ". . . *I wonder if I can arrange for a security guard for a while?*" Had Cohn done that, despite his wife's objections? Were they even now surrounded by armed men who were waiting for the right moment to break into the house and save the Europeans?

"I heard someone outside," Simon said, breaking into Riena's thoughts. She saw his grip tighten on his revolver.

An unearthly quiet descended on the room, and in the hush she could hear it too. Footsteps. She saw a shadow pass the curtains and the footsteps stopped at the front door. Nothing happened. Then the shadow passed again and the footsteps diminished as the person moved around to the side of the house.

Everyone expected the knocking to begin and yet when it did, they all jumped. All except Simon whose eyes had become deadly.

"You're going to have to answer it," he said to Riena. "I can't leave these people alone with you."

Riena stayed where she was.

"Go," he said. "Whoever it is, say there's illness in

the house and no visitors are being allowed in."

"What if the person doesn't believe me?"

"That thing in your hand isn't just for show. Use it if you have to; if you don't I will. Six is all we can handle."

Knowing there was no way she could shoot a human being—or anything else for that matter—Riena moved slowly across the room and down the passageway that led to the kitchen. Whoever you are, she prayed, please go away. For the love of God, please go away.

8

Riena entered the kitchen in slow motion. She could see a tall shadow behind the single glass panel in the door but there was no way to tell who it was. Not without opening the door or moving aside the folds of the lace curtain that covered the panel. It's a hawker, she told herself. Selling fruit door to door. Or a Mormon, selling Joseph Smith. John. Maybe it was John the gardener, deciding to work on Monday after all.

John. Missionary. Vendor. It made no difference to Simon's instructions: *That thing in your hand isn't just for show; use it if you have to.*

The knocking came again, gentle, yet insistent.

"Who is it?"

The shadow was mute.

"Who is it?" Riena's hand was on the door handle.

"Is Riena Parker there?"

"Yes. No." Riena froze. Who but Nkolosi could know that Elizabeth Riess was Riena Parker? Tom? He was long gone from the area.

"Elizabeth! What's going on out there?" Simon's voice carried easily down the hallway.

"Everything's fine," Riena called out. Unlocking the

door, she opened it a crack and peered out. Tense. Not knowing what to expect.

Her knees buckled and she let the door fly open. She was hallucinating, she told herself, closing her eyes and then opening them again.

"Riena? May I come in?" Jake said.

"Go away, Jake," Riena whispered. Gathering her strength as if she were a fighter preparing to face the world champion, she said loudly: "There's illness in the house, so you can't come in. And we have a vacuum cleaner, thank you."

"Riena, please, I have to talk to you."

"I told you, Sir, we don't need a vacuum cleaner." She lowered her voice. "If you value your life . . . my life . . . go away. Now."

She tried to shut the door quickly but she was not quick enough. Jake pushed against it and came into the kitchen.

"I know what's going on," he said. "I want to help you."

"You can help by leaving," she whispered. His shoulders sagged. He looks thin and haggard, she thought. "Master Barnard's dying. They don't want to see anyone," she said loudly. And then softly: "Stop trying to play Sir Galahad. It's too late for that, Jake. The best thing you can do for me, and for yourself, is to leave."

"Come with me."

"I can't. If you know what's happening—which isn't possible—you also know I have to go through with this."

"Elizabeth!" Simon sounded at the end of his patience.

"Coming!"

"Elizabeth?" Jake said.

"I have to go back in there."

"If you won't come with me, I'm staying here," Jake said.

"Don't get involved." He took her hand but she shook him off. "Please," he said. "I don't know what I can do but at least if I'm around . . ."

". . . Why?"

"Because I owe it to you and to our son."

It was a good thing she hadn't expected protestations of love, Riena thought. He was right, though. He did owe them. "Do what you want," she said, relocking the door.

"Tell him Nkolosi sent me because he thought you might need reinforcements."

She could feel his breath on the back of her neck. "How do you know Nkolosi? No, there's no time for that." She walked out of the kitchen and toward the dining room, with Jake right behind her.

"Who was it?" Simon asked Riena as she walked into the room.

"Ask him yourself. Nkolosi sent him," she said, watching Simon raise his gun and point it at Jake.

"Welcome to the club," Shari said. "Why don't you come in and join us. I'm sure this nice gentleman will give you membership at cut rates."

"Who the hell are you?" Simon said, ignoring Shari.

"Nkolosi thought you might need some help," Jake said.

"Do I detect an accent?" It was Shari again. "White American male comes to aid of Black bandit."

"Don't push me, lady," Simon growled. He looked at Jake. "I can use some help. Where's your weapon?"

For the first time since he'd come into the room, Riena thought, Jake looked as if he might come unstrung. "It was stolen," he said.

"Asshole. Elizabeth, give him yours. You don't know what to do with it anyway."

Riena handed Jake the gun. He took it from her and held it firmly.

"Good thing you're here," Shari said. "Elizabeth's not a very efficient revolutionary."

"Shut your mouth and put on the transistor," Simon ordered.

Shari didn't move.

"Do what the man told you," Jake said.

He was convincing, Riena thought, looking at the fa-

ther of her son. And attractive. Despite the past—or perhaps because of it—she felt a familiar stirring.

". . . It seems they have taken several families hostage and are holding them for ransom."

The eleven o'clock newscaster broke into her
thoughts and Riena changed position, embarrassed that at such a time her crotch was warm
and damp. But their summer was over. She was
sure of that now, realizing it would always be
that way for her with Jake—desire, followed by
embarrassment and love tainted by guilt.

". . . There is no need for widespread alarm. Talks
have already begun between our government and
representatives of the AFI . . ."

The voice repeated the litany.

". . . The police are holding off because they don't
want any harm to come to . . ."

Simon leaned across the table and turned off the
radio.

"How long do you intend to keep us here like this?"
Arthur Cohn asked calmly.

He was too calm, almost passive, Riena thought again.
Something in his face told her that he was asking the
question as a matter of form. That he believed rescue
was at hand. Either that, or he was playing a part to
comfort his family, in which case he was an actor wor-
thy of an Academy Award.

"A week? Ten days?"

"Why? Do you have a plane to catch? A ship that's
sailing, maybe?" Simon asked, obviously amusing himself. "Don't worry. You'll be free to go by next
Christmas."

Jake's look told Riena that Simon's words had triggered the same memories in him as they had in her. Their Christmas. Jake's gift to her a ten day break from his work at the university. Ten days for them to be together. She touched her neck, as if to feel the gold chain and pendant Jake had put there. It was long since around the neck of a jail attendant, she remembered, the pendant inscribed: "I love you. Jake."

"We can stay right here in this bed for ten days," he'd said. "That'll be your gift to me."

Except for business as usual," she'd said, knowing how much it hurt him but angry because she hadn't been able to buy him anything.

He'd taken out his wallet. Flung it at her, shouting: "Here. Take it all, just keep them out."

She'd started to refuse, to throw his wallet back at him. Then she'd thought of Ma who'd wanted a Christmas tree so badly. . . They'd bought the tree together, she and Jake, but she'd delivered it alone. Ma didn't approve of White men.

"I have to go to the bathroom," Riena said, knowing she would be sick if she didn't get some fresh air. Saying she needed to go to the bathroom seemed easier—a request less likely to provoke an argument.

"Go," Simon said, a benign dictator now that he thought he had a male helper.

Riena headed toward the outside bathroom. Instead of going inside, she sank down onto the concrete and leaned against the wall of the laundry room. Closing her eyes, she let the sun pour into her skin. The South African cure-all, she thought. "You have a cold; get some sunshine." "You had a nervous breakdown; get some sunshine." "You . . ."

An acorn landed on her lap and she looked up, surprised because she hadn't noticed any oak trees around the house. Fingering the acorn, she leaned back again. Staring at nothing. Thinking of nothing, until a second acorn dropped where the first had landed. The third was followed by a familiar body, striding boldly across

316

the garden.

"Tom!"

He put his fingers over his lips but his body proclaimed his right to be there so that watching neighbors would assume him to be a new gardener or a handyman. Then he was at her side, bending to help her up and she was holding onto him. A Piet-My-Vrou startled them both with its mournful cry and reminded them of the need for caution. They drew apart and their movement startled a lizard that had been sunning itself on the wall. It skittered down and under the nearest rock.

"I wish I could do that," Riena said.

Tom took her hand and turned it over, so that the palm faced him. "Everything's going to be all right," he said. "You have a long lifeline."

"What are you doing here, Tom?"

"Making sure you're okay," he said, letting go of her hand.

"Isn't that dangerous for you?"

"I suppose it is. What's happening inside? Why are you out here? I can't understand why Simon . . ."

". . . He has a new assistant."

"What?"

"Jake showed up, Tom."

"Jake? Your . . ."

". . . Yes."

"What the hell for?"

"Something about responsibility. . . . I don't know how he knew where to find me. He said something about Nkolosi—anyway, he's in there now pretending to be reinforcements."

"The man's a cretin to get involved."

"Not only that, Arthur Cohn's acting as if he knows help is on the way."

Faintly, as if it were happening in another world, Riena heard a bell ringing. Once. Twice. Then silence.

"The front door," Tom said.

"I have a feeling I lost my job sometime shortly before breakfast this morning," Riena said. "Let someone else answer it."

"Your attempt at humor is admirable, kiddo," Tom said, "but if you value your ass, you'd better get inside." His tone was light but his eyes were serious. Concerned.

Riena reached up and kissed him. "I love you, Tom," she said, knowing it was true. "See you in Teyateyaneng." As she turned and walked into the kitchen, she could hear that the ringing had resumed.

"Elizabeth!" Simon hollered. "Do something about that door."

As she walked past the dining room and glanced in, Riena saw the look of triumph on Arthur Cohn's face. She'd been right; she was sure of it now.

"Who's there?"

"Constable De Villiers here."

Riena waited for Simon to tell her what to do.

"Ask him what he wants," Simon hissed from the doorway of the dining room.

"What do you want? The old Master's very sick and I'm not supposed to let anyone in."

"I've come to report about Emily like I promised Mr. Cohn. I tried to telephone but there's something wrong with the line."

"I'll tell Mr. Cohn you came," Riena said.

"You'd better let me in so's I can check the phones. If the old man is sick they're going to need . . ."

". . . Let the bastard in," Simon ordered.

"You can't . . ."

" . . . I said let him in!"

Terrified, Riena opened the door. Then, flattening herself against the wall, she watched the *danse macabre* get underway, helpless to be anything but an observer.

"In here, De Villiers," Cohn yelled. "Fast."

Constable De Villiers was no mental giant, Riena thought, watching him take three hesitant steps forward

318

and stop short, waiting as if he were playing "Statues" and the caller had yelled "freeze." By the time he had lifted his foot to take a fourth step, it was too late. Simon had changed the game to hide-and-seek without telling the other player. His face impassive, he pumped three bullets into the Afrikaner policeman who was still playing Statues and sank slowly to the floor with the look of a bewildered child.

A pool of blood formed at Riena's feet. It trickled from the constable's wounds, finding its level around one parquet tile that was almost imperceptibly lower than the rest, spreading into the cracks around it to form a dark rim. A moat, Riena thought, big enough to float a toothpick boat with a postage stamp sail.

"Close the door," Simon shouted.

Riena looked up.

"You! Elizabeth. Close that fucking door."

Riena didn't move. She just kept staring, trying to blink and sure no part of her would ever move again. In some other level of awarness she could feel Simon's fury, and behind him, see Jake being tackled by Arthur Cohn. Though the newsman was much shorter than the American, and older, he was succeeding in his attempt to wrestle the gun away from Jake. Perhaps because he was acting for all of them, he seemed to have taken on the combined strength of his whole family.

Suddenly Cohn, victorious, straightened up. He was holding the gun the way he might have balanced a bagel, Riena thought, as Simon turned to face him.

"Return that gun," the Black man said.

Cohn shook his head.

"I'll shoot you."

Simon's words were matter of fact. Riena wanted to shout at the newsman and tell him to protect himself, but her tongue seemed to have frozen to her palate.

"Give it back to him, Art," Michelle Cohn pleaded.

Looking at his wife, Cohn slowly held the weapon toward Jake.

"Don't do it, Arthur!"

The new command came from Barnard Sr. who had stood up and was leaning heavily on the dining room table.

"Don't be a fool, Dad," Cohn said. "Mickey's right. Let's try to stay alive." He looked as if he were yelling, Riena thought, but the words emerged a barely audible whisper.

Giving his son-in-law a look of utter contempt, the old man lunged for the weapon.

"The door!" Simon yelled again, his voice muting the sound of his bullet as it sent old man Barnard spinning to the floor. He fell with a thud and jerked once or twice. Then he lay there. Unmoving.

Riena remained frozen to the wall, unable to move from its protection.

It took all the effort she could muster to turn her head enough so that she could see out of the open front door, the one Simon was still shouting at her to close.

"Damn you, woman!" Simon screamed.

She pushed herself into the wall, identifying with a curious kind of apathy the source of Simon's fury—a second policeman. He'd apparently stayed outside in the patrol car while his partner had gone to make his report on Emily. He came closer, running up the driveway. Past her. A Black man. His face a blur until he was crouching behind the dining room door-frame in the spot that Simon had vacated seconds before. In his uniform, Riena thought shuddering, he reminded her of Alfred. His spine had the same kind of rigidity, his eyes a similar hardness.

"Don't move, man." The policeman's gun was trained on Simon's back.

The AFI man's reaction seemed voice-activated. He whirled around and fired. The policeman reacted at least as quickly, flattening himself on the floor as the bullet cut the air and embedded itself in the wall behind him.

"Drop it!" he said.

Riena watched Simon's eyes turn murderous, a Buffalo caught at the watering hole by a crocodile, ready to fight to the end to quench his thirst. The policeman had seen the same thing. Without another warning, he fired. At almost point blank range, he had no trouble finding his mark.

Simon struggled to stay upright, fighting for each last second of life. He died with his eyes filled with venom, sliding down the door-frame like a half-filled sack of mielies and cursing every inch of the way. Was she dead, too, Riena wondered? A butterfly permanently impaled against the foyer wall—the pin through her center created by the trauma of watching men die. And for what? There could be no winners here. Only losers, she thought, listening to the silence.

And then she heard them. Running footsteps on the driveway outside the open front door. She didn't have to look to know whose they were and the knowledge released her at last from her paralysis.

"Tom!" She pushed herself away from the wall. "Get away from here!"

She was too late. The policeman was pushing her aside, his knees slightly bent, his gun arm raised and ready. When Tom's dark face and tall body appeared in the doorway, the policeman aimed and fired.

Clutching his side, Tom executed a quarter turn and fell. Riena waited, willing him to get up. When he didn't, she heard herself scream his name. Over and over. Then she was bending over him. Crying. Cradling his head in her arms.

Suddenly she felt strong fingers grip her elbow.

"Daddy! Art, it's Daddy! I think he's dead!" The voice was Michelle Cohn's.

The fingers tightened. Riena tried to shake them off but they were relentless. "Come one," Piet Barnard said. "I'm getting you out of here."

Riena twisted her head. She could see vague shadows

inside the house through the open doorway. Arthur Cohn moving toward his wife and daughter. Staring at her.

"Why don't you leave my arrest to the police and go to your father," she said quietly, wondering why she wasn't crying.

Barnard released her and handed her a handkerchief for the tears she couldn't feel. "I'm not arresting you. I'm trying to help you."

"Why?"

"No questions. Just come."

"Not without Tom."

"There's no time for that. We have to leave now or it'll be too late."

"Piet. Come here. Our father's bleeding to death, there's a bloody war going on and you're out there playing Good Samaritan to a stranger," Michelle yelled.

"I'm sorry, Sir, you can't go anywhere right now," the policeman said, looking up from the floor where he'd been examining his partner's body.

Piet Barnard took out his wallet and flashed a card at him. "I'm a prison warden," he said. "You have enough to handle. Let me see your badge; I'll make sure you get a commendation. Someone has to go for help."

"The patrol car's outside, Sir. I'll use the radio."

"That man out there, the one you shot, probably destroyed it," Jake said, coming out of the dining room.

The policeman looked torn, as if he wanted to say: "I'll shoot any bastard who leaves," but was afraid to tangle with the bureaucracy.

"You can't take the woman with you, Sir," he said finally. "She was engaged in criminal actions."

". . . Don't be a fool," Barnard said. "She's my niece."

"Can't you see she looks like me?" Shari added, coming to stand next to Riena who had been moved back into the hallway by the renewed pressure of Piet Barnard's fingers.

"But she's wearing a maid's uniform."

"It was that man's idea of a joke," Barnard said, nodding at Simon's body. "He made her put it on."

"What about that one?" the policeman asked, pointing at Jake.

"He's not one of them either," Riena said quickly, having anticipated the question and too confused to care why Barnard and Shari were protecting her. "He's an American who was playing along with them to try to protect us."

The policeman scratched his head. His fingers left a trail of his partner's blood along his forehead. "You mean one man was holding all of you?" he asked.

"I have to talk to Jake before we go," Riena said to Barnard, knowing the battle with the policeman had been won.

"Well, make it snappy," Barnard said.

Jake was standing a few feet away, looking as if he didn't really believe everything that had happened. Hearing his name, he woke from the stupor that appeared to have taken hold of him. "I'm coming with you," he said to Barnard.

"No, Jake," Riena said, pulling him away from the others so that only he and Barnard could hear what she had to say. "Help Tom, please."

"Who's Tom?"

"The man lying out on the front steps. He's been shot. Find his car—it's probably at the bottom of the hill—and get him on the next train to Teyateyaneng."

"If he's been shot he should be taken to a hospital."

"Put him on that train, Jake. Please," Riena said, making the assumption that Tom was alive but in no shape to drive his own car, even if he could get away from the house without Jake's help. As for the possibility that he might be dead, that was something with which she refused to deal—as if choosing to assume the best eliminated all chance of the worst.

"If you help him," she said, "you'll be wiping out

323

your obligation to me and to your son. You said you felt responsible. . . .''

". . . We have to go now, girl,'' Piet Barnard said. He took Riena by the arm and turned her toward the front door.

She shrank back. "Tom?"

"Don't look," Barnard ordered, angling his hand at the side of her eyes as if it were a blinder as he led her past Tom and toward the car.

"Your father . . . shouldn't you stay and make sure he's all right?"

"There's nothing I can do for him that the others can't," Barnard said, opening the car door and pushing Riena inside.

"What if he's dead?" Riena asked, verbalizing her fears for Tom through old man Barnard.

"If he's dead there's even less I can do for him," Piet Barnard said. "Don't look so shocked. He'd be the first to agree that it make more sense to help the living." He slammed the car door shut.

Riena watched him walk around to the driver's side, clamping her hands together to stop them from reaching for the door handle. She could feel her nails drawing blood. Barnard sat down beside her and she listened to the engine turn over.

"Are you going to make it?" Barnard asked, pulling the car quietly out of the driveway. "You look like you're in shock."

"I'll live." Riena could feel the tears this time, making their way down her cheeks. What was the point of living if Tom was dead, she thought. She looked back over her shoulder at the porch steps. "Please, Tom," she said, in a choked whisper, "be one of the living, too."

9

"You'll get a crick in your neck," Barnard said.

Riena straightened out and stared at the road ahead.

"Even if the American can do what you asked, it's going to take him a while to get your friend to his car. They couldn't possibly be behind us yet."

The man was right, Riena thought, but that didn't make it any easier not to keep turning around to glance at the ground they'd covered.

"Where're we going?"

"To a telephone box. I'm going to call a police ambulance and I have one other call to make." He hesitated. "I speak Swahili quite well, Riena—that is your real name isn't it? I spent several years as warden of a jail in Nairobi."

"I thought you could understand what Simon was saying."

"Why didn't you warn him?"

"If you hadn't understood, I'd have had to go to the police myself."

Barnard pulled up at the side of the road. "This shouldn't take long," he said. "When I'm finished, I'll take you where ever you want to go."

"Why are you doing this?"

"Because I have to," he said simply.

She watched him through the car window. His first call took less than a minute. The second one took longer. She could see him gesticulating, and when he replaced the receiver in its cradle it was with none too gentle a movement.

"Damn idiots," he said, getting back into the car and starting the engine. "I tried to get through to Government House but I got a flunky who didn't believe a word I was saying. I'm going to have to keep trying until I can get the Prime Minister."

"You don't have that much time."

"You're right." He stopped the car and reversed it until they were back where they'd started. "I'll try one more call."

This time Piet Barnard looked a great deal more satisfied when he returned to the car but he offered Riena no explanations. "Where to?" he asked.

"The railroad station."

"I'll buy you a plane ticket."

"No. Thank you. I have to take a train."

"Train it is," he said as if he were taking a guest on a tour of the city and tea at the Langham was the next stop en route to station.

"How far is the railway station?" Riena asked.

"Not far. About ten miles, maybe less."

"That last phone call. Did it do any good?"

"I think so. Let's find out, shall we?" He turned on the radio. "I called a friend of mine at SABC."

"I interrupt your morning music with the following announcement. As you know, several prominent South Africans families were taken hostage today by the AFI, Africans for Independence, a terrorist group who are conducting talks with high officials in our government. They have specific demands which, if met, will result in freedom for the hostages."

So far, Riena thought, she had heard nothing that related to what she had assumed was the topic of Barnard's telephone call.

"One family," the announcer continued, "has already escaped without the aid of mediation. A member of that family, newsman Arthur Cohn's brother-in-law Pieter Barnard, who recently resigned as warden of Cape Town's Roeland Street Gaol, called me minutes ago. He claims to have overheard details of a plot by the AFI to poison tomorrow's deliveries of milk if their demands are not met. Although Mr. Barnard mentioned a particular dairy chain, we urge you not to drink *any* milk delivered tomorrow. Do not buy any milk in the shops; stay with powdered milk. We have no idea how many dairies have been infiltrated. We will be broadcasting this warning every fifteen minutes for the next twenty four hours on all stations around the country."

Riena looked at Piet Barnard's profile. He seemed younger suddenly, as if what he had done and was doing had succeeded in relieving a burden that he'd carried around for a long time. She could understand his informing the country about the AFI's next move; what she could not understand, despite their newly discovered familial relationship, was the risk he was taking by helping her.

"Will you explain why you're doing this for me?" she asked.

"I helped you once before. Why shouldn't I do so again, especially now that I know who you are."

"How did you know I was the one. . . ."

". . . Who walked out on my hospitality? I didn't. Not until I got a call from Cape Town that Daniel Van Der Merwe was trying to track down one Riena Parker."

"And then you heard Jake call me Riena?"

"Yes. The pieces fell together nicely after that."

For a moment Riena wondered if Barnard had also recognized Tom's voice as that of the man who had warned him about the explosion. But since Tom and the warden—former warden—had not spoken to each other again except for those few minutes on Saturday morning, she dismissed the possibility as unlikely.

"Why didn't you stop me that night?" she asked, opening the car window slightly.

"I wasn't making a judgment about incarceration versus freedom, if that's what you're thinking," Barnard said. His voice was softened by the sound of the car's wheels, turning on the tarmac. "I don't know what

327

made me let you go. I'd had almost no sleep that week and I felt fragile. My imagination was feeding on shadows. By the time I realized you were real, it was too late to stop you. Besides, I was getting good at doing nothing.''

"Why didn't you admit to the papers that you knew it was an explosion that had been deliberately set?"

"It was easier to call it a freak boiler accident."

"I thought perhaps the system had rendered you incapable of distinguishing between the revolutionaries and bureaucrats."

"In a way, you're right."

"Was that why you resigned?"

Barnard turned his head to look at her. "I decided to take early retirement. Write a book. Play gold. And watch my country fall apart."

"Do you think nihilism is going to become a way of life? It may be the only way to wipe out all trace of the past."

"I don't know, Riena. Do you? Do you think a newly enlightened people can live harmoniously with their past masters?"

"I don't know that either."

"The only thing I'm convinced of is that the world is crazy," Barnard said.

Neither of them said any more for several miles, until they were driving across the overpass above the Central Railway Station.

"It looks like the Guggenheim Museum in New York," Barnard said, peering down at an enormous rotunda. "I wasn't crazy about that either." He parked the car, turned off the ignition, and pocketed the keys. "Stay here. I'll buy your ticket. Where are you going?"

"I'll need a third class ticket to Teyateyaneng."

"Third class? Second class, surely?"

"I'm going to try for Black instead of White."

"In case your friend makes it to the train and needs help?"

Riena nodded.

"Do you want something to read?"

"No thanks."

"Wait in the car," Barnard said. "If anyone asks, you're my maid. You've had a family emergency and I'm sending you home."

His words reminded Riena that she was still wearing Emily's uniform. She looked down at the thick stockings and started to take them off; they'd be sticking to her legs by the time she reached Teyateyaneng. She had barely removed them when Barnard reappeared.

"Hurry," he said. "The train for Bloemfontein's leaving from platform five in less than ten minutes and it's a good walk."

"Bloemfontein?"

"You'll connect there with the train to Maseru. It's the only railway into Basutoland."

"When will I be in Teyateyaneng?"

"Shortly after eight," Barnard said, handing her a ticket.

She was hardly on the train before it gave a fitful jerk. Snorting like a lazy horse that preferred lying in the sun, it began to gather speed for the journey. Please God, she thought, let Tom be on the train.

"It'll be better someday," Barnard said, shoving a fistful of notes into her hand. He was crying unashamedly.

Riena watched him until he was no more than a black dot on the grey surface of the platform. He did not raise his hand to wave.

Once Barnard was out of sight, Riena settle down as best she could on the hard wooden bench of her third class carriage. It was going to be a long journey, she thought, but by sunset she'd be in Teyateyaneng; it was midsummer, and the sun would set late over Thaba Bosigo—the Mountain of the Night.

It was hot on the train. Hot and stuffy. The seasoned travelers had closed the windows the moment the train began to move, and no pleading on Riena's part would budge them in their resolve to keep them closed. The bugs would come in, they told her, pointing at the bodies already accumulating on the glass. The soot and the dust must stay outside, they said.

If there were unwashed bodies around her, contributing to the smell and the closeness, Riena thought, it really didn't matter. With the windows shut, she'd soon smell like the rest of the passengers. Nor did the eating rituals that started almost at once help—the pooling of day-old bakery bread and whatever leftover meat and cheese had been hoarded for the journey. And beer—in bottles and cans—and liquor, what kind she could only guess at, in battered flasks, handed around the traveling community in the roar of singing and fighting and complaining that contributed to her feeling of claustrophobia.

Finally, unable to stand it, she stood and walked to the end of the carriage. She was in the first third class car; if Tom had made it onto the train, he'd be somewhere between her and the baggage compartment that doubled as a cattle truck when the need arose. Standing in the corridor, next to a window that she'd manage to open, she watched the tail end of the train snake around a bend; it was rocking from side to side, like a Matchbox toy on a Meccano set rail.

A big man leaned across her and closed the window, glaring at her as if she'd committed some dreadful criminal act. Muttering an apology, she moved to the end of the car and stepped across the metal connectors that linked the carriages. The ground, moving below, made her dizzy and she rocked precariously and reached out for something to hold.

"Careful, *gamat*."

She felt a strong arm encircle her waist, and beery breath on her face. With a mixture of gratitude and fear, she shook herself loose.

"Don't be so high and mighty," the man said, grinning. "I was just trying to help."

"Thank you," Riena said, swaying toward the entry door to the next carriage and hoping the man wouldn't follow her. As she closed the door behind her, he winked, and she wondered if he would be waiting for her when she came back.

Once inside the next car, Riena walked its length. She inspected every seat and knocked at the doors of the toilets that flanked either end of the coach. As she proceeded down the aisle of that carriage, and then the next, greedy hands grabbed at her legs; each time she had to cross yet another metal separator, she experienced the same dizziness from the speed at which the ground sped away beneath her. When she reached the baggage compartment, the train stopped at a siding. Having made sure that Tom wasn't inside, she stepped off the train and hurried back to her own carriage, pushing her way past a disembarking family who were saying tearful farewells to fellow travelers they hardly knew—as if they'd known them all their lives instead of only for the hour or so that the train had taken to get from Johannesburg Central to the siding.

Back in her seat, but not yet ready to face the fact that Tom wasn't on the train, Riena watched through the window as a car raced up to the station and stopped. A man and woman tumbled out, the man yelling "Wait!" to the conductor as he pushed the woman toward the train.

The conductor blew his whistle as the woman, disheveled but triumphant, was helped onto the train by someone inside.

"Thanks for chasing the train," someone shouted, as the huge iron monster lumbered into motion.

The man on the platform grinned and waved.

Perhaps that was what Jake was doing, Riena thought; chasing the train through the Transvaal and into the Orange Free State so that he could beat it to a stop and put Tom onto it.

Having made the decision that the two men were out

there somewhere, chasing the train, Riena stretched out on her seat and tried to relax. The movement of the train and the closeness combined to sedate her, and she soon fell asleep. Two hours passed. Then a third. She had been on the train for four hours before she was fully awake again.

"Want a drink?"

A man in the seat across from Riena handed her a warm can of beer, his eyes locked on her ankles. She accepted, tilted her head back, and swallowed. The man started to laugh at the expression on her face as the tepid beer hit her throat.

"It's not champagne but it's wet," he said, taking the can from her.

"How long have you been on the train?" Riena asked.

"An hour or so. Why?"

"Nothing. Thanks for the beer."

She stood up and walked into the corridor to begin another search of the train. If her theory was correct, Tom could have boarded the train at the same time as the man in her compartment—or at any one of the other stops she'd missed while she'd been asleep.

This time Riena's journey from her end of third class to the baggage compartment and back again was uneventful. She found the movement of the train far less unbalancing, and she was soon back in her compartment, staring out of the same dirty window. A month ago, she'd given birth to a son. Now, in less than a week, she thought, she'd lived through an explosion, escaped from jail, been exposed to Nkolosi and the Negwenya, and fallen in love with someone she'd known all of her life. And there was the AFI. . . .

Riena leaned her forehead against the window. The heat inside the train was making her feel feverish and the glass felt relatively cool against her skin. She was beginning to feel fragmented, she thought. Like a cracked seashell, at the mercy of a Mouille Point storm. She didn't want to believe that she had no control over her own fate, but it was becoming harder and harder to believe anything else. It was as if all of the internal mechanisms she had learned to trust had gone awry, as if both instinct and intellect had left her stranded. She didn't belong in the White world of the Cohns and the Barnards, any more than she belonged with Nkolosi and his Negwenya. Yet she was having trouble labeling any of them bad or good, as if the sorting process that usually helped her define right and wrong was no longer part of her consciousness.

As for what awaited her in Teyateyaneng, Riena thought, captivity seemed like a pleasant alternative compared with fighting Nkolosi and the Negwenya for repossession of her son.

Holding her breath against the smell of stale urine and unwashed bodies, Riena wondered how she could have been so naive as to have believed that she would come to terms with herself during the course of this journey. All she had really managed to do was to pose more questions. The AFI's concept of any means to an end made no more sense to her now than it had done in the beginning; at the same time, the existing system was irrational. To acquiesce to it meant that she was accepting hopelessness as a way of life—for herself, and for her son.

"Last stop, Bloemfontein. Everybody off the train. Last stop, Bloemfontein."

The conductor walked down the cars, warning everyone that the end of the line had come.

"Where do I get the train to Maseru?" Riena asked him.

"Follow me," a man said. "I'm making the same connection. The train for Maseru leaves in fifteen minutes, so we have plenty of time."

Riena followed the man through a maze of platforms and thanked him profusely when they got on board the train. The station was a central connecting point for the Orange Free State, and she might never otherwise have found her way through the throngs of passengers and porters.

"We still have five minutes," the man said, sitting down opposite Riena. He picked up a copy of the Basutoland News that someone had left lying on the seat and offered it to her.

She shook her head, and ignoring the glares of everyone around her, disobeyed train etiquette and opened the window so that she could stick her head out of it and look up and down the platform.

The whistle had blown before she saw them, Jake half dragging Tom toward the train.

"Wait! Conductor, wait!"

The man heard her and saluted. By the time he whistled again, Jake had guided Tom into the last car.

Before Riena could cross to the other side of the train to see if Jake had climbed off onto the far side of the double platform, the train began to move. Riena hesitated, torn between trying to wave goodbye to Jake and going straight to Tom. Sure the American would understand why she was not standing at the window, she started to run through the cars in the opposite direction to the motion of the train. Stumbling. Picking herself up and then stumbling again, until she reached the whipping tail of the train.

Tom was sitting with his back against a mound of suitcases. His chest was still heaving with the effort of boarding the train but he managed to smile at her. "Well, fancy meeting you here," he said.

Riena sat down on the floor next to him. He'd sounded jaunty enough but his eyes told her he was in pain.

"The bullet grazed a rib or two," Jake said from the opposite side of the car.

"Jake?"

"No one else."

"I thought you'd go back to Johannesburg."

"I will. Eventually."

Riena looked from one man to the other. "Will one of you please tell me what happened," she said, reaching out to touch Tom's face.

He caught her hand and held it.

"It's not all that complicated," Jake said. "The policeman had more than enough to do taking care of the Cohns and Anne Barnard. I just walked out, told Tom what I was going to do, and went to get his car."

"Well, it wasn't quite that easy," Tom said. "He had a helluva time getting me to the car."

"No one tried to stop you?" Riena asked.

"The police ambulance passed us at the bottom of the hill but there was no reason for them to be suspicious. I sat in the back of the car," Tom said. "We stopped at a Chemist and Jake bought bandages and tape; we got to Central Station too late for the train so we chased it all the way to Bloemfontein."

"We should probably go to Maseru and take you to a hospital, Tom," Riena said, seeing him wince as the train jerked.

"No." He sounded adamant.

"Then try to get some sleep," Riena said. "Lie down and put your head in my lap."

Tom did as he'd been told and was soon mumbling incoherently in a state of semi-consciousness.

"Is he in a lot of pain?" Riena asked Jake.

"I don't think so. I've been giving him Demerol."

"How'd you get it without a prescription?"

"Bribery."

"Thank you, Jake," Riena said, stroking Tom's moist forehead. When the American didn't say anything, Riena looked at him and smiled. "You shouldn't have come back, you know."

"I had to, Riena."

"I suppose so. Jake, what happened to old man Barnard?"

"I didn't wait around to find out. I suspect he was dead."

"I'm sorry."

"Why should you be?"

This time it was Riena who didn't answer. She didn't know why it should matter to her that Piet Barnard's father—her grandfather—survive. But it did. Perhaps, she thought, it was because he was the last of an old breed who, right or wrong, believed in themselves.

10

When the train slowed down at Teyateyaneng, Tom was barely conscious. Jake slid open the heavy baggage room door and propped a suitcase against it.

"You're going to have to help me with him, Riena," he said. "There's no way he can make it down this step without help from both of us."

Riena shook Tom gently. "Tom. We're here. Wake up."

"I can't move," Tom said hoarsely. "You two get off. I'm going to die on this cattle truck."

"That's the Demerol talking," Jake said, shaking Tom a great deal more roughly than Riena had done. "Come on, Tom. We only have a few minutes. Riena, you get off. I'll manage him as far as the door by myself, then you can give us a hand."

By the time Tom had been maneuvered off the train, the conductor was yelling, "All aboard." Jake kicked the suitcase back inside and the door slammed shut.

"I'm sorry," Tom said, leaning heavily on both of them. "It's taking all my strength to stay conscious."

As they stood in the hot South African sun, Riena tried to block out the certainty that Tom's wound was infected. The train was disappearing down the track and she distracted herself by wondering why the conductor hadn't come along to chase them out of the bag-

336

gage compartment. The distraction was brief because it didn't matter. He hadn't and they were here now, in Teyateyaneng. She looked around at the landscape. It was as bleak and barren as her thoughts. The dusty platform's only inhabitants were a dozen white-toothed, grinning *klonkies*—young Sesutos who stood close to the tracks, their round, distended stomachs hanging almost to their knees. Sweat glistened on their bodies through the haze of heat and dirt that rose behind the departing train and Riena watched as they shared the fruit and pennies they'd collected from the passengers.

"Let's get Tom into the shade," Jake said. "Over there, in the waiting room."

Together, they half-dragged Tom into the dubious shelter of a corrugated iron roof, held up by four slim wooden poles. There were walls on two sides, and against one of them leaned a slatted bench where they propped Tom like a rag doll.

"I'm sorry," Tom said again. He was holding his side but he sounded coherent. "My head's beginning to clear. I wasn't much help out there, was I?"

"Are you in much pain?"

"Yes, but I'd rather have the pain and be able to think."

A large railway map of South Africa, tattered but recognizable, hung over Tom's head. Riena looked at it, searching for the spot that marked Teyateyaneng. It was no more than a pinpoint and might not have been visible at all had someone not circled it with a greasy crayon. She looked at the Orange Free State to the northwest and the Cape to the South.

"I never realized how small Basutoland was," she said.

"It may be small on the map but if it gets dark before we find Nkolosi, it'll seem endless," Tom said. "What time is it?"

"Quarter past eight."

"Did a lot of people get off the train when we did?"

"Not that I noticed," Riena said. "Did you, Jake?"

The American shook his head and looked out at the

platform. "If they did, they're not around now."

"Will Nkolosi have the baby with him?" Riena asked.

"I don't know," Tom said. "Come to think of it, his place shouldn't be all that hard to find . . . it'll be the hut with a dragon guarding the door."

Riena didn't know whether Tom was joking or serious. Either way, he was right; it made sense to get started before dark. She walked to the far end of the shelter and looked outside. If she'd expected to find Teyateyaneng occupied by Nkolosi's army, she thought, she'd been misled. Everything was quiet. Normal. Standing with her back to the platform, she faced the outskirts of the village itself. She could see people going about their end of the day business: roadside hawkers, packing away their wares; children straggling home to bed; a stray dog, sleeping in the middle of the road near the only tree in sight.

She looked toward the west. The sun was hanging over a small *koppie,* a hill half the size of Devil's Peak. By no stretch of the imagination could it be called a mountain, yet Riena knew that it was Thaba Bosigo.

As she watched, a shadow moved across the sun. Winged and graceful, it floated in the sky like the mother of all Lightning Birds. Yet what she saw was no Lightning Bird with its smooth wings and underbelly as red as the hibiscus blooming out of the sand at her feet. This creature was black against the sun, its wings edged with lace, its tail curved.

Frightened, Riena turned to the two men. "The sun will be setting soon," she said, in a voice that didn't sound like her own. "The mountain will grow and Nkolosi's army will walk out of its shadows."

"Riena? What're you talking about? And what's the matter?" Jake asked. "Your voice sounds peculiar."

"I'm fine, Jake," Riena said, ignoring his first question. "Look, there's no need for you to stay here. I'll find a way to get Tom to. . . ."

". . . I'm not leaving, Riena."

"Why?"

"I don't know. I feel as if something's drawn me

338

here," he said, walking out of the shelter. "Why don't you stay with Tom while I try to find Nkolosi."

"No!" The word came out like a command. "We have to stay together," Riena said, more quietly. "If you can manage to support Tom without me, I'll lead the way."

"How can you lead the way when you don't know where we're going any more than I. . . ."

". . . I'll lead the way." Again Riena's voice had a strange intonation, a combination of the imperative and of involuntary speech, as if she were a ventriloquist's dummy being forced to enunciate words whose source was outside her own mind.

With Jake and Tom trailing behind her, Riena walked out into the sunset. It was an artist's palette of red and gold and auburn. She looked back to make sure that Jake was coping with Tom's weight; both men smiled at her. Reassured, she knelt on the ground, not really knowing what it was she sought but seeking it anyway. It was almost as if whatever was using her for a medium was telling her what to do in a foreign tongue she was on the brink of understanding. And then she saw it. Them. The fine tracings in the sand—a half-closed eye; a delicately scalloped wing.

"Look to your right," Tom said. It was his voice now that sounded strange. Hollow. The words directed from somewhere other than his own larynx.

Riena drew her eyes away from the image etched in the sand, and looked into the glow of the rainbow sunset. The figure was still there, performing its ritualistic dance high among the pink-tinged clouds. But this time it did not frighten her. She felt a sense of coming home, and nodded her head in thanks to her guide. Why she felt suddenly that the Negwenya was benign, she did not know. Nor did she understand why Tom wasn't screaming in fear of she who had haunted him for so long. What Riena did know was that it would be easy from now on to lead the way through the summer terrain.

She started to move again, no longer having to search

339

for the path that lay before her as clearly as if it had been hollowed into the ground: a lizard, not moving at their approach; a spray of berries; and always the tracings. First one, and then another, until there were no more and Riena had to stop and look up again at the sun. It was sinking fast and the Mountain of the Night was growing tall with the lengthening shadows.

"She's still there," Tom said.

"I know," Riena said. "I wasn't looking for her."

"What were you. . . ."

". . . I was looking for Nkolosi's army."

She stood until Jake and Tom reached her side. Then she pointed. "Do you see them?" she asked.

"I do," Tom said.

Jake shaded his eyes. "See whom?"

And soon he could see them too. Nkolosi's army. Men and women. Creeping out of caves and mud huts to straggle across the plains. In front of them. Behind them. Around them.

"Aren't you afraid?" the American asked.

Riena and Tom shook their heads.

"Why not?"

"I'm not sure. Maybe fear disappears when you accept your destiny," Tom said.

"Have you done that?"

"I have a feeling I don't have much choice," Tom said, shifting his weight. "Let's keep moving or my side'll stiffen up completely."

Slowly the three of them walked on through the village of Teyateyaneng, past children in ragged clothes playing in the sand, and adults with young old faces who left what they were doing and joined the threesome. They didn't stop again until they were at the far reaches of the town, approaching a small house that stood away from the rest, moving toward a man who sat cross-legged in front of an open door. He was staring at Thaba Bosigo, looking at it as if he alone had created the mountain, his dark brown shoulders gleaming in the final rays of the sun as it kissed the crest of the hill and disappeared.

340

The man looked down and began to draw in the sand. Slowly. Lovingly. The edge of his nail barely caressing the earth.

"Wait here," Riena said, turning to the two men behind her. They stopped and she saw Tom sink to the ground. Jake stood for a moment before he sat down beside him. Then, one by one, the villagers and the men and women of the caves did the same. Waiting. Crosslegged and motionless. Their African bodies wrapped in beads and blankets and growing out of the landscape, as if someone had planted an orchard in the middle of Basutoland.

"Nkolosi!" Riena called out, certain, though she was not yet close enough to see his face, that the figure outside the house was that of the witchdoctor.

Only Nkolosi's hand moved, tracing patterns in the sand.

"Where are Maria and my son?"

A woman appeared in the doorway behind Nkolosi. Though it was not Maria, she was holding a bundle in her arms.

Riena took a step forward. "Is that my son?" she asked, staring at the red satin blanket that trailed down the front of the woman's denim jeans. Riena took another step forward, but her progress was stopped by voices that cried out behind her.

"You have failed us, Nkolosi."

"We are not equal!"

"We are not free!"

Slowly, Nkolosi raised his head and stilled the motion of his hand. "Tomorrow!" he called out. "Tomorrow you will be free and equal."

"No, Nkolosi," Riena said. "You have failed them. The White man knows about your plan and they will be neither free nor equal tomorrow."

"Stop!" Nkolosi commanded. He held up his hand and his long nail glistened like a dagger in the twilight. "The Negwenya will become angry if she hears you."

"With whom will she become angry, Nkolosi?" Riena said, moving forward again. "With me? I think not.

341

With you, perhaps, with the Master who has failed her."

"You have failed!"

The cry came again, echoing against the fortress of Thaba Bosigo.

"Go home, Nkolosi," Riena said. "You do not belong here. You are not a Basuto."

Unfurling his body like a leopard preparing to defend itself against the enemy, Nkolosi stood. "I can succeed," he shouted. "I will succeed."

As he stood, straight and tall, the animal skin sarong he wore taut around his muscular legs, he looked up toward the summit of Thaba Bosigo. He had no sooner raised his head than the expression on his face changed, the arrogance replaced by pleading. Fear. He stepped backwards. Stumbled. Stood erect again.

"No."

It was a whisper. A plea. Again he stepped backwards, his body pressing against the mud wall of his hut.

Riena could feel the chill of a shadow overhead, but she didn't look up. She couldn't. The changing expression on Nkolosi's face commanded all of her attention. The man she had so feared because of the intensity and power that radiated from him throughout the country, into White homes and Black, into educated minds and into the hearts of savages, had become a prisoner pleading to be released from the ultimate punishment.

Turning his head aside as if he had been struck, Nkolosi whispered. "I am your servant. I can. . . ."

Riena watched the witchdoctor's eyes dilate in terror.

"Don't," Nkolosi screamed, reeling sideways, as if he had again been struck by a force so strong that he could not begin to fight it. Instead, with one bloodcurdling scream that seemed to come from neither beast nor man, he leaped high in the air. As he fell to the ground, he covered his face and lay crumpled and still, the arrogance gone from his body. Riena did not have to examine him to know that he was dead. Gingerly, she removed his hand from his face. His eyes were staring toward Thaba Bosigo, his face set in an expression of fear such as she had seen only once before, on Alfred

Mtshali's face that day in Zeekoevlei. She looked at the design Nkolosi had made in the sand and despite everything she felt sadness for the witchdoctor who had drawn each scale so tenderly. Each scallop on the Negwenya's wing spoke of love and pain and defeat. He had known it was over, she thought, even while he was drawing the portrait of the Negwenya—he had known.

That was when she heard it, the flutter of wings and the faint whisper of her name. She looked in the direction of the sound. There was nothing there. Even the sun had gone and the quiet of dusk had descended upon the plain.

"Riena."

She stood up and looked around. This voice was firm and clear, she thought, as the woman she had seen earlier standing behind Nkolosi stepped out of the hut and held out the bundle she'd been holding. Its satin covering glowed red in the twilight.

"Miss . . . Deanna?"

"Take your son," Deanna said, a look of sadness on her face. "I don't really want to give him up; he's beautiful."

"Where is Maria?"

"Safe in the village. I took her place."

"Why are you here?"

"I knew Jake would come to Teyateyaneng."

Riena turned away, leaving the child in Deanna's arms. Facing the village, she watched as one by one the squatting men and women stood, silhouettes now that the sun was gone. She looked up at Thaba Bosigo to find the shadow that had guided her to Nkolosi, knowing it, too, would no longer be there.

"Moshesh . . . Moshesh . . . Moshesh."

The chant began as softly as a lullaby. It echoed off Thaba Bosigo and into the farmlands and the countryside. Into the shanties and the thatched roofed huts.

Together, Tom and Jake rose and moved toward her.

"What is it they want, Tom?" Riena asked, when they were close enough to hear her.

"They want a leader."

343

"You, Tom?"

"No," he said, taking her hand. "They want the child. They are saying that the child is South Africa's future. Their future. Our future, yours and mine."

"He's your son," Deanna said, walking up to Reina. "Take him."

Riena took the child in her arms and held it against her. Breathing in the innocent perfume of her son's young body, she looked up at the evening star, and made a wish for him—not that he would be the leader of a nation but that he would survive and grow to manhood in freedom.

"He's your son, too," she said to Jake.

Jake moved into Deanna's shadow and Riena waited quietly until they drew apart. "Take him, Jake," she said. "Take the child to America where he can grow up proud to be a man." She was crying softly.

It was not Jake but Deanna who stepped forward and held out her arms.

"I'll come for him," Tom said, joining her. "But even if we can't, Africa will draw him back."

"I don't understand," Riena said. "He'll be raised as an American. Why should he care about Africa?"

"Moshesh . . . Moshesh . . . Moshesh."

Tom's answer was muffled by the chanting as it rose to a crescendo and filled the valley with the sound of a nation calling for a new leader. Then, slowly, it died to a murmur, and the people began to disperse.

When the four of them stood alone in the shadow of Thaba Bosigo, Riena looked up at the rising sliver of a new moon and at the three silent figures around her. The night made no distinction between Black and White and Coloured, she thought. It had leached their color to create silhouettes which stood equal before the Mountain of the Night.

Suddenly, Riena remembered Nkolosi. Someone had to bury him; his body couldn't be left for the hyenas and the jackals, she thought. But when she turned to the spot where the witchdoctor's body had fallen, the ground was bare.

344

"What happened to him, Tom?" she asked. "Did you see anyone remove. . . ?"

Tom shook his head, and Riena, chilled, hugged herself. She felt pathetically small and inadequate, she thought.

"Before we leave this place," Tom said, "there's something you have to see."

Riena allowed herself to be led to her son who was sleeping peacefully in Deanna's arms. She watched as Tom gently removed the infant's blanket and exposed a tiny thigh.

"Tom, what. . . ."

". . . Look." He pointed at the child's soft flesh.

Bewildered, Riena shook her head.

"When Nkolosi died, I heard the Negwenya's voice," he said dreamily. "It was like water flowing down the slopes of Thaba Bosigo. She told me. . . ."

". . . Tom, you have a fever. You're hallucinating."

"No, Riena, listen to me. She released me when Nkolosi died and she has chosen a new Master."

Riena looked closely at her son's leg. She could see it now. A tattoo. Infinitesimally small. So tiny that the tip of her finger was big enough to cover the scalloped wings and the twisted tail.

"No," she said. "It's just a *miggie,* a summer insect."

"Then brush it away," Tom said.

Giving up, Riena angled the child's leg so that the moonlight shone directly on it. The Negwenya was in bondage to Nkolosi like the rest of us, she thought. Now that he's no longer alive . . . She bent over and kissed her son. As she did so, she felt a gentle breeze on her neck and heard the whisper of wings.

She didn't look up.

"One day the Negwenya will call him home," she said.

"No," Tom said, covering the child against the encroaching chill of the African night. "One day Africa will call him home."

THE INSTITUTE

By
James M.
Cain

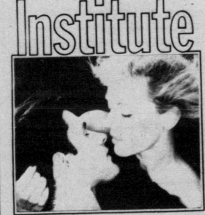

AUTHOR OF THE POSTMAN ALWAYS RINGS TWICE, DOUBLE INDEMNITY & MILDRED PIERCE.

"NOBODY ELSE HAS EVER QUITE PULLED IT OFF THE WAY CAIN DOES, NOT HEMINGWAY, AND NOT EVEN RAYMOND CHANDLER. CAIN IS A MASTER OF THE CHANGE OF PACE." —TOM WOLFE

James M. Cain
The Institute

THE FORBIDDEN LOVE THEY SHARED DREW THEM INTO A VORTEX OF VIOLENCE AND DEATH!

PRICE: $2.95
0-8439-1034-8
CATEGORY:
Novel

The brilliant career of James M. Cain, the celebrated author of "The Postman Always Rings Twice," "Mildred Pierce" and "Double Indemnity," reaches a shattering climax in this power-triangle of love, lust and greed.

When Professor Lloyd Palmer seeks financial backing from wealthy Richard Garrett, he meets and falls in love with Garrett's seductive wife.